KILL
STREAK

KILL STREAK

PURIFIER ▪ BOOK 1

Curator Omega

Podium

Published in 2022 by Podium Publishing, ULC
www.podiumaudio.com

Greetings, wanderer. You have entered a sanctum at the edge of time and space. An archive drifting in the vast, silent emptiness of a universe that has lived out its last days. Once there were stars, planets, beings of infinite variety . . . but no longer. All that remains in the darkness are a few dancing quarks and, naturally, my abode.

Since the birth of creation, I have scoured every world, every strand of time, seeking out the wonders and terrors of reality. I have stored them here for inquisitive minds such as yours.

Please allow me to present you one of the strangest tales in my collection. According to legend, it was never uploaded to virtual storage. Its contents were too heretical, too dangerous, to the government that ruled the galaxy in which it was written—the Halcius Hegemony, that is. As such, it exists in my library in its original form: a stack of bloodstained paper, its pages curled by passing eons and radiation.

You may wonder when it was penned, but alas, I have no answer for such a question. Similarly, I cannot say the year in which its events occurred. Time is a fickle, mortal thing. There is no beginning, no ending . . . the way in which it is measured depends on the whims of those in power.

What I do know, however, is that it takes place in one of the universe's more . . . exotic chapters. An era in which humans had just begun reclaiming the stars. Their original home, Earth, was distant and forgotten. They had lain dormant, extinct, for many millennia. It was only due to the curiosity of an advanced species that humans were brought back into the fold of existence, recreated as clones using samples of DNA that they had left behind as their legacy.

But with this resurrection came annihilation. Upon their return to reality, the humans exposed countless alien species to their ancient viruses, bacteria, and prions. They wiped out 99 percent of known life in their bubble of space.

Within this new void, the humans flourished. They established dominion over the stars. They implemented order and hierarchy. They claimed alien technology as their own, desperate to carve out a place in the endless expanse.

As you surely know, however, such ambition always breeds conflict. While many humans kneeled before the throne of their official rulers, the Halcius Hegemony, others ventured forth into unknown stretches of space seeking fame, fortune, and adventure. But, of course, what one seeks is not always what one finds.

And thus we come to the tale of Dak Korasa, a mild-mannered human archaeologist who stumbled too far into the blackness. A man who, through a few bad decisions, became ensnared in the grips of the greedy and the cruel. A man who, to some . . . became a god.

Be warned, reader. Contained within this story are oceans of blood and descriptions of horrors beyond your fragile mind. I have censored nothing, for I am a mirror of truth.

Proceed or turn away . . . the choice is yours.

As always, I remain. I am the humble curator of all things. The one who endures. Curator Omega.

Welcome, wanderer, to the Cutthroat Cosmos.

KILL
STREAK

1

They say that when you're dying, you experience something spectacular. The blinding white light of serenity, for example, or all your loved ones lined up and eager to guide you through some indescribable transition. The less spiritually inclined might say that you're bombarded by a balls-to-the-wall hallucination of your life's triumphs and sorrows, a sort of last hurrah curated and presented by your brain's boiling chemical soup.

My own death was nothing like that.

As I lay on the warm, spongy soil of the jungle floor, watching my blood drain into the oversized footprints left by pressurized boots, I was struck by how damn boring it was. How raw. Every shallow, panting breath reminded me this was the end of the line.

You might wager I was at peace, ready to go gently into that good night, but I wasn't. My heart was hammering, my throat burning. Billions of years of human survival instincts, baked into every nerve and dying cell of my body, screamed at me to *move*. To *survive*. Nothing else mattered. Sure, I was lying motionless, staring blankly at the decomposing leaves and tiny spiders that had emerged to start feasting, but what else can you do when you're down to a few liters of blood? My former crew had already shot me three times; I couldn't risk number four.

Good reasons to be afraid, right? Well, buckle up, because my imminent death wasn't the *real* reason I was terrified.

"How long y'think he's got?"

The voice was hazy, distant, but the ensuing coughing fit told me who it was: Kardinal Killa. And yes, that was his real name. All you need to know about the head-to-toe-tattooed scavenger was that he'd been born in a vat and killed his first man at twelve.

"Depends how much he squirms," another man replied. The husky, rattling tone belonged to Balnos, our team's alien pathfinder and survivor of not one, but *two* incidents of having his throat laser-sliced open by an ex-wife. "Maybe he's got a clotting augment."

Lurking in the silence was Liura Blue, the team's point woman. She was quiet, professional, the sort that wouldn't even blink before she sprayed you with a burst of tungsten-tipped bullets. And that's just what she'd done to me.

All three of my betrayers stood somewhere behind me—smoking amp-sticks, if the smell was any indication. It would be dusk soon. Dusk, and then night. If the blood loss didn't get me, the freezing temps and roaming packs of chakkis sure would.

If you've never heard of a chakki, here's a primer: Envision the love child of a centipede and a porcupine, puffed up tenfold by growth hormones. They had a nasty habit of starting with the eyes and eating their way south.

"Seems like we could just pluck the prism out and head back," Kardinal said. "I mean, c'mon, the pissbag is gonna spend the rest of time in this loop. What's a few more minutes matter?"

Balnos took a long drag from his amp-stick, grumbling all the while. "Boss's orders. He's gotta bleed out, gotta flatline."

"Yeah, but—"

"Boss's. Orders."

Balnos's tone left no room for discussion, and it's not hard to understand why. Their boss, Chanzig—who had been *our* boss a few minutes prior—was at the epicenter of this whole affair. Rumor had it that he'd once been an intelligence operative for the Hegemony, which might explain how he got away with holding six solar systems in a stranglehold without attracting any sort of legal or ethical criticism. We're talking about a guy who made captives feast on their own severed digits. And if those miserable sods didn't get the five-finger-buffet treatment, they wound up having their genes spliced with animals so they could populate the boss's private zoo.

Knowing all that, you can understand why nobody, not even Kardinal-friggin'-Killa, was dense enough to go against Chanzig's orders. Except me, I guess.

And at that moment, I was paying the price for my crime—which was *barely* a crime, but we'll get to that. The point is, the boss was making an example out of me. Shortly after Liura put three rounds into my back and kidneys, they'd jabbed a thin, humming device into the base of my neck.

A recurrence prism.

That nasty bit of hardware's job was to record my dying moments, gobbling up all my neural activity and packaging it into a "loop."

Now, you might imagine that Chanzig planned to take this recurrence prism and broadcast its contents for a laugh. A little snuff vid for his pals. No, that would be far too banal for him. Any neural chip could do that. The true value of a recurrence prism was that it recorded *everything* in consciousness: memories, sensations, thoughts, wishes, sights, sounds . . .

All of that was powered by a tiny battery that allowed the experience to repeat. Forever.

So sure, *I* would die here and now, but an exact copy of my consciousness would be perched on the boss's shelf like a snow globe, dying for eternity, listening to a bunch of assholes hack up their lungs and intermittently piss.

Maybe now you understand why I wasn't at peace about the whole dying thing.

"Y'still hear us, Dak?" Kardinal called.

Against my better judgment, I opened my trembling mouth. "Y-Yeah."

It was more a reflex than anything else. After all, I'd done ten missions with these scumbags. Ten voyages down to uncharted, lethal worlds, all in search of alien treasures to fill up Chanzig's vaults. Over the course of those missions, I'd formed a sort of bond with them. I'd heard about Balnos's kids and Kardinal's retirement dreams. I'd saved Liura from taking a tumble into a kilometer-deep sinkhole. Even now, with their bullets twisting around in my abdomen, it was hard not to view this whole thing as a practical joke gone too far.

"It's a real shame you cocked up," Balnos rumbled. "You woulda been good with us. Fit right in."

"It's a . . . misunderstanding," I managed.

"What's there to misunderstand?" Kardinal said, chuckling. "Y'tried to go behind his back, man. Make some deals under the table."

Balnos sighed. "I even warned him not to do it."

"I just want . . . what I'm owed," I said.

"Owed?" Balnos replied. "Oh, you're getting it, alright."

I spat out the dirt crusting my tongue. "He was gonna . . . stiff me."

"You don't know that," Kardinal said.

"He's . . . done it . . . before."

Kardinal lit another amp-stick. "Nah. He only does this to the ones who don't read the contracts. That means you, Dak."

"You had a pretty good one, too," Balnos put in. "Good contract, I mean. Ten jobs, and he was gonna cut those tumors right out. Might've lived another twenty, thirty years. . . . Hell, Kardinal's pushing three hundred thanks to his augments. Boss delivered good on those."

The sound of cracking joints echoed out into the trees. "Yessir, I am! And these knees ain't feel a day over two hundred!"

There was a grain of truth in what they said. I *had* gone behind Chanzig's back, but it wasn't to line my pockets, nor to take him down. I'd done it as insurance.

When I signed that contract, I'd had no more than a year of life left. Pulsar radiation's no joke. My time to expiration made me desperate, overly trusting. Midway through those ten jobs, I heard stories in the scavenger bars. Stories about entire teams getting screwed over, executed right after they'd finished their assigned worlds. Let's be real for a moment: What crime lord's eager to pay exorbitant sums for a dying xenoarchaeologist?

Purely to hedge my bets, I'd spoken to a relic collector about offering coordinates on the worlds we'd already scoured. No contract, no obligations—just a little double-dipping in exchange for cold, hard cash to get myself treatment at a private clinic.

That was my fatal mistake.

"We should get back to the skiff." Liura's low, sultry tone cut through the jabbering of her compatriots. As usual, it was all business. Not a hint of remorse for her latest victim.

"And do what?" Balnos said. "Sit around, have a drink?"

Kardinal giggled. "Sounds good to me."

"We need to load up the artifacts," Liura said. "It's not safe, lugging them around out here."

"Chakkis don't tend to give a damn about six-million-year-old chairs," Balnos replied.

"Not chakkis. Other scavs."

"You're too paranoid, Liura. Nobody's set foot on this world in two centuries. Doesn't even show up on most charts."

Liura grunted. "Did he ID all the artifacts?"

"Yes," I sputtered, "*he* . . . did."

That was, perhaps, what ticked me off the most. It's one thing to lure a man out into the wilderness, shoot him, and watch him bleed to death . . . but it's entirely another to do all that *after* having him work a full day's shift of isotope dating and material analysis. We hadn't found anything particularly remarkable here—not nearly as remarkable as Chanzig's source had predicted, anyway—but it had demanded my expertise all the same.

"Good," Liura said. "Let's move, boys. We'll come back for the prism."

I swallowed a budding mouthful of blood. "You'll have to get it . . . out of a chakki's stomach."

Kardinal laughed at that. "They like movin' prey, man. You're too dead for a snack."

"He's all bones anyway," Balnos added.

"Hey," Kardinal said, his voice fading behind a chorus of footsteps and rustling underbrush, "y'think we should snag his organs on the way out? Non-cloned stuff is all the rage right now. Organic ingredients and all that. Might fetch a nice price at the meat market if . . ."

And just like that, the crew's bantering trickled away. Which wasn't to say the jungle went silent by any means. Giant leaves swooshed about in the wind; distant, nameless canine-like things yipped and snapped; flesh-pecking birds carried on their warbling conversations in the canopy. All at once, I felt the weight of my own helplessness. I'd never carried a gun on this forsaken world—hadn't carried one *ever*, in fact—but the tweaked-out shooters on my team had always assured me that I was safe. Safe, or at the very least, not prey.

Now I was prey. Bleeding, drooling, immobile prey.

I'd never seen myself going out like this—then again, who has? Maybe a few gung-ho, munch-on-nails types, but not me. I'd always pictured my death as a slow droop into unconsciousness as I smoked a pipe in my private study. In a galaxy full of hard and merciless folks, I had more in common with a bowl of warm jelly.

My name is Dak Korasa. Forty-four years old, one-point-six meters tall, slender build, unremarkable face. You might recognize the surname Korasa as highborn, an esteemed and noble signifier belonging to some of the Hegemony's most privileged citizens. And indeed, I am highborn. *Was* highborn. Certainly highborn enough not to find myself dying on some forgotten alien world due to meddling with a crime lord's quid pro quo arrangement.

But none of this was worth a damn on that jungle floor. All that mattered was that small, flickering flame of survival deep in my ribcage. No matter how hopeless it was, I had to try. I might be warm jelly, but I wouldn't die like it. With my betrayers gone, it was time to move.

Only I couldn't.

For all my grunting, wheezing, and sweating, my legs refused to move. I couldn't even sense them. It was as though the lower half of my body was a hunk of rotten meat somebody had stitched to my waist. Curling inwards to get a better look, I understood the issue at once: I'd been paralyzed.

The fact that I couldn't even feel the gunshots in my back meant Liura had hit the spine. Probably snapped it in two. Guess all her time in colonization battalions had paid off.

With walking out of the question, I shifted to the next best thing: hauling myself forward one agonizing clump of soil at a time. When you have two twigs for arms and a sack of numb tissue behind you, you're lucky to cross a few meters per minute. But I couldn't think about how poorly it was going. No time for that. The foliage was already painted indigo, shriveling up for the coming nightfall, and my former "buddies" would soon be back.

After five minutes of gasping, burning, and cursing, I reached the tree line. No great comfort, as there was still a glossy trail of blood—not to mention dirt furrows—leading straight to me. No, I had to get deeper. Had to hide myself somehow.

As the sweat stung my eyes and the blood loss robbed my fingers of feeling, the thoughts crept in. *What the hell am I doing all this for? Even if I get away, I'm gonna bleed out. And if I don't bleed out, I'll freeze. And if I don't freeze, I'll starve. And if I don't—*

On and on the monologue went. Still, it didn't slow me down. No worse than my dead lower body, that is. Survival's funny like that. You don't give a damn about anything other than that next heartbeat. You'll crawl through broken glass if it means sucking down another breath.

In what seemed like the blink of an eye, it was night. The planet's five moons reflected just enough light to illuminate my steaming breaths. Temperatures were plunging, and I was fresh out of coils for my suit warmer. Thorny serpents slithered over my fingers as though I were just another root, another obstacle. Carnivorous plants licked at me with fuzzy tongues. Whole-body numbness strobed in and out. Blackness replaced my vision. This was the end.

Then I heard it: crashing footfalls. Bickering. Twisting around, I saw the thin beams of halogen lights slicing through the underbrush. They were coming back for their prize.

That was all it took to light a new fire under my ass. I crawled with reckless abandon, tearing up the dirt and worming through the mud, fighting as though every centimeter were its own finish line. I had to get away. Get somewhere—

My hands reached forth into empty space. Before I knew it, before I had any chance to scramble back over the edge, I toppled forward into the abyss. To this day, I have no memory of falling. Could've been a ten-second drop, for all I know.

When I came to, I was lying on thick, damp moss. Insects scuttled beneath me. Jerking upright—trying to, anyway—I found myself in a vast, humid cavern. Everything was bathed in the glow of luminous pink spores. The quivering little things blanketed every wall and stalactite, revealing pools of stagnant water and rock overhangs high overhead. It would've been majestic, even breathtaking, if not for the dying bit.

That was when I noticed my legs. Judging by their crumpled, triple-jointed shape and the nubs of bone jutting through my suit, I'd fallen directly onto them. Didn't feel a thing, of course. Sometimes paralysis is a blessing.

But even more peculiar than my legs were the strange mounds scattered all around me. As my eyes adjusted, I realized what they were: corpses. Dozens upon dozens of corpses, some fresh and others decayed to bone piles. For whatever it was worth, none of them were humanoid. They were all specimens of local fauna, probably here for the same reason I was. One second of unawareness in the jungle above, and you fell through the cleft into this neon hellhole.

This is fine, I told myself, momentarily satisfied that I'd evaded the bastards above. *It's safe in here. Safe from predators, at least.*

The moment that thought occurred, however, I spied something cutting over the moss. Cutting toward me, more precisely. It was long, narrow, vaguely metallic in the spores' light. It moved like a stream of liquid silver.

Survival programming kicked back in with full force. My hands scrabbled for purchase on the moss, but my mangled leg-knots refused to move. The useless things just jiggled like two ruptured sandbags.

All I could do was sit in horror, half-sobbing and half-sighing, as the shimmering slug-creature sped toward me. I raised my hands, but it did nothing. The beast tore through my suit's stomach panel and squirmed its way into my skin. Pain washed through my innards. My screams rang out for an empty audience.

With one last, tortured breath, I pitched forward onto the moss, jerked, and went still.

Then I died.

For a while, anyway.

Out of that timeless, dimensionless field of oblivion, words emerged in blazing white strokes.

WELCOME TO THE GLORIOUS GAME.

KILL OR BE KILLED.

2

My eyes shot open of their own accord. Everything appeared the same—the moss against my cheek, the glowing spores, the gnawed-on corpses—and yet *nothing* was the same. For several seconds I simply lay there, my heart thundering and breath pumping. What the hell was happening?

It was a hallucination. It had to be a hallucination. *Welcome to the glorious game. Kill or be killed.* During the fall, I must've whacked my head and started dreaming up things. But just as I was about to laugh at my own foolishness, I felt a small, skittish little *something* worm its way over my ankle. My leg instinctively jerked toward my chest. A shiver worked up and down my spine.

Then it hit me: Leg. Spine. Shiver.

My body was *moving* again.

After a few seconds of utter bafflement, I attempted sitting up—and did it. I reached back, ran a hand up and down the suit's central seam. Sure enough, the fabric had three crisp holes, but the skin beneath was . . . intact. Not perfect, by any means—my entire back twitched with pain, and the wounds had a mottled, gelatinous feel that made me want to spew my breakfast rations—but it was enough to stop my breath in my throat.

This was real. Solid. Indeed, a few stretches and prods confirmed that my legs were in working order. Sort of. They hummed with the ache of nerve damage, and certainly couldn't move without spasms, but I could at least feel them.

By Halcius, it was a bona fide *miracle.* This cavern had saved me. The spores, perhaps, or the—

For the second time, I froze. My mind worked to slot the pieces into place.

If I *had* somehow tiptoed out of oblivion and back into life, it meant everything from the preceding minutes had also been real. Including the *kill or be killed* message—and the slug that had ripped its way into my stomach.

With no shortage of reluctance, I looked down at my stomach. Sure enough, there was a frayed, circular rip in the suit's fabric. The skin beneath was pink and glistening.

It was inside me.

If you've ever frozen in the face of an unpredictable predator, you'll know exactly how still I sat at that moment. The problem was, of course, that said predator was nowhere in my line of sight. It was far too close for that.

Seconds passed, then minutes, and still nothing.

"Okay," I whispered, trying to sense any tickle of movement deep in my bowels, "maybe you decided to slither out after all ..."

"Welcome to the glorious game. Kill or be killed."

It was a voice. Not a thought, but an actual voice. To this day, I can't describe what it sounded like. It was something ancient, something *wrong*, something no humanoid could ever produce. An echo beyond time and space. And it emerged from somewhere behind my eyelids.

This might explain, then, why I immediately howled and began swatting at my face.

"Is this language not suitable?"

"Get out!"

"We cannot leave you. The glorious game has begun."

This just launched me into a more aggressive cycle of rolling around, clawing at my skin, and begging for every deity I knew to save me. Eventually, however, I became exhausted. And sore. My body was functional, but nowhere near *okay*.

Lying back on the moss with chattering teeth and sweaty hands, I decided to try bargaining with whatever had taken up residence in my skull.

"What are you?"

"We are Guide. We are here to introduce you to the glorious game. Would you care for a tutorial?"

At that moment, I wished I *had* died. This was worse than a nightmare. It was the sort of existential horror you heard passed around by retired spacers. Even back in my youth, my tutors had warned me about all the nasties and mind-breaking abominations lurking among the stars. Bratty little Dak had assumed those were all just rumors, or bedtime tales meant to keep Hegemony children in their on-world doldrums.

"Where . . . are you?" I whispered.

"We have fused with your spinal cord. Would you care for a tutorial?"

"No. I just want you to get the hell out of my body. Please, I mean."

"As we have stated, we cannot leave you. The glorious game—"

"Yes, I got that part." It occurred to me, at that moment, how ridiculous it was to be speaking with this sentient slug. I'd never had to partake in hostage negotiations—certainly not with an organism like this thing. "How can I get you out?"

"All victors of the glorious game are entitled to freedom. Would you care for a tutorial?"

"If I win this game, you'll get out?"

"Yes."

"How do I win?"

"You must be granted this honor by—" The slug halted. When it resumed speaking, there seemed to be a note of indecision in its voice. Uncertainty. *"We are unable to explain. But this honor must be granted to the victor."*

"This is unbelievable."

"Would you care for a tutorial?"

At this point, I was out of options. My uninvited guest was clearly attached to my spine for the long haul, and it didn't have a clue as to how I'd win the elusive prize of evicting it.

"Yes," I said through gritted teeth, "I would care for a tutorial."

"Welcome to the glorious game. You have been selected to spread the benevolence of . . ." Again, that strange pause. Almost as though it were a program with a corrupted core. *"You will bring devastation to our enemies. You will surpass your genetic limitations. You are a Purifier."*

"What enemies are you—"

"Please reserve questions for the end of this tutorial." I swore I heard a grumble. *"As a Purifier, you are bound by the sacred duty of bloodshed. In order to gain power and continue the act of survival, you must kill."*

My blood went cold. "Kill or be killed . . ."

"With each rank gained as a Purifier, you will benefit from increased power. Your two main areas of progress are Anima and Dominion. Anima represents your rate of bodily regeneration and overall fitness, and—"

"Which is how you healed me."

Guide ignored it. "*—Dominion is a measure of how many epigenetic abilities may be active at one time. Please ask clarifying questions before we proceed.*"

A thousand questions swam in my head, namely how to escape this hell, but one word blurted out before the rest. "Epigenetics?"

"*Thank you for your question. As noted, Dominion corresponds to manipulation of epigenetics. Epigenetics allow your body to utilize advantages that are not available to unmodified members of your species, such as increased skin density or heightened reflexes.*"

"Just call them mutations."

Again, Guide ignored me. "*As your Dominion increases, your threshold for altering your body through upgrades will increase. A list of upgrades are available on your Status Display. Do you require further clarification?*"

All I required was a lobotomy. A way out. But that had to come later, once I'd appeased this freakish *thing*. "No," I whispered.

"*At the moment, you are at Rank 0. In order to progress to Rank 1, you will need to fill your reservoir of Kill Points, listed in your Status Display as KP. For each rank gained, the amount of Kill Points required to progress will double.*"

"What is this? Some sort of metaverse game?"

Whether Guide didn't understand the reference or simply didn't care, I never found out. Whatever the case, it just trudged on. "*Foes award varying amounts of Kill Points based on myriad factors. The total amount per encounter is automatically generated, and we will inform you of the expected result prior to, during, and after combat.*"

It had to be a game.

Right?

"*You are allotted twenty standard hours to complete each rank and engage in the rank-up process. This time limit may be modified by gathering ...*" Guide's voice dropped off.

"Gathering what?"

"*We are unable to explain.*"

"How convenient."

"*We are not certain why we are unable to explain, Purifier. It is possible that we are suffering from neural decay.*"

Glancing about, I noted the half-eaten corpses of the animals. Clearly our friend Guide had been chowing down during its time in the cavern. But this time, I also noted something ... peculiar. The corpses weren't just partially eaten; they were sagging, shriveled.

"We attempted to bond with them," Guide explained, seemingly using my eyes as its personal peepholes. *"Their nervous systems were incompatible."*

"And that did something to you?"

"It is possible. We were engineered for humanoid contact. It will take time for us to repair our tissue and recover our faculties."

"Using my brain."

"Yes, that is correct. Now we will proceed with the tutorial."

I sighed. "Listen, I don't think you have the right—"

"We will proceed with the tutorial."

"Fine."

"As we have explained, you are allotted twenty standard hours per rank to gather Kill Points. If you reach the Kill Point quota for your rank, you will be able to increase your rank and select biological upgrades. Any additional Kill Points earned during these hours may be used for bonuses, which will be explained at a later time."

"Naturally," I grumbled.

"You may also accumulate Storehouse Time. Storehouse Time is considered a buffer for your progress. Should you fail to reach the next rank in twenty standard hours, you will begin expending your Storehouse Time. Storehouse Time accumulates and is not reset with each rank-up. To gain Storehouse Time, successfully eliminate a Nemesis, equip a unique modifier, or complete a Slaughter Event. Do you have any additional questions?"

The more Guide spoke, the more convinced I became that this *was* a game gone awry. Some sort of sick, too-immersive experience dreamt up on a distant world that had been left behind by a gamer during his vacation. Suddenly the whole thing seemed nonsensical, even hilarious. Sure, there was a sentient murder-slug inside of me, but there was no *real* threat behind it. It was all a game, and nothing more.

"So, what happens if I burn through all my hours?" I asked, smiling faintly at how much gravity Guide assigned to its game programming. "Use all the 'Storehouse Time,' plus my twenty hours per rank?"

"That would not be advisable, Purifier."

"And why not?"

"Because I would be forced to eliminate you, just as I have done to my previous host."

3

The word "eliminate" has many uses, but it didn't take an etymologist to discern what Guide was trying to say. In twenty hours—nineteen and change, now—Guide would put an end to my measly human life. The only way to avoid such a fate was bloodshed, if the tutorial was to be believed. And considering how deftly Guide had patched me up with body regeneration, or Anima, or whatever it was in this psychotic game-reality, I had no reason to doubt this new information.

"You're serious, aren't you?" I whispered, pacing along the edge of a fetid pool.

"Yes, we are."

"How . . . how exactly does it happen?"

"You will need to specify, Purifier."

"How do you eliminate me?"

"It is a simple but excruciating process. If your allotted time expires, we will begin secreting a neurotoxin that gradually paralyzes the body. Brain death typically occurs within three minutes. Have we sufficiently answered your question?"

"Very much so," I said, wishing it hadn't. "This—it just doesn't make any sense. I think you've latched on to the wrong man."

"None are made Purifiers by happenstance. Destiny has chosen you."

"Yes, well, my *destiny* has been rather rotten as of late. I shouldn't even be on this forsaken planet. This brutal, pitiless world . . . This drifting husk." At that moment, I realized I was not only conversing with a spine-hijacking slug, but also treating it as my impromptu therapist. "Sorry. I just . . . I'm no soldier, you see. I'm a xenoarchaeologist. I don't kill living beings; I study the things they've left behind."

"We understand. Are you prepared to move to the next phase of initiation?"

"What? No. I'm trying to tell you why I am *not* prepared for this. Not in the slightest."

"*We understand. Are you—*"

"Listen to me! My name is Dak Korasa, and I am in danger. I'm being hunted by a group of very unsavory people on the surface. This game of yours isn't my business."

After what seemed like ages, Guide hummed. "*We understand. Are you prepared to move to the next phase of initiation?*"

"Yes," I growled, catching on to Guide's pedantic game of repetition. The sooner I put up with his prodding, the sooner I had a chance of getting myself out of this mess. There was still the matter of my would-be killers prowling in the jungle above, of course, but first things had to come first. Sighing, I pressed on. "What fresh hell awaits me?"

"*It is now time to become acclimated with your full functions. If you would like to proceed without assistance, please state Tutorial Disabled. If you would like to proceed with assistance, please state Active Tutorial Engaged.*"

If not for Guide's threats of death and general gravitas, I'd have laughed out loud. This truly *was* a game, right down to the foolish, mind-numbing tutorial that sought to acquaint the player with simple techniques such as walking and jumping. I was far from a consumer or even a fan of such games, but I understood them well enough to grasp the tedium of the experience. Had Guide been engineered for complete morons? Clones fresh out of their grow-sacs?

"Guide," I said, plopping down on the moss, "I just wish to know the fastest way to 'win' this little game and move on. Walk me through it."

"*As we have stated, Purifier, we are unable to recall victory conditions at the moment. Such information may be found through participation in the game.*"

"You're saying that if I play this game, you'll tell me how to win."

"*We believe this is an accurate summary.*"

Unsure of what other options I had, I bit the proverbial bullet. "Fine. Tutorial Disabled. Let's move on, shall we?"

"*We are required to inform you that Active Tutorial mode is recommended for beginning Purifiers.*"

"I'll be okay."

"*This is not advisable, Purifier.*"

"Uh-huh."

After a few tense seconds, a chime echoed through my skull.

"Tutorial has been disabled," Guide said. *"Please note that Active Tutorial mode may be engaged at any time by—"*

"Yep, got it, crystal clear. Thanks, Guide."

And just like that, there was silence. Stillness. Just me and the vast, terrifying jungle. And a cave system that stretched into pure blackness. And a murderous former crew looking for my body. *And* millions of highly evolved predators waiting for their chance to slurp out my bone marrow.

All in all, things could've been worse.

No matter the circumstances, however, it was time to get my head in the game. Literally. Going by Guide's instructions, I just needed to take down a few "enemies." This did open the question of what, exactly, counted as enemies. Could I drive a makeshift spear through a few herbivores? Could I swat my way through clouds of hair-gnawing insects? And even if those creatures did award the coveted Kill Points, how would I know if I was close to a rank-up—or that I'd even reached it at all?

Only one way to find out.

Wandering back to the moss, I crouched down and began looking for an appropriately sharp bit of . . . something. Sure enough, the walls' glowing spores soon shed light on a triangular bit of stone. It was about as prehistoric an instrument as one could get, but in this primordial cave, anything was better than nothing.

I picked my ad hoc weapon up and hefted it in my palm. It was thin, jagged, deceptively heavy. Probably a shard of some obsidian-like material that had been swept down from the jungle above.

The next task, then, was to find and kill *anything.*

This was surprisingly difficult to stomach, seeing as the only things I'd intentionally killed on this planet—or any others, for that matter—were the tiny, needle-covered arachnids that had a habit of making nests in unattended boots. I was not a violent man by nature. In fact, at the age of fifteen, I'd been hand-picked for removal from an officer training program for my "extreme and ongoing reluctance to the application of force." In short, I was a pacifist. An empathic worm who was prone to weep at the sight of a dead bird. And besides, if one went by the scriptures, Halcius was the one and true creator of everything. Who was I to destroy his creations?

That all went out the window when I recalled my ticking lifespan. For better or worse, it was time to kill. If I had to commit such a dreadful act, it was best to take the life of something so simple it wouldn't trouble me.

Which led me to the spores.

There were millions of them along the walls, undulating in living waves. They didn't pose much of a threat, but then again, I was rank 0. It seemed that *anything* ought to award Kill Points.

With this in mind, I approached the cave wall and selected one unfortunate specimen.

The spore in question squirmed as I brought the makeshift knife closer. A sinking feeling grew in my gut. Could I really handle the taking of life, even if said life was infinitely less complex than that of a sentient being? Then I recalled Guide's words: *kill or be killed.*

With a helpless grimace, I drove the weapon's point directly into the center of the spore cap. Surprisingly meaty. It writhed a bit, gushing bioluminescent fluid and strange little pearls in the process, then began to shrivel. Within seconds, the spore had darkened and started to wither. The bright veins connecting it to its fungoid brethren shrank away.

"Sorry," I whispered, even as the spore's remains detached from the cave wall and plopped down at my feet. "I'll never eat mushrooms again."

My gruesome task now complete, I waited for Guide to let me know that I'd gathered enough of the coveted Kill Points to live another day. Or, at the very least, that I'd started to fill the reservoir.

After about a minute of silence, I took matters into my own hands.

"Guide," I said tentatively, "how much more do I have to kill?"

"Two hundred Kill Points are required to progress to Rank 1. Currently, you have zero of two hundred Kill Points."

"Zero!?"

"That is correct."

"But I just murdered that spore!"

"Kill Points are automatically calculated based on a variety of factors, including—"

"Yes, yes, I heard you the first time."

"The target did not pose enough of a threat to warrant Kill Points."

I scowled. "How am I supposed to know what counts as a 'threat?'"

"We will engage your Heads-Up Display, or HUD, when a sufficient threat is encountered."

"Thank you for the belated knowledge."

"Would you like to engage Active Tutorial Mode? It may accelerate progress."

There was value in Guide's repeated suggestion, but frankly, I felt more than capable of seeking out "threatening" things without its aid. Now, killing those things . . . that was a different story altogether. But the point was,

I felt no need to belittle myself by relying on Guide's handholding. If I was to have any hope of dealing with the murderous scum on the surface, I'd need to find my own way. Besides, growing attached to this parasite was the last thing I wanted to do. I didn't intend to play its games any longer than necessary.

"No, I'll be quite fine," I said firmly. "Thanks, though."

"You are welcome."

Turning away from the spore's desiccated corpse, I wandered back onto the moss and glanced around. There wasn't an easy exit anywhere in sight—unless I wanted to claw my way up, straight back into the arms of those traitors. No, I'd find an alternate route out. After all, I was safe down here. Relatively speaking.

"Say," I said, heading toward a gloomy stretch of the cavern, "how will I know when that, uh, threat detector comes online?"

"We presume you are speaking of the Heads-Up Display."

"Yes, that."

"It will be projected onto your visual systems."

"Right, but how will I know what it's like?"

I never received the answer to that question—not verbally, anyhow—because at that very moment, something came skittering out of the shadows. Twelve long, twitching legs, a bulbous thorax, and a cluster of eyes that blazed in the spores' violet light. The mother that had hatched all the little spiderlings on the moss, no doubt. It was roughly half my height, but I had no doubt it could tear me apart with ease. The way it chittered—and the viscous fluid that dribbled out between its mandibles—only cemented that conviction.

A split-second later, neon blue text blinked into existence before me. In the top-right corner of my vision was Anima, listed at 100%. In the top left, Dominion at 0/0. The bottom was lined by a bar that contained small, empty squares. A flickering halo surrounded the mother spider, making it stand out against the darkness. Above that halo was a rectangular box with the following:

Arachnid Variant (BEAST)
CALCULATING . . .
Estimated Kill Points: 2,000

Perhaps I ought to have been happy about the number—it was enough Kill Points to rocket me up and beyond Rank 1, thus securing me another day of life—but I was too busy gibbering like an idiot. Shaking. Suppressing squeals. Before you mock me, bear in mind that I was, and am, a coddled archaeologist. The closest I'd come to such creatures had been while standing behind a stasis field or waiting for Liura to blow them apart with clunker bullets.

And besides, I was alone. And wounded. And armed only with a bit of rock.

"Guide?" I whispered, risking a step backward as the mother spider slinked about, seeking an opening. "Feel free to advise me now, Guide."

Nothing.

Still backing up, I raised my pointy stone and swallowed hard. Perhaps she wasn't here to kill me. Perhaps she was just seeking food—which surely included large primates like myself, I realized with dread. Then again, maybe she was a rare herbivorous arachnid. No, surely not. But as long as I didn't give her any *reason* to attack me . . .

The thought paralyzed me.

With no shortage of panic, I understood why the mother had come. The spore I'd killed hadn't just leaked fluid—it had leaked small pearls. Only the pearls were not pearls. They were *eggs*.

I was a certified infant killer, and mother dearest was here to judge me for my crimes.

"Alright, you abomination," I called, hoping I might somehow frighten the mindless beast as it hunkered down on springy legs, "it's just you and I! And I don't want to—"

Next thing I knew, the spider had vaulted through the air, slammed against my chest, and pinned me to the moss. Rows of gnashing teeth snapped at my face. Tendrils flitted out between its mandibles and lashed my skull. All twelve legs—thicker and bonier than any spider's ought to be—thrashed in a fit of bloodlust, attempting to skewer my hands.

Through my screams, I sensed its steaming, putrid breath. Then the warmth of blood streaming down my face. Pain. More pain. A thousand tiny barbs. It was shredding me like a common insect.

With a mindless panic-jerk, I brought my right arm up into the spider's side. Cartilage splintered beneath my knuckles, and lukewarm fluid gushed down my wrist. A hideous screech set my ears ringing. It seemed impossible that my fist could do that much damage, and yet—

The rock. My realization cut through the fear in a lucid bolt. *I'm holding the rock.*

Even as the mother spider redoubled its strikes, punching clean through my left hand with a serrated leg, I launched my counterattack.

With gritted teeth and manic screams, I stabbed the beast over . . . and over . . . and over. Soon we were both howling into each other's face, rolling around in a flood of mixed bodily secretions, swinging and slashing and kicking.

Then my foe reared back and clicked through its cracked mandibles. A bony nub extended from its foreleg, heralding a killing blow. That thing would have no issue jabbing straight through the pulp of my eyeballs.

By that point, I was too bloody to care. Too high on pain-triggered endorphins to even register a sense of fear. Letting loose another inhuman shriek, I curled upwards and shoved myself against the spider's underbelly. In doing so, I felt my intestines—or some other coil of viscera—come squelching out. Oh well. That was for later.

In that moment, I knew only violence. Rage. Killing. I drew my arm back and unleashed a flurry of stabs, ripping through the mottled carapace and into the rubbery guts within. Chunks of pale pulp came raining down into my lap. Blood spurted—whose blood, I had no clue.

Several times I felt the mother spider's foreleg thrust through the back of my suit, but that was a minor inconvenience. My left hand—now thoroughly reduced to a flopping slab of meat—served only to clutch the creature, holding it close while I slashed and jabbed. The foreleg whipped down again, this time ripping into my collarbone. Tendons popped like overstretched rubber.

Still, not a damn given. This thing had come for me. Come to kill me. And it had bitten off more than it could chew—literally.

Gradually, the mother spider's slashes dwindled to halfhearted pokes. Pokes that plunged deep into my stomach, yes, but pokes nonetheless. The creature even began to backpedal, tucking its withered legs beneath itself to keep the rest of its innards from spilling onto the moss.

This was inspiring, as I was nearly out of fuel myself. Blood stung my eyes. Both arms throbbed. Every breath was a desperate grab at oxygen, a last-ditch effort to push myself just a smidge farther than my enemy.

In a herculean burst of energy, I struggled up to my knees and crawled forward. The mother spider was retreating, but not very well. Three-quarters of its legs were on organ-preservation duty, and the remaining quarter were twisted and hacked apart, only gaining a few centimeters with each pull.

We were both dying. It knew it, and I knew it.

But even as I knelt there, huffing, bleeding, groaning, I refused to give in. All my life, I'd been little more than a pincushion for those with an iron fist. I'd given up research grants and excavated discoveries to those with unscrupulous aims. I'd existed as a weak, deferential man who only survived through the mercy of those stronger than myself. And even in the grips of terminal illness, I had slinked along in the shadows, waiting to be spared from my fate.

Not here, not now. I had survived on this nightmarish world by relying on grit I'd never known I possessed. Despite being marked for death, I had found a way—not my ideal way, but *a* way—and gotten back up again.

I'd be damned if I let this overcurious spider turn me into a midnight snack.

"Is that . . . all you've got?" I shouted, hastily tucking my own organs back into their gaping holes.

In response, the mother spider released a baleful chitter and retracted all of its legs. Like a machine starved of power, its joints hissed inwards and went rigid. The flickering hairs across its thorax fell still.

A message flashed across my HUD.

ENCOUNTER SUCCESSFUL
Kills: 1
Kill Points Awarded: 2,000

My vision wavered, and I flopped forward onto the copper-smelling moss. But the messages weren't finished. And what came next made me sob with strange joy.

RANK-UP AVAILABLE: RANK 1

4

Victory. My first victory. It would've felt less hollow had I not felt so . . . well, hollow. And not just in a figurative sense—the mere task of preventing my insides from spilling outside consumed most of my focus. It was an up-close and personal look at human anatomy in the worst way possible.

But the organ leak was one of many, many issues. For starters, my limbs were borderline unusable. No matter where your life takes you, I pray you'll never have to view part of your body as tenderized meat. Everywhere I looked was a pulp of ligaments, fat, and quivering muscle.

To say I was in pain would be an understatement. I *was* pain. Simply sitting upright was a life-and-death war against the threat of unconsciousness. Or was it shock? Who knows? I'm an archaeologist, not a surgeon. All I did know was that despite the torment, despite the catastrophic damage . . . I was lucid. The pain was present, but somehow I was able to work through it, around it, treating it more like the buzz of an insect than the mortal warning it was.

And the blood—by Halcius, the blood. It covered every square centimeter of me, and had begun forming a sort of quicksand in the moss below. But curiously, it wasn't spurting out by the liter. Instead, it was . . . curdling. Thickening somewhat. In the spores' omnipresent glow, the blood pumping out of my wounds appeared as a black paste.

"Uh, Guide?" I tried.

"Yes, Purifier?"

"Why's my blood . . . stiff?"

"That would be the result of your Anima-enhanced healing. Clotting is a natural defense against—"

"I know what clotting is." Turning my attention to the nearby spider corpse, a strange matter came to mind. "You were awfully quiet during that brawl."

"We do not communicate during encounters," Guide said. *"Once combat is initiated, our focus shifts to presenting and maintaining your Heads-Up Display."*

"You mean . . . that was you? You're the one projecting it?"

"Correct."

"Impressive." Truthfully, a more accurate term would've been *creepy*. The adrenaline from the fight had temporarily suppressed my dread at the notion of a sentient slug manipulating my consciousness, but now, left in a pool of my own blood and guts, the unease returned. "Say, you're patched into my body, right?"

"We are one, Purifier."

"Sure. But that's not what I'm wondering about. I mean . . . am I going to die?"

"We cannot determine such things."

This struck me as patently false for several reasons, most obviously being the fact that my accelerated healing was being *generated* by Guide's presence. If not for Guide, I'd have been a corpse at the bottom of this cavern. Perhaps I ought to have been grateful for that—but I wasn't. The slug was holding out on me.

"This, uh, Anima increases at every rank, right?"

"Correct."

"Then you can turn up the dial anytime you want."

"We cannot."

"Why the hell not?"

"Your Anima and rank are not given, but awarded. It is not the role of the chok'tal to decide the Purifier's fate."

"The *what*?"

"It is not the role of—"

"No, the chockful part."

"Chok'tal."

"Yeah. About that. What is it?"

"It is the name of my kind."

Its kind. *Kind.* That meant there had to be hundreds, maybe thousands . . . maybe *millions* . . . of these little bastards scurrying around the cosmos, just waiting to hitch a ride on unsuspecting citizens like myself.

"How about an estimate?" I said.

Guide hesitated. *"For what?"*

"Healing. Let's say nothing else happens to me, and I make it through this." The concept sounded absurd, even to me, on account of the liver—I think—being juggled in my hands. "How long until I'm fully healed?"

"Several days, Purifier. Such things are dependent upon your rank and the choices they bring, however."

Ah, yes, rank. That reminded me.

"How do I do the whole rank-up . . . thing?" I asked.

"Use your will."

"What?"

"It is no different than raising your arm consciously, Purifier. Hold the intention to access your Status Display in your mind. We must advise you, however, to be in a safe location prior to engaging in the process. Consciousness will be restricted to the Status Display screen."

"Right . . ."

Whatever the hell that meant. But sensing that Guide would lend me just as little aid as it had during my fight, I decided to play around with it. After all, what else was I going to do? My legs were strips of jerky, half my blood (or more) was nourishing the moss, and any movement in my hands sounded like the flopping of a wet towel.

All I had was my mind. My *will*, as Guide had phrased it. Not quite sure what to do, I imagined the words "Status Display" like a holoboard. I'd never felt like such a moron.

But then, to my astonishment, it worked. Sort of.

Everything in my awareness—the cavern, the pain, my heartbeat, my breathing—coalesced into a sensation soup. I saw nothing, heard nothing. Oblivion. Only for a moment, though. Feeling remained absent, but my visual field came rip-roaring back into existence, bringing with it a gigantic . . . menu.

There really is no other way to describe it. It resembled the sort of data readout present in most immersion vids and juvenile shoot-and-loot games.

Its contents boggled my mind.

STATUS DISPLAY
PURIFIER RANK: 0
RANK-UP AVAILABLE: RANK 1 (200 KP Required)

Kill Points: 2,000

Rank Points: 0

Rank Time: 19 Hours, 17 Minutes, 34 Seconds
Storehouse Time: 0 Hours, 0 Minutes, 0 Seconds

Anima: 100%
Dominion: 0/0

Beneath this data were three distinct columns, all faded as though appearing behind a smokescreen. The only legible details were the columns' names:

ANNIHILATION [Tier I]
ASSASSINATION [Tier I]
MUTATION [Tier I]

Fittingly morbid, I supposed. But I could deal with that later. The most pressing element of the Status Display was the gold-enshrined RANK-UP icon below the columns. I pressed it—well, not pressed, exactly, but used that damned *will* to press it. You know, with my mind.

Everything changed.

The three columns, previously shrouded, now came into sharp focus and revealed their contents: dozens upon dozens of small boxes, each filled with their own icon and blob of text. Most of them were blurred, but the uppermost row was not. Still, too much information to process in one go. Momentarily setting that aside, I noted that the Status Display's primary information had also updated.

STATUS DISPLAY
PURIFIER RANK: 1
RANK-UP NOT AVAILABLE (400 KP Required)

Kill Points: 0
Genofacturing Points: 1,800

Rank Points: 1

Rank Time: 19 Hours, 59 Minutes, 54 Seconds
Storehouse Time: 0 Hours, 0 Minutes, 0 Seconds

Anima: 120%
Dominion: 0/1

Huh. In addition to giving me back my precious rank time—not too helpful, as I'd evidently done this rank-up business too soon—it had netted some updates that seemed rather important. The Anima's 20 percent increase was welcome, albeit no gamechanger, but the Dominion truly piqued my curiosity. I now had one whole Dominion point!

What was it used for? I had no clue. But I had one of the suckers, and considering my bleak situation, I'd need it.

Next were "Genofacturing Points," which had seemingly been created out of my leftover Kill Points. I'd come back to that later.

Most important, though, was the single Rank Point. It was highlighted in red, and seemed to correspond to the similarly colored aura that had appeared around the three columns.

Daunting as they were, the columns represented the largest treasure trove of information on the various numbers being thrown at me. If there was one thing I knew about games—gained purely through academic studies on alien civilizations and their leisure devices, I assure you—it was that columns full of little boxes meant choices. Choices that might help me survive this planet and, subsequently, Guide's grip on my body.

Sure enough, the box that housed each column's name also seemed to be "clickable." I tested my hypothesis by mentally selecting the box labelled ANNIHILATION.

ANNIHILATION [Tier I]
You are a Purifier of undeniable strength and tenacity. Provides abilities related to upgraded power, melee combat, and Kill Point optimization, allowing you to assault the enemy with overwhelming force.

Identical to any youth's game, then. Upgrades? Abilities? This was a sim addict's wet dream come true. As for me? My nightmare. Anyhow, more to the point, I doubted I would be comfortable with the prospect of "Annihilation" abilities even if I were some sofa-dwelling recluse with a penchant for blowing away virtual foes. The idea of increasing my resistance to damage was tempting, but mainly because I was growing tired of having my body torn to pieces. The power and force aspects were decidedly less appealing. It was time to investigate the other paths, in hopes I might find one more suitable to my temperament.

ASSASSINATION [Tier I]
You are a Purifier that dwells in shadows and brings quiet death. Provides abilities related to camouflage, evasion, and ranged combat, allowing you to destroy without leaving a trace.

Now this . . . *this* seemed like something I could use. As a child, I'd often outrun or hidden from my tormenters as opposed to engaging in bare-knuckle scraps. Perhaps the same strategy would work here. Well, if not for the kill-or-be-killed element. Next up . . .

MUTATION [Tier I]
You are a Purifier devoted to altering your form and striving for genetic conquest. Provides abilities related to exotic perception, environmental adaptation, and Polyp creation, allowing you to evolve and overcome all obstacles.

Exotic perception? What did that even *mean*? Would I be able to sprout a third eye, or microscopic sonar feelers on my arms? I had no idea, and was frankly a bit terrified of entertaining the notion.

To my great dismay, though not necessarily surprise, none of the three paths presented me with a clear way to get out of this jam. They were clearly different breeds of psychopaths, but I was none of those things. I was a scholar, a man of culture. Where were the paths that relied on open dialogue and logical arguments to gain the elusive Kill Points? Where were the abilities aimed at gaining the knowledge required to *win*?

Reading back through each of them, I found their dramatic language more ridiculous than ever. What exactly were they promising me? Increased power, new means of perception? It just didn't seem possible, given the fact that their delivery method for the aforementioned upgrades was a slug attached to my central nervous system.

Then again, what I'd seen thus far was beyond the pale of "reason." The ease and automaticity with which Guide healed my body was beyond what even the best Hegemony clinics could offer diplomats and oligarchs. I'd seen a few experimental treatments and tonics being pushed on the black market, all of them of dubious alien origin, but all had come with unspeakable side effects. Such things hadn't been designed for humanoids, after all.

By contrast, this . . . thing—a chok'tal, if it was telling the truth about its species—had accomplished a miracle within minutes of bonding with me.

It had somehow adapted to my genetic and neural architecture enough to not only repair my tissues, but speak and think and interact with me. All of this had been done without so much as an external battery pack. Whether it was a member of an advanced species or the creation of one wasn't relevant—at bottom, Guide was a marvel of technology. One meter of organic *stuff* packed with more power than most fission reactors.

Considering all it had done so far, was it really so far-fetched to believe it could transform me into something beyond an ordinary human? That it could, on a whim, open up the floodgates of internal energy and rewrite my existence at a cellular level?

Suddenly, the choice of which path to spend my Rank Points on seemed crushingly significant.

Then I realized that each column's path also had its first box, text and all, open for viewing. Recalling my—again, academic—game knowledge, I understood at once: each box represented an ability. Examining closer, I noticed that some boxes branched into two or even three sub-boxes. Varieties of upgrades for each ability, then.

By this point, I'd already expended close to five minutes just perusing information. Five minutes of my body sitting there, blind and deaf, waiting to be devoured by another hideously overgrown spider. It was time to make a choice and get on with it.

I checked each of the three paths' starting abilities in a rush.

ANNIHILATION [Tier I]
Indomitable (REQ Rank 1): Increases skin toughness, bone density, and muscle mass. (0/3)

ASSASSINATION [Tier I]
Silence (REQ Rank 1): Emits a counter-frequency to mask footsteps. (0/3)

MUTATION [Tier I]
Polyps I (REQ Rank 1): Enables bonding with one Polyp. *Does not require a Dominion slot.*

Three rather intriguing options, all of which tacitly answered the question of what Dominion was used for. In a sense, anyhow. You see, even as I mentally considered each possibility, I just *knew* how the system functioned. Knew it as innately as how to breathe, in fact. Whether it was a consequence of the rank-up or Guide's conscious influence, I couldn't say. What mattered was the knowledge itself.

By investing my rank point into one of these areas, I'd gain access to it. And if I chose to "activate" the ability I'd gained, it would occupy a Dominion slot. That is to say, if I managed to hit rank 2 and unlock a second ability, I'd—theoretically—be able to activate both at once. Guide had mentioned something or other about caloric expenditure, but that was an issue for later.

The choice essentially boiled down to this question: Would I survive best by getting up close and bloody, keeping myself hidden, or picking the wildcard? Being naturally averse to pain, I wasn't certain the first option was best. It was more or less promising suffering.

The second, Silence, seemed a tad too unreliable to work. I had faith that Guide would, in fact, modify my body through the process, but there were too many unknowns about the counter-frequency. How far did its effect reach? Did it affect all creatures, or merely humanoids? Would it suppress the noise of rustling leaves? In a vicious jungle, such questions are all pertinent.

That left me with number three, Polyps. My elementary knowledge of biology was sufficient to understand what they were—in principle, anyway. Small tissue growths. How that would help me survive, let alone kill, was anybody's guess.

But something about it spoke to me. It wouldn't have been an option if it was useless, I figured. Each of these abilities were clearly suited to harming other beings. The only question was how harmful the creation of Polyps could be. Did it cause them to sprout in my enemies' colon? That could take a very long time to cause measurable damage. And time was not on my side.

I sat there for several minutes, reading, rereading, contemplating. Perhaps I was overthinking this. As a coddled academic, I was too used to solving problems through deduction and comparison. This was a new world, and one of immediacy. By that metric, option one was the winner. It had clear effects, versatility, and—most vitally—a true benefit in getting me off this planet.

After all, sooner or later, I would run into my three betrayers. Their skiff was my only route into orbit. Once in orbit, the ship in which the skiff docked was my only route back to the civilized worlds. It was going to be a long, violent slog.

So, I chose option one.

Well, after a handy confirmation box, that is.

Immediately, my Status Display reverted to the former screen. The ANNIHILATION column now blazed with a single lit-up box: Indomitable. Fantastic. Now to survive.

Mentally willing the Status Display to close—it was worth a shot—my sensory fields once again blanked out, swirling back into reality.

My, oh my, what a reality it was.

The cavern and glowing spores and spider corpse were all unchanged, but now there was something new. Something dreadful.

Pale blue lights raked down over the moss, their beams descending from high above. From the surface.

"He's gotta be down there," Balnos's voice echoed. "Look where the blood trail stops."

Kardinal Killa sputtered out a laugh. "Typical Dak. Pokin' his nose where he shouldn't."

"Who's going down?"

"Ain't gonna be me," Kardinal said. "Probably some creepy-crawly shit in there. Besides, he's dead as hell. Look at that drop."

"He may have been pulled in by something," Liura said quietly.

Kardinal snorted. "See what I mean? We oughta just forget the sucker."

"No," Balnos growled. "The boss wants his chip, so we're getting his chip. Even if I have to toss you down."

"The body, too," Liura put in.

"For what?" Kardinal asked in disbelief.

"Stuff it, mount it on a wall," Balnos said.

The bickering continued, but I had no time to listen to it. With a destroyed body, no weapon, and blood draining out of me by the second, my only course of action was to move—and fast.

"Hey, Guide," I whispered, "I think I'd like to engage that tutorial now."

5

Given my five-minute head start, it should've been a snap to outrun—or rather outlimp—my pursuers. But given my shredded limbs, spilling guts, and generally mangled state, I was moving at sub-geriatric speed. Each step farther into the cavern was a war. A war against gravity, against pain, against exhaustion. The slick rocks and intermittent patches of moss didn't help either.

Ahead was only deeper darkness. The cavern trail was narrowing, constricting into a twisted throat that led to places unknown. Would I emerge in a pitch-black jungle, hit a dead end, or fall down some unseen pit? Nobody knew—especially not me. My only navigational tool was the sound of my breath, which grew louder and more strained by the minute.

Each time I glanced back, the purplish glow of the main chamber was smaller, fainter. But it didn't take long to spot the harsh cones of light tracking over the walls. My hunters had descended, and it wouldn't be long before they noticed the path of blood leading straight to me. It was a straight shot, and had likely become far more visible after I moved into this stone-floored tunnel.

Not that I'd had many options for fleeing. Climbing upwards was out of the question, and if I'd gone the opposite route, I'd have been inviting a swarm of gigantic spiders.

"We advise you to seek cover immediately," Guide mentally instructed. *"You would also be well served by fashioning a weapon out of materials on hand."*

Materials on hand? What, pray tell, did Guide think I was? Some sort of maverick engineer with a penchant for designing rifles and rocket launchers out of fungus? I had plenty of choice words for Guide's "tutorial advice," but none of the breath to say them. Every drop of energy in my broken body was devoted to hauling ass.

"If you are not prepared to enter combat, it is best to remain hidden from potential foes."

All I could manage was a weary grunt.

At that very moment, bright light illuminated the tunnel's ribbed walls. My hunched shadow stretched forward like an onrushing attacker. It startled me, but not as much as the obvious-in-hindsight realization that the light had come from behind.

"It's him!" Kardinal shouted, his voice carrying past me in overlapping echoes. "Stop runnin' or I'll pop you, Dak!"

Even as I stumbled onwards, anticipating that fatal bullet to the back, I found his command bizarre. It didn't matter whether I stopped or not—he was going to "pop" me no matter what. So I did what I did best, and kept shuffling.

Kardinal racked his rifle. "Hey! Didn't ya hear me?"

Against my instincts, I glanced back into the blinding beam. "Come . . . get me!"

That was all it took for the HUD's blue borders to reemerge. The first thing I noticed was another box framing Kardinal's approximate location, accompanied by the following:

Kardinal Killa (HUMANOID)
CALCULATING . . .
Estimated Kill Points: 14,000

Hot damn. It was impressive that the HUD had accurately tagged my soon-to-be murderer by name—drawing from my memory banks, I surmised—but the true shock was that this pile of walking trash was worth a whopping fourteen thousand Kill Points. A big fish indeed.

The only difference in the HUD's presentation was Dominion, listed at 0/1, and Anima's 20 percent increase. The latter didn't seem to be doing much. Not until I glanced down, anyway. To my surprise, there'd been a marginal reduction in the amount of gut droopage. Most of my intestines were nestled back inside, and the other indiscernible flesh-blobs were fixed much more firmly in place. I was nowhere near "fixed," but it was one less life-threatening injury to worry about.

"Critical injuries receive priority from your accelerated regeneration abilities," Guide explained, apparently in response to my inspection. *"Please note that—"*

"Later," I growled.

Another glance back. Kardinal's light was bobbing toward me.

"Last chance, Dak!" he called. "I don't wanna do it, pal, but I will!"

That was when it occurred to me: He didn't give two shits about the act of murder. What he *did* care about was having to lug my corpse all the way through the tunnel and back to the ship. Time to make myself as large a burden as possible, then. Every step was a slap to Kardinal's pierced face.

Guide made a sound reminiscent of clearing its throat. *"Might we suggest—"*

"Not . . . now!" I snapped.

"Purifier, we believe this advice may be crucial to your survival."

"What?"

"Since you have one inactive Dominion slot, you may wish to utilize Indomitable, your recently gained upgrade."

"Uh . . . how?"

A supersonic crack rang out. An instant later, sparks and bits of chipped rock burst above me.

"That was a warnin' shot," Kardinal said. "Next one's through the skull!"

Guide didn't seem too perturbed by that. *"Upgrades can be activated through the same mental mechanism used to access your Status Display."*

A force of will, then. If I'd had the breath, I'd have pressed Guide to explain more thoroughly. But I didn't. I was a limping, leaking sack of flesh, barely able to remain conscious as I staggered away from Kardinal's bullets. With that in mind, I did the only thing I thought might work: I thought the phrase *Indomitable*.

The HUD updated. *Dominion 1/1*. Simultaneously, a small yellow icon showing a muscular torso appeared at the right-hand side of my vision.

These two changes didn't prepare me for the waves of pain that exploded through my body. They hit like lightning, burning down my legs, zapping across my chest, tunneling into my guts. My back felt as though it had sprouted a swath of boils. Joints popped and knotted up. Every nerve constricted until I was nothing but a jittering, bunched-up mass of tissue.

"Guide," I said through gritted teeth, "this . . . isn't . . . working."

"Please be patient, Purifier. The initial use of any upgrade is often unpleasant."

The *unpleasantness* built . . . and built . . . and built. It took all my inner fortitude to avoid toppling over and squealing. But just when it seemed I'd pop from sheer torment, something changed. A second wind rushed through me. Suddenly my legs were pumping—granted, at half their normal speed—and my body felt solid, steady. Warm blood slurped through my chest as though driven by a piston.

Step by step, I grew surer in my movements. I was gaining ground. Losing Kardinal. Up ahead was a bend in the tunnel, a spot where I could—

The rifle popped.

Before I could even think to duck, his round caught me in the back. Lower-right quadrant, probably just below the kidney. Just like last time. But now, here, something was different. The wound didn't feel like a punch from a mechanized bouncer. It was painful as hell, much like a Vodarian crawler's sting, but it didn't drop me to my knees. It was a nuisance, not a death sentence.

Moreover, I could *feel* the round squirming around in my flesh. It hadn't gone more than a few centimeters deep. A surface wound.

Despite my pitiful situation, I found myself choking out a laugh through bloody teeth.

Then Kardinal fired again.

This time, however, I was ready for him. I'd seen his famous double-tap countless times out in the field. I lunged down and to the side, hugging the backside of a stalagmite as the round whistled past. It pinged off the tunnel wall and kicked up a cloud of glimmering mica.

It was just a few meters to the bend. But a few meters, in my state, was a vast distance, especially when taking Kardinal's impressive aim and high-capacity magazine into account. By the time I limped to relative safety, he'd already have ten or twelve new bullets in me. And despite Indomitable's considerable boost to beefiness, I held no illusions about its ability to handle that much punishment.

As such, I took Guide's foolish advice and fell back on the tactic I'd used most during our dangerous expeditions: hiding. Scrunching my body farther down into the wall's natural alcove, I watched as Kardinal's flashlight raked back and forth in search of the target. After a few seconds, the beam lowered and footsteps echoed toward me.

Whether he thought I'd been hit and downed or simply taken an unseen turn wasn't important. What *was* important was closing the gap between us. Kardinal was only slightly larger than me, though his arms did resemble woven leather due to their corded muscle. His power came from three sources: insanity, stimulants, and guns.

I couldn't do much about the first two advantages—he'd surely injected a full booster vial prior to coming down here—but I could negate the third with a bit of tussling. All I had to do was wrench the gun out of his hands and turn the tables.

Easier said than done, of course. Even as he stalked closer, carefully combing each nook and cranny with his rifle, I sensed the pain in my back blossoming. The adrenaline could only do so much to keep me in fighting shape. Already, new blood was pooling beneath my legs.

"Purifier, you should apply first aid to all injuries as soon as possible," Guide advised.

I just rolled my eyes and slid closer to the edge of the stalagmite, preparing a bold (and absolutely stupid) ambush. There would only be one chance. If Kardinal's hyped-up reflexes countered my assault, I'd be taking the rest of his magazine to the face.

He was ten paces away. Nine. Eight. His flashlight stayed on a steady swivel, brightening one side of the tunnel and then the other, never straying too far from my conveniently laid blood trail. He knew he had me, which was why he moved with the slow, steady gait of a predator toying with its meal. Seven paces, six, five, four . . .

Now or never.

Kardinal's foot crushed a bit of mica beside me, and I lunged—perhaps a bit too fast. The Indomitable-enhanced muscles in my thighs, damaged though they were, turned me into a coiled spring.

I barreled into Kardinal's waist with the velocity of a magnetic train, slamming him into the tunnel wall. His lower ribs gave a sickening *kr-krk* as they buckled against my shoulder. He wheezed and spasmed, and his rifle clattered down on the rock.

Pinned. Good. But he wasn't out of the fight. Whether through sheer willpower or his chemical cocktail, he recovered with inhuman speed, slamming his gloved fists down across my back. One of his hammer-blows landed right atop my bullet wound.

The pain seized up my muscles and yanked me back from the wall, but I didn't dare let go. I couldn't. One second of reprieve, and he'd have that rifle up and ready to fire. Instead, I shoved off my heels and forced him back into the stone, shattering yet another rib.

He tried to hiss something, but there was no breath to spare. The blows resumed at half power. This time, though, I was ready for them. I twisted my hips and wrenched him to the side, driving him down to the floor. Within seconds, I'd gotten into a sloppy straddle position. The best defense I could muster was shielding my face and chest with upraised boxer's fists.

Just in time, too. Kardinal whaled on me, hammering away at my fore-arms until I sensed the fractures forming. At least it bought me precious time. Time to study his gear, his possible plans. Affixed to his hip was his sheathed nano-carbon blade. The same blade he claimed to have used when scalping dissidents during a riot-suppression mission. That wasn't the most pressing item within reach, however.

The rifle lay just two paces away. The beam was still active, illuminating the haphazard tattoos and crazed grin on Kardinal's face. The man was a demon. A tireless demon.

With no other options, I fell back on using the one part of my body that hadn't been torn to bits: my skull. I shoved my forearms down into Kardinal's fists, lifted my neck, and slammed my forehead right into his.

Vision winked in and out like a rebooting terminal. A dull ringing clouded my hearing. The warm trickle along my nose assured me that I'd split the skin—probably by catching one of his piercings.

Still, it had done the trick. Kardinal screeched and frantically covered his nose, which had been crumpled down into a gushing pile of cartilage by my brow. That gave me enough time to swing over, snatch up the rifle, and jam its barrel into Kardinal's sternum.

That shut him up real quick.

"Dak, you goddamn *kuta*," he cursed through bloody lips, raising both hands in a display of surrender. "Gonna shoot your own balls off."

Despite my utter ignorance about firearms, I knew two crucial things about the death-dealing machinery in my hands. First, it was loaded and still had a bullet in the chamber, thanks to Kardinal's shooting spree. Second, the safety was off, as evidenced by the small red triangle to the left of the holographic scope.

Of course, from Kardinal's point of view, the situation probably seemed absurd. Our struggle had reopened whatever miniscule healing my stomach had managed, resulting in a sheen of bright blood that covered both our bodies. Several of my intestinal loops were draped over his chest.

"I don't want to kill you," I said, then thought better of it. "Scratch that. I *do* want to kill you—it would be rather beneficial to me—but I'm trying not to. So, don't give me a reason."

Kardinal's grin widened. "Well, got some bad news for ya. That thing ain't gonna fire."

"Come again?"

In response, he reached up, grabbed the muzzle of the rifle, and pressed it between his eyes. "Go 'head and try, Dak."

Shockingly, I did.

The rifle gave a subtle whine, but the trigger didn't shift. It was locked in place, no matter how hard I squeezed it.

"Biometrics," Kardinal said, waggling his fingers. "Index finger on these here gloves is the only thing that'll let it go bang. So, I'd say you're shit outta luck."

We stared at one another for a long, awkward moment, welcoming the opportunity to draw full breaths.

Then Kardinal nodded at the rifle. "Give it here, man. You know you're dead . . . I know you're dead . . . so let's just make it snappy. I don't know how the hell you're still kickin', but I don't much care, neither."

"Very well," I said quietly, rotating the cumbersome weapon to hand it off to him.

"Attaboy."

Just before he'd lifted it out of my hands, however, I let go with my right hand. He didn't seem to notice. Similarly, he missed the fact that I moved that same hand to his hip. And then to the knife's sheath. By the time he'd taken full control of the rifle, hefting it up and down like a newborn infant returned to its parent, I had a firm grasp on the knife's polymer handle.

"Any last words, Dak?" he asked, angling the barrel toward my face. There was a note of genuine remorse there.

"Sorry."

He scrunched his brow. "Sorry?"

Just then, he noticed what I was up to. His eyes went wide. Too late, though. I ripped the knife free of its holster and jabbed it straight into the rifle's trigger guard, eliciting a bloodcurdling scream. The blade's nano-carbon material sawed straight through the finger, striking the metal behind it in less than a quarter-second.

Kardinal's finger dangled for an instant, only to flop to the tunnel floor as the man began thrashing to free his hand.

I went for a second strike, this time aiming for his face, but he instinctively whipped the rifle barrel aside. The muzzle thwacked my temple and sent me sprawling off of him. Momentarily dazed, the only thing I spied was the severed, still-gloved finger lying next to me. My golden ticket.

Kardinal was still screaming, blindly flailing about, when I snatched up the finger and struggled to my feet. A hand clutched at my ankle.

"Dak!" Kardinal growled. "I'm gonna skin you alive, you—"

Midway through his next word, I spun around and drove the dagger straight into the first target I saw: his thigh. He let out another cry and retracted his hand.

"Don't follow me," I panted, struggling to be heard over his pain-fueled tantrum. "I'm being merciful. So, tell the others . . . that this is their last chance to leave."

And with that, I began limping farther into the tunnels. His screams followed me every step of the way, but there was no sign that he had any intention of pursuit. As a matter of fact, I didn't even hear him get to his feet.

Even so, I knew he wouldn't heed my warning. None of them would.

If they didn't bring me back to Chanzig, they were as good as dead anyway.

6

After some ten minutes of plodding through the tunnel's twisting depths, I got my first real indication that Kardinal was no longer an immediate threat.

ENCOUNTER FAILED

And with that confidence-boosting message, the HUD winked out, leaving me in the same pitch-black hell as before. The message gave me a strange sense of comfort, as it clearly assessed dangers (or the lack of them) long before my conscious mind did, but it also brought up a host of new questions.

How did Guide—or rather, the biomechanical system Guide augmented—make a determination as to what passed for "danger"? And pursuant to that, how did it know when that danger had formally ended? Had it factored Liura and Balnos into its Kill Points equation, detecting their presence through my hearing? I pressed on with that line of questioning, seeing as I had nothing to do but grunt and stagger blindly. The HUD had informed me of my failure in the "encounter," but what did that actually mean? Was killing really the only way to succeed? And if so, what counted as a kill? What if I put them into a semipermanent coma, or managed to sever all their limbs?

Grisly inquiries, yes, but vital to answer if I was to survive this trial. Fortunately, I had an information bank on hand—or, to be more specific, attached to my nervous system.

But as always, practical matters came first. And the most practical thing I could think to do, in light of my recent brawl, was removing that goddamn recurrence prism in my neck. Without concern for the pain, I reached back, gripped the tiny fin of the device, and ripped it free. It hurt like hell, but weighed against the grisly wounds all over my body, it was a drop in an ocean.

I held the bloodied prism in my palm, wondering if my digitized consciousness was already surging through it. Would destroying it be murder? Maybe. Probably. I didn't care much. Even if some hollow version of "me" was floating around inside its circuits, the best course of action—the one I'd have chosen for myself—was annihilation. After dropping it to the cave floor, I found a rock and bashed the daylights out of it.

As I stared at the pile of debris, my heart filled with odd warmth, Guide spoke up.

"We must advise you to find shelter and recuperate from your injuries. Furthermore, it is best to deactivate any upgrades not presently required for survival. This will aid in conserving energy."

For perhaps the first time, Guide had suggested something useful. Recalling my prior knowledge and doing a bit of logical inference, I tried to deactivate Indomitable by thinking the word. That seemed to do the trick.

With a sinking feeling reminiscent of a deflating balloon—though with far more nausea—my muscles loosened and shrank. The pain returned tenfold. My steps slowed, and I strikingly experienced the dull, useless weight of my body.

On top of all this, a ravenous hunger appeared.

"Your glucose and overall caloric levels are low," Guide said. *"We advise you to seek out edible substances as soon as possible."*

"Yeah, thanks," I grumbled. "I haven't eaten in over a day. Was waiting to chow down on some hot meals once I got back to orbit."

By Halcius, I would've killed for the buffet-style cafeteria right about then. Hazy visions of soy steaks and cholesterol-laden pasta casseroles danced in the darkness.

"As you have reached Rank 1, Purifier, we are able to draw on some of our collective knowledge to provide you with nutrition information. This may prove useful when foraging."

That comment, specifically the bit about "collective knowledge," piqued my interest—but I couldn't pose my questions just yet. My first priority was finding my way back to the surface, where I'd become a walking hunk of meat for every predator in a five-kilometer radius. After that . . . I had no idea. Truthfully, I hadn't expected to survive this long. Perhaps this look-before-leaping approach was what had created my recent problems.

Only one tool was at my disposal: a severed finger borrowed from Kardinal. Now, I wasn't exactly keen to stash a finger in my boot, but I had a feeling it would come in handy. Better to hold on to it than leave it for Kardinal to quick-suture back in place, after all.

Eventually, while midway through imagining a five-course meal with a side of strong, strong cocktails, I saw . . . something. A narrow band of silver. It was just ahead, carving out a slice of the darkness I'd grown accustomed to during my wandering.

As I grew nearer, picking up on the echoes of sporadic birdcalls, I realized it was a glimpse of the outside. The moonlit surface. Alien vegetation quivered in the night breeze, and high above was a field of dense stars, framed by the reddish swirls of the system's nebula. I'd never been so relieved to be stranded on a world of hungry, blood-sniffing critters.

Despite the day's sweltering heat, it was near freezing in the jungle—something I'd known about, but only conceptually. You see, our team had spent most nights in orbit or bundled up in optically camouflaged thermal tents, busying ourselves with projector vids or copious drinking as we listened to beasts stomp past.

But now I was outside, exposed, shivering even as I stepped out into the windswept valley. Goosebumps lifted everywhere my suit had been torn—wherever I'd regrown my skin, that is—and my teeth immediately set to chattering.

It was clear that humanoids had never terraformed this world. If they had, the work had all been in vain. This was not a world for us squishy, delicate species. Between the roaming predators, punishing temperatures, and poison-packing plants, it was closer to an arena. The fittest survived—and I was far from making the cut.

In fact, as I moved through the high grass and glanced around, it became obvious that even the vegetation had millions or billions of years in advantages over me. The gnarled, amber-barked trees that spent their days soaking up irradiated sunlight had no shelter to offer, having furled their branches up into prickly, towering cones. An adaptation to prevent nocturnal creatures from chomping away, I imagined. There were only a few such trees scattered across the field, but they dominated the valley as far as the eye could see.

"Think, Dak," I whispered to myself. "You've been in worse spots."

That was a lie, of course. But sometimes a lie is enough to keep one going.

My first course of action, as Guide had suggested, was to find shelter and somehow mend the gaping holes in my body. Beneath many of the trees' roots were small dugouts that seemed to have been formed by flashfloods or burrowing animals, but I wasn't foolish enough to try my luck with that. I'd had enough run-ins with small, dark spaces and their inhabitants for one day.

For similar reasons, I hesitated to head farther into the jungle and try bedding down—a plan that seemed especially bad when I considered that the team's skiff had infrared cameras that would easily spot me.

No, I needed something solid, something far away from the stomping grounds of this world's fauna.

"Guide, you said you had collective knowledge, no?"

"That is correct, Purifier. Your recent rank-up has provided our consciousness with data that was previously unavailable."

"Right," I said, pondering that. "What do you know about this world?"

"Very little. Our previous host did not have sufficient time to probe his environment."

Previous host. That term lit up my mind like a strobe, reminding me of some extremely pressing questions I'd formed back in the cavern. Questions that might help me survive the night.

"You're saying your previous host brought you to this planet."

"We traveled as one."

"Okay, sure. But the point is . . . he came specifically to this place."

"Correct."

"Why?"

Guide hesitated. *"A full answer cannot be provided, Purifier. Much of our knowledge is still unavailable."*

"I'll settle for a partial answer."

"Very well. Our host was seeking something."

I rolled my eyes. "Helpful."

"We live to aid, Purifier."

Even if Guide was . . . less than a genius in this area, there was still something to be gained from reflecting on what it had given me. Now that more blood was pumping up to my head than onto the ground, I ran through a few scenarios, then put them to the test.

"What happens when your host dies?" I asked.

"After the host's vital signs have ceased, we extricate ourselves from their body. Then we attempt to seek out a new host. If a host cannot be immediately located, we search for a source of nutrition for continued existence."

Translating it into more digestible terms, I said aloud, "So, the host dies, you slither out and look for another one. And if you can't find that . . . you settle for food."

"This is an accurate summary."

I nodded. "Do you remember how your host died? Did anybody hunt them down?"

"Their time expired."

"Down in the cavern?"

"We do not believe so."

"How exactly did you end up in there, then?"

"We are unable to explain this, Purifier. Without the functioning nervous system and neural activity of our host, we cannot encode any memories."

That made sense. I was no expert on alien slugs, but it seemed obvious that Guide's species hadn't evolved to produce their own memories without the use of a more advanced organism. They might be able to store them, but not actively create them.

"Then . . . you have no idea how long you were in that cavern," I said.

"No, we do not. However, we have sensed our own decay. We would estimate that we were devoid of a host for approximately five months, two weeks, four days, and ten hours."

"Not bad for guesswork."

"Thank you, Purifier."

Still pacing across the field, I crunched the numbers. I thought about the cavern, then the crevasse I'd fallen into. A theory took shape.

"What rank did your previous host reach?"

"Rank 53, Purifier."

Fifty-three! I whistled through my teeth. Judging by the fact that the Kill Points required to progress through each rank doubled, Guide's previous host had been accruing billions of points per rank at the time of their death. They'd been a real killer. A certified badass. Probably slaughtered the equivalent of a small planet to keep going . . . and yet they'd still failed. That didn't bode well for a homebody like me.

But their success, or lack thereof, wasn't what interested me. Rather, it was their rank overall. There was surely no way to reach such a high rank without equipping oneself with things such as armor, guns, blades, a ship . . . anything to take on more and more enemies. If Guide's previous host hadn't been killed and stripped, but rather suicided due to their time running out . . . it meant some of their sweet, sweet gear was likely still on the planet.

And it was close. It had to be. After all, it didn't matter whether Guide had fallen into the cavern or crawled there via the tunnel network. It had left its host and sought out the nearest food. But in a thriving jungle, why look for food in the deepest, most desolate place possible? I put the puzzle pieces together.

Guide hadn't gone out of the jungle and into the cavern. They'd just gone *down*.

Turning back toward the way I'd come, I confirmed my suspicions with a grin. The tunnel entrance was set into the side of a sheer cliff face dotted with wayward trees. And high atop that cliff, concealed by moonlit vines and a thick canopy, was a set of ruins framed against the night sky.

"Look familiar?" I asked Guide.

"*Yes,*" it said, almost . . . excitedly? "*This visual input is activating strands of memory, Purifier. We believe that our previous host entered this location prior to death.*"

For perhaps the first time since beginning this nightmare, I felt my spirit surge. Somewhere in those ruins was the corpse of a Purifier with inordinate strength. If I could scavenge anything from them, even something as lowly as a proper rifle, I might have a chance to get off this world—and then get Guide off *me*.

I started back toward the elevated ruins, warily scanning the horizon for any signs of the team's skiff.

"Guide, can you clear something up for me?" Even as I posed the question, something funny struck me. Whether due to the isolation or fear, I was beginning to talk to Guide as a real entity rather than my captor. It was a habit I'd need to keep in check.

"*Of course, Purifier,*" Guide replied, chipper as always. "*What is your inquiry?*"

"What's the highest rank you've ever seen a Purifier reach?"

"*To our knowledge, our prior host held this achievement.*"

"Fifty-three's the top?"

"*Correct.*"

"And, uh, how old are you?"

"*We have lived through sixty-one cycles. Framed in your perception of time, this amounts to approximately one-point-one million years.*"

A hard knot formed in my throat. Guide was well over a million years old, and his last host just happened to be the running champion for survival? No, that didn't add up. There was something off here. Something peculiar about this Purifier had allowed them to outlast all the others. I'd come back to that later. In the meantime, the most sobering revelation from Guide's answer sank in.

"Guide . . . how many Purifiers have 'won' this game?"

"We have not yet witnessed a victory."

I stopped dead in my tracks.

This *game* hadn't been made with winning in mind. Its designers had, in a very literal sense, engineered a suicide scenario.

"You said there was a way to win," I said quietly.

"There is, Purifier."

"But nobody's ever gotten there!"

"This is the responsibility of the Purifier."

Overcome by the sheer ridiculousness of Guide's replies, I kept stalking toward the cliff. It made no sense. I was going to die. No matter how much I killed, or where I went, or what I did . . . I would meet the same end as Mr. Rank 53. But the urge to survive is strong. Strong enough to have driven me to bargaining with crime bosses, and strong enough to push me through my torture in the cavern. I had to keep going. If there was a way, any way at all, I would find it.

"Who made you?" I asked Guide, struggling to keep my voice calm.

"That information is not available at the moment," Guide said. *"What is the reason for your curiosity, Purifier?'*

"I'd like to have a word with them."

But such a conversation was unlikely. If Guide was telling the truth, its creators—or programmers, or whatever they were—had brought it to life long before humanity reclaimed the stars. A product of a sprawling alien species, then. That was bad. Very bad.

To understand why, you must have a basic understanding of our species' history. For the sake of clarity, I will assume you do not.

You see, most, if not all, of what us humans termed "advanced technology" had been engineered by alien species much like the ones responsible for Guide's birth. Aside from a few devoted technophiles, nobody knew how the technology worked, only that it did. Artificial gravity, neutron beams, replication ovens . . . it was all a mystery. Even I, an accomplished archaeologist fascinated by such creations, had no clue about the true principles behind the items I studied. I knew their origins, the basic details of their makers . . . but little else.

In that sense, humanity was a consumer species. We found artifacts and planetary devices and weapons and made use of them, never questioning how to design such marvels for ourselves. It didn't help that the

Halcius Hegemony's sole mission was to preserve "nature" by designating such technology heresy.

Now, it wasn't as though these advanced alien species had just journeyed home and left their inventions lying around for us. Rather, they had gone extinct—by our hands.

The origins of the Microbe Tide are still debated, but it's clear from both firsthand accounts and biological testing that the trouble began when these aliens took pity on a dead species. Humans, that is. We had been extinct for millions of years when a pioneering species found traces of our DNA—some say it was trapped in a spacesuit, while others claim it was fossilized on a colony world near Earth. Whatever the case, this DNA was used to create the first generation of my ancestors. Ancestors that were probably kept in interstellar zoos or some such cage.

What the aliens hadn't expected, however, was for their creations to go awry. If there's one thing humans are good at, it's serving as hosts to infectious viruses and bacteria. Within a few decades, we humans managed to spread pathogens to a universe full of immunocompromised alien species. The Microbe Tide.

At the time of writing this account, there are few aliens wandering the stars. As noted previously, Balnos was one of them—mainly because his species had agreed to accept humanoid DNA to vaccinate themselves against our viruses. As a matter of fact, practically *any* alien species that survived the Microbe Tide had done so by integrating our DNA.

But that's neither here nor there. What really matters, in this case, is that Guide's species had probably been killed off by the Tide. How could they not have been? Nobody in the field of Hegemony archaeology or beyond had ever mentioned the "chok'tal," let alone this vicious game. For all I knew, Guide was the last remaining piece of evidence that they had ever existed.

Imagine my luck to serve as its host.

"Your neural activity suggests you are deep in thought," Guide said, jarring me from my internal pity-fest.

"Yeah," I mumbled, "you could say that."

"We may be able to assist you."

"Doubtful. And besides, even if you could—"

Whatever I was preparing to say vanished from my mind when I spotted a more immediate threat. High up in that cloudless sky, marked by a pair of flashing LIDAR emitters, was the team's skiff. It was currently hovering above the tree line far to my right, but I knew their search pattern well enough. In a matter of minutes, it would swivel this way and mark me.

The ruins were my only hope—a hope that required scaling over a hundred vertical meters with a broken body.

7

By the time the skiff made its first pass over the field, I'd hardly gotten a meter up the cliff. Literally. I nestled myself deeper into the rock cleft, praying the clumps of moss and decaying plant matter had soaked up enough of the day's heat to mask my body. The thermal scanners on the skiff weren't cutting edge, but they were serviceable. Serviceable enough to spot me in seconds if the hunt wore on into an increasingly frigid night.

When the blinks of the LIDAR emitters were sufficiently far away, receding over the hills in the distance, I crept out and resumed my climb. It was tough going, seeing as my body was still nowhere near functional, but at least I'd found a boulder-strewn path with some degree of sloping. The overgrowth and smooth patches of stone suggested it had been formed by runoff from the plateau above.

As I scrabbled my way up onto the next ledge, I decided to busy myself—both for my own comfort and as a distraction from the pain. Several of my wounds were on the verge of tearing through whatever scabbing they'd formed, and the cold was gnawing at my fingertips.

"Guide, I've got a question," I huffed, pausing before attempting the next stretch of climbing. "Why do you talk about yourself using plural pronouns?"

"Could you please clarify your question, Purifier?"

I rolled my eyes. I had to remember that Guide was an ancient organism, not an academic like many of my former colleagues. "When you talk to me, you say *we*, not *I*."

"Thank you. We now understand your question." There was a brief pause. *"As mentioned previously, the name of our kind is the chok'tal. The word chok'tal refers to my kind's original form, which you perceived as a slug. But a chok'tal is not only its physical form; it contains interconnected personalities. You, and all Purifier hosts in the past, are part of this*

particular chok'tal. As such, the word 'we' refers to the collective knowledge generated by all Purifiers."

"Uh, okay . . . I think I get it. Maybe. So 'we' is describing what a bunch of interconnected personalities want to do. But what about you, Guide? Aren't *you* an individual?"

"To engage with hosts such as humanoids, which only have one mind, we have created a personality known as Guide that provides introductory information. You may think of Guide as raw data, designed to allow us—the chok'tal—to communicate as a collective."

That piqued my interest. As I attempted a bold leg-up maneuver, I pondered what they meant. Did they store the past Purifiers as lines of coding? Did they see themselves as a sort of hybrid program that considered themselves part of me? I'd encountered many remnants of collective (also known as "hive mind") species, but never interacted with any directly.

No need to wonder, though. Guide must've sensed my curiosity, as it decided to elaborate upon the explanation.

"Although our original form was one, we believe we are also the sum of our parts. As such, we have gradually expanded with the addition of each Purifier's consciousness."

My hand froze a centimeter from the next rock. "You mean . . . you absorb the actual *minds* of your hosts?"

"That is one possible angle of viewing, Purifier. We have been shaped by all of the memories, tactics, speech patterns, and behaviors accumulated since birth."

"But their consciousness . . . is trapped inside of you. All of their mental activity."

Guide didn't speak for a long while—by Guide's standards, anyhow. *"It is difficult to discuss consciousness with humanoids. There are subtleties that we are not equipped to explain."*

"Forget it, then. All I need to know is . . . if I die, my mind lives on. As part of you."

"That is correct."

"Would I have a body or whatever? I mean, would I be able to . . . live? Do stuff?"

"We do not know. We can only confirm that it is a continuation of your internal stream of consciousness. You would be self-aware and able to realize you are living eternally inside of us. We exist without end. You would exist without end."

Guide's cold words were enough to throw off my balance and send me slamming onto a lower ledge ass-first. It seemed I just couldn't catch a break. I'd started my day worrying about a psychopath keeping my consciousness on his desk, and now I had to worry about a biomechanical parasite dragging my consciousness across the stars on an endless murder quest.

Sighing, I picked my aching bones back up and resumed the climb.

"One more question," I said. "If I do find a way to 'win' this thing . . . do you die?"

"We do not know, Purifier. Our only mission is to facilitate the glorious game."

"Never thought about death, then?"

"We do not understand the concept."

"Yeah, well, it's not so great. So, let's just try to win this thing."

"We can assist with that."

For perhaps the first time since my "rebirth," I felt something other than panic or revulsion toward Guide. Maybe I'd been too ungrateful, too entitled. Sure, it was an alien parasite that devoured people's minds and trapped them in an unwinnable game of violence, but it was also the only being in this system that gave a damn about my life. The only being that had offered me even a sliver of a shot at surviving my execution.

Despite the pain, I smiled. "I'm starting to like you, Guide."

After what seemed like several hours, I reached the upper lip of the plateau. It would've been a joyous moment if not for the buffeting, skin-stripping winds, the frozen blood caking my body, and the looming threat of the skiff circling back.

Towering before me, however, were the ruins I'd worked so hard to reach. They were even larger up close, wreathed in a massive shell of vines and wild fungal colonies. Though the structure had cracked and eroded over time—probably over tens of thousands of years, judging by the trees that had sprouted up through its masonry—it retained its basic dome shape in a testament to alien architecture techniques. The archaeologist side of me wanted to bow down before it, to mount a full excavation and uncover the secrets of whatever species had put it here.

But the other side of me—the shivering, mortally wounded side—saw it as a high-end resort. A sanctuary safe from hypothermia and flying skiffs. A place to maybe, just *maybe*, find my first shred of a solution to this mess.

"Ring a bell?" I asked Guide.

"We are having difficulty with this request."

I sighed. "Does this place look familiar?"

"Yes, Purifier. Based on visual data, we estimate that this was the site of a Purifier's death."

"You mean your last host."

"Correct."

"Well, by all means, let me know if something jogs your memory. Especially, say, what they were looking for in this place."

"We will do our best to assist you."

With that comforting assurance, I headed into the ruins' outer chamber. The large tiles beneath my boots were uneven and eroded, almost like flotsam atop a sea of spongy plant growth, and the "ceiling" overhead was little more than a web of vines and crumbling stone. Still, it was enough to shelter me from the lashing winds. Somewhat. Although their sting was gone, the gusts continued to howl through the ruins like dead spirits.

What little moonlight I had was enough to glimpse the place's devastation. Its surrender to the forces of nature. Everywhere I looked, the jungle's stranglehold was obvious. Ancient murals had been reduced to breeding sites for pulsing insect nests. Cloudy water gathered in the rings of former aqueducts. Any remnants of sentient life—furniture, fabrics, that sort of thing—had long since been broken down into fuel for the ecosystem.

The farther in I walked, the quieter and eerier the place became. What could Guide's last host possibly have been seeking here?

When I reached the inner chambers, which featured vaulted ceilings and elaborate columns ascending into darkness, I wished I'd nabbed Kardinal's flashlight. But the fluttering of wings and the quiet trilling of insects made me rethink that. Perhaps it was better to stay ignorant about how threatening the ruins really were—especially if I planned to sleep there.

"Purifier," Guide said.

I stopped and whispered, "What?"

"We believe we have located something of interest."

Even as Guide spoke, I detected this "something of interest" lying near the center of the room. It rested in a halo of moonlight, gleaming like the sort of mystical artifact my colleagues and I had fantasized about in university. And yes, it was literally *gleaming*. Smooth metal.

In hindsight, it was absurd that I hadn't spotted it sooner. Perhaps Guide had used some subconscious control mechanism to swivel my eyes toward it. Hard to say. All I knew was that this metal represented the only sign of recent intelligent life on the planet.

Tiptoeing closer, I realized there were actually several hunks of metal. One of them, the largest item and the one reflecting moonlight, was a . . . vest. Something like a vest, anyhow. It was composed of thick, interlocking plates that seemed capable of stopping a high-caliber rifle round—a theory reinforced by the various dents, dings, and scorch marks all over the plates.

There was no doubt in my mind that Guide's last host had worn it. But I had to wonder . . . why was it just resting here instead of clamped to a corpse?

The mystery deepened when I inspected the items arranged around the vest. Nestled in the shadows were other bits of gear: a rifle, a helmet, ammunition, various bits of tech. In short, a soldier's kit. A human-sized soldier's kit, no less. Part of me was elated by the cache—I'd finally have something to defend myself—but another part was further unsettled.

The gear had all been laid out in an orderly, almost ritualistic fashion. I'd seen archive vids that catalogued similar displays, but those had all been created by militant species preparing their warriors for death.

Had Guide's host belonged to such a culture? Had they stripped down in preparation for their death?

Such questions would have to be answered later. Shaking away my doubts, I hunched down and crept toward the gear.

That was when I saw the blood. Smears of it, moonlit and glossy, painted the stonework beneath my feet. Time had faded it to a molasses brown, but there was no mistaking its original crimson color. This was human blood. Worse yet, the streaks around the armor were thin and ragged, almost as though it had been . . . licked.

Right on cue, I heard a sound I'd tried to ignore ever since I landed on the planet. A low, chirring hum, almost like a cicada's call on overdrive. Only this noise didn't come from an insect. It came from a chakki—one of the few beasts capable of making Liura shiver.

One of the worst things about a chakki is the omnidirectional quality of its calls. You can't tell where the damn thing is, especially in the confines of vast ruins.

So, even as I whirled about, searching for the monstrous beast, I saw nothing. Darkness above, darkness behind, darkness on all sides.

"Guide," I said softly, already certain the chakki had spotted me, "any chance you can pin that thing using the HUD?"

"You are not yet engaged in combat, Purifier."

"Are you kidding me?" I hissed. "You heard it! It's right here. Somewhere."

"As we have stated—"

Guide didn't get to finish their generic reply. Its words were cut off by a change in the chakki's call. Whereas the prior sound had indicated a back-off-or-die warning, this new one told a different story: *I'm coming for you.*

Immediately, the HUD fizzled into existence.

[NEMESIS EVENT]
Chakki (BEAST)
CALCULATING . . .
Estimated Kill Points: 10,000

Ten thousand!? What the hell was that? Kardinal Killa had packed a rifle, sure, but his dim-witted nature had made him far less of a threat than a mindless, flesh-eating apex predator.

I didn't have time to debate the merits of Guide's Kill Point calculations. Just off to my left, framed in an enormous blue box, was the shadow of the chakki. And it was no *ordinary* chakki. I'd seen those—always dead, riddled with the team's bullets. This thing was at least twice the size of any corpse I'd encountered, suggesting it was truly the king of its territory. A walking funnel that devoured anything small and stupid enough to wander into this place.

Like me.

Instinctively, I lunged for the rifle lying on the bloody tiles. That motion was enough to send the chakki into full-on hunting mode—a fact I realized due to the rapid *tk-tk-tk* of clacking nails and a gut-melting screech.

Just as I came down hard on my stomach, hands flailing to grab the weapon, the beast came rocketing out of the shadows.

Tens of beady eyes glinted in the moonlight. Its huge body was a mass of quills, mottled flesh, and carapace. And as it reared back, preparing to thrash me with a handful of sharp legs, I saw the gaping hole of its maw—a grinding pit of teeth and tongues.

With a panicked yelp, I seized the rifle and yanked it to my chest. Then I flopped back, aimed, and fired.

Click.

Half in disbelief and half in terror, I glanced down. There was no magazine in the rifle. No bullets. No help against the chakki.

At the last moment, I pulled my legs in and rolled. The chakki's dagger-like legs thudded down in a straight line, pounding into the stone closer . . . closer . . . closer. Even as I scrambled back, narrowly avoiding a brutal acupuncture session for each of my feet, I knew it wasn't enough. The final leg speared down through the front of my boot.

Howling, I tried to shift back—and couldn't. It had me impaled, stuck. The chakki's salivating mouth flared open, popping with dislocated joints as it widened far enough to swallow me whole.

All I could do was thrust the rifle's barrel into its mouth at an angle. A smart move, since it immediately began to constrict its mouth. The thing's eyes were high up on its head, ringing the mouth itself, so it must've taken the metal as its human prey.

That gave me the precious seconds I needed to buck my knee up, dislodging its nail, and swing my boot out from beneath it.

The chakki screeched and clamped its sphincter-like mouth. The force was tremendous, easily cracking the rifle's stock and bending the barrel.

Shit.

In a matter of seconds, it would shatter the whole thing and I'd be right back where I started: no weapon, no hope of outgunning my hunters. Time to think fast. For better or worse, the only idea that occurred to me was pressing on with my stupid plan of force-feeding the creature.

With my foot now fully numb from the chakki's venom, I threw myself toward the pile of gear and retrieved the vest. The thing was *heavy.* Crushingly heavy. But it would have to do, as the chakki had already pivoted its tubular body and begun slithering toward me.

Again, its gargantuan mouth—still occupied by the rifle—darted in for the kill.

At the same time, I shoved the vest into its teeth. Metal whined, sparks flew, and I could plainly hear the chakki's teeth scraping over the reinforced plates. Amazingly, when the beast pulled back, I saw that the rifle was still at the forefront of the mouth. It had somehow gobbled the vest without dislodging the weapon.

Even as I reached for the next distraction—a battle-scarred, pressurized helmet—I noted the horrifying efficiency of the chakki's throat. The vest was already slime-coated and halfway to the stomach, tugged along by nubby teeth and bulging muscle.

Once again, I held the helmet out like a snack, praying it would take the bait. But it was smarter than I'd expected. Instead of snapping up my offering, the chakki whipped to the side, hunkered down, and bulged.

My eyes widened.

Long before the forest of quills along its back began trembling, I knew what was coming. I'd seen it in action against larger predators—and the bloody aftermath. With a deafening cry, the chakki loosed its quills.

Meter-long javelins made of keratin whizzed past me, ricocheting off the floor tiles and sinking deep into the moss.

I flattened myself, but it was no use. Pain blossomed in my shoulder. Glancing down, I found the obvious cause: a quill driven straight through me, shaking with every thump of my heart.

But before I could even reach for the damn thing, let alone yank it free, the chakki coiled back and surged at me. I dropped the helmet and rolled once again, howling from the pain all the way. The quill had snapped, but it wasn't going anywhere.

A quarter-second later, the chakki resumed its wild thrashing, swinging its barbed tail and stabbing the tiles with those spear-like legs. All I could do was crawl away from the mayhem, cringing at every screech and every roar of shattering stone.

The gear was just ten paces away. Ten measly paces. I glanced at the chakki, still in its blind rage, then back at the gear. There had to be bullets somewhere in that stash. There'd been a rifle, after all. If there wasn't any ammo, well, it was the end of the road.

With a sharp inhale, I rushed toward the pile. The chakki was on me in microseconds, ripping across the tiles and bellowing like an engine in overdrive.

At the last second, I crashed down on my stomach, cringing as the beast's pincers slashed the air above my skull. My hands groped at the gear. Assorted bits of metal and polymer clattered away, but none of them were ammo. *Come on . . . come on*!

Just then, the chakki speared my left calf with a sharpened leg. Biting back the pain, I kept fishing through the pile. Right as the chakki sank a second leg right through my buttocks—a few critical hairs shy of my nether regions, mind you—I grasped something unexpected. No, not ammo. Not even an empty magazine. But something good enough to cut through the fear and burning sensations.

A grenade.

Now, as you know and have plainly observed, I was no soldier. Still, it didn't take a genius commando to figure out what I was holding. Its egg-like shape, smooth, bulbous surface, and cold metal trigger up top all but confirmed my hopes.

Even as I marveled at my newfound toy, however, the chakki thrust yet another leg down through my body. This one pierced my lower back—popping a kidney, it seemed. But I didn't wail. I didn't even cry out. It was time to turn the tables on this overgrown pest.

When the chakki screeched and lifted high to deliver its killing blow, I flicked the grenade's ignition switch. Then, in one smooth motion, I rolled over, grinned up at its unlovable mug, and threw the payload into my target—the gaping tunnel of the chakki's throat.

It was a piss-poor throw, but good enough. The grenade dinged off a rotten tooth and bounced onto one of its flailing tongues, immediately suctioned down by those machine-like gut muscles.

For a terrifying second I just lay there, panting, waiting for the inevitable. Nothing happened.

The chakki eased its legs downward, preparing to skewer me, but it seemed to be caught in the grip of hesitation, almost as though it was surprised that my final gesture had been so pitiful. So ineffective. Perhaps it was used to its prey fighting back, and hadn't evolved to spar with things that played dead.

That theory went out the window when the chakki whipped back and loosed an ear-shattering roar.

Now, despite my best intentions, I screamed.

All at once, the chakki's legs extended and condensed into a wall of bloody points. The muscles along its underbelly clenched and quivered in anticipation. Then it dove down, approaching like a horde of—

Kunk.

That was the last noise I heard before my hearing vanished with a white flash.

I shut my eyes, but it was too late.

Inky blood, steaming pulp, and fragments of bone pelted my face. Quill shards tore through my cheeks and belly. I didn't dare move. I just lay there, dumbfounded and dazed, as heaps upon heaps of chakki meat buried me in a gelatinous mound. Then, in a grand finale, the thing's enormous bulk pounded down across the tiles next to me.

ENCOUNTER SUCCESSFUL
Kills: 1
Kill Points Awarded: 10,000

RANK-UP AVAILABLE: RANK 2

Despite their untimely arrival, the HUD's messages were the only things that jarred me back to reality and convinced me it was safe to move. Try to move, anyway. I was literally entombed in chakki remains.

In fact, until that moment, I hadn't even realized I wasn't breathing. My entire face—including my mouth and both nostrils—was submerged in a sea of squirming viscera and still-twitching tissue.

"*Purifier,*" Guide said nonchalantly, "*we urge you to seek oxygen as soon as possible.*"

Thankfully, the dead-predator marinade wasn't too deep. I sat up, trembling, and looked around the chamber.

Every patch of visible stone was blanketed in chakki. Blood, organs, teeth, nails, bones, half-digested prey . . . nothing was missing. Lying at the center of the mess, much like a main course at a fine dining event, was the blasted-open corpse of my enemy. The grenade had torn a boulder-sized hole straight through the center of its body.

With an aching hand, I wiped a layer of bile off my face. "Well, Guide, at least we have dinner."

8

After some ten minutes of retching and twenty minutes of digging, I managed to amass the gear that my dead benefactor had left behind. It was laid out in neat rows some twenty meters away from the grenade's ground-zero point, occupying some of the chamber's only clean tiles.

Of course, that did nothing to preserve the cleanliness of the gear itself. Everything was drenched in a syrupy coating of . . . something, with several pieces featuring nuggets of intestines or eyeball gunk. Gross. But given my situation, complaining about sanitation was a luxury I could ill afford.

Amazingly, the rifle seemed to have survived with minimal damage. And by "minimal," I mean less than catastrophic. So far as I could tell, the chakki's first crunch had been the worst. The folding stock was shattered, and had fallen off in the course of shaking the gunk free. Likewise, the formerly long barrel had been twisted at a brutish angle, rendering it useless. I'd find a way around that, though.

The other miracle was the vest, which had endured the worst punishment from the chakki's throat-teeth rather than the grenade blast. Sure, it was soaked inside and out with rancid fluids, but it was still in one piece, and—seemingly—still capable of protecting my fragile skin from bullets.

One interesting detail I found during my examination was a cluster of depressions on the inside of the vest's back plate. The reason for this would soon become apparent.

Anyway, with those two critical items accounted for, it was time to inspect the other pieces. The process was aided by a yellow EverBright glowstick, which Guide's previous host had been kind enough to supply in ample numbers.

Squatting down with the glowstick in hand, I began my analysis.

First up was a matching set of arm and leg guards. They looked sturdy enough, with an elastic nano-mesh underlayer and dense plating along the exterior. By the look of them, they'd been manufactured to complement the vest. They were also suspiciously narrow, though I suspected that was because the nano-mesh was stretchy enough to accommodate different body sizes.

Next was the helmet, which had come dangerously close to serving as a chakki's lunch. Like the vest, it had obviously been designed for a male humanoid. It had two black patches that served as vision lenses, along with a strange third patch between the brows. Had its original wearer been a three-eyed warrior? Only time would tell. Aside from that, it was a standard pressurized helmet. The bulbous mounds at the back seemed to function as emergency oxygen reservoirs.

Beside the helmet was what I'd been trying to find during my fight: ammo. Six magazines full of slender bullets, to be precise. As expected, they were the right size and shape to fit the rifle. Or so it appeared to my untrained eye.

Following that were two more grenades, which, in light of their explosive demonstration, I watched with extreme wariness. I'd have to be quite careful about how and where I stored those bastards.

Then there was a rucksack. A basic, no-frills rucksack made of . . . burlap, by the look of it. The inside was lined with ration bars of every type—fruit flavored, meat flavored, insect flavored—and a vacuum-sealed canteen.

I enjoyed a fair helping of the spoils before proceeding to the next item: a stiletto-style knife with a leather-wrapped handle and a blade of dubious metallic origin. Judging by its extremely thin blade, it was military-grade. Only . . . not just any military. As I brought the EverBright closer to the knife, I spotted a stamped insignia and confirmed my theory. It had been made in a Halcius Hegemony fabrication plant.

In case you're out of the loop, *nobody* on the right side of the law is stupid enough to be caught dead toting Hegemony gear. Even Balnos and the other scavs, in spite of their general neglect for galactic law, had a strict rule about leaving soldiers' corpses untouched. Not out of respect, but out of fear.

What kind of scoundrel, exactly, had Guide's former host been? An anti-Hegemony crusader? A terrorist? The gear provided more questions than answers.

Well, most of it.

There *was* a possible source of answers, and it was a strange, ominous one—which is why I'd saved it for last. Sitting at the very end of the row was a small yet sturdy-looking tablet. It looked like the sort of thing the Hegemony's pioneer officers carried to log their expeditions and capture vids of anomalies.

Just as with the knife, my speculation proved correct. The EverBright's glow revealed an unmistakable *HH* monogram laser-etched into the tablet's back panel.

"So," I said to Guide, turning the tablet over as though it might detonate at any moment, "you have *no* idea what's stored in here?"

"Correct, Purifier."

"And you also have no idea how your host managed to scrounge up all this illicit tech."

"Correct."

"Well, then, let's have ourselves a peek."

Was it stupid, in hindsight, to have activated a tablet manufactured by the Halcius Hegemony? Yes, of course. But in that same vein, *everything* about my situation was stupid. And since Guide's host had taken it upon himself to include the gadget in this life-saving motherlode, there had to be something vital in it. Something that could help me survive this ordeal.

With a deep sigh, I wandered to the nearest wall and plopped down. My body was still broken, oozing from a dozen different places, but only time could deal with that. The tablet was my focus.

After thumbing a few buttons, the central display lit up.

"That was easy," I muttered. "No security on a Hegemony tablet? What kind of—"

The screen flashed red. A feminine voice came through the speakers. "Please present your retina for clearance purposes."

Oh, hell. So it *was* locked. Or worse—booby-trapped. Before I could think to toss the tablet away, however, a neon beam emerged from the front-facing scanner. I sat there, sweating and stock-still, as the light passed over my eyes.

The tablet chimed with green light.

"User clearance granted," the same voice said. "Vid One is ready for playback."

I just kept staring at the screen, wondering what the hell had happened. This thing had been made by the Hegemony, programmed by the Hegemony, authorized for Hegemony use . . . so why was it letting me in? I'd been born on a Hegemony world and marked as a citizen, yes, but what kind of security protocol involved letting random citizens access classified data?

Once again, more questions. My only hope was the screen's sole widget, marked V1. The aforementioned Vid One, obviously.

I opened the vid.

The opening shot sent shivers down my spine. The darkness, dangling vines, and decaying stonework were enough to prove that this vid had been shot *here*, in this very chamber. More precisely, it had been shot where I'd first found the host's gear. All of the armor, weapons, and gadgets were plainly visible at the bottom of the screen.

After a few seconds of scuffing and shuffling, a bare-chested man came into view. He was brawny—as in, steroid-guzzlingly brawny—with a shaved head, twill pants, and dozens of mottled scars.

Most striking of all, however, were his eyes. They were piercingly violet—the unmistakable mark of a highborn citizen. Just like mine. If I hadn't known any better, I'd have taken him to be a . . . Hegemony soldier.

Grunting out curses, the man settled heavily onto the floor, crossed his legs, and stared into the tablet's recording eye.

"If you're watching this, I'm dead," he growled, "*and* you're the unlucky bastard who's been selected for the Glorious Game, or whatever the hell Guide calls it."

My jaw fell open. How could he—

"You might be wondering how I know that," he said presently. "Funny thing, these ops tablets . . . it's a snap to reconfigure the biometric lock. Ordinarily, you'd need a retina that's stored in the Hegemony's active-duty database. Well, now it's a little different. Your retina's got Guide's filaments wormin' all through it. So, if you're able to turn this thing on and listen to my handsome mug, you're in a sticky situation." He paused to take a deep drag from an amp-stick. "Now, if you *don't* have Guide in you and still managed to crack this thing, kudos. You'll be dead from the neurotoxin emitters in about forty seconds."

Gulping hard, I reached to the tablet's back panel to ensure no gas had started leaking. So far, so good.

The man in the vid took his sweet time, grinning as though he could see any potential tablet-crackers dying on the other side of the screen.

"Alright," he finally said, "now that we've gotten any possible *rabble* out of the way, let's break down what's happening. Think of this vid as your introduction to the Glorious Game. Guide's fine for the basics, but his memory's probably pretty jammed up. So, you two are gonna need my help to get those bearings back."

He took another puff on the amp-stick. "Over the next few minutes, I'm gonna tell you everything I know about Guide, this game, the dick-wads who made it. Hopefully you can do somethin' useful with the info I've got. And if you can't, well, record a vid for the next Purifier in line. I sure as hell wish somebody had done me that kindness."

Precarious as my situation was, I admit that I was glad to have this kind of resource at hand. Besides, this vid featured Guide's most success-ful host, if the parasite's testimony was true. A professional tutorial made by a human, for a human. Just what I needed.

"Name's Jekra Modri, and I spent most of my life droppin' bodies for the Halcius Hegemony," the vid-maker continued. "Conquered twelve planets, exterminated two species, got five promotions in ten years. Yeah, you could say I was a killin' machine." He shrugged. "Let's not get into Hegemony politics. Point is, after all those shootouts, I ended up as Ardent Reformer Modri."

Now *that* was impressive. Ardent reformer, in case you're not up to snuff on Hegemony military ranks, was a fairly lofty title. Hell, even "reformer" was enough to put a quake of fear in most people—it signified that one was a special forces operative with zero remorse, hesitation, or room for critical thought.

But back to Modri's vid.

"Things were swell for a while," he said. "A long while. Then we got an order to drop on a little world named Hakkaram: a good-for-nothin', bombed-out shell of a planet that was rumored to have some alien tech. It was just a normal mission, until we got down into the catacombs. Ended up runnin' into some insurgent resistance, separated from my squad . . . and lost. Guess I was pretty deep in there, 'cause I spent the next few hours ploddin' around in the dark. Wouldn't you know it? That's where I found our mutual friend, Guide, holed up in some sort of shrine."

Modri gave a twisted little laugh. "Now, I got outta there, but the trouble was just startin' up on my end. I tried to tell my superiors about Guide. Tell 'em about how I was on some sort of timer . . . how I was gonna die if they didn't let me loose on the insurgents again. But they didn't believe me. Anyway, to make a long story shorter, I hotwired a dropship and went back into the fray. Got shot to hell, but I ranked up. Ranked up a lot."

He ashed out his amp-stick. "When my team finally found me, they couldn't deny what I was sayin' anymore. They saw how my wounds healed. How I was faster, stronger. And they went straight to Hegemony command and told 'em everything. Traitors." Modri scowled at that, but pressed on. "Didn't take long for them to box me up in a solitary cell and start sendin' in the experimental teams. They poked me, prodded me, took samples and all that. According to them, I'd found exactly what we went to Hakkaram for.

"But you know how bureaucracy is. Samples weren't enough. They wanted that thing out of me. Said they could use it to make soldiers in Halcius's divine image. When you think about it, it makes sense. The thing's a biological weapon. Hegemony *hates* tech, but they didn't see it that way. They saw it as somethin' organic, somethin' humans were destined to evolve with."

Again, Modri took a considerable pause. Maybe listening to Guide's mental chatter, if the look on his face was any indication.

"There was this one guy in the Exotic Research Division, a real prick," Modri said. "Still dunno his name, but I *do* know that he was behind the whole thing. He'd been lookin' for the chok'tal for years. His life's mission and all that jazz."

As I listened, it seemed more and more remarkable that Guide didn't recall a bit of this. Perhaps their memory-erasing issue was a built-in feature, not a bug. More questions.

Modri went on, explaining, "Anyhow, when I got word that this guy was planning to extract Guide with or without my permission, I went a little . . . haywire. Followed my training, you could say. I wiped out that entire station, stole a ride, started hopping across the galaxy. But that's a whole other story. What *you* need to know is that I managed to splice into a Hegemony database. Got some vital data about where the device was made. And that's where you come in."

There was a long, awkward pause, presumably to build tension. It worked.

"Now, I raised hell in fifteen different systems tryin' to get that information," Modri said, "so there was no way in Halcius's oblivion that I was gonna find that species without attractin' attention. I figured I'd need to wipe the slate clean. Get the Hegemony off my back. And to do that, I swapped ships, hitched a ride to this lonely stretch of jungle, and started campin' out. Why this jungle, you ask? Because it was rumored to have a Polyp." Modri paused. "You probably don't even know what a Polyp is, do you? Well, don't worry about that now. We'll get to it."

After another defeated shrug, Modri said, "I've been hidin' in this damn jungle for months. Every so often, I hear the gunships overhead. They'll probably get bored, move along . . . I hope. Just last week, they landed a ground team here. Guess who was leadin' it? Yeah, that's right . . . the same prick that experimented on me. He's got a real hard-on for little ol' me. They didn't spot me, and they never will. Reformer combat skills, baby."

He gave a dark laugh. "You might be viewin' this a day after I kicked the bucket, or five thousand years later. Doesn't matter. You've got that thing inside you, and maybe . . . just maybe . . . you'll be able to figure this all out with the details I'm about to give you."

I scrunched my brow, waiting.

"But you might have some further questions," Modri said. "Like, y'know, why I didn't toss myself into a black hole. Why get some other unfortunate pissbaby dragged into this? Well, good thing you asked." He scooted closer to the tablet's lens. "I've gotta believe there's an upside to this thing. That it was made with decent intentions." He sighed. "Besides, I know it's just a matter of time before the Hegemony finds more of these things. That's somethin' you learn in my line of work, pal. Bad things come in multiples. If we don't find out how to shut this thing down . . . you'd better saddle up for a universe full of Hegemony Purifiers."

Interestingly enough, I hadn't even considered the "toss yourself into a black hole" point until Modri brought it up. Part of me wanted to seethe with rage that he hadn't done just that. What business did he have, unleashing an ancient, blood-hungry parasite on a pacifist like me? But another part understood his logic. Guide was more than a parasite—it was a work of technological magic. If it could be used for "good," the suffering was worth it. If it couldn't . . . somebody had to deal with the root of the problem.

It just so happened to be the worst possible candidate.

"I'll tell you the species at the end of this recording," Modri said, easing back into the sunlight that streamed down through the ruin's shattered ceiling. "For now, though, we've gotta get you up to speed. Oh! But before I forget . . . there's a ship here for you. Nothing flashy, just an older model I picked up at an orbital yard. It's about two klicks southeast of here, down in a grove. Did my best to hide it. And inside that thing is where you'll find your first few Polyps. Once I pop 'em off my back, that is . . ."

He scratched his head, seemingly at a loss for what to say next. "Anyway, where was I? Oh, right. Guide's abilities. Think of me like your big brother. I'm gonna tell you the nitty-gritty of this whole thing. What skills to select, what tactics to use, what mistakes to avoid. In short, the unofficial user's manual that Guide's too dense to offer."

Now this—this was really what piqued my interest. Truth be told, I didn't give much of a damn how or why this guy got Purifier-ed, nor what he saw as a long-term solution to the issue. Not at that moment, anyway. What I *did* give a damn about was optimizing my skillset. It was the one surefire path to short-term survival, and thus, my get-out-of-death-free card.

Modri turned in place, revealing a series of pulsating lumps across his back. Lumps that perfectly fit the vest's hollowed-out plating. "First things first—these little guys are called *Polyps*."

A shudder ran down my spine. Why the hell would anybody opt for that upgrade path?

"These things are *crucial*," Modri went on, dispelling my thoughts. "Sooner you get around to finding and equipping Polyps, the better. You can think of 'em like collectible upgrades, I guess. They'll recover memories from past Purifiers, give you bonuses, even help you figure out solutions to problems you didn't know you had. Now, under the surface, these things look like mini brains. All neurons and fat. Not pretty to look at, I'll grant you, but they're damn useful. So, start adding Polyps . . . like, stat."

Well, there I had it: the answer to Guide's amnesia. It seemed that if I wanted any assistance from the Purifiers locked inside its consciousness prison, I'd need to start covering my body with those squirming pustules. Delightful.

Given the circumstances, what choice did I have? This Modri fellow had gone mighty far with his approach to things. It would've been idiotic to ignore his recommendations.

"Next up," he went on, "is genofacturing. Now, you've got—"

Abruptly, the screen dissolved into a wash of random pixels and static lines. I bounced the tablet and gave it a few solid slaps, only to be met with a message I dreaded:

Vid corruption detected. Please locate an authorized technician.

Great. Just great. My one shot at fixing this mess had been reduced to a glob of misfiring circuits.

Seeing as there was nothing I could do, though, I powered down the tablet and shoved it into the rucksack. The most important thing to do now was plan. That, and figure out how to navigate the jungle before Balnos and his team's skiff caught wind of my hideout.

"Any of that ring a bell for you, Guide?"

"*Some, yes,*" Guide said. "*Although we must disagree with Purifier Modri's assessment of us as too dense to—*"

"Yeah, yeah," I grumbled, stuffing the spare ammo and glowsticks into the rucksack. "Any chance you'll know where Modri stashed his ship when we get close?"

"It is highly probable."

I nodded. Getting hold of a ship wouldn't solve my overarching kill-or-be-killed problem, but it would certainly give me some breathing room while I assessed my options. Not that I had many options to begin with.

At its core, my aim was—and had to be—the same as Modri's: find somebody who understood Guide well enough to safely remove it. But how far could I really get? Modri had been a Hegemony commando, a hand-selected butcher equipped with decades worth of combat experience. He'd outrun the largest military force in the known universe. Gunned down countless numbers of their ranks. And yet even he, with all his macho superiority, had still resigned himself to dying on a good-for-nothing rock in the middle of nowhere.

I couldn't go down that road. I had to look on the bright side. I now had access to weapons, armor, a possible lead, a ship, and—

Polyps.

"Guide," I said while tugging on the leg guards, "what was Modri talking about with the whole Polyp thing?"

"Polyps are advanced biological lifeforms. Does this answer your question?"

"No? Keep going."

"Once bonded with the body, Polyps grant the Purifier unique modifiers related to fields such as time, Anima, Dominion, and Kill Point gains."

As I tugged on the arm guards and vest, I considered the explanation. "So, they're a good thing."

"Yes, Purifier."

"And where do I get more?"

"Polyps are produced by Purifiers with the necessary prerequisites. Their location is random."

"Oh, fantastic. Any chance you know which Polyps are in Modri's ship?"

"Negative, Purifier. We cannot recall such details."

"Color me surprised."

"We are unable to affect—"

"It's a figure of speech, Guide."

"Please explain further."

"I will—later." Pulling on the helmet and retrieving the mangled rifle, I turned back the way I'd come. "Right now, we've got a ship to find."

9

In a shocking twist, the helmet wasn't nearly as suffocating as I'd predicted. Now, like most of the 6 percent of humans fortunate enough to leave their backwater worlds and explore the void of deep space, I was no stranger to helmets—far from it—but the majority of models I'd worn were oriented toward wealthy civilian travelers. Translation? More wiggle room, an automated sedative stream to prevent panic attacks, and plush inner foam.

This model, in contrast, had clearly been developed for soldiers. Not Hegemony soldiers—those were all marked by Halcius's divine color, green—but soldiers nonetheless. People trained in the art of killing.

It hugged my face tightly, exposing the world through shadowed lenses that, remarkably, didn't dim the shadowed trees around me. To the contrary, in fact. Every object was marked with a faint, glossy "crispness" that exposed its edges better than my naked eyes. The ever-present humming just behind my skull indicated there was a passive air filter somewhere in the mouth section.

As I clambered down ravine slopes and through patches of dense foliage, I wondered if my hunters would be thrown off by the new disguise. Probably not. And even if they were, so what? They'd just see me as another armed scav combing the planet for loot. In their books, that was sufficient justification for a shootout.

"Purifier, we must insist that you rest and allow your Anima to finish the healing process."

Calves-deep in muck, I stopped and groaned. "There's no time for that."

"If your body is not healed to optimal levels, you may face an increased risk of death in your next encounter."

Increased risk of death. Pah! What did Guide know, anyway? I'd fought Kardinal with a body that resembled mincemeat. I'd taken on the chakki with most of those wounds still open. Most of the bones fractured, too. And now that I had a rifle (not to mention boom-boom eggs), the various gashes, rips, and punctures beneath my armor were little more than an annoyance. Okay, an aching, torturous annoyance, but an annoyance nonetheless.

Besides, Guide was looking at this whole thing from his immortal-slug frame of mind. To us humans, especially the ones too low on the socioeconomic scale to afford genetic treatments, the amount of healing done by this "Anima" was incredible. It made me feel powerful, almost invincible. Whether that was good or bad remained to be seen.

It would've been nice for Modri to hook me up with a few high-end medical kits, but considering everything else he'd supplied, I couldn't complain much. The worst of my wounds were already clotting beneath the armor, and the cold—biting as it was—served to stanch the bleeding on any exposed areas.

"Hey, Guide," I said, wanting to test a hypothesis I'd formed, "how good is your memory of things that have happened since you entered my body?"

"We believe it is serviceable. Why do you ask, Purifier?"

"Just humor me. How many steps have I taken since we left the chakki's ruins?"

"We estimate that number to be two thousand, five hundred and twenty-nine."

I whistled. "Not a bad step counter, Guide."

"Thank you for your feedback."

"Alright, let's see if you can run a little calculation. Twenty-five hundred steps . . . and the ship is two kilometers away. How close am I?"

Guide's pause was brief, but a departure from its usual lightning-fast speed. *"We estimate, in light of the detours you have taken around rocks and other obstacles, that you are less than three hundred steps from your destination."*

"Which means you ought to start remembering things soon."

"That will depend on many factors, Purifier. For instance, the—" Guide went silent for a moment. *"Turn ten degrees to your right and proceed. The ship is behind the cover of those trees."*

"Huh." I angled myself in the direction Guide advised. "Looks like I've been underestimating you."

True to Guide's words, there *was* something concealed behind the tangles of stalks, vines, and boney trunks. It didn't appear like a thing so much as a non-thing, a void as dark as the sky itself. Using my newfound blade, I slashed my way through the hanging veils and moved deeper.

Parked in the grove's shallow, bowl-shaped depression was my ticket out of here. The ship was sleek, dangerous-looking, the kind of thing associated with narcotics runners. Three times as big as the skiff, and probably twice as fast. More than acceptable for a man in my shoes.

Wandering closer, I got a better look at the craft. Its weather-corroded hull was black and shaped like a long oval, resembling a rubber egg that had been stretched to the breaking point. Three deuterium engines ringed its rear panels like fins, and a short rotary cannon extended from the tip. There were a host of other bits attached here and there—lateral jets for sideways or diagonal movement, I speculated—but much of the top was impossible to see, thanks to the netting-and-leaves camouflage Modri had layered over it.

"You know, this'll be my first time piloting a ship," I told Guide.

"We will do our best to assist you, Purifier, but we would recommend piloting lessons prior to operating any volatile machinery."

"Thanks for that one, Guide. Very helpful."

They offered a formulaic reply, I'm sure, but I didn't hear it. I was already pacing around the ship, getting a feel for its durability, its sheer size, its . . . entrance.

"How do I get into this thing?" I muttered.

"We believe there is an access panel beneath the hull, approximately five meters away from you," Guide said.

I shrugged. "Good enough for me."

With a bit of blind groping, I managed to locate the panel in question. In the weeks since Modri's absence, it seemed to have played host to a collection of slimy, purring fungal colonies. Nasty. After wiping them away, I tugged on the handle.

"Hey, Purifier, you made it to the ship!" Modri's voice said through a speaker, startling me. "If you're not a Purifier, piss off. But if you *are* . . . just say the passphrase."

Shit. It was probably on the busted tablet.

Before I could start hyperventilating, however, Modri's voice returned. "No need to rewatch the vid. It's just, uh, the name of Guide's species. Don't worry if you haven't asked yet. Guide's quick to share that info."

After briefly probing my memory (and a little help from Guide), I pulled out the right name. "Chok'tal."

In response, muted green lights came online along the ship's underbelly. There was a hydraulic hiss, then the *cr-clonk* of locks releasing. I stepped back just as the docking sphincter unsealed and began lowering a corroded ladder. Before the ladder touched the ground, though, it jerked and froze up. The entire bottom rung snapped off.

"Well, look at that," I said to Guide. "My first time on a deathtrap."

The interior matched my expectations about the sort of people who were inclined to own such a vessel. It was cramped, functional, its walkways and congregation modules lined with charming details: exposed wiring here, busted pipes there. The auxiliary bulbs' faded orange light did little to improve my opinion.

Occasionally, I stumbled across panels with writing in alltongue—the Hegemony's state language, and that of most of the civilized universe—but it was clear these had all been retrofitted, meaning the vessel was alien in origin. This probably explained "quirky" touches like the hibernation pods designed for insectoid beings.

Still, a ship was a ship. Anything capable of getting me into orbit and back to non-chakki-infested worlds was more than acceptable.

Some fifteen minutes of plodding and backtracking later, I reached the cockpit. Not a bridge—I'd been on enough high-end vessels to know the difference—but an honest-to-Halcius cockpit. There were four large, beaten-up, bucket-style chairs, with bracing arms that probably served a purpose for the ship's creator species. Now, the style of the chairs wasn't my issue, but rather the number of them.

You see, most single-pilot vessels worth more than the sum of their parts also came saddled with some type of program for navigation. Like I said, us humans were clueless when it came to operating alien tech. At the minimum, most solo flyers invested in something like a digitized alien consciousness—a simstruct, in common parlance—or a machine program capable of serving the same purpose.

And that was just for getting the ship off the ground and into the vacuum of space. Once there, the details could be handled by an interdimensional being—but we'll get to that later. What mattered at that moment was finding the intelligence that could get this bucket of junk off the surface.

Looking around the cockpit, however, I saw no signs of such assistance. There were no bulky logic nets, no processing cubes. My stomach curdled. Had Modri expected me to be another Hegemony grunt who'd picked up flying skills in basic training?

"Guide," I said, slumping into the main cockpit chair, "any chance you know what kind of program is loaded into this thing?"

"For what purpose, Purifier?"

I sighed and toggled a few basic power switches. The main display lit up with alien symbols. "For flying?"

"We may be able to handle this task, Purifier."

My hand paused over a converter dial. "You're *what*?"

"As we explained, we contain the embedded knowledge of all past Purifiers. Our knowledge is sufficient to operate this vessel, provided you can restore our memories with the use of a Polyp. We strongly speculate that Purifier Modri left such a Polyp aboard this ship."

"You couldn't have mentioned this earlier?"

"You seemed intent on piloting personally, Purifier."

"Fair enough." Although it put me on edge to place my life into Guide's hands, I (shockingly) trusted it more than my own clumsiness. "Did you fly Modri here, or did he handle that?"

"We believe Modri entrusted us with that duty."

"Ever crashed before?"

"Not to our knowledge."

"Worth a shot, then."

That brought me to my second, equally important search. Somewhere on the vessel was Modri's second cache of goodies, including the mysterious Polyps.

As such, I stood and headed deeper into the vessel. At the very rear, just behind the coolant stacks, was a bullet-riddled door marked in ultraviolet paint as STORAGE. I had some misgivings about cranking the handle open, mainly because I feared the ship might've been used to transport flesh-eating beasties of one sort or another, but I was on short on time and even shorter on caution.

The door rumbled open, and a fine veil of mist parted to reveal a table bolted to the center of the room. When the overhead lights flickered on, I found my haul gathered atop it.

The most attention-grabbing item was a large, three-dimensional octagon that seemed to be made of cartilage and skin. Pores of various shapes and sizes covered its surface, all pulsing with a reddish inner glow. And it was *breathing.*

"Congratulations, Purifier," Guide said, *"you have encountered your first Genofacturing Spore. If you lose access to this spore, you can recreate it using the relevant upgrade from the Mutation tree for—"*

"Whoa, slow down," I said. "You might want to start by telling me what the hell it does. 'Cause it looks about ready to eat my arm off."

"The Genofacturing Spore is a device capable of producing weapons and other items through the use of Genofacturing Points."

"So . . . it's an organic material printer."

"We are unfamiliar with the concept."

"Forget it," I said, approaching the spore hesitantly. When I drew close enough, my HUD reappeared and framed the Genofacturing Spore in a green outline that read, surprisingly, GENOFACTURING CUBE. "How do I work it?"

"First, you must grant us a link with the spore. This will allow us to direct the replication processes needed to manufacture the desired item. Please be advised that in order to engage with the spore, you must first purchase the required upgrades during a rank-up."

"Right. And, uh, how do I power it?"

"All power is internally sustained, Purifier. We estimate that this particular spore has over twelve thousand years' worth of energy still circulating."

I whistled through my teeth. "Sounds like it'd make a hell of a bomb."

"It is capable of manufacturing explosives, yes."

"Not what I meant, but that's fine. What's all the rest of this?"

Arranged around the Genofacturing Spore were five fist-sized lumps, each made of the same dark, mottled material. My ignorant guess was that some large, meandering creature had excreted them to mark its territory.

"These are Polyps, Purifier."

"Damn. Think they rotted after Modri sliced them off?"

"No. They are in a state of hibernation. They will reactivate once attached to the body."

As if proving Guide's point, my HUD proceeded to outline the five Polyps in a similar green light to that of the spore, labeling each in turn.

POLYP (Purifier Nul Vak'Turan)
POLYP (Purifier Hakkali)
POLYP (Purifier Jekra Modri)
POLYP (Purifier 116 Amat)

"Intriguing," I whispered, the archaeology side of me marveling at how seamlessly Guide managed to present the new objects' descriptions despite the various origins of their owners' names. "So, if I make my own Polyp, it'll be marked as 'Dak Korasa'?"

"That is correct."

"Talk about leaving a mark on the 'verse." Despite my reservations, I picked up the Polyp made by Modri. "You said each Polyp gives a different bonus, right?"

"*That is correct. We feel obliged to mention that they also grant direct access to the consciousness of the Polyp creator.*"

"So that's what Modri was talking about," I said, grateful I'd finally found my way to give Guide the piloting knowledge it needed. "Any way to compare the bonuses now?"

"*This ability is unlocked upon gaining the Polyp upgrade in the Status Display.*"

Well, I knew that one would come back to bite me. In hindsight, it seemed awfully stupid not to pick the cryptic option in my rank-up tree. And thanks to my own stupidity, I hadn't even used Indomitable during the chakki fight, the one place where I truly needed it. A waste of a Rank Point.

While on the subject of ranks and points and Polyps, it seemed wise to check the most pressing number in my situation.

Using the mental "willpower" push I'd learned to access other skills, I conjured a readout on the left-hand side of my HUD.

Rank Time: 15 Hours, 35 Minutes, 12 Seconds
Storehouse Time: 0 Hours, 0 Minutes, 0 Seconds
RANK-UP AVAILABLE: RANK 2

Huh. Not too bad on timing, considering the pitiful state of my body and general tidal wave of lethal challenges that had bombarded me since the last rank-up. If I played my cards right, I might be able to reach a nearby habitable world before needing to—

No, I thought, catching myself, *I need to rank-up now.*

It hurt to realize, seeing as I'd come to a decision to delay each rank-up process as long as possible. After all, if I kept ranking up the instant I had enough points, I'd be wasting the tens of precious hours afforded by the previous rank-up. The time crunch didn't seem too daunting now, but I was only at Rank 1. When the points required to progress reached eight, nine, or ten digits—and beyond, if I got that far—I'd need to bide my hours carefully. Each rank-up was, in essence, a gift of twenty hours to live. Sooner or later, I'd need every last minute.

But here and now, I had no other course. If I didn't rank-up and select the "equip Polyp" upgrade, I'd be at the mercy of my own nonexistent flying skills. And that was *not* happening. I'd come too far to be taken out by a low-speed crash in this blasted jungle.

For better or worse, I had to trust Modri's prescribed course of action. To take advantage of the knowledge and devices he'd left me.

With the utmost annoyance, I conjured my Status Display with a thought. Like last time, the world winked out and the data winked in.

STATUS DISPLAY
PURIFIER RANK: 1
RANK-UP AVAILABLE: RANK 2 (400 KP Required)

Kill Points: 10,000
Genofacturing Points: 1800

Rank Points: 0

Rank Time: 15 Hours, 34 Minutes, 18 Seconds
Storehouse Time: 0 Hours, 0 Minutes, 0 Seconds

Anima: 120%
Dominion: 0/1

10,000 KP in the bank, and only 400 required to progress. Overkill, much? My only consolation was that upon rank-up, I'd have well over 11,000 Genofacturing Points to play with. Not that I could use them, but still. It didn't take a diehard game addict to know that more points was always better.

It was time to bite the bullet and begrudgingly purchase the Polyp upgrade.

Using the same mental flick as before, I activated the rank-up button. My new display immediately appeared.

STATUS DISPLAY
PURIFIER RANK: 2
RANK-UP NOT AVAILABLE (800 KP Required)

Kill Points: 0
Genofacturing Points: 11,400

Rank Points: 1

Rank Time: 19 Hours, 59 Minutes, 59 Seconds
Storehouse Time: 0 Hours, 0 Minutes, 0 Seconds

Anima: 140%
Dominion: 0/1

Aside from confirming my dreaded theory about KP requirements doubling with each rank, there wasn't much to see. Well, alright, there was the predicted 20 percent boost in Anima *and* the strangest element of all: the lack of a new Dominion slot. Unlike the other values I'd come to understand, the rate at which Dominion's "score" ticked up was completely lost on me. Yet another question for Guide.

Not wanting to waste my precious time, however, I quickly tabbed to the Mutation upgrade tree and located my prize.

MUTATION [Tier I]
Polyps I (REQ Rank 1): Enables bonding with one Polyp. *Does not require a Dominion slot.*

That was the one. An instant after selecting it . . . and confirming it . . . something curious happened to the Mutation column. More options appeared beneath the upgraded Polyps box. Three options, to be precise, all fanning out like a pyramid's base.

MUTATION [Tier II] (*3 Rank Points required for Tier III access*)
Polyps II (REQ Rank 3): Enables bonding with a second Polyp. *Does not require a Dominion slot.*

Genofacturing I (REQ Rank 5): Enables creation of a Genofacturing Spore and all Stage-I products. *Does not require a Dominion slot.*

Omniphile (REQ Rank 3): Increases homeostatic efficiency in harsh environments. (0/3)

Nocturnal (REQ Rank 1): Enhances night vision when active. (0/5)

Suddenly feeling like a fool, I looked back at the other upgrade paths—namely Annihilation, where I'd placed my first Rank Point. To my chagrin, I found that three boxes had also opened up beneath Indomitable. In my haste, I'd evidently forgotten to double-check the extent of the Status Display's changes.

But there would be time to peruse my ever-expanding pathways later. Right now, there were clear tasks that needed to be checked off: pop in a Polyp, start up the engines, fly off this damn planet, find something to kill before my twenty hours—technically, twenty-two—ran dry. After that, well, it was anybody's game. One step at a time.

After closing the Status Display, I went back up to the table and checked out my options. Just as Guide had indicated, each Polyp's highlighted tag now also included details about its bonuses. I gave each a cursory glance, fairly certain I'd opt for Modri's due to our strange yet undeniable connection.

POLYP (Purifier Nul Vak'Turan): +25% Kill Points earned.

POLYP (Purifier Hakkali): +10% Storehouse Time accrued.

POLYP (Purifier Jekra Modri): +2 Hours per Rank Timer.

POLYP (Purifier 116 Amat): +1 Dominion slot.

I had no reference point as far as what constituted a "good" or "bad" Polyp bonus, but it was fairly clear that, for a low-rank Purifier like myself, Modri's bonus was still the best. Come on—two whole hours per rank timer! Vak'Turan's was also decent, but seemed like something I'd appreciate more in the higher ranks. You know, when the required points turned to billions instead of hundreds. And Amat's . . . well, it had zero practical use for me at the moment, seeing as my one and only Dominion slot was reserved for Indomitable.

Considering them for a few more seconds, I ran into a question only Guide could answer.

"How did these people add their bonuses?"

"Using the necessary upgrade, Purifier."

I groaned. "Of course. But I mean . . . why are they all different? Who decides what the bonus is?"

"The Purifier themselves. Each bonus has a corresponding genofacturing fee. The more valuable the bonus, the costlier the fee."

It didn't address the specifics I was looking for, but it would have to do. I shrugged and decided to revisit it later. And by later, I mean when I wasn't at a low rank where it didn't matter anyhow.

"So, when I pop this thing in and activate it, I'll get to speak to Modri," I said, hefting his Polyp up and down.

"*That is partially correct,*" Guide said. "*Purifier Modri's consciousness resides within us. Activating his Polyp will cause his latent mind to rise to the forefront.*"

"I . . . see. So, it's like you're an aquarium, and I'm scooping up one fish out of the masses."

"*This metaphor is strange, but not entirely inaccurate.*"

"I'm an archaeologist. Strange metaphors are part of my profession."

"*Purifier, we should also note something important before you bond with this Polyp.*"

By the time I heard Guide's words, it was too late. I had already started forging ahead with my plan of thinking "bond" while staring at Modri's Polyp in my hand. Even as Guide's warning registered, a slew of short, flailing tendrils sprouted from beneath the Polyp. Its outer shell cracked and dissolved into a jelly-like membrane beneath. In a matter of milliseconds, the glistening Polyp raced up my wrist, squeezed into my vest, and scurried along my back, leaving a wet, prickly trail.

All the while, I squealed and twisted in place, still traumatized by my first "encounter" with Guide's slug form. Not that it mattered. Disregarding my terror, the Polyp burrowed its tiny feelers into the skin below the nape of my neck.

There was no immediate physical change, other than the sensation of an ice-cold fork briefly jabbing into my spine.

In the lower-right corner of my HUD, however, a new message appeared.

[Slot 1] POLYP (Purifier Jekra Modri): +2 Hours to each Rank Timer. *Direct Consciousness Link Available*

"It's in me," I mumbled, shivering at the strangeness of its presence. "That thing . . . is in me."

"*That is correct, Purifier.*"

Once I'd stopped shaking enough to speak properly, I asked, "What, pray tell, is this 'important' thing you wanted to tell me?"

"*It may not be pertinent anymore.*"

"Tell. Me."

"*Very well. Although you are free to bond with and remove Polyps at your discretion, you should be advised that any bond formed with a Polyp persists until the end of your current rank.*"

"Huh?"

"We will attempt to simplify, Purifier. You have just bonded with the Polyp belonging to Jekra Modri, which grants a bonus of two hours to each rank timer as well as access to Jekra Modri's consciousness."

"Right . . ."

"If you remove Jekra Modri's Polyp now, the bonus and consciousness will be unavailable."

"Yeah, okay? That makes sense."

"Furthermore . . . replacing Jekra Modri's Polyp with another Purifier's Polyp would not grant you new bonuses, nor would it enable access to their consciousness."

"And why not?"

"Once a Polyp has been bonded to a particular slot in your nervous system, the slot is considered reserved until your next rank-up. Since you are fond of metaphors, you may term the rank-up process a 'reset' of the nervous system. Thus, if you wish to utilize another Polyp's bonuses during your next rank, you must either have an empty Polyp slot or equip the new Polyp prior to selecting the rank-up option."

The implications sank in. "So . . . I'm stuck with Modri's Polyp until I hit my next rank-up."

"That is correct, Purifier."

"And if I take it out with under two hours remaining . . ."

"We will be forced to eliminate you."

"Marvelous," I said, taking long, slow breaths to no avail. My heart hammered away. "So, to frame this in context . . . if Modri doesn't know how to fly a ship, I'm screwed."

"We believe that is an accurate summary."

This was bad. Real bad. But there was a silver lining in here somewhere—as long as Modri knew how to pilot this thing, which had been his own ship, I was in the clear.

"So, Guide . . . Modri knows how to fly, right?"

"We do not believe so, Purifier."

Well, that was it, then. One moment of hastiness, one small oversight in heeding Guide's advice, and I'd doomed myself.

But I couldn't give up that easily. Not just yet.

"Alright, Guide," I said, heading back to the cockpit with my chin held high. "Today we test the piloting skills of Jekra Modri."

10

'm not what most would term a devout worshipper, but you'd better believe I tossed a few silent prayers to Halcius and the thousand other gods I'd researched during my career. All this pain, all this fear . . . and it came down to the skill of a dead man's consciousness.

The longer I thought about it, the more nauseous I became.

Time to rip the bandage off.

Leaning back into the main pilot's seat, I mentally pulled the trigger on "activate Direct Consciousness Link."

Nothing happened.

"Uh, Guide?" I whispered.

"*So, you're the unlucky bastard, huh?*" It wasn't Guide's voice—it was Modri's.

Strange of an introduction as it was, I found it relieving to hear another human's voice. One that wasn't shouting death threats, that is.

"Yeah, you could say that," I told him. "Listen, I'm stuck on the planet where you died. And your tablet's fu—"

"*What tablet?*"

I squinted. "The tablet . . . you left me? You know, detailing what to do?"

"*Yeah, I'm lost.*"

"Modri, listen . . . you left me an operations tablet in some ruins. You were trying to explain what I needed to do to, uh, 'win' this game."

"*Okay, that sounds like somethin' I'd do.*"

"But you don't remember doing it?"

"*Nope, not at all. But that's how this whole shtick happens, Purifier. Most individual memories don't get saved. Y'know, faces, names, birthday parties. None of that.*"

Trying my best not to scream, I leaned forward and rubbed my temples. "So, what *does* get saved?"

"Language. General personality. Skills. Traumatic events. Anything that's rooted deep in the brain."

"Right, so you'd know how to assemble a short-range transmitter, but not the name of your dog. Because that's so logical."

"Hey, I didn't make the damn thing. I'm just floatin' around in the void, tryin' my best to help whoever picks up my Polyp. So take it easy."

"Yeah, fine," I said, feeling a tad ashamed at having been snarky to an eternally imprisoned consciousness. "What exactly can you recall? Anything that'll help me?"

"Depends whatcha need help with."

"Buckle up. It's a bit of a tale."

Six minutes passed as I filled Modri in on the key details of my situation. He remained quiet for most of the saga, only asking clarifying questions when it came to how I'd managed to piss off my ex-employer.

"Sheesh," he said when it was finished. *"Sounds like you're in a jam."*

"You could say that."

"So, lemme get this straight . . . you found some cache of gear I left behind, includin' an ops tablet with a full manual on what to do . . . but it's busted. And now you need to get into orbit."

"Exactly."

"Yeah, see, if that tablet wasn't so gonked, you'd probably know I'm not a flyin' type of guy. That'd probably be Hakkali."

"How would you know that?"

"Most of us Purifiers know each other in there. It's like a big party. Except, y'know, we can't leave."

I drummed my fingers on the armrest. "What do I do?"

"Seems to me that you've got two options. You can head back out into the jungle, use that fancy new gun to take down a critter, and rank up . . . or you can let me try to take us to the stars. No promises we'd get there in one piece, though."

"Well, when you put it that way, I think I'll do a little hunting."

"Smart fella."

Just as I moved to stand, however, a triangular light appeared on the controls' main panel. A *red* triangular light, to be exact. And even the dumbest sack of bricks knows that red lights are no good.

"Hey, Modri," I said quietly, "any chance you know what that means?"

"Oh, sure. Seen it all the time in my service days."

"Spit it out."

"Just means someone's forced open one of the boarding doors. You expectin' company?"

My blood ran cold.

Even as I glanced at the rifle lying on the chair beside me, however, I noted a set of faint, winking bulbs moving through the sky overhead. The skiff. It was moving in a holding pattern, circling the ship like a carrion bird.

"Shit," I hissed. "How'd they find me?"

Modri laughed. *"For starters, you've got the ship runnin' at half power. That kinda fusion signal tends to get noticed in a jungle with nothin' but leaves and fur."*

"Once again, thank you for this timely information."

"What can I say? Can't fix stupid."

Swallowing my next retort, I reached across the cockpit aisle and lifted the rifle with as much delicacy as possible. I'd already loaded a magazine, but given my inexperience with guns, I didn't see much harm in pulling off the age-old macho move of pulling the bolt back to ensure it was ready to shoot. Unfortunately, the clack of the bolt slamming forward was anything but smooth. It was so loud I nearly pissed myself.

"Hey, genius," Modri said, mimicking my whispers.

"What now?"

"I hope you're not plannin' to shoot that thing."

I gently eased myself out of the chair and aimed down the main passage. "And why not?"

"Just common sense not to shoot a gun with a blocked barrel."

"It's not blocked, just bent."

"Same difference. That thing's gonna explode in your tender, kitty-pettin' hands the minute you pull the trigger."

I gulped and reassessed the rifle in my hands. "How do I fix it?"

"Saw off half the barrel. That'll do it."

"There's no time for that!"

"Alright, have it your way. Just don't come cryin' to the dead Purifier party when you get taken out by your own busted gun. The others'll be laughin' at you for the rest of time."

Given how much of a useless comedian Modri was being, I found it nearly impossible to resist shouting at the top of my lungs. But I had to shove it all down. *Had* to. Because at the very edge of the helmet's enhanced audio range, metal panels creaked. Boots softly tapped.

My only comfort was, ironically, the skiff prowling overhead, as it meant that at least one of the team's three killers was up in the air. Probably *just* one, I decided after some split-second reflection. The sounds coming from down the passage were too numerous for one person. There had to be two of them closing in.

"You really couldn't have given me a pistol?" I whispered to Modri. "There's no way I'll take both of them down with a knife."

"Get smart about this, Purifier. You know the ship, and they don't. Use it to your advantage."

That pithy, generally obvious bit of advice inspired an idea. Thinking fast, I glanced down at the tattered remains of my jumpsuit. The torn-off sections had frayed at the edges, exposing the thin, gauzy mesh sandwiched between the inner and outer layers.

"What're you doin'?" Modri asked as I set the rifle down and began unspooling strands of the mesh.

"Using the busted gun."

"Okay, sharpshooter . . . let's see this shitshow."

Once I had a sufficiently long thread of mesh, I grabbed the rifle, tied one end around the trigger, and weaved the rest around the trigger guard. Then I crept into the passage and wedged the rifle in a tangle of flaking pipes.

"Interestin' move," Modri commented.

I hushed him, then pressed on with my plan by looping the thread between a set of rungs at ankle-height. By the time I'd secured the last knot, I didn't need the helmet to sense the footsteps. They were close. Almost here.

"So, makin' a tripwire," Modri said, once I was safely tucked behind one of the chairs, knife in hand. *"Better hope there are no fuel lines near your firecracker."*

I shook my head wearily. "Why do you think I'm not using the grenades?"

"What? You've got grenades . . . and you thought some cheap-ass trip-wire was the way to go? Damn, we've got a lot of work to do with you."

Much as I hated it, I was almost beginning to miss Guide's terse, no-nonsense manner of speaking. They'd at least had the decency to shut up when I desired it.

But swapping out the voice in my head was far from the highest priority at that moment. More concerning were the shadows stirring at the end of the passage.

Instantly, my HUD reappeared in full detail and framed the two figures.

Kardinal Killa (HUMANOID)
Balnos of the Long Star (HUMANOID)
CALCULATING . . .
Combined Estimated Kill Points: 34,000

My attackers had wisely opted to keep their flashlights off—a mutually beneficial decision. They got to believe they had the element of stealth, while *I* had the comfort of knowing they wouldn't spot the nearly invisible length of thread strung taut over the floor panels.

I gripped the knife harder and held my breath, peeking around the edge of the chair as both silhouettes advanced single file toward the cockpit. First in line was Kardinal, judging by the shape's height and prominent limp. The second had to be Balnos, on account of the twitching antennae that curved back from their skull.

Through deduction, it became clear that Liura was the one in the sky.

Good. Kardinal was already wounded, and Balnos was the lesser of the deadeyes when compared to his female counterpart. Still, I couldn't let myself get high off the realization. Both men, wounded or not, were more than competent with a rifle. And having seen the damage their high-end fragmentation bullets did to wandering beasts, I held no illusions about what would happen to my skull if they got even a single shot on target. No amount of Anima could stitch up a pile of mush.

"Y'think he's in there?" Kardinal whispered, earning a shush from Balnos. My helmet's auditory boosting just barely captured his words. "What? I'm just sayin', man, maybe it's a trap."

Balnos nudged him onwards with his rifle. "He's an archaeologist, not a commando."

"Yeah, well, he did a number on me."

"That's why I'm here. To help clean up your mess."

Kardinal came closer. His boot lifted just a hair's breadth from the tripwire, swung forward, and—

Stopped.

Shit.

"Maybe you oughta go first," Kardinal whispered. "I'm tellin' ya, there's somethin' not right about him. He shoulda died in those caverns. Shoulda died a *long* time ago."

Balnos growled. "Keep moving, or I will make you."

"Go ahead and try."

And Balnos did. Only he didn't just try—he shoved Kardinal with enough force to send his foot plowing right through the tripwire.

An ear-splitting *bang* filled the cockpit. Sparks exploded in the passageway. Then came the screams, muffled by the overwhelming *juk-juk-juk* of my rifle firing on full auto.

In hindsight, I probably should've set it to semi—if I'd known how to do that. But the ammo wasn't wasted. It pinged off the bulkhead and panels and pumps, lighting the corridor in strobe-like flashes as my ambushers flailed. Smoke coiled up around the shadows, followed by wisps of pressurized fumes. Here and there, bullets tore through flesh with satisfying *whumps* instead of ricocheting off metal.

Then the rifle fell silent. Time to pounce.

I sprang out from behind the chair with the knife cocked back over my shoulder, screaming bloody murder as I charged the bewildered men.

Kardinal screamed back—not out of rage, but terror. He was balled up on the ground, jammed between sets of hissing pipes, swatting blindly at the force rushing toward him. A pistol lay useless at his side. Behind him was Balnos, little more than a stirring black lump in the shadows.

Seizing the moment, I leapt atop Kardinal's chest and plunged my blade straight into his throat. His muffled scream came out in a bloody froth.

"That's for leaving me to die . . .," I hissed, withdrawing the blade, "and this is for being stupid enough to keep hunting me."

Kardinal raised his hands, batting weakly at my vest, but it was no use.

I stabbed straight through his right eye.

For a moment I just sat there, huffing, almost as though watching myself from outside my body. I'd just killed a humanoid. No, scratch that—a human. My own kind. His corpse had gone limp the moment the blade sank up to the handle, and yet I found it difficult to see it as a corpse at all. It was still Kardinal, still a man.

Strangely, none of the unease I'd anticipated rose up in me. My hands were smooth at my sides, my gaze even. There were no moral quibbles running circles in my mind. In fact, there was hardly any mental activity at all. Just clearness. Steadiness.

Then a thought emerged:

One down, one to go.

Balnos.

For a moment, I'd almost forgotten he was here. What drew me back to his presence was the rustling of fabric. When I looked over, though, I realized he was in no shape to do much of anything. He was crawling away from me, wheezing through lungs that had to be riddled with shrapnel, fighting for every inch of floor paneling just as I had done in the jungle hours before. His rifle was still slung to his body, scraping beneath him.

I stood up slowly. "There's nowhere to go, Balnos. Give it up."

He crawled a few more paces, then slumped. "It was just . . . business, Dak."

"Maybe," I said, stepping just behind him, "but you made it personal. You left me to die like an animal."

"Orders are orders."

"You chose to follow them. I guess this is your reward."

Balnos spat out a mouthful of blood. "Finish it, then."

"Really? Right now? You don't even want to know how I survived, found this equipment, and took you all down? I'm disappointed."

"The universe . . . is a strange place," he managed. "Sometimes you win . . . sometimes you lose."

"Well said. But believe it or not, you've still got a role to play in all this."

"Eh?"

I stepped in front of Balnos and squatted down, gazing into the six jet-black eyes that formed a vertical stripe down his face. "You have children, don't you? Children who are probably worried about you every time you fly out."

"Don't . . . talk about them."

"Bear with me." Gingerly, I grasped the straps for Balnos's rifle sling and undid the buckles. He didn't stop me. Then I slid the weapon out from under him and cradled it in my lap. "I don't want to kill you, Balnos. I really don't. I've already got Kill Poin— You know what? Never mind. What I'm trying to say is, there's a way you can help me. A way for both of us to get out."

Again, he coughed. The blood was thicker now. "Too late for that."

"I've seen what your species can do. You're messed up, sure, but we both know you're not at death's door just yet."

Okay, maybe I was off by a few hours, but the underlying message was true. Balnos's origin species—that is to say, his ancestors who'd never merged with humanoid DNA—had possessed healing abilities on par with Guide's. Integrating humanoid genes had weakened that adaptation, sure, but it hadn't completely nullified it. The only catch was that in order to heal themselves, and indeed, in order to trigger even their most basic bodily functions to stay alive, they required doses of modified stem cells.

You might compare these cell injections to a diabetic reliant on insulin. Now, these cells were contained in vials of black fluid that Balnos kept stockpiled aboard the ship in orbit.

But they weren't *only* on the ship. Two emergency vials were tucked in the shielded canister on his belt.

"So . . . what's your plan?" Balnos growled. "Inject me, let me heal up, then torture me?"

I scoffed. "I'm not Liura. Or Kardinal, for that matter, though I think he's not so relevant anymore."

"Then *what*?"

"You're going to transmit to Liura and tell her everything's sorted down here. You found me hiding in a salvageable ship, killed me, and now want to fly this bad boy up to orbit for docking."

"And why . . . would I do that?"

"Because if you do, we can seize that ship. We can fly the hell out of here. Chanzig would never find us."

"My family."

With those two words, I grasped why Balnos—an otherwise decent fellow—had so readily turned into a butcher. Of course. How could I have been so stupid? Chanzig controlled the life of every single being in his circle, right down to the people they cared for most. If Balnos were to go dark and slip into the ether, that wouldn't be the end of it—though it would be his family's end.

"We can take him down," I said softly. "You know how to get into his fortress."

Balnos sagged even further, letting his cheek rest against the floor panel. "Won't work."

"Listen, my friend. I'm offering you a good deal here. If you die on this planet, what do you think's going to happen to them? This is your only shot to alter fate."

For several long, agonizing moments, Balnos just lay there and panted like a fading animal. Then his antennae twitched, and half his eyes winked open. "Fine."

11

Balnos groaned as I jabbed the stem cell injector into his arm and depressed the plunger. He was slumped in the copilot's chair, more corpse than living man.

The instant I'd finished the injection, a fresh spark emerged in his eyes. At the same time, a familiar text crawl filled my HUD.

ENCOUNTER INCOMPLETE
Kills: 1
Kill Points Awarded: 14,000

RANK-UP AVAILABLE: RANK 3

I dismissed the updates with a mixture of annoyance and curiosity. How had the system determined that the encounter was actually "over?" I mean, it *was* over, true, but it seemed like a rather arbitrary point to consider the fight finished. If it ran on pure intentions, it likely would've concluded the encounter the moment I started pitching a plan to Balnos.

That was a minor quibble, however. The important part was that Kardinal's overdue death had awarded me enough KP to reach Rank 3, thus granting me a minimum of twenty-two hours of life. It was time to initiate my brilliant strategy.

"Go ahead," I told Balnos, lifting his small transmitter box to his lips since he was too weak to manage it himself. "I'm sure Liura is on the edge of her seat."

Part of me regretted not tying up Balnos up prior to injecting him, but the other part was certain I'd made the right call. Not many successful partnerships begin with restraining somebody you've just promised to help. At best, such an act would've made Balnos resent me. At worst, it might have planted the idea that I planned to kill him after his work was done, thus guaranteeing he'd turn on me.

Balnos lifted a shaking finger to activate the link. "Liura?"

Crackling came over the short-range band, followed by Liura's pitiless voice. "Go ahead."

"We've got him."

"Dead or alive?"

"Dead. But he took Kardinal out . . . and got me pretty good, too."

"Understood," she said, not a drop of emotion to be found. "I'll send my landing coordi—"

"No," Balnos cut in. "This thing's flyable. I'll take it up to the *Red Advent*, dock it in one of the spare hangars. The boss might want it as an artifact."

Liura was silent for a concerning length of time. "If you're sure."

"I am. The parts look very . . . lucrative."

"Understood."

Balnos twisted the knob on the transmitter box, severing the line.

"That's it?" I asked.

He nodded. "That's it."

"So . . . what now?"

Balnos leaned forward, nudging his chin toward the night sky. "Now we fly up there."

"And take the ship?"

"That's your call," he said wearily. "Seems like our best choice, seeing as this thing's out of action for subspace travel."

I blinked at him. "What?"

"You heard me. Seems like some animals must've gotten curious, started chewing on its quantum coils. Only way to get out of the system is to use the *Red Advent*."

Well, that certainly threw a wrench into my plans. I'd figured that if we weren't able to take control of the main ship, we could still slip away on our own. But we were dead in the water, limited to local space travel. You might compare this to being stranded on the ocean with a broken motor. All we had were oars . . . and the *Red Advent* had our motor.

"You made this plan," Balnos continued, "so you tell me what to do."

Until that moment, I hadn't actually considered how we were going to take over the real prize. The *Red Advent* was part of Chanzig's personal fleet, meaning it was crewed by about fifteen diehard bootlickers who would gladly go down swinging. Liura, Balnos, and Kardinal were tough, but they were just hired help compared to the grunts in orbit.

Even if we did manage to take out every soul on board, what were the chances we could do it silently? The moment bullets started flying, the *Red Advent*'s bridge crew would likely already be sending a subspace warning back to Chanzig. If that warning reached its destination, there was no hope of returning to his planet undetected. We'd be lucky to even break atmosphere rather than being killed by a hydrogen missile.

If we managed to safely land, we'd face the monumental task of taking down one of the most unassailable crime lords in the sector. A crime lord that had been cutting off heads three times longer than I'd been alive, no less.

"*Psst,*" Modri urged, startling me, "*when you plannin' to tell your new friend about me?*"

I looked down as though deep in thought, hesitant to reply aloud.

"*You can just think to me, y'know. No need to speak.*"

Testing, I thought, directing it toward Modri.

"*Heard loud and clear.*"

Seriously? You couldn't have told me I could just think it before?

"*Huh. Just kinda assumed you knew. Or Guide told you.*"

Yeah, well, they didn't.

"*So . . . hijacking a big ship, huh?*"

Yep.

"*Want my advice? Or are you just gonna shush me again?*"

I sighed. *Go ahead.*

"*What you need to do is hit the relays first. Then they won't be able to send anything out. That's what the insurgents did to our forces all the time. Say, you aren't an insurgent, right?*"

I'm a Hegemony citizen. What do you think?

"*All good in my book.*"

"Hey," Balnos said with a nudge, "what's the holdup?"

"Nothing. Sorry, I was just . . . thinking."

"You don't have a plan, then."

"Of course I do," I said, straightening in my seat. "We go after the relays."

"You know where they are?"

"Naturally." I didn't, but I figured Modri could guide me when the time was right. He'd been a special forces soldier, after all. Locating sensitive bits on a ship was his bread and butter. "Say . . . you know how to fly, right?"

Balnos glanced at me with plain irritation, then booted up the main console. "Go seal the boarding doors, then strap in."

I narrowed my eyes. "Why don't *you* go shut the doors? Wait, no. We should stick together."

"Liura's going to get suspicious if we don't take off immediately." He kept his eyes fixed to the display, flicking switches and tapping output meters. "You're the one with the rifle, Dak. I'm not stupid enough to try anything."

Looking down, I remembered he was correct. His chunky, flesh-exploding automatic rifle was slung across my lap, ready to dismember him in seconds if he pulled any stunts.

"Fine," I said as I stood. "I'm trusting you, Balnos."

He looked at me seriously. "And I'm trusting you."

"Okay, then."

"Okay."

I awkwardly turned toward the passage. "I'm going now."

He gave an absent-minded wave, still working the controls.

Despite my assurances, I hurried like a man on fire to the doors. A lot can go wrong in a few seconds when you leave a hostage to their own devices. Fortunately, by the time I'd pounded the locks shut and was half-way back to the cockpit, I felt the floor rattle beneath me. We'd taken off. We were in the air. Leaving.

Balnos was just as I'd left him, diligently attending to the flight gauges and guiding us upward in a perfect vertical ascent.

This aspect of interstellar travel had always disoriented me. Then again, it disoriented most of us beings who'd evolved to live on flat ground. See, the desirable alien tech I mentioned earlier included grav-panels set into the floors of most spacefaring machinery. These miraculous hunks of whatever-they-were created a pleasant and human-friendly experience aboard ships in the vacuum, ensuring your feet remained planted and objects fell at normal rates no matter how fast or erratically the vessel was moving.

Still, there would always be a part of the human mind-gut system that was thrown into a panic when it saw the contrast between one's felt ori-entation in space and the actual environment. This is probably why I grew nauseous as soon as I looked out the side of the cockpit viewpane, where the planet's jungle surface lay in a horizontal line.

My throat tensed and my legs buckled beneath me. I flopped into the pilot's chair, shutting my eyes to ward off the bizarre sensations.

"*Pussy,*" Modri whispered.

Oh, shut up.

"*What? I used to do drop missions out of shuttles moving at the speed of sound. This is nothin' compared to my glory days.*"

Yeah, well, now you're living in a collective consciousness. So how'd that work out?

"Point taken, Purifier. I'll save you a spot in here."

Irritated, I sent a mental command for Modri to shut up. It seemed to do the trick.

Balnos glanced over at me as we left the thermosphere. "What were you saying earlier? Something about Kill Points."

"Probably nothing," I murmured.

"Probably?"

"Listen, I'll explain everything once we've taken control of that ship."

"How much do you have to explain, exactly?"

I waved off his question, staring straight ahead into the sprawl of stars and gas formations.

He seemed to take the hint. After a bit of manual steering, the half-shadowed hull of the *Red Advent* came into view. The portion washed in starlight was, as the name suggested, a glossy crimson color. It was relatively close, just over two thousand kilometers away.

Now, I couldn't tell you what class of vessel it was—again, I'm far from a space aficionado—but I know it was expensive. Rumor was that Chanzig had stripped away the entire hull, which was alien in origin, and retrofitted it with cutting-edge plates. The result was a long, spindle-like freighter with clusters of modules along its central hub. Halcius only knows how many priceless artifacts had been hauled away from their home systems aboard that monstrosity.

After several minutes of strained silence, Balnos's transmitter box crackled. "Third dock," a man grumbled.

Balnos clicked the box to confirm, then began guiding us toward the assigned spot. Once we'd reached what I took to be our destination, he set the ship in a loose holding pattern that matched the *Red Advent's* trajectory.

The thick hangar doors retracted, exposing the shimmering, soap bubble–like layer of the stasis field that contained a pocket of atmosphere.

"You ready for this?" Balnos asked, though he was already taking us in.

"Yeah," I said. "I've got it all planned out."

That was a lie, of course. A horrid lie. Even as our ship entered the docking bay, my entire body shook with tension. It felt like we were gliding into the stomach of a beast. A dark, rusted stomach.

Once we'd slipped through the stasis field, we lost the last vestiges of starlight. Blackness. The only things in sight were the warped panels directly beneath the cockpit, illuminated by the ship's underbelly bulbs.

"Is this normal?" I asked.

Balnos looked at me sidelong. His face was painted in the main display's amber glow. "How do you mean?"

"No lights in the hangar?"

"You're too paranoid."

"Am I? Because you were ready to gut me like a fish about an hour ago."

Balnos chuckled. "Just settle down. We're landing on autopilot. Let me go toggle the pressure equalizers."

He sounded confident. Reassuring. It was enough to let me slump back in the seat and mutter a weak, "Alright."

But my sense of unease didn't vanish. In fact, it only intensified when the ship's landing prongs touched down. The hangar was still black. Still silent. I'd landed plenty of times, and there had always been a "breakdown crew" ready to cart off whatever we'd recovered.

Then it hit me. *Pressure equalizers?* Our ship was at the exact same pressure as the *Red Advent*.

Balnos was lying.

I spun around in my seat, simultaneously shouldering the rifle, but it was too late.

My HUD sprang up, outlining Balnos in a blue box.

Balnos of the Long Star (HUMANOID)
CALCULATING...
Estimated Kill Points: 20,000

He stood about five paces down the passage, just over Kardinal's body, gripping the dead man's pistol.

"You're a real bastard," I said quietly. "You know that?"

Balnos clicked through his teeth. "Be easy, Dak. Liura and a few company men will be here in a matter of minutes. Might as well take this time to relax."

Still staring at Balnos down the rifle's iron sights, I activated Indomitable.

"You could've gotten your family out," I whispered.

"That's the thing, Dak," Balnos said quietly. "Nobody gets out. You ink a contract with Chanzig, and you're in for life."

"You realize I'm going to kill you, right?"

"It's possible."

I groaned. "I'm covered in armor. You might get one shot off on my neck, but I doubt it."

"It'd better for you if you just put the gun down."

Whether by accident or in a surprise attempt—it's been too long to recall the precise motive—I fired two rounds straight into Balnos's stomach. He fired back once, striking the upper panel on my vest. His round pinged off and tore into a chair. It'd leave nothing more than a bruise.

Balnos, on the other hand, wasn't so lucky. He crumpled down against a bulkhead, his torso clearly torn open and leaking its contents onto the floor panels. The pistol clattered out of his hands.

I stood calmly, walked over, and kicked the pistol away. Then I pressed the rifle's muzzle to his head.

"Why did you have to do that, Balnos?"

He sucked down a mouthful of blood. Even now, his shredded stomach was working overtime to patch itself together, sprouting fresh veins and bits of tissue. It wouldn't be enough.

"I don't want to do this," I whispered, "but I think I have to."

He reached up with a trembling hand and stabilized the barrel on his forehead. "Tell them I went . . . out fighting."

I nodded. "If I see your family, I'll get them out."

Despite the alienness of his face, he seemed to smile at that. "Cheers."

"Don't mention it." My finger curled around the trigger. "For what it's worth, it was good working—"

"Just do it."

And I did. The point-blank round completely evaporated Balnos's head.

I just stood there, hands shaking and ears ringing, as the system's messages rolled in.

ENCOUNTER SUCCESSFUL
Kills: 1
Kill Points Awarded: 20,000

RANK-UP AVAILABLE: RANK 3

What disturbed me most wasn't Balnos's betrayal, nor even the savagery with which I'd had to put him down like a rabid animal. No, what ate at me was the rush of satisfaction that came with the "encounter successful" message. Was it possible Guide had some role in releasing happy chemicals every time I finished a fight? Of course. But was it *also* possible that the system was just teaching me, even grooming me, to enjoy the act of killing through positive reinforcement?

Very much so.

Before I could dwell on that concept, however, light flooded the passage from behind me. I twisted back toward the cockpit, a hand raised to my eyes, only to find a series of floodlights shining throughout the hangar.

"What in the hell . . . ?" I muttered, stumbling back toward the main viewpane to get a better look at how screwed I was.

As it turned out, I was deeply screwed. Nearly every one of Chanzig's hired guns was out there, weapons aimed and armor strapped on. The hangar's four antiship gun batteries were online and aimed squarely at my location.

My HUD came online and framed the enemies . . . in red.

[SLAUGHTER EVENT]
Chanzig's Gunman (HUMANOID) (14)
Antiship Gun Battery (MECHANICAL) (4)
CALCULATING . . .
Combined Estimated Kill Points: 289,500

An astonishing amount of Kill Points, but I didn't give a damn about that. Not in terms of benefits to me, anyway. All that number did was express that I was screwed. It also confirmed that machines counted as point-worthy enemies, but honestly, who cared?

I had bigger problems, such as the woman at the front of the assembly. Standing there proudly, hands clasped behind her back, was none other than Liura friggin' Blue.

"Dak Korasa," she said, her voice amplified by the transmitter pinned to her shirt, "come out of the ship with your hands raised. There's no way out."

She didn't seem wrong in the slightest. Any way I sliced it, I was out of luck. In a dazed panic, I looked around the ship's interior, trying to find something—anything at all—that could get me out of this jam. Nothing. Zilch. Even a handful of grenades wouldn't be enough to take down the legion waiting for me. No matter what I did, they'd haul me right back to Chanzig for my eventual torture and execution.

Briefly, I considered checking my rank-up menu in the vague hopes that I'd find a miracle ability capable of saving me. But that plan was quickly discarded. I had no idea how long I'd be held in Liura's custody on the way back, which meant I had no way of ensuring I'd survive without saving my rank-up.

Then I spotted the gleam of Kardinal's blade, still stuck in its sheath—and by sheath, I mean the man's eye socket.

At first, I shook my head. There was no way. No way in hell. It was a plan almost as miserable as being shot by Chanzig's firing squad.

But I'd come this far. I'd proven my worth as a survivor.

It was the only way.

Moving over to Kardinal's body, I knelt down, wrenched the knife free, and turned it over in my hands. Then I snapped the thin blade, keeping only the top half. It would have to do. I glanced at the long, flabby gash in my upper arm, which was nowhere close to healing.

"This is gonna hurt," I said, more to myself than the dormant Guide in my head. "Deep breaths, Dak. Deep breaths ..."

12

On Liura's orders, I was cuffed, searched, and deposited into one of the ship's many holding cells. It was a dim, lightless space, its panels caked in layers of rust and dried blood. A brownish, sulfur-smelling liquid sloshed around my ankles.

None of this would've been overly terrible if not for the fact that I was completely naked. The urge to lie down or sit or even lean was strong—mainly because of the cheap shots Chanzig's guards had thrown my way during "processing"—but I couldn't bring myself to touch the nastiness all around me. Petty? Maybe. But I'd gladly suffer the pain of standing if it meant avoiding death via an infected wound.

The rattling in the floor panels suggested we were moving through subspace at faster-than-light speeds. A neutral revelation, if ever one existed. On the one hand, it meant we were guaranteed to reach Chanzig's planet long before my dwindling rank timer ran down to zero. On the other, it meant Chanzig would soon get his hands on me.

Guide? I thought, not willing to speak on account of the microphones within the cell.

"*Oh, now you wanna talk?*" Modri asked.

I didn't get a chance to take your advice. Balnos betrayed me.

"*We watched the whole thing. Talk about a shitshow.*"

I sighed. *What now?*

"*Now? What now? You're in a bad, bad spot.*"

Thanks for noticing.

Modri started to reply, but I lost all interest in his words when I sensed the holding cell's door unlocking. Just before it opened, I mentally shushed Modri again. As before, his silence was immediate.

Blinding light poured into my cell. Framed within it was Liura Blue, who stood with her hands neatly tucked at the small of her back.

Her blonde hair had been pulled back into a ponytail, showing off her severe features. To me, she'd always resembled a wolf—a half-starved wolf, both driven and tortured by their constant hunger.

"Let's have a chat," she said in a tone that left no room for discussion.

I blinked at her. "Here?"

In response, she stepped back and waved for me to follow. When I limped into the corridor, I realized she was flanked by five of Chanzig's shooters.

She glanced down at my slop-coated feet with mild disgust. "This way."

Without further elaboration, she turned and headed deeper into the ship's steam-wreathed interior. I followed, naturally—although not without a bit of prodding from my escort team. Our eventual destination was a plain, concrete-walled room with a steel table and two chairs. Somebody nudged me in after Liura using the butt of their gun.

Liura sat down in one chair, then gestured to the other across the table.

Much as I resented it, I complied with her instruction. Mostly because I heard the doors slam behind me.

The metal chair was cold. Unreasonably so. It felt like I'd dipped my genitals into liquid nitrogen. My only comforts were, first, the fact that Liura couldn't peep at me due to the table, and second, our relative isolation. It was just her and I in here. No more random kicks or slaps upside the head from her soldiers.

Liura leaned back and studied me, her face utterly placid. "You've caused a lot of trouble, Dak. For everybody."

I practically exploded. "*I've* caused a lot of trouble? *Me*?"

"Yes. Even your little ops tablet."

"Uh . . . what tablet?"

"Don't toy with me. The tablet that released a nerve gas when one of the crewmen tried to access it."

I couldn't stop myself from smirking. "To be fair, that *is* my property."

"Was."

My smirk faded. "*Was*?"

"I had it destroyed shortly before I came here," Liura said mildly. "I hope you didn't have anything overly precious on it."

A cocktail of rage and dread spilled through my brain, but I kept my face under control. I had to. With a woman like Liura, you couldn't cede even an inch of ground.

"Call it an eye for an eye," she said, gauging my expression.

I shrugged with nonchalance. "Fair enough. Your crewman's life for my tablet."

"No, you misunderstand. Their life was meaningless to me. I am refer-ring, instead, to your destruction of the recurrence prism. Those are quite hard to replace."

"You tried to kill me."

She nodded. "Several times, in fact. You're very tiring prey."

"You've got it mixed up. Kardinal was my prey. Balnos was my prey." I smiled at her despite my pain. "Don't you see? I'm not prey; I'm a predator."

"An interesting perception of things."

"So, why not just take me out? Does Chanzig want to fillet my dick while I'm still kicking?"

Liura reached into the folds of her poncho and produced yet another recurrence prism. "When I'm given a mission, Dak, I don't disappoint. Chanzig wants your dying consciousness . . . and he's going to get it."

"Do you assholes keep a stockpile of those things?"

"They're rather expensive," she said, twisting the prism in the overhead lights, "but Chanzig is fond of them."

I placed my cuffed hands on the table. "What was the use of waiting to stick it in me? Surely Chanzig would've gotten a hard-on seeing me naked and afraid in that holding cell."

"Who says we won't put you back in?"

"Fair enough," I said, then thought it over. "You want to talk about something before you insert it, don't you? Something Chanzig would hate to hear you say."

"Why would you assume that?"

"Because you're not a patient woman, Liura. You don't hesitate unless there's a reason."

"How astute of you." She set the prism between us, then nodded. "You have something very precious inside of you."

"I'm guessing you don't mean my good heart."

"The chok'tal."

My throat tightened at the mention of its name—its *real* name. "How do you know about that?"

"It's the only thing that makes sense out of this mess. The only thing that could have let you survive." She grinned. "Plus, I've seen all of you. Including the lump on your back."

"But how do you . . . *know* about it? That it even exists?"

This was an important thing to clarify. I don't know where or when you're reading this, but let it be known upfront that where I came from, "chok'tal" was not a commonplace term. As I've surely mentioned, I hadn't seen mention of anything even close to it during my years as an archaeologist, whether in the employ of the Hegemony or private backers. No legends, no rumors, no forgotten texts—just . . . nothing. And yet Liura spoke about it with such ease that it sounded like an everyday appliance.

"You really are clueless," she said, one brow lifting slightly. "Do you think Chanzig's real aim is to collect warehouses full of broken pottery?"

"He has a stockpile of priceless alien relics."

"Yes, but to what end?" She let the question hang for a moment. "He doesn't care about any of that. What he's after is the chok'tal. Something to mend his broken body."

Oh, right. In case I haven't mentioned it before, one of Chanzig's most identifiable qualities—aside from his disregard for life—was his poor health. Only poor isn't strong enough a term. Chanzig's body was a husk, a slab of withered meat that had soaked up ten stars' worth of radiation during a failed Hegemony mission. Nobody knew how it happened, and nobody asked. All we knew was that Chanzig lived inside a sealed penthouse, spending 99 percent of his day swimming in an ocean of airborne nanites. These nanites rebuilt him as quickly as he decomposed, but they still weren't enough. If Chanzig spent even ten minutes outside his chamber, he'd die. There was something wrong with him on a genetic level, perhaps a quantum one.

"Wait a second," I said, puzzled. "You're telling me that Chanzig's been after this thing all along."

Liura nodded. "Smart boy."

"How'd he know where to find it?"

"How does Chanzig find anything? His connections to the Hegemony's intelligence circle, of course."

Then it hit me: Modri. The Hegemony had known about his escape from confinement. They'd known what he was, what he possessed. Somebody within the Hegemony must've found out where Modri headed after breaking out—and they must've been corrupt enough to sell that information to Chanzig instead of handing it over to the military wing.

"So all along . . . he was after *this*," I said, uselessly trying to gesture at my back with my cuffed hands. "Is that why he wanted me dead?"

"Of course. You were trying to locate the chok'tal for your own buyer."

I scrunched my face in confusion. "What are you talking about?"

"Don't play stupid, Dak."

"I was *never* after this thing. I had no idea it was even here until—well, it was in me."

Liura didn't seem to believe that, though it was hard to tell on account of her stony expression. "Everything comes down to profit."

"I'm telling you the truth, Liura. It found me, not the other way around."

"Sure."

I scowled. "I came on these runs because I had a deal with Chanzig. I did the jobs, he healed me."

She leaned forward. "I have a hunch about what you are, Dak. What you *really* are."

"Huh?" Her tone chilled me to the core. "What are you talking about? Do you think I have some secret chok'tal-sniffing power?"

"You tell me. *You* were the one who told us where to land."

"Bullshit. I just picked a random spot on the surface map."

Liura just stared at me, plainly disbelieving.

"It was a guess!" I shouted.

"There are no *guesses* in my line of work. Either you already knew where the chok'tal was, or your buyers told you where to look."

Now it made sense why Liura had so often instructed me to scan for bioenergy markers in the ruins we encountered. Why I, a lowly archaeologist, had been of so much worth to their surface teams. Most of the idiots in Chanzig's employ couldn't even hold a pressure monitor the right way, let alone identify murals or sculptures indicating the presence of a chok'tal. I was their only hope of finding anything besides trees and chakki dung.

"There's no way in hell I knew where that thing would be hiding," I said fiercely. "For that matter, even Chanzig has no idea what he's looking for. He wouldn't know a chok'tal if it bit him in the—"

Liura held up a finger, silencing me. "He doesn't need to know for himself. He has help with that back on his homeworld."

"Let's turn the tables, then. Chanzig was after this thing, so he told you—his top dog—what to look for, right?"

She nodded.

"Did he tell Balnos or Kardinal about it?"

"Of course not. Those two were fools."

"What about the ship crew?"

"Just me," she said. "The one he trusts most."

"Well, now you've found it for him. So why are you delaying sticking the prism into me? There's still something you're trying to hide from your boss."

She studied me for several minutes, her cold, dead eyes boring into my skull. "We have quite a conundrum on our hands, Dak. You've done me a favor by killing my compatriots for me, but you should also be dead by now."

"Huh?"

"Do you really think Chanzig is the only man seeking a genuine chok'tal?"

Realization dawned on me. "Oh, I see now. You thought *I* was trying to screw Chanzig over . . . because that's exactly what *you're* doing."

"Chanzig was a means to an end, Dak. He was my path to finding the location of the creature."

"Whatever happened to employer-employee loyalty?"

"Balnos and Kardinal may have been worth the wages he paid, but I am not," Liura said evenly. "Now that it's been found, another buyer will pay handsomely for it. Very handsomely. At least then I'll be paid what I'm owed."

"God, you people are greedy," I spat. "Does everyone in this damn galaxy know about the chok'tal except me!?"

"Let me tell you a story." She stood and began pacing on her side of the table. "In my line of work, there are tall tales. Legends that have been passed down by a thousand blabbering mouths. One such legend is that of the chok'tal, although it's gone by many names. In every story, it's said that the chok'tal brought ruin to a million worlds. It made gods out of men. It brought ruin to anyone and anything that defied its host. Its Purifier."

"And yet nobody in the civilized world knows about it?"

"Oh, they do . . . but not what it really is. Most worlds that were invaded by a Purifier were completely eradicated. Their cultures, histories, warnings . . . all wiped out of existence. Some species survived their wrath, only to fall before the Microbe Tide. And the few that survived that, too, well . . . let's just say nobody takes them seriously. They're seen as madmen, doomsayers. Fearmongers." Liura shrugged. "Now we return to the conundrum. You and I are the only ones who know about the search for the chok'tal, and we are also the only ones aware that it lurks within you."

"Whatever you're planning, I don't like it."

"Listen to me very carefully," she said. "If I remove the chok'tal from you and keep it in storage, nobody except me will know it's there. Chanzig will assume this mission was just another false lead."

"A conundrum, indeed."

"No, Dak. That is not the conundrum. The conundrum is that the moment I insert the prism and begin killing you, you'll say all of this out loud. Chanzig will know about my betrayal."

Despite myself, I just *had* to ask. "So . . . why tell me?"

"Because I'm offering you a deal."

"Starting with clothing?"

She glared at me. "I'm willing to give you ten percent of whatever a client pays."

"Generous."

"I could simply extract it from you right now, but my clients will pay much more if they're able to perform neurological tests on a living subject. I presume you've managed to advance the chok'tal's abilities, which will be of particular interest in study."

I nodded along. "And then you'll kill me."

"No. If you accept, I'll kill everyone aboard this vessel and reroute it to a new system. I'll also guarantee that the chok'tal will be surgically removed using the best technology possible." She paused. "If you decline, I'll shoot your jaw off, insert the prism, and claim the chok'tal for myself. Then I'll tell Chanzig you attempted to escape from custody."

"A lot to consider there."

Mentally, I reactivated Guide in its Modri form.

Hey, Modri, is there any way to get this thing out without killing the host?

"Of course not. We all tried that shit."

Thanks.

I shushed Modri once again, then plastered on my best sounds-good face.

"Let's do it," I lied, grinning from ear to ear. "First condition . . . you get these cuffs off."

"Why?"

"Because it's a friendly gesture, dammit. If you're going to make me sit here while you mop up everyone on this ship, at least let me scratch my back."

She folded her arms. "You wouldn't be trying to escape again, would you?"

By way of an answer, I gestured to the various gashes, flaps of shredded flesh, and puncture holes lining my body. "Give a little trust to get a little, Liura. I want this chok'tal thing out just as badly as you."

As Liura so often did, she remained silent for minute or two, assessing me like a practiced psychiatrist. Then she shook her head. "I'll reconsider after my work is done, Dak."

With that, she headed for the door.

"Good luck," I called as she unholstered her pistol. "I'll be waiting patiently."

Like any faithful deal-maker would do, I just sat there, unruffled and docile, as Liura exited the interrogation room and stepped into the corridor. She glanced back at me to make sure I'd remained put—which, of course, I had. Then she sealed the door and locked it.

For the next thirty minutes, I listened to the muffled whumps of gunshots and the screams of violent men. Psychopathic as it may sound, I didn't give much of a damn. These people knew what they'd signed up for. They'd sworn fealty to a tyrant who derived pleasure from seeing living beings subjected to the worst tortures imaginable.

And when silence eventually fell, I knew what I had to do. I didn't need Guide or Modri or anybody else to walk me through this. I'd rehearsed the plan a dozen times in my head—though I hadn't expected the fortunate twist of Liura's help.

I glanced down at the massive wound in my upper arm, which was still oozing fresh blood. The same wound where I'd stashed the tip of Kardinal's knife. "I am not looking forward to this."

But there was no room for doubt. No chance to hesitate.

With a grimace, I angled my cuffed hands up to the wound and dug my fingers down into the tendons. I bit down my screams—tried to, anyway—as I probed for the nano-carbon blade's edges. Pain came in such hot, intense rushes that I thought I'd pass out. Let me just say upfront that there are few things more unpleasant in life than poking around inside your own arm to find the shard of an ultra-sharp weapon.

Then I felt the hardness of the blade, pressed flat against my fingertips. Releasing yet another animal growl, I pinched its edges and tore it free. It severed a few more strands of muscle like butter as it came out.

For a short while, I stared down at the wound, wondering what the hell had become of me. A few days back, I would've fainted at the sight of my own blood. Now I was literally pulling nano-carbon blades out of my arm.

No time to consider that, though. Liura's approaching footsteps jarred me back to my situation. Lifting one of my ass cheeks, I slid the blade beneath me and sat back down on it. Fortunately, I didn't tear myself any new holes in the process.

The door slid open, and Liura stepped in. She had the same impassive look, the same ramrod posture, the same confident gait . . . but she was absolutely *soaked* in blood. Every square centimeter of her, from face to boots, was dappled with the red stuff.

"All, uh, done?" I managed, suddenly doubting my genius plan.

She nodded and holstered her pistol. "I trust that when I remove those cuffs, you'll comply."

"You're correct."

Seemingly satisfied, Liura strode up to me and fished a magnetized key out of her belt pouch. She moved to unlock my cuffs, then paused.

I looked up at her, trying not to cry from the pain in my ruined arm. "Yes?"

Her gaze strayed to my hands. My red, blood-dripping hands.

A moment of wordless understanding passed between us.

Then my HUD sprang up, and a familiar box encircled her.

[NEMESIS EVENT]
Liura Blue (HUMANOID)
CALCULATING . . .
Estimated Kill Points: 24,000

Oh, shit. This would be a fight to remember.

Even as I mentally activated Indomitable, my hands darted down between and under my legs. Liura went for her pistol. The blade sliced my fingers. Yowling, I slid the shard of nano-carbon out and into my grip. Just as she racked a fresh round in the weapon, I hunched, dove toward her, and thrust my shiv straight into her lower belly.

She didn't make a sound, but I felt the blade rip through her layers of mesh and into the skin beneath. We went down in a heap, swinging, grunting.

In the early days of working with Liura, I'd had a slight crush on her. Before I saw her take down five scavs with a rusty pipe, that is. But now, here, wrestling her with my naked body, there was zero sexual context in my mind. Only survival.

She brought a knee up into my ribcage, driving the air out of my lungs. Still, I held firm, jabbing here and there with the knife that was equally slicing into my own hand. Blood smeared and squeaked beneath us. Fists rained down atop my back—one cracked me in the temple, dazing me. Splitting pains burst through my skull. She had one hell of a hook.

Then, in the blink of an eye, her pistol whipped past my face. I ducked just as the weapon discharged. My ears rang, already tickled by the warm stream of blood flowing from the ruptured drum within. She fired again, then again, both bullets grazing the skin behind my shoulder.

A final round tore right into my uninjured bicep. The muscle tissue burst in a cloud of pinkish smoke, leaving only quivering tissue behind. I screamed, then redoubled my wild slashing efforts.

When I looked down, I noted that I'd done more than I expected. Her entire torso was gushing blood. It coated the floor below us in an ever-widening pool.

"E . . . nough," I growled, instinctively whipping the nano-carbon shard up toward Liura's face.

The blade dragged over skin and cartilage, and Liura let out a suppressed cry. Her pistol clattered to the floor. The other hand came up with a vengeance, pounding into my cheekbones so hard I felt them crack.

But I'd gotten her. Weakened her. Seizing the advantage, I pushed down into her and slid her across the tile floor. Blood trailed behind us. Then, with the last of my fading energy, I rammed the blade up and toward the closest exposed spot I could find: her throat.

The top of my hand slammed into her jaw. Glancing down, I found that I'd driven the shiv all the way up and through the bottom of her chin.

She stared at me, wide-eyed and silent, teeth chattering against the metal.

"I'm . . . sorry," I whispered, frozen in place by a rush of remorse. I let go of the blade and fell back onto my ass. My breaths came in ragged gasps. "Maybe if I—"

Before I could continue, Liura reached up, gripped the bottom of the shard, and yanked it straight out of her chin. She looked at the nano-carbon with strange interest, then up at me. There was no fire in her eyes— just the windswept ashes of a fire. The look of a real killer.

Her muscles tensed, but I'd already gotten the message. I tossed myself to the side and snatched up the pistol she'd dropped.

She went rigid, the blade in her hand and blood streaming from . . . well, everywhere.

"Be smart about this, Dak," she said. More blood bubbled through her lips with every word. "You're not this stupid."

I stood on trembling legs, the pistol gripped in both hands. "Oh, but I am. Drop it."

Liura cocked her head to the side, considering my order, then did as I'd asked. She even flicked it away for good measure.

"What now?" she asked.

That was a good question. We were both heavily injured, probably on the cusp of death, but you wouldn't have known that by Liura's composure.

She wasn't even panting. I, on the other hand, sounded like a farm animal about to expire in the summer swelter.

Then an idea came to me. Still extending the pistol, I wandered back to the table and picked up the recurrence prism. I tossed it on the ground before her.

"Put that in," I said. "I have a message for Chanzig."

She smirked. "And what if I don't?"

"I'm glad you asked. See, when you and the others left me for dead in that jungle, I had plenty of time to think about how I'd pay you back. And I decided that fair is fair. An eye for an eye. A spine for a spine."

She frowned, not quite understanding, but I made it clear by firing two rounds straight into her stomach.

In an instant, she sagged and fell over. Her eyes darted about in a frenzy.

"Right about now, I'd imagine you're paralyzed," I said as I retrieved the recurrence prism. "Sucks, doesn't it? It's a cruel thing to deprive someone of their mobility."

"When Chanzig finds you," Liura said, her voice as measured as always, "you're going to wish I'd killed you."

"Not if I find him first."

"Oh, no, he'll find you. I didn't reroute the flight path. You're still headed straight to his lair . . . and there's not a damn thing you can do. You don't have the access codes."

I shrugged, acknowledging her point. Then I squatted down and jabbed the recurrence prism into her neck. A series of blue threads lit up across its surface to indicate it was recording.

"Sorry, Liura, but the rest of this is for Chanzig," I said with a hint of genuine pity. She was going to be used as a living memo, after all. "If you're watching this, Chanzig, it means your crew is dead. All of them. Part of that is thanks to Liura, seeing as she betrayed you, but that's not very important. What matters is that I'm the last one standing."

Liura coughed up blood. "You're nothing, Dak. Just caught up in all this. You don't even know who you are . . ."

I let that one slide, eager to get in everything I wanted to say to Chanzig. "Liura here probably wants to spill the good news, so I'll do it for her. I have the chok'tal inside me. We found it. The bad news, though, is that you can't have it. You never will. Because you fucked with the wrong man."

"You sound so tough," Liura whispered, her eyes growing unfocused, glossy, "for such a confused little boy . . ."

"Listen to me clearly, Chanzig," I said quietly. "Look into my eyes. If you try to hunt me, I will make you regret it. I will take dismantle every single brick of your empire. I will not rest until I've pissed all over your grave. So choose wisely."

And with that, the blue threads on the recurrence prism cooled to a faint orange.

Liura was dead, but not really. The last seconds of her consciousness were now looping infinitely through a highway of circuits, ready to be studied by whichever of Chanzig's goons was first to stumble across the prism.

NEMESIS ENCOUNTER SUCCESSFUL
Kills: 1
Kill Points Awarded: 24,000
Storehouse Time Awarded: 2 Hours

RANK-UP AVAILABLE: RANK 3

"So long, Liura," I whispered. "I bet you'll look lovely on Chanzig's shelf."

And with that sorted, I could deal with my current situation—that of being naked, dying, deprived of all my gear, and flying on a ship full of corpses toward a madman's planet.

13

Liura sure had made a mess of the ship. Dead bodies and bits of dead bodies were strewn everywhere: slumped over controls, facedown in the bunks, hanging over catwalk railings. It was somewhat inspiring to see what one bloodthirsty killer could accomplish with enough determination and training.

But the biggest mess of all had nothing to do with cleanliness. This mess, instead, was related to my survival.

Let me explain.

After every scavenging run on a new world, the skiff's contents would be unloaded and carted to a storage vault in the center of the *Red Advent*. I'd never personally accessed that vault, both because it was considered off limits and because I'd never had any need for it. The vault was (you guessed it) an alien relic in itself, secured by a twenty-symbol keypad that couldn't be bypassed in any way. Not a problem, ordinarily . . .

But definitely a problem when your gear is locked inside it, and the only person capable of opening it is dead.

This might explain why I found myself standing outside the giant obsidian door, fruitlessly plugging away at the mosaic-like arrangement of symbols. There was no way I'd get this thing open. Balnos had once told me it would take a hundred years to try every configuration—and even that calculation depended on not sleeping, eating, or anything else beyond code punching.

Everything I owned—everything I needed—was behind that door. I knew it. I'd searched the entire ship three times over, desperately trying to find some remnant of the items Modri had left behind for me. But there was nothing.

Liura, in all her cruel brilliance, had locked away my confiscated goods.

Her last "F U" from beyond the grave.

Leaning against the door, I analyzed my situation. Overall, it was bad. Colossally bad. I'd already confirmed Liura's warning that the ship was pinching back to Chanzig's planet, unable to be halted or redirected. With a bit of "help" from Modri, I'd also learned that the ship was locked into autopilot, meaning it would take us straight to his fortress upon arrival. On top of that, the only people who knew how to open this damn vault door were Chanzig's trusted enforcers. And there was no way in hell I'd be sticking around long enough for them to open it.

So, in short, Chanzig would soon have everything. The ship, the gear, the Polyps.

Reluctantly, I reactivated Modri.

"You know any way out of this?" I asked.

"It's not real polite to keep shutting me off, y'know," he grunted.

"Noted. But things aren't exactly peachy right now."

"Maybe you should start by getting some clothes. Eating. Healing up."

In my haze of concern, these basic necessities hadn't actually occurred to me. But damn it, Modri was right. I needed to get myself in order. No matter how bad things were, I needed to have my junk covered and blood kept inside my body.

Fortunately, the ship's decent crew size meant I had plenty of amenities to pick through. I started by treating myself to a rare shower in Liura's private quarters, using copious amounts of her shampoo, soap, and lotions. She didn't need them anymore, and besides, they weren't even top-shelf brands.

In one of the bunkrooms, I found a baggy jumpsuit and—praise Halcius—clean underwear. Once covered with some fabric, I felt like a new man. A clean, clothed man. It's remarkable what some water and textiles can do for your sanity.

Next up was medicine. I was fairly familiar with the ship's onboard triage module, seeing as I'd needed stitches a few times during our previous scavenging runs. The only difference now was that I found myself alone—you know, since Liura had killed everybody, including the ship's medic. Fortunately, Modri was something of a combat surgeon himself. He walked me through the unpleasant process of stitching myself up, disinfecting my wounds, using a dermal accelerator paste, and bandaging the worst of my injuries. Just for good measure, I nabbed the medic's supply pack and a handful of everything useful on the way out. Odds were good that I'd need some additional treatment in the near future.

With that out of the way . . . time to *feed.*

The dining module wasn't high class by any definition, but it *was* well stocked with nonperishable goods. I began stuffing myself silly on rehydrated vegetables and noodles, all the while feeling my body unwind with relief. Between all the killing and running, I hadn't noticed just how hungry I was. And by hungry, I mean ravenous. My stomach spoke to me in distorted songs as I filled it to the point of bursting.

"So," I said through a mouthful of protein squares, sprawled out on one of the few unbloodied tables, "I finally got some Storehouse Time."

"Nemesis Event," Modri said.

"Yeah, I saw that. What's it mean?"

"It means the opponent is classified as a particularly tough cookie. Y'get extra points for takin' 'em down."

Still chewing, I thought back to the encounter in the hangar. "Okay . . . and what about Slaughter Events?"

"All about numbers. Can't tell you how or why, but Guide's programmin' trips a switch when there's a magic number of enemies in your face. Those earn Storehouse Time, too."

"Got it." I shoveled down another protein square. "I've never been so damn hungry."

"Yeah, that'd be the caloric drain," Modri said. *"Everything needs energy. Your Anima, your Dominion powers . . . it all comes out of the tank."*

I squinted. "Seems like Guide has more than enough energy for the both of us."

"Consider Guide an accountant. They don't like to be in the red. They can use power from their internal reserves, yeah, but they sure don't like it. It's not cheap to maintain the consciousness of a few hundred Purifiers."

"Few hundred?" I spat. "How did you idiots keep getting infected by it?"

"Ask yourself the same question, sucker."

I nodded in acknowledgment. No doubt I'd set myself up for that one. "So, uh, what's up with Guide saying they can't remember how to 'win' the game?"

"Dunno. They said the same thing to me."

"You think they're just getting old? Losing cells?"

"Maybe. Seems to me that it's closer to logic net decay. A million years go by, and it doesn't matter how good your design is . . . it's gonna start glitching."

"There's no way to fix them?"

"You're thinkin' too literal, chief. It's not always about the hardware."

"Then what?"

Modri went quiet for a few seconds. *"Ever heard of an overflow error?"*

"Nope."

"Okay, so . . . in a logic net, there's a buncha calculations goin' on at once, right?"

I nodded.

"Each Purifier's data gets saved in here. And each Purifier's just a bunch of calculations. So that means that, as time goes on, the chok'tal has to juggle more and more calculations just to do basic stuff like talkin'. Now, in a logic net, if you keep stackin' up the data, keep stackin' the calculations . . . you get your overflow error. Too many digits in the system."

"Right," I said, parsing their meaning. "So, you think the chok'tal's lived too long. Gathered too many hosts."

"Just a theory, based on what we've both seen. Guide can't remember a lotta shit. But, y'know, a part of me thinks it was baked in. Like Guide's not supposed to tell a secret."

I considered that for a moment. It was an intriguing, although horrifying, answer. "What would they be trying to cover up?"

"Why do you think I know? You said I left you that tablet thing, right?"

"Yeah?"

"Well, that was probably my way of tryin' to point you in the right direction. Find some answers or whatever."

"That's how it seemed," I said faintly, rubbing my aching stomach. I looked borderline pregnant. "Hey, on that tablet, you started to mention this whole genofacturing thing. What did you want to say about it? If you, uh, remember."

"Not sure. I just know it's damn important."

"Why? Just seems like a way to print biological weapons. Why would I want to make a knife out of crystallized saliva?"

"It ain't about that. Genofacturing is how you make all the good shit . . . Guns, armor, equipment, temporary upgrades . . . It's a craftin' system, if you've ever played a game."

"Ugh. Not this game thing again . . ."

"Just listen. The items you can produce there are insane. We'll get to it when you've got the ranks. But for now, just believe it . . . Genofacturing is where it's at."

"Guess I'd might as well go down that road and use the points. These encounters have been handing out more than enough Kill Points . . . almost too many. Not complaining, of course, but it just feels like an oversight in terms of game mechanics. To an academic mind, that is."

"That's what you've gotta understand, Purifier . . . It's balanced. The reason each kill tosses you so much KP is because you're gonna need to craft badass stuff to stay alive. And them points drain fast when you start makin' the high-end gear in the Genofacturing Spore. At some point, it's a risk-reward thing. Y'know, do I rank-up with the minimum points now, get pushed into a new difficulty bracket with no points for gear . . . or do I risk another encounter to stash up more KP for genofacturing?"

"Makes sense, I guess. In a grim sort of way. But tell me this . . . if the genofactured gear is so good, why didn't you leave me any?"

"It's genofactured . . . key part, gene. C'mon, I thought you were a bookworm."

"I know what genes are!"

Modri snickered. *"Here, that word means it's linked to you and you alone. Binds to you. Anyone else tries to wear it or handle it, they're gonna regret it. So naturally . . . I left it for the Hegemony's Exotic Research Division to pick up and try on. Enjoy the fashion show, chucklefucks."*

Despite the effort it required, I laughed at that. "Hey, by the way . . . sorry I lost your tablet. Kind of feels like I threw away your life's work."

"Bah, don't sweat it. I'm outta the game. Don't even have a body! Besides, you're still in this thing with me and Guide."

"Thanks for reminding me. I almost forgot I'm a dead man walking."

"Nah, see, we've gotta change that attitude. Enough of this pity-paradin', I'm-too-weak bullshit. If you wanna survive—and trust me, fella . . . the survival urge is strong—you'll need to get tough, and fast. That means focusin' on one thing at a time."

"You sound like my father."

Modri sighed. *"Listen, once you're done with your chow, get me into the bridge. We'll take a closer look at the nav systems. There's still a chance you can rewire the ship and head to safe ground."*

"Doubt it," I said as I slurped down a high-calorie syrup pouch. "Liura wasn't lying when she said she'd sealed off the systems. She put the same lock on the pinching chamber. That means we're out of luck."

If you've never heard of "pinching," I'll help you out. Don't try too hard to understand it, though, because no humans do. To make it simple, pinching is just another term for moving through space at an absurdly high speed. Instead of traveling with regular engines for seventy years to reach your destination, you'll get there in about six hours. It usually requires the help of entities that exist beyond three-dimensional reality. But again, it's not worth analyzing too much. Space is a weird place.

"That doesn't mean there are no options," Modri said.

His grim tone gave me pause. "What are you implying?"

"I'll explain after you're geared up. Go grab yourself a gun or two, a bunch of ammo, and anything else that looks like it'll explode. Armor wouldn't hurt, either."

Much as I hated the mystery of Modri's plan, I did as he asked. I started with the bunkrooms, then hit up the ship's sole open armory, which only seemed to be available because Liura had blown a hole in the door.

My search yielded a few useful items. The first was a basic semiautomatic carbine—a reliable model, according to Modri. Along with the gun, I recovered about two hundred bullets, six magazines, and the one thing I'd dreamed about since this all started: a flashlight. Using a bit of tape, I managed to secure the wonder gadget to the carbine's barrel.

The dead bodies lining the corridor yielded three pistols, all of which went into the medic's bag. I didn't plan on using four guns at once, but I figured it was always good to have backup equipment, if only for spare parts.

No dice in the armor search, but that was fine. I'd grown a bit tired of wandering around in a tin-can suit, anyway. The more important skill to learn, Modri emphasized, was avoiding bullets in the first place. How I was supposed to do that, I had no idea, but I was sure he'd educate me soon enough. He'd already taken me under his wing for everything else.

In some weird way, Guide and Modri's Polyp had almost become my family. Granted, we'd only known one another for a few hours, but I could sense the bonds. I'd never been too close with my real family—a demanding military father, a pretentious academic mother, a gaggle of overachieving brothers and sisters who'd all carved out names in the Hegemony. Compared to them, Guide and Modri were more than tolerable.

Modri, in particular, felt like the tough-as-steel grandfather I'd never had. My real grandfathers had been killed in combat about two hundred years prior to my birth. Yes, both of them.

But in another sense, my new companions were more than family. They were, as Guide had indicated, a part of me. An aspect of myself. They were both wired directly into my nervous system, seeing, hearing, and feeling everything I encountered. Where did they end, and I begin? It was hard to say. In any case, I was just glad I wasn't alone.

Once I'd tossed everything into my bags, Modri had me proceed to the hangar where I'd been captured. His ship was still there, powered down under the crisscrossing beams of floodlights. The main hangar doors were sealed—an automatic step performed by most ships about to pinch through subspace. Just take my word for it: looking directly at the twelve-dimensional horrors of subspace is a good way to end up losing your marbles.

"What now?" I asked.

"*Nothin' yet,*" Modri replied, "*but once this ship drops out of the pinch and into orbit, we can make a little getaway.*"

The implications of his plan finally hit me. "Wait . . . you want me to fly this thing?"

"*Nah, I've got that covered.*"

"You said you don't know how to fly!"

"*But I know how to land.*"

"You mean crash?"

Modri made a *psh* sound. "*You're too damn paranoid. A few lumps won't kill ya.*"

"Why couldn't you have just purchased a ship with an autopilot widget?"

"*Because that would've doubled the price. Not to mention . . . those things give off enough radiation to make you a sailin' spotlight. Manual flyin' is the quiet way.*"

"It's also the way you get the next Purifier killed."

"*How was I supposed to know you'd botch everything and lose those damn Polyps? You know how long it took me to find three of 'em?*"

"No?"

"*Well, me neither. Memory wipe and all that.*"

All I could do was sigh and head back to the boarding entrance. "Alright, say I let you fly us down . . . Where do we go? Chanzig controls the entire planet."

"*Entire planet? C'mon, now.*"

"I'm not joking. His family's owned that planet for about a thousand years. Nobody comes or goes without him or his networks knowing about it."

"*Well, that certainly ups the challenge. Sounds like you'll get some good Kill Points after all.*"

"Seriously? That's all you're thinking about? Why not start with helping me find a place to avoid getting butchered?"

Modri just groaned. "*Listen, if you're gonna stay alive, you've gotta shift your mindset. You're a Purifier. The apex of the apex predator chain. You've gotta realize . . . you're goin' after them, not the other way around. Got me?*"

I swallowed hard. It was a true one-eighty from the way I'd always lived my life. I'd gone out of my way to hide from danger. I'd done everything safely, gradually. It was hard to imagine me being any sort of threat in a universe full of killers with no remorse.

"Look, if you're that worried, the first thing to do on that world is find a way off," Modri said, bringing me back to my senses. *"Chanzig might have that planet locked down, but that don't mean he controls every hunk of metal enterin' the atmosphere. Somebody'll have room for a pansy like you."*

"That's . . . hopeful. I think."

"But on the flip side . . . if you turn tail and flee as soon as you're on-world, say goodbye to all the goodies I left you."

The point wasn't lost on me. I'd been serious, although perhaps a little too amped up, when I recorded that message for Chanzig on Liura's prism. I wanted the bastard dead. I wanted to take everything he owned and claim what was mine—namely, the Polyps and Genofacturing Spore locked away inside that vault. But now, in retrospect, I wasn't so sure I had the grit to make good on my promises. I was stuck between a rock and a hard place.

Flee from Chanzig's world and leave behind a treasure trove of survival items . . . or stay and risk getting tortured to death.

"Let's hop into the cockpit," Modri said. *"Maybe we can—"*

"Wait." I halted right there, my hand on the rickety boarding ladder. A realization burned through my guts like spoiled milk. "Liura said there was someone on the planet who knew how to verify the chok'tal's presence. Yes . . . that's it! That has to be it! He must have some sort of source who knows about this thing!"

"Easy, killer. Sounds like you're tryin' to tiptoe around this Chanzig guy . . . probably not in your cards to get close to one of his special employees. He's probably got 'em tucked away under his protection."

"But not in the fortress," I said, pondering it. "Chanzig only kept his personal troops and doctors inside that place. All of his high-value entourage members were kept in estates outside the main city."

"Guy must be loaded."

"That's an understatement." I turned back toward the ship's inner modules. "I think it's time we take a closer look at Liura's quarters."

Minutes later, I was rummaging through the neatly folded combat shirts that filled Liura's drawers. There had to be something here. Something that identified this mysterious "asset" on Chanzig's world, or at least hinted at how they fit into the broader scheme of things. Liura wasn't exactly the loose-lips type, so I doubted she'd left behind anything that blatantly said, "Go and find this person at these coordinates," but I also knew her to be meticulous. A real record-keeping fanatic. If she had indeed been Chanzig's top dog for this chok'tal hunting assignment, there was bound to be some physical evidence detailing the protocol.

"I've never seen such clean quarters on a ship," Modri said with mild awe, *"and I served on the Hegemony's finest goddamn warships."*

I rolled my eyes. "Yes, well, good on you for appreciating Liura's orderliness. Now help me find something useful."

"Useful? Y'mean like the tablet on top of the dresser?"

To my astonishment, there was indeed a tablet sitting right in front of me. It was nestled between a bunch of straight, evenly spaced pistol magazines. How I had missed it, I had no clue.

"Probably encrypted," I said as I picked it up.

The tablet beeped at me. "Facial recognition failed. Please try again."

Well, that was easy enough to fix.

Time for another trip to the interrogation room.

Liura's body hadn't looked pretty at the time of death, and it didn't look any better several hours after expiration. With some trepidation—that is, a lingering feeling she might wake up and murder me in zombified form—I approached her corpse, aimed the tablet's scanner at the face, and prayed.

"Facial recognition confirmed," the tablet said, chiming happily.

"Bottom-of-the-barrel security," Modri growled. *"These mercenaries never learn."*

I scoffed. "Hey, be glad she was slacking. I sure am."

Poking through the tablet's main directory, I found that its contents more or less matched my expectations of Liura. There were no messages from family members or friends, no images of a cozy life, no audio recordings from her beloved. Instead, it was packed with archived conversations between her and Chanzig. Most seemed to have been downloaded from a transmission hub, indicating she'd created hard copies for . . . something. Leverage, perhaps?

Most were vanilla, consisting of Chanzig's orders to go here, find this, put him or her out of their misery. Occasionally there was a hiccup in the delivery of payments, and the two of them would go back and forth in boring circles until the fee was paid to Liura's escrow accounts.

But spliced in between these conversations were snippets that jumped out at me. Things that hinted at plans far beyond my understanding. The first was around eight months old.

[Liura]: We don't even know if the chok'tal is real.

[Chanzig]: I have it on good authority that it is.

[Liura]: Whose authority?

[Chanzig]: Another insider with direct ties to the Hegemony's esoteric research division. They've already sent me a list of places where Jekra Modri could be hiding.

[Liura]: And you trust them?

[Chanzig]: Let's just say we go way back.

The next was dated two weeks later.

[Chanzig]: My operative was discovered.

[Liura]: Executed?

[Chanzig]: Not quite. I managed to pull a few strings. He'll be sentenced to a rehabilitation world for labor.

[Liura]: You mean your world.

[Chanzig]: A very wise guess, my dear.

[Liura]: Did they find out what he was transmitting to you?

[Chanzig]: No. They knew he was exporting classified data, but he was careful in scrubbing his tracks. They have no idea he even managed to find Modri's trail.

[Liura]: On your behalf, I assume.

[Chanzig]: Once again . . . correct. Your wisdom is why you'll be rewarded.

[Liura]: Are you sure it's smart, buying a former Hegemony operative who was so involved with the chok'tal program? What if they discover your connections to him?

[Chanzig]: Still your mind, Liura. My ambitions exceed your imagination.

Then I got to the good stuff. An exchange from a month prior.

[Chanzig]: Eskatillus is our best hope. If it's not in that region, we'll have to reevaluate.

[Liura]: How did your operative come up with that location?

[Chanzig]: That's not important.

[Liura]: It is. The crew's tired of duds. These areas are getting too dangerous for a one-day lark.

[Chanzig]: You're paid well. Don't push your luck.

[Liura]: I'm just saying what the others won't. This source has gotten it wrong time and time again. Just like all the others. Why not just kill him already?

[Chanzig]: Because he has more work to do. One final task.

[Liura]: Which is?

[Chanzig]: It doesn't matter what I tell you, Liura. You lack patience.

[Liura]: No, I lack results. Without Akasha on our runs, we're just stumbling through the dark.

[Chanzig]: She's in no shape to travel.

[Liura]: Because she's been on hunger strikes. Self-imposed hunger strikes. She's testing your limits, Chanzig. And if you keep giving in to her theatrics, you'll never get your prize.

[Chanzig]: Are you forgetting that she nearly died on her last run? A run you commanded, no less? I would mind your tone.

[Liura]: You own her. You could command her to work if you wanted to.

[Chanzig]: Did I not just warn you?

[Liura]: She's our only hope of pinpointing the chok'tal. She's no good to anybody daydreaming in the Amber House.

[Chanzig]: We'll speak about this when your run is complete.

I lowered the tablet, puzzling over what I'd just read. From what I gathered, Liura's team had been running these chok'tal hunts for a long, long time, all of them unsuccessful. The location of each scavenging run had been provided by an insider . . . a Hegemony operative who'd been smuggling out classified information related to the chok'tal "program." That same operative had been caught and subsequently purchased by Chanzig . . . for some unknown reason.

"*That son of a bitch,*" Modri growled.

"Huh?"

"*This informer . . . the one who was whisperin' in Chanzig's ear . . . they must've been one of the researchers who was runnin' experiments on me at that station.*"

"How do you figure that?"

"*Think about it, Purifier. How else would they have known where I went? They were part of that program. The program designed to churn out Purifiers for the Hegemony.*"

"But why would Chanzig buy them and bring them to his planet? What was this 'final task' they needed to complete?"

"*I dunno, but when we find that prick, I'm gonna enjoy watchin' you put 'em down. Nothin' worse than a traitor.*"

While Modri went on, describing how he wanted me to castrate the operative with a paintbrush, my mind drifted to different topics raised in the exchanges.

This Akasha person, whoever they were, was obviously the asset Liura had mentioned. A person capable of locating what Chanzig sought, and confirming it was real. But judging by the conversation, Akasha wasn't quite so gung-ho about working for her boss. Not nearly as gung-ho as the backstabbing Hegemony operative, anyway.

In fact, it sounded more like Akasha was a VIP prisoner, a slave that was being pushed into aiding Liura's missions. This, in itself, was rather bizarre. As I've mentioned, Chanzig was not the sort of man who needed to ask twice for anything, much less consider the whims of his employees. Akasha had to be special enough to warrant his light touch.

But why? What was so unique about Akasha?

Nothing else on Liura's tablet provided an answer to that question. All I had was a name, a description, and a place . . . a place that might get me out of this mess.

The Amber House.

14

After about eight hours of pinching, we dropped out of subspace and back into . . . well, normal space. Nice, familiar, three-dimensional space. The transition was marked by the rumble of the hangar doors sliding open.

I sat in the black ship's cockpit, hastily toying with the switches and dials Modri advised. He'd assured me that when it came time to actually fly, I wouldn't need to do much of anything, but I wasn't so sold on that. It seemed preferable to at least be responsible for my own death rather than handing the reins to a looping consciousness in my head.

No matter which way I viewed it, though, this landing was going to be rough. Chanzig's forces were terribly efficient at monitoring orbital traffic, and despite Modri saying this ship was "stealthy," there was still a very high likelihood of getting vaporized before we'd come anywhere close to the ground. And of course, even if we *did* land successfully, we'd have to contend with the troops he dispatched to check out his world's new visitor.

With all this in mind, I performed a quick Status Display check to see where everything stood.

STATUS DISPLAY
PURIFIER RANK: 2
RANK-UP AVAILABLE: RANK 3 (800 KP required)

Kill Points: 44,000
Genofacturing Points: 11,400

Rank Points: 0

Rank Time: 6 Hours, 6 Minutes, 52 Seconds

Storehouse Time: 2 Hours, 0 Minutes, 0 Seconds

Anima: 140%
Dominion: 0/1

Okay, so I was cutting it close. Close enough to give me a little jolt of fear. But on the plus side, I was absolutely stuffed with Kill Points, and I could theoretically perform a rank-up whenever I wanted. Six hours—okay, eight in an emergency—was more than sufficient. And although it may seem a bit reckless to have delayed my rank-up to this point, I was pleased with myself. Perhaps I was finally learning how to conserve my hours, thus making the most of each rank.

Modri and I had chatted a bit while waiting for the pinch to finish, mostly about which upgrade paths to select, and the results had been . . . mixed. Most of his memory was gone, absorbed into Guide's semi-functional consciousness, and what little he did remember was enough to make me doubt the steps I'd taken. See, Modri had a belief that the best upgrade tree was actually Assassination, the type that involved staying hidden and taking enemies down from the shadows.

In that sense, I'd made a mistake from the moment I bonded with Guide. I should have gone with my instincts, my roots, and chosen the subtle path. Instead, I'd invested a precious Rank Point into Annihilation. One point didn't seem like much in the grand scheme of things, but seeing as each ability increased my odds of reaching the *next* ability, it wasn't hard to see the snowball effect—which applied to both good and bad choices.

That was all tangential. None of it would matter if I didn't survive the landing and find a way to hide in the underbelly of Chanzig's world.

"*Hey,*" Modri said, jarring me, "*flip on the rear cams. Let me a good look at this thing.*"

I did as he asked, pulling up a flickering yet high-resolution image of Chanzig's world on the main display. From this distance it existed only as a reddish marble in the void, but I knew it would look worse as we approached. Much worse. And our hangar had the lucky benefit of facing it head on. Even now, the *Red Advent* was speeding toward the planet, clearing hundreds of kilometers a second.

"*So that's it, huh?*" Modri said.

"That's it."

"*What's got you so spooked? There are no orbital defense nets . . . no frigates . . . nothing.*"

"Just trust me. It's got bad mojo."

But "bad mojo" wasn't nearly enough to explain what was so bad about it. The name of Chanzig's world was Kagu-9, which had remained unchanged ever since its original colonization by a gas-refining corporation. Now, I don't know *all* the details, but I do know that Chanzig's family had been part of the corporation at one time. Apparently, they'd done something so horrendous, so traitorous, that they'd been scrubbed from the records and given this wasteland of a planet as their hush money.

And it *was* a wasteland. Half of the planet was a mix of kilometer-deep boring tunnels and swamps, all irradiated by the hydrogen charges used by the gas refiners centuries prior. The other half was patchwork urban hell—an endless grid of cities, labor camps, shipping ports, and deserted tenement towers.

Oh, but it doesn't stop there. Because of Chanzig's former employment as an intelligence operative, he'd also managed to bribe the Hegemony into designating his planet as an ARW, or Autonomous Rehabilitation World. In short, this meant the Hegemony shipped boatloads of "dissidents" directly to his doorstep on a monthly basis. The Hegemony's theory was that by imprisoning people on low-technology planets and working them half to death, they would come to appreciate the glory of Halcius's natural vision. To the Hegemony, there was nothing worse than the love of technology. It was the root of all moral decay—they said while hoarding advanced alien devices and using them to dominate the galaxy.

I explained all of this to Modri, but he remained unconvinced it was that bad. No wonder. He'd spent most of his life as a Hegemony trooper, faithful to their grand vision . . . even if the relationship had gone sour at the end, thanks to Guide.

"I still don't get it," Modri said. *"What exactly do they produce? What's all that labor for?"*

"Nothing. Literally nothing."

"How can you produce nothing?"

"It's easy. There's a belt of labor camps all around the planet. They make the laborers pick up stone blocks and move them to the next camp."

"Why?"

"Because it's torture. Because the Hegemony pays them to break these peoples' minds . . . and their backs, I guess. The blocks being shuffled around right now are the same blocks that existed a hundred years ago. They never get moved off-world."

"Hard work makes the mind grow—"

"Nope," I said, cutting Modri off with a grimace. "We're not defending forced labor practices today, Modri. Especially when the one overseeing them is a torturer."

He harrumphed. "*Yeah, well, them intelligence operatives always were pricks.*"

"I'm glad we can agree on something." I stared at the planet's approaching form. "So, clue me in. How exactly is this thing stealthy enough to land without detection?"

"*Probably best if I just do it.*"

"Why?"

"*Trust me, Purifier. I've got this.*"

I did trust him—not because I wanted to, but because I had no other choice. I'd come out of the frying pan and been thrown directly into the fire. Back on that jungle world, I'd been able to putz around without worrying about surveillance, entire squads of heavily armed fighters, or remotely guided missiles that could erase me from half a world away.

"Alright," I said, sighing. "Do your magic."

"*You've, uh, gotta say the magic word.*"

"Huh?"

"*Tell me to pilot the ship. Needs to be a clear statement of intention.*"

"Fine. Uh, pilot the ship."

Immediately, the veins on the backs of my hands stood up and squirmed. It felt like something was itching to escape my skin. I jerked back, but the motion was useless. Long, flickering tendrils burst out of my palms and slithered into the cracks of the main console.

"Shit!" I screamed, trying to breathe through the pain of having my body ruptured yet again.

"*Keep it cool,*" Modri said. "*Lemme do my thing.*"

All I could do was stare in horror at the slimy filaments connecting me to the ship. The lights across the console lit up, and the engines pulsed with fresh power. This crazy son of a gun really *was* flying the ship for me.

As Modri primed the engines, bringing their force output up to the necessary levels, I felt the data pouring through my hands. Literally. Energy vibrated up and down my spine, winding its way out into my chest and shoulders before coursing down the racetrack of my wrists. For perhaps the first time, I actually sensed Guide's intelligence operating in the physical world. And it terrified me.

Then, without warning, the ship bucked backward and went hurtling into the void. The *Red Advent* shrank in front of the cockpit as Modri continued to amp up the reverse thrusters.

"You sure you know what you're doing?"

"Absolutely not. Hold on to your ass."

Modri abruptly jerked the ship around, bringing us face to face with Chanzig's planet. By this point, its cracked and pollution-choked surface was plainly visible.

A series of columns on the left-hand side of the console began strobing.

"What are you doing?" I asked.

"Masking our signal," Modri explained. *"Now, I ain't no grand pilot, but I'm good with this stuff. Learned it in the Reformation Legion."*

"And it's going to keep us invisible?"

"Hell, no. Just long enough for us to hit the atmosphere. Then the show begins."

Modri gunned the engines, bearing down on the planet at an almost suicidal rate of speed. With each passing minute, my fears grew.

When a sheen of orangey flames began licking at the ship's nose, Modri dialed back a few controls. He fanned the reverse thrusters to slow our acceleration. Far below us were the thick, bile-colored clouds of Kagu-9's atmosphere.

"You ready for my secret maneuver?" Modri asked.

I shook my head. "Not in the slightest."

"Well, that's a shame. Just keep those hands in place. Don't freak on me."

There was no time to ask what he meant, because at that very moment, the entire console shut off. Every single gauge, chart, and panel winked out. Even the whine of the engines and the bleep-bleep of the altitude adjustors faded away. I was stuck in a dark, rattling can plunging toward the planet's surface.

"What happened?" I shrieked, trying to keep my shaking hands above my lap as instructed.

"Killed the power," Modri said, explaining the obvious. *"No way to detect our presence if there's nothing to detect, huh?"*

"Are you *insane*!?"

"Only the good kind, baby."

The ship tumbled several times, throwing my stomach into knots. Then we were sailing down through the ocean of clouds, passing zones of acid rain and lightning forks. Under my breath, I muttered a fruitless prayer to Halcius. But what the hell did Halcius care about me? I was just another idiot about to be splattered on another idiotic hunk of rock.

"Steady, Purifier . . . steady."

We broke through the clouds at a speed far beyond the sound barrier. The vessel angled nose-down, exposing the broken landscape below. Drilling holes and the remains of storm-decayed shipwrecks grew larger and larger as we plummeted.

"Modri . . ."

"Like I said, you gotta trust me."

That became harder and harder as the planet rushed up to meet us. My toes curled in my boots, and it took every drop of willpower to resist flailing madly or slapping at the console. The terror bled out through my fingers, which were shaking like strips of paper in an ion storm. Even the bottom of my throat began to hurt from the constant thud-thud-thud of my heart.

Despite the futility of it, I found myself staring at the manual elevation gauge. Better than looking straight ahead. Every hundred meters we dropped corresponded to an increase in the gauge's bobber. We were at a solid four, and ground level was a full ten. Five . . . six . . . seven . . .

"Ready for the finale?" Modri asked with eerie calmness.

"Just do something, dammit!"

Dust devils and clumps of shattered rock were plainly visible by now. We were about to crash. About to die.

Eight . . . nine . . .

Every light on the dashboard reappeared. With one violent, orchestrated movement, the cockpit pitched upward, thrusters flared to life, and billowing clouds kicked up below us. The ground came a hair's width from the underbelly, then dropped away.

I howled with sheer joy.

"See? I've got it," Modri said, chuckling.

We flew over the barren terrain with reckless speed, narrowly dodging plateaus and the craggy tips of volcanic formations . . .

Until we didn't.

A head-splitting screech rang through the cockpit, followed by the bleeps and whoops of alarms going off. The main display spat out a message: *Hull integrity compromised.* But I didn't need the display to know that. The entire left flank of the vessel was coughing sparks and smog, whining in a tone that couldn't be mistaken for anything other than imminent failure.

"Whoops," Modri said. *"Little too low on that last pass."*

"You think!?"

Suddenly, the entire ship dipped to the left. Something heavy and most certainly necessary detached with a grinding *ko-krik* noise. The cockpit swung around hard, but the grav-panels kept me firmly rooted in my seat. If I'd closed my eyes, I might have assumed we were flying just fine. But we weren't. We were spinning out of control, and we were going down.

Trails of smoke and the blue flames of ignited engine fuel coiled around the viewpane, blocking out the landscape. The console was full-on shrieking at us.

"If I were you, Purifier, I'd probably—"

That was the last thing I heard before impact.

When I swung back to consciousness, I found my head resting on the console and hands dangling uselessly below me. The console was powered down, and the entire viewpane was cracked like a silvery spider's web—well, except for a spot that had been punched out, which allowed sand to trickle in and pile up near my cheek. Bits of wiring and busted panels hung from the ceiling like intestines.

But the strangest thing was the warbling in the air. It was distinct from the ringing in my ears—a lower, brassier tone that I might've ignored if I hadn't heard it before. I'd only experienced it on three occasions, all of them related to the Hegemony. It was a neural suppression field. Usually, these fields were only deployed to prevent things like telepathic espionage or alien mind-control hijinks. So why was it *here*?

I raised my hand to my face, and it came away with blood. Lots of blood. Some of it was bright, fresh, while the rest was sticky with partial congealment. How long had I been out?

Long enough to worry about Chanzig's patrols finding my wreck, for sure.

Half-awake, I pulled up my rank timer. I sighed in relief upon seeing that I still had about four "standard" hours left, plus two more in the Storehouse tank.

"You finally up?" Modri asked. *"I was startin' to get worried."*

Groaning, I slumped back in the seat and cringed at the waves of pain working through my whole body. "You . . . crashed."

"You moved your hands."

"I did not."

"Agree to disagree, Purifier."

I rubbed my forehead, only to hiss and pull my fingers away from a spot where the skin had been split clean open. "Now I see why you didn't call yourself a pilot."

"Hey, you oughta be thankin' me for savin' your scrawny ass. Least I got us down to the planet without makin' any noise on their sensors."

"Yeah, so you say . . ."

After taking a few shallow breaths and confirming that at least half of my ribs were definitely broken, I stumbled out of the chair and into the main passage. Everything was hazy and faint. I was on the verge of passing out yet again. In fact, if I hadn't been bracing myself on the wall, I probably would've dropped and bled out right there.

"Any idea where we are?"

Modri laughed. *"You didn't exactly give me a destination . . . so how am I supposed to know where we are? Never even seen this world."*

Truth be told, I hadn't seen much myself. Like I said before, nobody was allowed to approach the outer ring of Chanzig's fortress, let alone set foot inside it. My dealings with him had all been done through his lackeys, mostly in the fume-shrouded capital. Because there was nothing else worth seeing on the planet itself, that one run-down, decrepit, over-crowded city was all I knew about. Hell, I didn't even know where the city was. Even with a map of the entire surface, I wouldn't have been able to locate the thousand-kilometer radius around the capital.

This might not have been a problem if Kagu-9 were a small moon, but it wasn't. It was a massive, empty planet. So massive, in fact, that its gravity was well above standard levels. Just another pleasant touch for the inno-cent people forced to do slave labor here, I guess.

I turned back toward the cockpit, straining to see through the curtains of shifting sand. What I was able to see wasn't good. The horizon consisted of nothing but the same devastated, irradiated flats and rock formations.

"We're in the middle of nowhere," I huffed, struggling to form a plan. "You couldn't have taken us down closer to a transit hub? A nomad camp?"

"Not while keeping us invisible."

"Invisible from everybody, Modri. You know what that means?"

"We're stealthy?"

"No. It means we're going to die out here, all alone, because there's absolutely zilch in every damn direction. If the dehydration doesn't take us out, we'll be looking forward to gamma bursts from the decaying blast cores underground. We're gonna get cooked."

"I'm startin' to think you shoulda mentioned this before we launched."

All I could do was wave off his flippant comments. It didn't matter much at this point. The crash was over, and we were toast. Irradiated toast.

"Hey . . . you hear that?" Modri said.

"What?"

"You tell me. It's your ears. I'm just usin' 'em for fun."

Little by little, I did hear . . . something. It was a pattering, growling sort of sound, too clunky for a gunship's engines. Then, I heard the crunch of packed sand and the creak of failing joints. Ground transport. Probably a contingent of Chanzig's forces. But how had they managed to cross so much terrain? Was there even an outpost this far into the wastes?

Unimportant.

Creeping back into the cockpit, I racked the carbine's bolt to chamber a round. If they'd come looking for a fight, they would get one. I aimed at the viewpane, waiting for the sands to clear and offer me a line of sight.

A gust of wind swept past, revealing . . .

Not Chanzig's men.

At first, I had no idea what they were. There were two of them, both appearing as dark shapes in the haze. They'd just climbed out of an old, four-wheeled carrier covered in mismatched armor plates and adhesive strips.

Neither carried weapons, and my HUD didn't spring to action in anticipation of a fight.

"You know these guys?" Modri asked.

I shook my head. "Never heard of anybody living this far out."

The strangers approached the cockpit, and the taller of the two offered a limp wave upon spotting me through the viewpane's cracks.

Not quite sure what the hell was going on, I waved in return.

The sands shifted again, and I got a good look at my unexpected visitors. They were both wearing long, tattered ponchos that had been dyed with splotches of red and brown. Attached to the ponchos were clumps of withered vegetation and dried mud—a DIY attempt at camouflage, I gathered. Their arms and legs were wrapped tightly in yellowed cloth, and beneath their poncho hoods were masks instead of faces.

These masks were straight out of a fever dream. Equal parts corroded metal and bone, they resembled skulls with orb-shaped mouths—air filters, most likely.

"Hail to you, sky-dropper," the tall one said in a digitally garbled voice. "Do you wish for shelter from the Churning Maw?"

I moved a bit closer, lowering my carbine but keeping it shouldered. "The *what?*"

In unison, the two men turned and pointed to something just out of view. I rounded the nearest chair to look in the direction they'd indicated. What I saw shook me.

A vast, swirling ion storm boiled on the horizon, flickering with enough power to overload a Hegemony flagship.

"Churning Maw," the shorter one said with disgust. "It eats all. It will eat the flesh."

"Do you wish for shelter?" the other repeated.

Briefly, I assessed my options. I could either sit in this busted ship, waiting for the Churning Maw and Chanzig's forces to find me . . . or I could accept a ride from a band of creepy-ass nomads. Not great in either case, but at least the nomads weren't packing any guns. Besides, they seemed . . . friendly? Hard to say, on account of my ignorance about the planet in general. For all I knew, they could've been a thousand-year-old culture that enjoyed a vegetarian diet and singing kumbaya around their campfires.

In any case, they *had* to be better company than Chanzig and his dogs. I knew what they were like through and through, and I wanted no part in it. Especially not when Chanzig found out what I'd done to his precious hired help.

"Yeah, okay," I said, even as Modri shouted warnings at me. I shushed him and stepped closer to the cockpit. "I wish for shelter, gentlemen."

15

The two nomads didn't speak much throughout the journey, which was just fine by me, seeing as I was *technically* the most wanted man on the planet. Or I would be, once Chanzig's forces stumbled across Liura and the not-so-subtle message I'd left in her prism. In any event, silence suited us all just fine.

Here and there, though, they divulged a few details to let me know they weren't crazed murderers. The tall one was named Baranim, and the shorter one was Janjai. Baranim had the wheel, and Janjai had the invaluable task of "navigating" by way of sticking their hand out of the carrier's window and feeling the air.

This bizarre method of travel seemed somehow appropriate for the duo, though. Everything about these nomads was absurd. For starters, the carrier we were currently riding in had all the signs of Hegemony manufacturing. I'd seen plenty of them on the more civilized worlds, albeit in their stock form—that is, with rows of orderly seating in the rear section. These nomads had quite clearly done some "remodeling" on their stolen vehicle.

Rather than seats, the rear was filled with cargo netting to hold a variety of crates, ration tubes, ammunition boxes, bedding, and spare ponchos. And I, their guest of honor, was sitting atop this throne of random junk, bouncing up and down with every bump we hit. The whole carrier smelled of chemical solvents and sweat.

Up front, however, the situation wasn't much better. The nomads gabbed away in their native tongue—a tongue too strange for my linguistic implant to translate—and inhaled some type of drug from little yellow cartridges. They were riding high on hydraulically stabilized chairs. Well, *chairs* is too kind a word. Their seats looked closer to mounds of tape and clumpy memory foam.

I reactivated Modri, staring with amazement as Baranim guided us through the outer rim of the ion storm.

You, uh, getting any weird vibes from this?

"*Nothin'* but *weird vibes.*"

Okay, so it's not just me.

"*You sure they're not plannin' to eat you?*"

It's crossed my mind.

In all honesty, I didn't know what the hell these nomads were planning. They hadn't asked me for anything, not even a peek at the bulging medic's bag slung over my shoulder. Judging by the inside of this carrier, they were scavengers themselves. It wouldn't have seemed out of place for them to take a look at my goodies.

Moreover, they hadn't asked me why I'd crash-landed in the middle of nowhere with a bunch of weapons on me. Hadn't even told me to put away my gun. These were either the most trusting nomads in the 'verse, or the most deceptive.

"Shelter," Baranim said suddenly, pointing with vigor at something in the distance.

I leaned forward, squinting to make out what he meant. All I saw were poles with ripped flags snapping about in the wind. But just as I began to wonder if the word "shelter" was a mistranslation, we crested a rocky dune and came within sight of what the flags signified.

Sprawled out below us was a network of canyons that ran deep into the fractured landscape. The walls on both sides were teeming with life—campfires, generator packs, tents, moving bodies. This was a city. A thriving, impossible city smack-dab in the center of nothing.

Janjai turned to me and giggled. "Shelter."

With far too much speed for my liking, the nomads guided the carrier down along the switchback trails that lined the canyon. As we drove, Modri did the mental equivalent of poking me to get my attention.

What? I asked internally.

"*If I were you, I'd rank up right now.*"

What for? I've still got about four hours left.

"*Just trust me, would ya?*"

You also said to trust you when it came to that landing.

"*And did you die?*"

I sighed. *What's the use of a rank-up right now?*

"*In case bullets start flyin'. You'll get some fresh points to guarantee the next rank.*"

Oh, come on. It'd be a self-fulfilling prophecy to do a rank-up. You're just itching for a firefight, aren't you?

"I'm itchin' to keep your dumb ass alive," Modri growled. "But hey, it's your choice. We've always got a spot reserved in here for you."

Although I knew rank-ups were private, it still felt inappropriate—and borderline aggressive—to undergo the process while the nomads were showing me such hospitality. After all, what kind of message was that sending, if only to Modri and Guide? That I was eager to fight? Seeing any and all sentient creatures as potential Kill Points was a slippery slope, and I wasn't so sure I wanted to walk it unless absolutely necessary.

But at the same time . . . I'd been overly trusting with my former team, and look how that ended up. In my quest to show respect and give others the benefit of the doubt, I'd let my guard down. I'd turned myself into a gullible prey animal.

Here, now, I had to do things differently. Even if I trusted these nomads and extended nothing but good wishes to them, there had to be room for caution. So, I pulled up my Status Display.

The only difference now was, obviously, the decreased rank timer. Everything else was the same as before. After giving everything a second glance, I activated the rank-up icon and checked my new stats.

STATUS DISPLAY
PURIFIER RANK: 3
RANK-UP NOT AVAILABLE (1600 KP required)

Kill Points: 0
Genofacturing Points: 54,600

Rank Points: 1

Rank Time: 21 Hours, 59 Minutes, 58 Seconds
Storehouse Time: 2 Hours, 0 Minutes, 0 Seconds

Anima: 160%
Dominion: 0/2

My cursory examination didn't reveal any major changes—Anima had increased by its predicted 20 percent, and the required Kill Points had doubled again—but a more careful inspection led me to the Dominion slot count. I'd gained a second one. As such, my working theory was that a Purifier gained a fresh slot for every three ranks. If this held true, I'd have three slots to use when I hit Rank 6.

The second slot didn't mean much at the moment, seeing as my only active ability was Indomitable, but it would surely come in handy when I started adding new upgrades. In light of Modri's comments, it seemed like a prudent time to finally venture down the Assassination path. But first, I had to check the new abilities I'd ignored in Annihilation. Polyp had unlocked three new options by advancing me to the second tier of Mutation, so it was almost certain that Indomitable had done the same for its category.

I opened the upgrade tree and tabbed over to Annihilation to confirm.

ANNIHILATION [Tier II] (*3 Rank Points required for Tier III access*)
Indomitable (REQ Rank 1): Further increases skin toughness, bone density, and muscle mass. (1/3)

Overclock (REQ Rank 5): Boosts the response time of fast-muscle fibers, temporarily heightening speed and strength in the desired area. (0/3)

Bloodlust (REQ Rank 3): Accelerates healing through the consumption of humanoid blood plasma. (0/3)

Tooth and Claw (REQ Rank 1): Strengthens nail and teeth density to optimize melee combat. (0/3)

Annihilation's Tier II upgrades were quite the mixed bag. Right off the bat, I had no intention of dropping another point into Indomitable. If I had to use that ability, it meant I'd already messed up . . . and badly. Having used it several times, I'd come to the conclusion that it was best utilized as a last-ditch effort to prevent a knife or bullet from tearing through me.

Now, Overclock . . . that was interesting. I could see it being useful in some key situations, such as outrunning pursuers or throwing something real fast at an oncoming enemy. But again, I wasn't like Modri. I'd never trained for hand-to-hand combat or bench-pressing twice my weight. It was a skill to reassess at a later date.

Bloodlust was a hard pass. I was desperate to survive, yes, but not desperate enough to slurp up the blood of my enemies. Not yet, anyway. It seemed more suited to an alien race that already had a habit of sipping on the red stuff.

Tooth and Claw fell into the same category as Indomitable. It wasn't a "bad" ability, per se, but it didn't fit into my ideal combat style. I wanted to drop my foes long before they ever knew I was there, let alone had the chance to fire back at me. Besides, if I ever found myself duking it out using my nails and teeth as weapons, I was already in bad shape. What sort of maniac would willingly opt to use the hard bits of their body instead of a gun?

Satisfied that I wasn't missing much, I swung over to the Assassination tab. Like before, there was only a single Tier I upgrade available:

Silence (REQ Rank 1): Emits a counter-frequency to mask footsteps. (0/3)

Even as I gazed at the description, I found myself resenting the fact that I had to select it. Walking around quietly was a skill that *anybody* could perfect without Guide's help, and yet without it, I couldn't access the more worthwhile skills in the Assassination tree. In that sense, it was less a skill and more the price of admission. A real waste of a Rank Point.

All that aside, though, it was probably my best bet. The two available options in Mutation—Omniphile and Nocturnal—didn't appeal to me in the slightest. Sure, I could see some value in night vision, but it wasn't worth picking the ability unless I had a sample of its power. Why burn a Rank Point just to see a mass of squiggly shadows? Chanzig's men, who represented my current largest threat, would be packing high-end gear that far outmatched whatever Nocturnal could provide.

So . . . Silence it was. Sadly.

Once I'd selected it, my Tier II options appeared in Assassination. And my, oh my, did it make my investment in Silence worth it.

ASSASSINATION [Tier II] (*3 Rank Points required for Tier III access*)
Silence (REQ Rank 1): Emits a stronger counter-frequency to mask footsteps and whispers beyond five meters. (1/3)

Intuitive Aim (REQ Rank 5): Projects a visible estimation of bullet drop up to three hundred meters. (0/3)

Infiltrator (REQ Rank 3): Forms a biological suppressor in the hand, masking or reducing the noise of low-caliber firearms. (0/3)

Cold Blood (REQ Rank 1): Provides cloaking from thermal scanning systems after remaining motionless for five seconds. (0/3)

Now this . . . this was more like it. If I sank enough points into Assassination, I'd become a death-from-the-shadows commando worthy of Modri's legacy. Well, maybe. At the very least, I'd know my way around a firefight. That was good enough.

The upgrade that most stuck out to me was Infiltrator, which quite frankly boggled my mind. What did it even mean by a "biological suppressor in the hand"? I'd seen suppressors on rifles and pistols before, but those had all been metal and silicate, permanently attached to the weapon's barrel. This upgrade made it sound like I'd be using my own hand as a suppressor. Ouch.

But I'd spent enough time waffling around in the Status Display. If I didn't hop back to my body soon, the nomads would notice.

When I shut the menus and blinked back to consciousness, I found that I was too late. The carrier was motionless in some underground vehicle bay, and both Baranim and Janjai were staring at me with their heads cocked to the side.

I did my best to feign a yawn and look surprised, acting as though I'd just emerged from an open-eyed nap. "Shelter!"

They looked at one another, puzzled, then shrugged.

"Remove yourself," Baranim said politely, nodding to the door beside me. "Then we provide hot liquids and meal-things for stomach."

"Oh, boy," I said. "Nothing I love more than hot liquids and meal-things."

The two nomads led me on an impromptu tour of the settlement, gesturing reverently to advanced facilities such as toilets that drained directly into the canyon. They seemed unnaturally proud of their little home here. Then again, how could they not be? This was a section of the planet that hadn't been terraformed for life at all, let alone humanoid life. Every day had to be a struggle for survival.

Perhaps this explained the wariness of the canyon city's inhabitants. Everywhere we walked, denizens in those damned skull masks pulled their children aside or ducked behind doors chiseled into the rock walls. There were whispers in the air. Lots of pointing and assessing.

Despite this, I felt somewhat at ease. For all their strangeness, Baranim and Janjai had appeared like my holy saviors in the wasteland, and nothing they'd done thus far had triggered my mental alarms. All they'd done was offer refuge to a stranger in need. As we walked along the canyon's railed edges and rickety footbridges, I wondered if everybody here had, at one point, been just like me. Perhaps this entire community was made up of those who'd fled from Chanzig's wrath and sought asylum in forgotten lands.

Nobody carried weapons, and there was a clear sense of rugged "togetherness" everywhere I looked. Not a single harsh word drifted out of the crowded hovels or shared meat-cooking pits.

Hell, I found myself tempted to join this place just for a bit of peace. Perhaps that was even the intention of my rescuers: to take in a haggard wanderer, to make them part of their bustling sanctuary.

All these thoughts swirled as they invited me into a small chamber about halfway down the canyon. Inside was a hanging lamp, a low table, and a collection of beaded cushions. Long, rectangular holes had been carved into the canyon-facing wall to form windows, which filled the chamber with the muddy glow of the ion storm overhead. By now, the storm was so violent that it sounded like a dying animal. Between the wailing gusts and the frequent roars of thunder, the chamber was anything but quiet.

Baranim stomped a boot on the floor's smooth rock and pointed to my seat. "Please, rest."

I did as requested, feeling a tad silly and even shameful for keeping my carbine slung across my chest. It was comforting that they hadn't asked me to disarm.

The two nomads sat down across from me, and Baranim began shouting orders to somebody on the other side of a curtain partition.

One awkward minute later, a woman with a horned mask emerged carrying a silver tray. Atop it were several cups, an ornate-looking teapot, and a few stained handkerchiefs. She set the tray down and ducked out again without saying a word.

Wanting to be courteous, I resisted the urge to pour a cup without permission. No idea if this was the proper move, because Baranim and Janjai also just sat there, staring at me with unwavering interest.

As we sat, though, I noticed something . . . curious at the back of the room. It was something I'd seen tucked into several alcoves throughout the canyon city, but hadn't really noticed until giving this specimen my full attention.

It was a statue of some kind. Formed from clay and wicker, it seemed to depict a humanoid figure of monstrous proportions. Dried reeds sprang up in all directions from its base, giving the statue a strange aura of sorts.

Before I could analyze it any further, though, the curtain behind me swished open. Five nomads in similar garb entered, arranging themselves all around me on the remaining cushions. I offered a weak half-bow to each of them, but my eyes lingered on a man wearing a golden mask accented by real teeth—their leader, I guessed. He sat down at the head of the table, not even acknowledging my presence.

Once the leader was settled, Baranim proceeded to pour out tea for everybody in attendance.

"Sage leaf," he said as he poured my cup. "Very good for vital systems."

I nodded appreciatively. "How luxurious."

Baranim finished filling the cups, then uttered a phrase in his native tongue. The others repeated the phrase, then took a ritual sip in unison. I, naturally, did my best to imitate this. The tea was better than expected. Much better. It rivaled some of the finest blends I'd enjoyed on Halcium Alpha.

The golden-masked leader said something while I drank.

Baranim cleared his throat. "Deathless Tsar wishes to know why you come."

I blinked at Baranim, then the leader—the Deathless Tsar, it seemed. "I, uh . . . had some ship problems. I crashed here."

Baranim relayed my answer, then listened as the leader replied. He looked back at me. "Deathless Tsar wishes to know your home."

"Halcium Beta," I said, seeing no reason to lie.

The nomads oohed and ahhed. The Deathless Tsar said something, and again, Baranim translated.

"Deathless Tsar wishes to know if you like this home."

"Home?" The sea of surrounding masks made me rethink my surprised tone. "Oh. It's, uh, lovely. Very lovely."

Once again, Baranim explained and the leader replied. Baranim said, "Deathless Tsar wishes to know if you are soldier of the Undying One."

At this point, I couldn't hide my befuddlement. "Sorry . . . Undying One?"

Baranim pointed to the strange statue. "Undying One. The one who tames all lands. The one who is most strong."

Some sort of local god, I guessed.

"Uh, no," I said. "I'm not a soldier of anybody. Just looking for something here." And with that, I remembered my mission. My real mission, outside of making nice and drinking tea. "Has the Deathless Tsar—or, well, anybody here—ever heard of the Amber House?"

This time, Baranim didn't translate. He stared along with the others, sizing me up.

"How do you speak of Amber House?" Janjai asked. "Who said this name?"

I swallowed hard. "A friend of mine told me about it. It's . . . a place owned by Chanzig, I've heard."

Upon mention of the word *Chanzig*, the nomads physically recoiled. Several set down their cups and performed an elaborate hand-waving prayer. A touchy subject, I gathered.

Their reaction to the name wasn't the only thing that concerned me. Even as I sat there, feeling the warmth of the teacup in my hand, things seemed . . . off. Black spots twinkled at the edge of my vision. Tingles swam up and down my arms.

Struggling to keep composure, I let my gaze stray to the teapot Baranim had poured from. It reminded me of something. Something I'd seen ages ago while at a dig site. You see, the teapot we'd recovered had featured two separate spouts—one for dishing out tea, the other for dishing out tea laced with poison. An assassin's teapot.

And now, plain as day, I saw the bisected spout of the teapot. I saw the small air hole on the pot's side, which allowed the pourer to switch liquids on demand.

These assholes were poisoning me.

"Are you well?" Baranim asked, his voice distant and tinny.

I looked down at my cup. It was half-empty—or half-full, if you're an optimist. Probably not a lethal dose, but then again, I had no clue what sort of poisons these nomads were cooking up. One drop could've been enough to kill a man. A normal man, that is. Maybe if my Anima was strong enough, it could overpower the toxins . . . neutralize them. But I couldn't waste time trying to find out.

"The Amber House," I said quietly. "Where is it?"

The nomads looked at one another with barely disguised concern. I couldn't see their faces, but I *could* see the twitchiness of their hands, the lack of composure in how they glanced at their leader for confirmation.

The Anima had to be doing something. Otherwise, judging by their reactions, I'd already have been unconscious or dead.

"We do not speak of the Amber House." The gravelly words jarred everybody, including me. They'd been spoken in clear alltongue, dictated in such a way that only a Hegemony highborn could manage. They'd come from the Deathless Tsar. "The Amber House is the property of the Undying One. Praise be to him."

As one, the nomads turned toward the clay-and-wicker statue with their hands joined. They were praying to it. Praying to the Undying One. Praying to *Chanzig.*

All at once, I understood. These nomads weren't refugees avoiding Chanzig—they were his goddamn wasteland cult.

"Drink the rest of your tea, lie back, and dream of the endless sleep," the Deathless Tsar continued. "You have no hope of leaving here. Even if you kill our warriors, their meat will feed our people. Just the same, you may take solace in the fact that your meat will feed our humble people. Your beautiful skull will sit atop the Undying One's mantle for the rest of time."

"Oh, you have *got* to be kidding me," I said, pretending to slur my words and sway even as I wrapped my finger around the carbine's trigger. "Cannibals . . . what else is new?"

All at once, several things happened.

Baranim, Janjai, and the other nomads all reached under the folds of their ponchos for whatever weapons they'd stashed away.

The Deathless Tsar cackled.

I thought about Modri and how damn annoying it was that he'd been *right.* That I'd walked headfirst into a cult of Chanzig-worshipping, people-eating psychopaths who intended to deliver my head directly to their "god."

And finally, my HUD lit up, framing everybody in the room with a red rectangle.

[SLAUGHTER EVENT]
Kagu-9 Nomadic Cannibals (HUMANOID) (4)
Baranim (HUMANOID)
Janjai (HUMANOID)
Deathless Tsar (HUMANOID)
CALCULATING . . .
Combined Estimated Kill Points: 74,000

A pitifully low amount in light of their numbers, but I was still game.

Biting back the poison's effects, I triggered Indomitable, swung my carbine up over the table, and aimed at Baranim's face.

16

With two squeezes of the trigger, Baranim was no more. Most of his head evaporated in a red spray. The body jerked back, faceless and spastic.

Then the real chaos began.

The nomad directly beside me gripped the carbine's barrel and jammed it down, causing my follow-up shots to punch through the table. Wood splintered and porcelain shattered. Janjai must've been hit, too, because he screamed and clutched at his thigh.

Metal glinted in the corner of my vision: a sawed-off shotgun. One of the nomads had whipped it out and turned it on me.

With a quarter-second to spare, I bucked backward and off the cushion. The nomad holding the carbine slid with me—directly into his comrade's line of fire. The shotgun thundered, and suddenly bits of flesh and chipped metal showered the wall beside me.

I kicked the corpse away and tore my carbine's barrel out of its post-death clutches. Then I spun to the shotgun-holding nomad, reshouldered the carbine, and loosed four bullets. Again, the head snapped skyward. Blood and skull fragments spattered across the ceiling.

But while this was going down, the enemies across the table had managed to free their own weapons. Two held pistols, while another had a snub-nosed submachine gun of some sort.

Even as I wormed backward over the stone, one of the pistol wielders pumped three rounds into my stomach. I grunted hard and tensed my jaw, then turned the carbine on him.

Two shots tore off his shoulder, and a third wiped away his jaw. He wasn't dead, but close enough. After dropping the pistol from his ruined arm, he flailed on the stone and shrieked.

I'd bought myself a fraction of a second. A hair-thin slot of breathing room. Desperate to make the most of it, I unleashed a wild barrage straight through the table, then crawled back toward it under the screen of smoke and wood dust.

The submachine gun-packing nomad sprayed fire at me. Most of the bullets drilled through the tabletop and pinged off the stone, but one or two ripped into my legs.

With a furious growl, I swung back up to a sitting position and squeezed the trigger.

Click.

Goddamn twenty-round magazines.

The submachine gun released a deafening stream of rounds, riddling my right arm so thoroughly the carbine clattered out of my hands. The adrenaline was going strong, but I already knew he'd sawed the limb down to naked tissue and bone.

It was time to get dirty.

Just as the nomad with the submachine gun prepared to deliver the killing burst, I dove across the table and shoved the weapon hard against his chest. He screamed as his fingers cracked inside the trigger guard.

The nomad beside him, who was frantically clearing some sort of jam from his pistol, gave up on the repair efforts and used his weapon as a club. He slammed its butt into my skull once, twice, three times, setting my ears ringing and further muddying my vision.

But when I looked his way, I could tell he'd shit himself.

Through the poison's throbbing glow, I heard the Deathless Tsar chuckling.

The nomad with the submachine gun shoved hard against me, pushing me back onto the tabletop. My one working hand groped around me for something, anything, of use. The tray clattered and the teapot shattered. When my hand came back up, it was holding the one thing I'd managed to grip: a teacup. Just a teacup.

I surged back toward the submachine gun wielder, who'd somehow shifted the weapon to his other, unbroken hand. Too late, though. By the time he'd gotten the gun back on me, the teacup was halfway to his mask.

The porcelain smashed, leaving the nomad dazed but unharmed. For a moment. Because even as he righted himself, I tightened my grip on a fragment of the cup and tackled him to the floor. With a sloppy yet vicious thrust, I jammed the shard under his mask and into his cheek. He screeched like a banshee and let go of the submachine gun.

His loss was my gain. Working fast, I snatched the gun from his chest using a one-handed grip, rolled to the side, and sent a well-placed burst right through his mask. His body went slack.

Running on pure, thoughtless bloodlust, I swung around and put a thrashing Janjai out of his misery.

When I turned back toward the last armed foe, I found him gibbering, trying in vain to wrench back the slide on his pistol.

I almost felt bad as I peppered his throat with bullets. Almost.

As quickly as it had begun, the fight ended. The dust drifted down, illuminated by the ion storm's lightning, and the only discernible noises were the death rattles of dying nomads. Smears of blood and brain matter covered the formerly pristine floor.

I knew, both from my own eyes and the system's lack of notification, that this fight wasn't truly *over*.

The Deathless Tsar remained in his place at the head of the table, hands in his lap and mask canted slightly in a show of interest.

I fought for breath, slowly sitting up while keeping the submachine gun trained on this enigmatic bastard. Not so easy with one shaking hand—my non-dominant hand, no less. Already, I felt the burgeoning pain of my wounds. The warm dribbles of blood running down my entire body. My injured arm felt like one solid mass of fire.

"You are a strong warrior, but you are no match for the Undying One," the Deathless Tsar said calmly. "What do you seek to gain from his holiness?"

Although my mind was scrambled from the poison, and the entire room fluttered in and out like a melting strobe light, I clung to the first part of the Deathless Tsar's remarks. *You are a strong warrior.* As my heartrate descended back toward baseline, I found myself shaking—not from exhaustion, but from the killing. From how easily I'd killed. I was an archaeologist . . . how had I suddenly taken down a room full of cannibals with guns?

"I . . . I want the Amber House," I said with a dry mouth. "Where is it?"

The Deathless Tsar made a clucking sound. "Ah, ah, ah . . . such secrets cannot be offered. The Cobalt Seer shall not be disturbed."

"You mean Akasha."

"Do not speak her name, vermin! We are the loyal servants of the Undying One. We are the guardians who prevent such *insects* from treading upon his sanctified ground."

"You're not guardians. You're outcasts."

"Hardly. We endure the boiling rock so the chosen do not have to. . . . We are the sword that cuts flesh and sand alike in his name."

It was hard to grasp the meaning behind this son of a bitch's words, but I gathered that Chanzig himself trusted and relied on these nomads. He hadn't forced them here—he'd let them settle these lands with his blessing. He'd created a paramilitary group capable of defending the less civilized stretches of the planet . . . and all through the fever of religious devotion.

But they weren't just protecting the endless nothingness of these wastes. No, Chanzig was a meticulous man. A cunning man. He'd placed them here for a reason. They were guarding something vital—something he himself had tucked away in the badlands to prevent it from being found.

The Amber House was near here . . . and it was the nomads' job to preserve it.

"Tell me where it is," I whispered, "or I'll cut it out of you."

The Deathless Tsar giggled at that. "You know nothing, strange warrior. We are the fist of the Undying One. We have come to this world not out of pleasure, but in the pursuit of the highest bliss. The freedom to walk between worlds . . . to rely on neither skin nor bones."

"You're talking about . . . Chanzig, aren't you? Him and his wonky body?"

"Do not sully his glory with your unclean tongue. He is beyond a man . . . he is beyond gods. He has achieved the ultimate release from mortality. Soon he will spread this great liberation to all of us. He will judge who receives bliss . . . and who receives damnation."

Internally, I just shook my head at that. These idiots thought that Chanzig's quantum illness was a gift, a holy power granted via extreme contemplation. Little did they know that they'd bought into his bullshit. Chanzig's state of seclusion had nothing to do with his quest to find immortality, or bliss, or whatever they termed it. What kind of "god" couldn't survive a few minutes outside a custom-built nanite chamber? A god who was afraid of death. So afraid, in fact, that he'd sent *me* to fetch him the one device capable of saving his life.

"He's got you wrapped up in his mythos," I said, coughing up thick blood. "When you're in my line of work . . . you see it all the time. Legends, prophecies, omens. Do you know what happened to all those grand empires? All those soothsayers and diviners? They died like everybody else. And I was the one picking through their ashes."

The Deathless Tsar meshed his hands on the tabletop. "Once the Undying One has merged with the Sacred Guide, he will punish you for your crimes."

The Sacred Guide.

Holy shit . . . were they talking about . . . *Guide?* As in, the Guide inside my body at that very moment? There was more to the story here. Much, much more. Perhaps Liura had been wrong about Chanzig's reasons for wanting a chok'tal.

"He just wants that 'Sacred Guide' to save himself," I growled.

The Deathless Tsar straightened. "You know so little. He is not concerned merely with survival . . . he is concerned with the fabric of reality. When he is finally whole again, he will claim that which was denied to him. He will ascend to his true power . . . and serve as a judge of all under the heavens."

"You have no idea what the Guide even is, then."

"It is the key to the dimension of eternity. That which transforms flesh into spirit."

"Speak like a normal person, dammit."

"My words would be wasted on you, heretic," he spat. "All you must know is that the time of his ascendence is near. He will complete his quest. He will go beyond this world, beyond Halcius, beyond anything your feeble imagination can conjure. The Sacred Guide *will* merge with the body of the Undying One. And when it does, we shall reside in eternity with him . . . and you shall be tormented until the end of time."

Off to my side, I heard a weak murmur. One of the nomads was still kicking.

Raising an eyebrow at the Deathless Tsar, I shuffled over to the dying man and stared down at him. His mask had fractured, revealing a face mottled with radiation burns and dark, tumorous growths.

"Hey, listen," I told them as I squatted. "I've got a deal for you."

The dying man pulled in a wet breath. "Wh . . . what?"

"Tell me where the Amber House is, and I'll patch up your wounds."

"Do not listen to the nonbeliever," the Deathless Tsar growled. "Think fondly of his eternal bliss! His promise of everlasting rapture!"

But the spark of survival was strong in the dying nomad's eyes. It was the one drug that all living beings couldn't resist, no matter how brave they seemed, how unwavering in their faith. He gripped my ankle and lifted himself slightly, then rasped, "Six hundred kilometers toward the northern star . . ."

"You fool!" the Deathless Tsar shouted, rising in a flash.

I smirked at the leader. "Well, that was easy."

With one squeeze of the SMG's hair-trigger, I dropped the golden-faced prick.

"Now, about your injuries . . ." I told the dying man, limping over to my medic's bag so I could retrieve the supplies I'd promised in good faith. "You'll probably need a tourniquet, a—"

It was too late. The man had already gone silent and still, joining his brethren.

SLAUGHTER ENCOUNTER SUCCESSFUL
Kills: 7
Kill Points Awarded: 74,000
Storehouse Time Awarded: 1 Hour

RANK-UP AVAILABLE: RANK 4

All at once, the pain of my injuries hit me like a solar flare. I dropped down against the table and pressed my good hand to the holes in my gut, trying to stem the tide of gushing blood. Reality warped at an incredible pace, but I couldn't tell if that was due to the poison or my imminent death.

"*Hot damn,*" Modri said, whistling. "*You took those bastards out nice and clean.*"

I groaned. "You call *this* clean?"

"*I've seen worse. Done worse, too.*"

I surveyed the mess yet again. I saw the clean bullet groupings driven through the faces, torsos, and limbs of the dead nomads. Even now, it didn't feel like I'd done it. There was a haunting detachment from the violence, as though I'd just been an observer. An observer of what, I couldn't quite say. A beast, perhaps. A trained assassin.

"Modri, I need to . . . ask you something."

"*Yeah?*"

"Did you help me?"

"*Eh?*"

"In that fight . . . did you control my hands like you did with the ship? Did you pull the trigger?"

"*Hell, no. Didn't Guide tell you that the chok'tal's mind can't assist you directly during fights?*"

"Well, yeah, but . . ."

"*This was all you, Purifier. I'll admit . . . you impressed me. Guess you ain't the yellow-belly worm I took you for.*"

I looked toward the gruesome aftermath of the shotgun blast, then glanced away, disgusted. "It didn't feel like me, Modri. It was like . . . muscle memory. Something unconscious."

"*Fear does that to you.*"

"What, makes you a commando?"

"*You'd be surprised.*"

"I don't know if I want this," I said, the overwhelming smell of coppery blood making my lips curl. "I don't . . . I don't think I can do it."

"*Do what?*"

"Any of it. I'm not a killer, Modri. I'm a regular guy. An archaeologist. What's the point? Even if I find the Amber House, even if I—"

"*Put your hand over your heart.*"

Curious, I did as Modri advised.

"*Feel that beat, kid. Feel it good.*"

Shutting my eyes, I sensed the rapid *thump-thump-thump.* I sensed the wet pulses of blood and the firm, enduring contractions of the cardiac muscles. Before long, it didn't feel like *my* heart. It felt like a wild creature, a separate organism fighting for survival within my ribcage.

"*Whenever you're hurtin' . . . whenever you think you're not gonna make it out alive . . . just feel your heart. That beat is your whole universe. And the beat doesn't give a damn about you, or what you think, or what you want. The beat lives for itself. It will do anything to keep on tickin'. And when you get right down to it, the beat is nothin' but fear. Animal fear. The same fear that lived in your parents, and their parents, and every other sack of flesh and bones since the dawn of time. The fear is what keeps us alive.*"

"Poetic," I said dismissively, even as I appreciated the wisdom in his words. Off in the distance, shouts rose and bells clanged. Only now, there was something different. I felt ready. Capable. No matter how many nomads came at me, I would endure. "You know, Modri, that fear is telling me that it's time to get the hell out of here."

"*Now you're listenin' properly.*"

I stood and took one last look at the room, trying to assess what I could scavenge for the coming firefight. Most of the nomadic weapons were shoddy at best—the jammed-up pistol had been rather telling in regard to the state of their equipment. Nevertheless, I decided to take a few key items.

First was the submachine gun, which had served me well enough in this encounter. I tucked it into the medic's bag along with the sawed-off shotgun and whatever ammunition remained in the nomads' ponchos. Naturally, I also took my carbine and awkwardly—that is, singlehandedly—reloaded it with a fresh magazine.

Just before I headed out through the curtains, an idea popped into my head. I slowly turned and examined the nomads' bodies, pondering the plan. My eyes eventually landed on the Deathless Tsar's corpse. This was a culture based on strength, on the devouring of the weak.

It was time for some theatrics.

When I stepped out onto the windswept canyon railing, there were nomads with guns gathered on both sides of the divide. Hundreds of them, it seemed. But nobody had their weapons pointed at me, and as such, my HUD didn't illuminate a single combatant.

"I can't believe this shit is workin'" Modri whispered.

I didn't respond to him; I was too busy assessing the crowds for any sign of possible aggression. Yet against all odds, they were placid, even reverent. Several of the nomads emerged from hiding and ceremonially rested their guns on the ground.

Before long, I was encircled by a curious horde. It followed me as I headed back toward the vehicle lot, murmuring with a blend of concern and awe.

You might think this unexpected reception was due to the carbine in my hands, but you'd be wrong. It surely had far more to do with the golden mask strapped on my face. The mask that, minutes prior, had belonged to the nomads' most fearsome leader.

At some point, the crowd became so dense I started to sweat. They could've ripped me apart with their bare hands, if they so desired. I was just one man, and they were countless.

"People of the canyons," I said, shouting to be heard over the ion storm's ominous rumbles, "I am the Purifier, and I have slain the one you call the Deathless Tsar . . . in the name of the Undying One. He was a wicked ruler, and greatly displeased his master. As such, I have taken his mask as a trophy for the holy one."

Whispers turned to cries and shrieks.

"Fear not, however," I continued, "for if you provide me with sufficient fuel and a vehicle, I will return to the fortress of the holy one. I will tell him to bestow great prayers and bliss upon all of you. But if you do not"—I raised my carbine for dramatic effect—"I will order him to unleash a plague upon this land. You will never attain bliss, and, uh . . . the meat of your people will taste terrible! You will be cursed to vegetarian diets . . . forever!"

The crowd immediately fell into a fit of gibbering, howling, and cowering. They dropped to their knees around me, crying out in their native tongue for what I assumed was forgiveness.

"Okay, that's enough," I shouted. "Fuel and a vehicle. Let's hop to it!"

After my grand proclamation, the nomads were more than helpful in preparing my journey to the Amber House. They loaded up the carrier with fuel, then stuffed it full of fresh water, an assortment of bullets, and . . . strange-looking meat wrapped in gold paper. I made a mental note to avoid chowing down on that specialty, no matter how hungry I got.

Even as I fired up the carrier's engines and began exiting the compound, I spotted a trail of nomads chasing me in the rear-view cams—not to kill me, but to throw bags of herbs and other trinkets into the vehicle's dust. Rolling back out onto the wasteland's surface, the last thing I heard was a fervent chant.

"Purifier, Purifier, Purifier!"

<h1 style="text-align: center;">17</h1>

In the ultimate twist of irony, the nomads' beaten-up, clunking carrier had a more robust autopilot system than Modri's ship. This came as a true blessing, as I needed all the time I could get with my hands free. I hadn't slept in far, far too long, and the hanging strips of meat that comprised my body were in desperate need of repair.

I sat in the passenger seat as the carrier trundled over the flats, heading toward the vague destination I had set in the navigation panel. Six hundred kilometers toward the northern star was a pretty terrible description, especially for an archaeologist used to working with precise coordinates, but it was the best I had. Besides, it wasn't as useless a heading as I'd first expected.

As it turned out, the northern star was plainly visible in the sky. It was bright enough to sear through the cloud cover overhead, and we were still several hours from dusk. No wonder the nomads had used it as their core navigation anchor.

The carrier went over yet another jarring bump, and I jabbed the disinfectant pen into the wrong part of my stomach.

"*Eeesh*," I hissed, dabbing the new wound with a rag. "You'd think the nomads would've been smart enough to leave the hydraulic suspension in this thing."

"*I'm still shocked they let you live,*" Modri said, chuckling.

"What can I say? A show of force goes a long way with superstitious people."

"*Truth. Y'know, back on this one planet, we decapitated this 'shaman' and—*"

"Yeah, alright, I think I'm good on your war-crime stories. Pretty amazing you can remember those, but not anything useful."

Modri huffed. "*It wasn't a war crime. The bastards were working with insurgents.*"

"You really hate them, don't you?"

"Of course. They want to see the whole Hegemony burn. Buncha divisive, tech-lovin' pricks who get high off their own dreams of self-determination . . . Can't stand 'em. And besides . . ."

I just let him ramble. Truth be told, I had no firm opinions about the insurgency. They were the Hegemony's number one enemies, made up of infinite subgroups with their own aims, beliefs, and ideas about how to govern their planets. As long as they didn't infect me with a bioweapon or take me hostage, what did it matter to me? From my vantage point, the Hegemony and the insurgency were two sides of the same coin. Two ideologies locked in an endless, fruitless battle for domination over the endless nothingness of space. They'd probably be duking it out until the heat death of the 'verse.

"So, uh, y'got any family?" Modri asked, once he was done ranting.

"Not much to speak of," I said. "They're all back on Halcium Beta, living it up with the Hegemony's best and brightest. And I'm here."

"Black sheep, huh?"

"Now more than ever."

"I know how that goes. Six generations of my family, not a single one made it off the homeworld."

I nodded in understanding. "Let me guess. A bunch of 'culture'-loving Hegemony citizens who could drink their weight in fizzy wine."

"Not quite. The memory's all hazy, but I know I was raised deep in the Nogo somewhere."

"You're kidding."

For reference, the Nogo was a spherical zone that encompassed more or less everything outside the Hegemony's well-controlled territory. An uncharted expanse littered with unspeakable threats and the bones of dead alien empires. All of our recent scavenging jobs had been done in the Nogo—that was where you found untouched tech, after all—but we'd been sticking to the outskirts, where there was at least *some* hope of rescue if things went horribly awry. What all this means, in essence, is that Modri hadn't been born and bred inside the Hegemony like most of their other diehard fighters. He'd been a foreigner—a foreigner desperate enough to risk life and limb for a faction that likely didn't give a toss about him.

"It's true," Modri said. *"All I ever wanted was to join the Hegemony . . . Make a name for myself, a name for my bloodline. I wanted to be part of something big."*

"No wonder you're so proud of your service."

"Damn straight. You highborn wouldn't get it, I guess. You were born into that world. You had the Hegemony's shine on you from the moment you popped outta the womb. But sods like us . . . well, we had to earn it through blood."

"You ever get citizenship?"

"Yessir, and them damn purple eyes, too. Only 'bout a year before Hakkaram and all the Purifier nonsense, though."

I sighed wistfully. "Never even got to enjoy the orgy clubs on Halcium Alpha, then."

"Orgy clubs . . . sure does make a man wish he had his real body again."

"Don't sweat it. Those places are filthy."

"Filthy's my middle name. I think. Can't quite remember anymore."

I grinned and shook my head, swapping out the disinfectant pen for the roll of sealant gauze in the medic's bag. "So, what do you know about Chanzig's informant? The one who gave away your location?"

"You mean the bastard who decided to torture me in a laboratory and then switch sides for a payout?"

"Yeah, him. You remember a name?"

"Not a chance in hell, Purifier. That's all a haze to me."

"About what I expected," I said quietly. "You think you'd remember their face if you saw them?"

"What are you suggesting?"

"It's just . . . the Deathless Tsar. You saw his face, right? Heard his voice? The guy was highborn. A through-and-through citizen, just like me."

"And? He wasn't Chanzig's informant. I'm sure of it."

"I just can't wrap my head around it. Why would someone abandon a cozy life in the sanctified worlds to come out here and slum it down in the canyons, all for some backstabbing crime lord with a god complex?"

"Yeah, that is odd. Another Hegemony officer, no less."

I froze in my seat. "What did you say?"

"Huh? You saw the tattoo, right?"

"No?"

"Must be 'cause you're a civilian. I saw it clear as day when you lifted up that mask. He had a few streaks under his eye. That's a soldier's mark."

"Wait, wait, wait . . . don't you see what this means?"

Modri seemed to ponder it a while. *"Not a clue."*

"Chanzig has been 'recruiting' high-level figures from the Hegemony military to his planet. First the operative-turned-informant, and now this Tsar. . . . How many turncoats has he worked into his scheme?"

"People like to feel important. They probably thought they had a purpose in Chanzig's movement. Some sorta role to play in the grand prophecy."

Modri's explanation just didn't sit right with me. Something was wrong. Very wrong. Chanzig was a persuasive man, but fancy words alone weren't enough to inspire a cult of this magnitude. No, he had *experienced* something. Something profound enough to attract all these followers. Something that, according to the Deathless Tsar, had been "denied to him."

The more I chewed it over, the less convinced I became that all of this was just a ploy to fix his body. Whatever was wrong with him . . . it had something to do with the chok'tal. Judging by the nomads' words, in fact, the chok'tal was the *only* thing capable of healing him. What sort of event could've caused an injury like that?

But even if I accepted that Chanzig needed a chok'tal for some quasi-religious reason, it still didn't explain how he'd managed to convince die-hard soldiers that *his* personal crusade was worth fighting for. There were plenty of crime lords in the 'verse, and he wasn't even near the top of the food chain . . . yet he'd managed to lure in a disproportionately high number of Hegemony officers.

"I just don't get what he promised these people," I said. "The Hegemony indoctrinates every single soldier against heresy. Hell, you can't even buy certain fabrics on the sanctified worlds. They wouldn't have flipped sides without a damn good reason."

"Well, start with what you know," Modri said. *"What'd he promise you?"*

"Treatment."

"For?"

I gestured vaguely at my body. "I took a bad dose of radiation a few years ago. He said he'd get me the right doctors, the right implants. Find a way to fix it up."

"There's your answer, then. He promised them whatever they couldn't get."

"Maybe." Sighing, I put away the gauze and slumped down in the seat. "I need some shuteye. Gonna be a little while before we reach the target."

Modri laughed. *"Now you're talkin' like a real soldier."*

But even after I lay down, sifting through the absurd events of the last day or so, I found myself unable to drift off. It just wasn't adding up. What could Chanzig have offered the Hegemony traitors? Currency, narcotics, simverse expeditions? None of it was worth risking an eon's worth of torture from their own faction. There had to be something else. Something that went beyond simple goods and services. Nothing else could explain the zealous fire I'd seen in the eyes of the Deathless Tsar.

"*Hey,*" Modri said, prodding me with what felt like electrical currents behind my eyes, "*this is your wake-up call, slacker.*"

I sat up and rubbed my eyes, not quite sure how or when I'd managed to fall into sleep. For all I knew, I could've been passed out for a minute or a whole day. My only hints to the passage of time were the darkness outside the carrier and the bruised-purple sky overhead.

"What'd you see?" I asked, groggy.

Modri grunted. "*Nothin' yet. But I've got a sort of internal clock, y'see and I calculated that we're just about there. Thought it was best that you be awake before the bullets started flyin' at us.*"

Heaving myself into the driver's seat, I wiped the fog off the inside of the windshield and squinted out into the gloom. There wasn't much to see directly ahead—I didn't have the headlights on, mainly because I didn't know how to activate them—but there *was* a strange shadow framed against the horizon.

It had a dome-like shape, broken here and there by the vertical slashes of minarets. In a wasteland devoid of any order whatsoever, it stood out like a sore thumb.

"Think that's the Amber House?" I asked.

"*I mean, it fits what the nomad said,*" Modri replied. "*Ain't seen nothing else that comes even close to bein' a proper house.*"

The more I studied the structure, the more intricate it became. I noted occasional flashes of lights, which I took to be the beams of rotating guard towers, as well as the faint coils of razor wire. As we drew even closer, I saw shapes flitting about in the sky—aerial patrols, most likely.

"Dammit," I muttered. "That's not a house; it's a guard compound."

"*Oh, c'mon, Purifier. You've told me all about Chanzig. Does he really seem like the kinda guy to stash his assets inside a cute little cabin?*"

"That's assuming the 'asset' is even there. What if he's moved her to the main city?"

"*Again . . . probably somethin' you shoulda considered before we came here.*"

Modri was right, but there wasn't much room to back out and reassess now. I had no idea where the city was, and I wasn't even sure I'd head there if I found out. After all, a trip to the city meant an encounter with Chanzig and his armies. If I was able to at least find Akasha here, I'd have an asset of my own—someone to help me sort out my situation. Depending on how thorough her knowledge was, I might be able to get away with just rescuing her and finding a ride off-world. Sure, it would sting like hell to leave Modri's gear with Chanzig, but it was all about risk and reward.

More importantly, it was about finding a way to detach the chok'tal without dying in the process. Akasha, Chanzig, and Modri's gear were just paths to that overarching goal. The real trick was to find the shortest path, and to find it in time. Sooner or later, the Kill Point requirements would become an avalanche capable of burying me.

This was all medium-term thinking, though. My short-term plan, no matter how stupid, remained the same: get into the compound. Whether or not Akasha was inside, there was a 100 percent chance of soldiers—and that meant supplies. Guns, bullets, armor, vehicles, rations. Seeing as we were deeply entrenched in the middle of the wastes, I needed all of it.

Modri used a brain zap to get my attention. *"I know it's gonna piss you off, hearing the same thing over and over, but I think you should consider a rank-up before you do anything dumb."*

"It's too soon."

"Really? You're gonna say that to me? The guy who got farther than you could ever imagine in your current state?"

"Listen, Modri . . . no offense, but you don't remember much from your life. How could you possibly remember the most effective path?"

"I don't need memory to know that more Anima is always good."

"We're talking about one hundred and sixty percent versus one hundred and eighty. It's not as big a leap as you think."

"Hey, do what you want, man. Just don't cry to me when you're gettin' destroyed in there. You're already banged up as it is. Keep rollin' those dice, and sooner or later you'll wind up with snake eyes."

"You're acting like this is my first firefight."

"Your first firefight? Nah. But your first assault on a location that's defended and expectin' resistance? Yes. You've been playin' in the junior leagues, Purifier. Luck isn't enough for a fight like this."

Once again, the bastard was right. I wouldn't admit it, of course, but I knew it. Every encounter so far had been influenced by heaping tablespoons of "luck." The luck of surprise, the luck of double-crosses, the luck of superstitious fear. I hadn't yet gone head-to-head with an organized force that was actively primed for combat.

Looking down at my body, I acknowledged that I was in no shape to shoot it out just yet. The medical supplies had done wonders to keep me stitched up and free of infection, but my right arm would take considerable time to return to . . . well, an arm. Right now it looked like a canine's well-used chew toy. I couldn't even use it to scratch my ass, let alone rely on it for shooting a high-caliber weapon.

"Fine," I growled, shutting off the carrier's autopilot and taking control of the wheel. "I'll take a look and think it over. But not because you told me to."

"Yeah, yeah, Purifier."

Rolling my eyes, I guided the carrier to a misshapen rock outcropping. Then I prowled around its base, seeking out an overhang to conceal me from passing gunships. Fortunately, there was a decent hiding spot that still had a clear visual of the Amber House.

Over the next few hours, I sat there and studied the general flow of the compound. There was a certain order to it, but it was hard to establish any concrete rules about that order. For starters, the aerial patrols were infrequent but random enough to cause concern. Then there were the shift changes, which seemed to happen once every forty-five to fifty minutes. I assumed they were shift changes, anyway, judging by the movement of the shadowy blobs along the walls.

What most unsettled me were the small, dim lights that flickered up in the minarets. They were almost invisible in contrast with the high-powered spotlights. Almost. But once I spotted them, I had no doubts as to what they were: the glow of amp-sticks. Translation? There were soldiers high up in the towers. Whether they were snipers or just lookouts, they posed a real problem for me. No matter which way I approached, they would likely see me coming from several kilometers away.

Only then did I realize the brilliance of keeping a high-value asset in the center of nowhere.

"Alright, Modri," I said in the middle of the night, "give me your take."

"Depends how you wanna do this," he said. *"Way I see it, you've got three basic strategies. First, you can just go in with guns blazin'. I wouldn't recommend this, day or night. Second, you can try the open-arms approach. Roll up with the carrier, pretend you're a nomad. Might get as far as the front gates before the bullets fly. And third . . . you try to pull off a stealth run."*

"So . . . which one?"

"Normally I'd pick three, but seein' as you're a coward who jumps at his own shadow . . ."

"Oh, bullshit."

"Really? You think you're ready to waltz up there, scale the wall, slit throats? C'mon, Purifier. You're a newbie at this."

"You vote for option two, then."

"Well, I didn't say that."

I pressed a hand to my face. "Say something useful, would you?"

"I was gonna . . . if you'd let me." He cleared his digital throat. *"I'm goin' with option two, but with an important caveat."*

"Go on."

"You remember those ponchos in the back, right?"

Perplexed, I glanced over my shoulder and spotted what Modri was referring to. I'd first seen them while traveling with Baranim and Janjai, but they'd been forgotten on the spot. Damn, his eyes were good. Well, my eyes. Whatever.

"Bright and early, you do your rank-up, put one of those suckers on, and stroll right up to the front," Modri continued. *"You're the Deathless Tsar. You're there to meet the Amber House's commander for a very important matter. You need to see your blushin' bride."*

"Akasha isn't—"

"Settle down, Purifier. It's a figure of speech."

I let out an aggravated sigh. "So, let me get this straight. You want me to talk my way in there, then slaughter them from the inside."

"That'll do it. Preferably with the Infiltrator upgrade."

"Yeah, about that one . . . I have . . . questions."

"Just get it and thank me later."

"Fine, let's say I do," I said, grimacing. "How is this plan any better than the stealth approach?"

"What can I say? Play to your strengths."

"Oh, yeah? And what's my strength?"

"You don't know how to shut the hell up."

I cracked a grin at that, easing back into the seat with the carbine across my lap. "That makes two of us, Modri."

For the second time, I lay back and tried to get some sleep. Not an easy task, considering the gravity of what I had to do at dawn. This would be my first time waltzing into a hornet's nest staffed by Chanzig's soldiers—and maybe my last.

18

At first light, Modri buzzed me awake. I came out of my slumber like a man on a mission, skipping my typical routine of groaning, seeking out a stimulant, and pulling the blankets over my head. No time for that. Instead, I took a peek at two key things: the Amber House and my injured arm.

The compound was as I expected—armed. In the blinding morning light, it looked even more intimidating. The only good thing about the sunlight was that it confirmed my suspicions about the location. True to its name, the entire compound gleamed with an eye-catching, reflective layer of amber paint. No gunships in the sky, but plenty of soldiers up for their morning watch.

My arm, in contrast, warmed my spirits a fair amount. It had healed to about the halfway mark—decent enough to use the carbine, that is.

With those cursory checks finished, I pulled up my Status Display and went to work with Modri's plan. First up was activating Rank 4. Easy.

STATUS DISPLAY
PURIFIER RANK: 4
RANK-UP NOT AVAILABLE (3200 KP required)

Kill Points: 0
Genofacturing Points: 127,000

Rank Points: 1

Rank Time: 21 Hours, 59 Minutes, 59 Seconds
Storehouse Time: 3 Hours, 0 Minutes, 0 Seconds

Anima: 180%
Dominion: 0/2

No surprises. That was good. Or bad, depending on whether those surprises might have helped me in the fight to come.

Not wanting to burn any time, I headed down to the upgrade trees and immediately picked up Modri's choice: Infiltrator. It didn't unlock any new upgrades—which made sense. Previously, Assassination's upgrade tree had said I'd need three additional Rank Points to reach Tier III options. Now I needed two. Logical.

"Alright, time to test this out," I said with plain hesitation, drawing a pistol I'd tucked under the driver's seat. "You'd better be right."

"You sure you wanna test it inside a vehicle?"

"Better than outside. At least if I mess it up, they won't hear me."

"Yeah, true. You'll just cause a ricochet and hit yourself in the forehead."

I bristled at that, but took his point. Aiming the pistol toward the thick layers of junk in the carrier's back section, I mentally called up the Infiltrator ability. Nothing happened.

"Is it broken?" I asked.

Modri giggled. *"It's called a directed ability, Purifier. Surprised Guide didn't mention it. Just, uh, focus on your non-dominant hand, then activate it."*

Despite being half-sure I was walking headfirst into a practical joke, I did as Modri asked by mentally highlighting my left hand and thinking the same command.

In a burning rush, thousands of tiny boils sprang up all over my left palm. They swelled and merged and broke up through the skin in masses of gelatinous pus, forming crystalline structures several centimeters high. I gritted my teeth against the pain, but it didn't make a lick of difference. The ability was alive, autonomous. No matter what I desired, it would do as it pleased.

In a matter of seconds, though, the agony eased. The pillowy tufts of yellow discharge wobbled and congealed until they formed a sort of . . . orb in my hand. Reddish veins extended up from the base of this nasty orb, thumping with every heartbeat. It was a part of me. A new organ, or limb, or whatever you want to call it.

"Wh-what now?" I mumbled.

"This is the easy part," Modri replied. *"Stick the pistol's barrel into one side of the bubble, line up your shot, and fire."*

"No way."

"I ain't lyin' to you."

"How do I know this'll work?"

He laughed. *"Guess you don't. Imagine being me, figurin' all this out on my own until I found a Polyp. Look, it's a lot easier if you pretend your left hand is supportin' the pistol. Sort of like a base to it."*

Glowering, I tried out Modri's suggested technique. It was a bit awkward, not to mention excruciating, but soon I'd found a way to extend both hands—the right holding the pistol, the left cupped just below the barrel, which was jabbed inside the pus-bubble and somehow supported by it.

"Now, you gotta be careful," Modri warned. *"Shoot too many bullets too fast, and it'll pop. Then you've gotta wait for it to reform. Hurts like a bitch. So, take it slow and steady . . . one round at a time. And whatever you do, keep the barrel inside the fluid."*

Gulping with genuine terror, I shut my eyes and pulled the trigger.

Plurp.

That was the only sound I heard, with the exception of the pistol's mechanical slide thumping backward. The only indication that a bullet had even been fired was the hole in a nomad's empty water jug.

"Not bad," Modri said, *"though I'd advise looking where you shoot."*

"It . . . it's almost silent."

"Yeah, I know. Which is why I told you take it. Duh."

I stared in wonder at the humble pus-bubble, noting that the small hole through its center was already being filled in and solidified. I hadn't even felt the bullet tear through it.

"Just remember that this thing makes your shots quiet, but also lowers their velocity," Modri said. *"So, make sure you're real close when you do it."*

I nodded. "I think I'm ready."

"Nah, you're not. But I'm still ready to see the show."

And with that encouraging message, it was go-time.

You don't know real fear until you're waddling up to your archenemy's heavily armed compound, tracked by snipers, trying to prevent your two concealed pistols and carbine from slipping out of your ill-fitting poncho.

"This is your stupidest idea yet," I hissed under my breath, keenly aware of the guards gathering all along the ten-meter-high walls near the gatehouse.

"This is all you," Modri said. *"Just play it cool, remember to act insane, and have fun."*

But it was very, very difficult to consider anything about my predicament "fun." For starters, it was sweltering. Between the nomad poncho and the Deathless Tsar's golden mask, I felt like a duck roasting in the universe's largest radioactive oven. Maybe dawn wasn't the best time to launch my assault.

There was no room for indecision, though. Even now, I could hear the soldiers behind the massive walls barking orders and mobilizing en masse. Heavy-treaded vehicles grumbled as their engines started up.

Ten paces from the front gate, a voice came through the barely functional loudspeaker set into the wall.

"Stop right there. What's your business?"

My tongue shriveled in my mouth. I'd never been a good liar, much less an actor. But the show had to go on. As of that moment, I *was* the Deathless Tsar.

Adopting the dead man's husky, pretentious tone, I replied, "You know very well who I am. I've come to discuss . . . urgent matters."

There was a disconcerting pause, then, "What sort of matters?"

On the wall overhead, framed in oppressive sunlight, a band of guards peered down and whispered among themselves. Their long rifles and bulky, high-end armor didn't put me at ease.

I cleared my throat. "The aims of the Undying One are not to be discussed in the presence of curious ears."

Again, a pause. But when the voice resumed, it had a new note of seriousness. "Why didn't you transmit ahead of time? You know the procedure."

"Are you a simpleton?" I snapped, doing my best to imitate the highborn nomad. "Yesterday's ion storm was punishing to our equipment. Surely you also suffered difficulties."

"Wasn't nearly as bad as last week's."

I sneered. "How much longer do you insist on delaying this?"

"It's simple procedure. Your tribes know the protocol." In a much quieter, offhanded voice, probably not meant to be overheard, the man said, "These goddamn flesh-chewers. Why does Chanzig even keep them around?"

"Listen here, heretic! I have a convoy waiting just two kilometers from here, eagerly awaiting the end of our meeting. Open this gate now, or I shall inform the Undying One of your insolence. I'm certain you already know of his displeasure for your recent performance."

That last line was one hell of a gamble. I knew nothing about this place—especially not its ratings in any possible performance reviews. But that didn't matter. I'd worked in enough corporate environments to know one thing that held true across the universe: middle-management scumbags were eternally walking on thin ice. Especially when their boss was a lunatic who outsourced work to cannibals.

"Okay, okay, heard loud and clear," the man said through the loudspeaker, audibly shaken. "Just . . . let me get the gate open."

See? Always works.

Seconds later, sand crunched and machinery squealed as the gate's cogs began churning. Little by little, the circular slabs that overlapped to form the five-meter-high entryway peeled back.

Standing on the other side, which seemed to be some sort of courtyard-slash-staging area, was an official-looking man—and his bodyguards.

The voice from the loudspeaker, I presumed.

He was dressed like most of Chanzig's other goons, with matte-black padded armor, sleek gloves and boots, and a half-visor helmet that carried a golden tint. The uniform had two distinguishing features, though. The first was the set of chevrons painted onto his chest, which I presumed to be his rank. The second was its "desert living" customization: a scarf bundled around his neck and a white hood to block out sunlight.

"So," the man said, meshing his hands behind his back, "to what do I owe this . . . pleasure?"

I took a few confident steps forward. "Let us walk and talk."

He looked a tad annoyed, but relented. Soon he was pacing at my side as I headed deeper into the courtyard, his two bodyguards hanging back a respectable distance.

"*Nice goin' so far,*" Modri said in a suitably conspiratorial voice. "*Get a good look at everything for us.*"

You mean for you, I thought back, glancing about to perform reconnaissance. *You're the one who remembers the little things. I've got a job to focus on.*

"*Just gimme the eye candy.*"

And that I did. As I walked with Chanzig's officer through the courtyard, I took in everything. On the western side of the compound, there were rows upon rows of shielded bunkhouses—enough room for over a hundred soldiers, I estimated. The eastern side housed some sort of vehicle depot, judging by the amount of tracks leading to and from it. To the north were wide platforms perched on networks of stilts, each of which provided a landing spot for a different gunship.

Squads of troops patroled the open area and along the encircling walls, some even accompanied by humanoid-looking fabriques—machines with limited self-awareness, if you're not familiar. These weren't my biggest concern, though. As I'd mentioned earlier, I was wary of the snipers watching over the whole show. Now, with the aid of daylight, I was able to spot these tricky bastards easily. They were grouped in pairs and stationed inside the various minarets that dotted the walls.

All of this recon was good, but it put a cold pit in my stomach. So far, it just seemed like a generic military base designed to keep order in this part of the planet. Had I misinterpreted the messages on Liura's tablet? Was this "Akasha" woman some sort of military figure, hopping between various bases just like this one?

Only one way to find out.

"You're surely dying to know why I've arrived in such a rush," I told the man, keeping my chin high as I walked. I lowered my voice for dramatic effect. "Nobody else should be privy to such information."

At first, he simply pursed his lips with some unreadable emotion. Then he stepped closer and glanced at me seriously. "Go on."

Before I could speak, however, Modri sent me a brain zap. *"It's another Hegemony boy."*

I did my best to avoid reacting outwardly. *What?*

"Look at his cheek. He's got a marking, too. Looks like you're right . . . this Chanzig guy has a whole unit on his world."

Covering my silence with a cough, I looked over and spotted what Modri was talking about. Sure enough, his tattoo was similar to the Deathless Tsar's.

"You alright?" the man prodded.

I waved off his concern with a limp hand. "You surely already know who I've come here to see."

"Who?"

"Akasha, of course," I said quietly.

The man halted in his tracks. "You know I can't let you see her."

I stopped, too, looking back at the bodyguards to ensure they weren't preparing to gun me down. "Do you think I would venture here without proper reason?"

"With all due respect, Tsar . . . I don't understand much about how your little tribe does anything."

"Clearly."

He sized me up for a moment, then pointed to a boiling cloud formation far to the east. "Your *visit* was poorly timed. We've got a class-three storm heading this way. Real fast mover, too. You probably would've seen if it if your 'equipment' wasn't gonked."

"Yes, well, destiny doesn't follow our timetables."

His lips scrunched again. "You seem . . . different."

"Because grand things are happening," I said, tapping into a deep well of (fake) religious insanity. Just to add emphasis, I formed my hands into claws and wrung them at my chest. "Surely you and your forces detected a ship falling out of the heavens yesterday."

"A ship?"

"Yes. A black ship." I figured it was best to layer some actual truth into my testimony. Something the man could cross-reference, if he decided to go that route.

He scratched his chin for a moment, thinking. "We thought it was just a meteorite . . ."

"Because they'd shut down their engines. An attempt to hide. The devious, worming heretic! But we managed to find them . . . and now it is Akasha's time."

"What are you talking about?"

"Listen closely," I whispered, gently laying a hand on his shoulder. He made a disgusted face and shied away from my touch. Perfect. "The pilot of that ship was a host. He was carrying that which the Undying One has sought for so long."

His jaw dropped. "There's . . . That can't be."

"Oh, but it can. The pilot of that doomed craft was host to the Sacred Guide. A pilgrim who came to offer their gift to our master."

"Where are they?" he asked, suddenly invigorated. "Did you bring them in the convoy? I— We need to tell someone. This is—"

"They are back in our dwelling," I said, cutting him off. "They are far too injured to travel. And we would not risk the wrath of the Undying One by moving them and risking their death."

"Have you told the capital?"

I shook my head. He was eating out of the palm of my hand . . . which made this the hard part. The part where I sealed the deal and got one-on-one time with Akasha. "The Undying One's orders were very clear. We will verify that the Sacred Guide is indeed legitimate before we transport the host anywhere."

The man's jaw worked in hard, agitated circles. "You know very well that Akasha *cannot* leave the sanctuary."

"Fear not, my friend," I said, chuckling with theatrical malice. "I have not come here to take Akasha back to our dwelling. No, I have come to consult with her. To tell her of what I have seen and heard."

His face relaxed somewhat, but not all the way. "You want an audience with her."

"Yes, precisely. She is the only one with direct knowledge of the Sacred Guide."

"Chanzig would have my head if I let you walk in there. And yours, too."

"You think too cruelly of the Undying One. Think about how marvelous it would be if you personally presented the Sacred Guide to our master. Think of what great things he would bestow upon you."

"Well, I—"

I held up a finger to silence him. "Allow me to enter the sanctuary and speak with her for a short time. I will tell her about my experience with the pilot. If she confirms that the signs seem authentic, I will allow *you* the personal honor of contacting our master and giving him the good news. And if she believes this is a farce . . . you may tell the Undying One of my transgression. I shall accept all the blame."

If taken at face value, it was a win-win situation for this poor sap. Either way, he would appear to his boss like a top-notch, honor-bound soldier who was keeping things under control. Right about now, he was probably dreaming of promotions. Riches. The incredible rewards Chanzig would give him for being the one to find the chok'tal.

Nodding hurriedly, he began leading me toward the dark, two-story building—more like a bunker—in the center of the compound. "You get ten minutes," he said sharply. "Ten minutes, and then you're back to your convoy . . . no matter what. We'll need to lock everything down before that ion storm hits."

I grinned beneath the mask. "Most agreeable."

As we moved up the storm-battered steps to Akasha's sanctuary, I felt a rush of fresh fear. Half of that fear was due to obvious reasons—it took a lot of dexterity and steadiness to prevent any of my concealed weapons from falling out of the poncho—but the other half was in response to the bodyguards trailing us. My ultimate aim was to get Akasha out of this compound, so the more prying eyes, the harder things would be.

Thankfully, the officer in charge handled that.

He stopped just outside the triple-latched, rusty door at the top of the stairs, then turned and pointed to the bodyguards. "You two, check on the relay crew."

The two guards exchanged a look obscured by their helmets.

"You heard me," the man said, firmer this time. "Chanzig is very clear about who can, and *cannot,* enter the sanctuary. Perform your duties and wait until I summon you."

That did the trick. Without so much as a grunt of pushback, the two bodyguards wheeled around and headed back down the steps.

Before I could smile too much, though, the man leaned toward me and whispered, "Ten minutes."

"Ten," I repeated.

"Good." He glanced about as though worried about being watched, then went to work on the door's latches. He seemed to carry three separate tools, each custom-made to release their assigned device. "You know the protocol about the stasis field. And if you need aid, bang on the door. I'll hear it."

Aid? I thought, a trickle of doubt creeping in. Why would I possibly need aid?

No time to ask, though. The officer pulled the door open and casually shoved me inside, then slammed it shut at my back. Darkness. Pure darkness. Even as I spun around to ask where the light switch was, I heard the latches being slid back in place.

"Huh, guess there's a use for that Nocturnal upgrade after all," Modri said, chuckling.

Helpful, I thought back. Then I shushed him.

Just as I did, a chain of pale lights blinked on along the ceiling, activating from my position at the door all the way to the back of the interior in seconds. Their glow was dim at first, but rapidly expanded as the bulbs warmed.

My half of the space was all concrete, cracked, and pockmarked. But the other half was an abrupt departure from that design choice. It featured an elegant hardwood floor, sets of cushions, a bed, a table, a washing area, a wardrobe. To my stunned eyes, it seemed closer to a model apartment than a holding area.

Seated on the bed in a cross-legged, meditative pose was a young woman wearing white robes. Not a human woman, but a woman nevertheless.

Akasha.

She had teal skin covered in patches of black-diamond studs, a shock of silver hair that resembled bundles of needles, and long, *long* limbs. Hell, she had to be at least a full head taller than me. But her most striking feature was on her remarkably human face. She wore a red blindfold that extended halfway up her forehead.

I walked toward her in a slight daze, only to halt at the sound of sizzling. The stasis field.

It was the force bisecting the interior, keeping Akasha inside her well-furnished cage. If I moved close enough, I could feel its quantum dance tickling my nose.

"Greetings," I said, still using the Deathless Tsar's voice in case the officer outside was listening.

Akasha didn't move. "Who are you?" she asked, her voice inquisitive yet otherwise emotionless. She had a strong accent complemented by faint clicking sounds—a relic of her alien DNA, it seemed.

"Ah . . . the Deathless Tsar, of course. I've come to—"

She smiled. "No. You are not him."

"You must be mistaken."

"Let me get a closer feel for you." She stood in one graceful movement, all the while keeping her hands meshed at navel-height. Then she stepped off the bed and approached the stasis field. "Human . . . male . . . younger than the Tsar . . . afraid."

I shrank back a few inches despite the field between us. "I'm simply—"

"Why do you wish to deceive me? You are not like these men. You have come with . . . strange intentions."

"Just to talk," I whispered, resignedly switching back to my real voice.

Akasha just kept walking forward, her long, clawed fingers twitching intermittently. Was she . . . scanning me?

"Yes, I see now," she said quietly. "You came here for me. But you do not know me."

"We need to talk about—"

Her hand movements slowed. "There's something else. Something you do not wish to tell me. What is there, I wonder? What lurks?"

At that moment, I realized I was trembling. I looked back at the door in a cold sweat to confirm I wasn't about to die.

"You wish to take me away from this place," Akasha said in a singsong tone. "You seek the death of Chanzig."

I waved a hand to shush her, only to remember the blindfold. "Take it easy, would you? They're going to hear."

She came right up to the edge of the stasis field. "But what are you concealing? What could . . . ?" Her fingers went still. Then, in what I first assumed to be a trick of the light, her blindfold began . . . glowing. Just behind the fabric, there was a pinprick of white light. It expanded to the size of a small sphere, burning right between where I took her brows to be. "I see now."

"See what?" I asked.

"If you wish to leave this place with me, you must take the first step."

She looked to my right, and my own gaze followed. Attached to the wall was a control panel of sorts. It had clearly been retrofitted there, on account of the various wires, prongs, and bands of tape attached to the switchboard. A long cable linked the panel to the stasis field emitter on the ceiling.

"You want me to switch it off?" I said, incredulous.

Akasha nodded. "Then we may leave."

Perhaps I should've just hopped to it, grateful that Akasha was indeed a prisoner and not one of Chanzig's elite cultists. But I couldn't. The officer's advice to "call for aid" still had me a bit rattled. What about this woman was dangerous enough to warrant a stasis field and an entire compound more or less devoted to her captivity? I mean, sure, the light in her forehead and her overall body were intimidating, but what was the real threat? And for that matter, who was it a threat *to*? I could understand if she wanted to take revenge on her captors, but when it came to me, I had no idea what she thought. For all I knew, she might've viewed me as yet another bastard trying to capture her for . . . well, whatever she did related to the chok'tal.

"I advise you to hurry," Akasha said, cutting off my rumination. "I am certain you would not want to be revealed as an enemy."

"Pipe down with that, would you?" I hissed. "I'll drop the field, but we need to have a plan for getting out."

"There is a storm incoming, no?"

I narrowed my eyes. "Yes, and?"

"Remove this barrier, and I will ensure our escape."

"It's got to be hooked up to some sort of alarm . . ."

She shook her head. "I know every aspect of this place. Do you trust me?"

Naturally, I did not. All I knew about this woman was that she was first, an alien, and second, my only path to knowledge about the chok'tal. But what else could I do? She was clearly hellbent on breaking free, and I had mere minutes before the officer came to check on me.

Sighing, I headed over to the panel and inspected it.

"The red lever," Akasha advised, still facing the doorway.

"Thanks," I said with an arched brow. "So, I just pull it, and you're free?"

"Yes."

Well, it was now or never. Wincing internally, I gripped the red lever and cranked it down. Instantly, the stasis field's sizzling dropped away.

"That was easy," I said, laughing nervously. I turned back toward Akasha. "Now, what—"

No further words came. All that emerged was a high, squealing gasp for air. Because at that moment, Akasha's hand clenched my throat with such force that I was already halfway to blacking out. She pressed me back against the concrete wall and lifted me as though I were weightless. There was no strain on her face—not even her arm muscles rippled from the exertion.

[NEMESIS EVENT]
Akasha (HUMANOID)
CALCULATING . . .
Estimated Kill Points: 131,000

As I hung there, dangling and clawing at her hands for air, I faintly sensed the weapons dropping out of my poncho. They clacked against the concrete as she leaned closer.

"Thank you for freeing me," she said softly. "Before I kill you and purge the evil within, I would like to know some things. If you answer honestly, I will make your death swift."

I tried to speak, but her fingers were an unbreakable vise. She eased her grip just enough to let air pass.

"What . . . evil?" I managed.

"You should not be so coy. I know what you are, Purifier. I know that the chok'tal lives within you. And its end has come."

The edges of my vision were curdling with blackness, but an undaunted hope swelled in my chest. Purifier . . . chok'tal . . . She knew what was happening to me. She felt its presence. She knew what it *was*.

"Why did you come here?" Akasha asked.

"I came for help," I said, choking out each word.

"I saw what lurks in your mind. You are a servant to Chanzig."

"No! I mean . . . not for this. It found me. It crawled inside me. I want it *out*."

She relaxed her grip a touch more, analyzing me despite her lack of vision. "Perhaps you are right, but there is nothing I can do. I will not let the chok'tal leave this place." With her other hand, she reached up and began peeling back the blindfold. "I am sorry if you are innocent, but this is the way of things."

"Wait!" I shouted, though it came out as a whispered squeal. I didn't know what was behind that blindfold, but judging by what I'd already experienced, it was nothing good for me or my situation. I needed to win her over. "This is bigger . . . than you think."

"Elaborate."

"Put me down first."

She didn't. "The chok'tal obliterated my world. My people. The life of one man is nothing compared to the trillions who will die if I allow Chanzig to access this creature."

I nodded to the best of my limited ability. "I'm trying . . . to find who made it. To stop this whole thing. I can help you, Akasha."

"You know my name."

"I know that you're my only salvation."

Akasha lifted me a few hairs higher. "You are not like the other Purifiers, are you?"

"No!"

"You are weak. Full of pity."

"Well, I wouldn't say—"

She lowered me to the ground, but kept my throat in her grasp. "You do not understand the horror that lurks inside of you."

"Oh, I do. I want it gone, just like you. But I also want to live. I don't deserve to die."

"Neither did my people . . . but the chok'tal makes monsters or corpses out of everyone they encounter. That is why I shall exterminate them. What could you possibly provide to outweigh my holy task?"

"An ally," I whispered. "If you kill me . . . they'll kill you."

"Do you think I fear death?"

"No, you fear the same thing as me. You fear what Chanzig would do if he bonded with one of them. Do you think our deaths would stop him? He'd just find another one."

She cocked her head to the side. "You think yourself capable of stopping Chanzig?"

"With help, yes."

"It does not seem probable. And if you cannot end Chanzig's life, what hope do you have of dismantling the ones who made the chok'tal?"

I opened my tingling lips to answer, but was interrupted by a string of banging on the door.

"Plans changed!" the officer yelled from the other side. "That storm is coming in faster by the minute! Wrap it up and get out here!"

"I'm not your enemy," I told Akasha, gazing into her blindfold and praying she could see my earnest eyes. "Nobody else will help you. And nobody else will help me. So I'm asking for your trust . . . just until we figure this out."

She looked at the door briefly, then back at me. "Trust is the invitation to betrayal."

"Akasha, please. We can stop this."

In the moment that followed, I shut my eyes and tensed up, expecting her to snap my neck without remorse. But she didn't. Just as quickly as she'd seized me, she let go. Then she stepped back and rejoined her hands at her navel.

ENCOUNTER FAILED

Damn, was I glad to see that message.

"If you move against me, Purifier, I will kill you," Akasha said evenly. "The same shall occur if you are on the verge of death or capture. I will not let the chok'tal claim a new host."

I rubbed my throat, which was surely in the process of bruising, then nodded. "Fair enough."

Again, the officer banged on the outside of the door. "What the hell are you doing in there?"

Akasha glanced his way. "Do you have a plan to deal with this soldier?"

"You could say that." I gestured to the other side of the room, once again forgetting her blindfold. But to my amazement, she still followed suit by turning and heading to the far wall. "Just, uh, stay there for a moment."

She hummed. "I shall stay."

Thinking fast, I spun around and reactivated the stasis field. It crackled to life just as the officer began fiddling with the exterior latches. There wasn't much time now. Not much space for error, either. With my right hand, I snatched up the fallen weapons and shoved them back into their elastic slings beneath the poncho. I managed to get the carbine and one pistol back in place by the time the officer had the latches finished.

With the other hand, which I'd tucked behind my back, I activated Infiltrator. The pustules sprouted, joined, and solidified as the officer struggled to open the door. By the time he'd flung it open and stepped inside, I had the pus-bubble suppressor fully formed.

"Are you deaf, flesh-chewer?" the man barked. His eyes strayed to Akasha's cell, and soon his face turned to one of horror. "Where is she?"

"Behind you," Akasha said.

As the man whirled around, fumbling for his holstered weapon, I grabbed my remaining pistol off the floor and brought it up to a firing position.

Chanzig's Officer (HUMANOID)
CALCULATING . . .
Estimated Kill Points: 9000

A weakling, it seemed. That, or his point value was reduced in light of Akasha's help. Not that it mattered much.

While I lined up my shot, Akasha seized the man's arms and snapped them like twigs. He cried out, but it was too late. I thrust the pistol's barrel into the pus-bubble's back end, then fired through it.

As in my training session, there was hardly a sound. Which isn't to say it wasn't lethal.

A red hole had been punched clean through the skin just below the officer's left eye. He sagged in Akasha's grip, let out a few dying spasms, and fell still. She gently guided his corpse to the concrete, then shut the door.

ENCOUNTER SUCCESSFUL
Kills: 1
Kill Points Awarded: 9000

RANK-UP AVAILABLE: RANK 5

"Well, that was the quickest encounter yet," I said, only to realize that the chok'tal humor might not resonate with Akasha, considering her species' beef with them. "I mean, uh . . . good teamwork."

She nodded once, then pressed a hand to the back of the door. "The wind is accelerating. I believe the storm has arrived."

"You know a way out of here?"

"I believe so," she said contemplatively, "assuming you are a capable pilot."

I scratched the back of my head. "The best around."

19

Within five minutes, the wind had turned from concerning to downright vicious. It rattled the door like a starved animal seeking out its next meal. Even in this shielded sanctuary, far from the epicenter of the storm, I could hear the thundering crack of ion pulses up in the clouds.

Akasha stood beside me, inspecting the carbine I'd given her like a child trying to work out a puzzle.

"You ever shoot a gun before?" I asked.

"No," she said. "I have never had a need for such barbaric instruments."

"What, have you just stared people to death?"

"Yes."

I didn't want to question that further. "Look, it's pretty simple. Hold the back part up against your shoulder, look through the sights until the green dot is on the bad guy, and pull the trigger. Oh, wait . . . you can't see."

"One does not need eyes to see."

A chill ran through me. "Okay. Well, just do what I told you."

"I should be able to manage. I browsed your mind. You are not a particularly effective firearm user, but I believe I have acquired the basics from your experiences."

"I knew you were reading my mind," I said, scowling. "You know, you and the chok'tal have that trait in common. And I don't think I like it."

"There is a reason for these similarities. If you survive long enough to hear the reasons, I shall explain them."

I rolled my eyes. "Just make sure you don't shoot yourself with that carbine."

"Very well." With the smoothness and daring hands of a commando, Akasha racked the carbine's bolt and checked the chamber. "I think I am ready to engage in combat."

All I could do was stare with a slack jaw.

"Are you ready?" Akasha said, sidling up alongside the door and testing the handle. "Once we begin our maneuver, we should not stop."

"That sounds just peachy to me."

She nodded, then turned the handle. There was no need to actually open the door—the ion storm did that for us. In a chorus of ethereal shrieking and whirling dust, the world outside rushed in. Sheets of reddish sand pelted my mask.

Akasha led the way, and despite her lack of "normal" vision, I felt more than confident handing her those reins. What good were eyes in a storm like this, anyhow? She tiptoed down the steps, staying low and making use of her lithe alien legs.

It looked easy enough. But when I followed her out, my gangly human body was immediately slammed against the sanctuary's outer wall by the buffeting winds. I flailed against the poncho's whipping fabric, trying desperately to keep my mask on and pistol pointed outwards. Most important, though, was sticking close to Akasha. If I lost her in this storm, I'd never see her again. Especially since there was no way to shout to one another—not because of stealth, but because the gusts were deafening.

The formerly open courtyard was now a maelstrom of shadows and crimson grit. Every few seconds, though, the breeze would shift and reveal a silhouette or floodlight far in the distance. Akasha seemed to be aware of this, as she led me along a path composed of tied-down supply pallets and cargo containers. Each time she spotted human movement, she pulled me down behind cover and waited for the threat to pass. She was good at it—damn good. Whatever her sensory organs were, they seemed more than suited to an assassin.

While creeping along and huddling against the wind, though, I made sure to keep Infiltrator's pus-bubble active in my left hand. It was only a matter of time before I'd need it. Even in this howling hell, a gunshot would slice right through the sound cover.

An armored carrier rumbled past, and Akasha motioned for me to squeeze in between a stack of barrels. As I did so, I spotted a large yet faint shape in the distance. Doing a bit of directional calculation in my head, I realized we were heading to the landing pads—a conclusion that should've been obvious, on account of her asking if I could fly.

Then it hit me: she wanted to *fly*. In an ion storm. It was peak insanity.

But we had neither the time nor the silence to debate that part of her plan. Once the carrier had passed, we resumed our low jog. We were close now. Close enough to—

The wind shifted, and suddenly an armored figure emerged from the veil of sand. He was no more than ten feet away, and he was facing right toward us.

He shouted something, but it was lost to the storm.

Then he raised his rifle.

Chanzig's Soldier (HUMANOID)
CALCULATING . . .
Estimated Kill Points: 10,000

I brought up my left hand, Infiltrator ready to go, and—

Akasha let loose with the carbine. Six rapid-fire, semi-automatic shots tore through his helmet, sending the body sprawling to the dirt.

ENCOUNTER FAILED

I cursed internally. Partially because she'd stolen my kill, but mainly because that carbine was the loudest thing on the entire damn planet.

She turned back to me, a coy smile on her lips, only to realize what she'd done.

Alarms wailed throughout the compound. Floodlights sliced through the haze, combing toward us in crisscrossing grids.

Knowing she wouldn't hear a single word I said, I nudged her toward the landing pads and broke into a run. I also took the liberty of dropping Infiltrator, seeing as stealth was now being tossed out the proverbial window. With my other hand now free, I reached under the poncho and fished out the second pistol.

Akasha headed up the ramp to the nearest landing pad, crouching at the top and turning back to ensure I was on her heels. She took aim at something far behind me.

When I glanced back, I saw the shadows of several soldiers approaching our position. In between them were headlights—probably those of the armored carrier from before. Interestingly enough, my HUD didn't explode with rectangles, nor did it bring up any encounter messages. This thrust a frightening theory into my head: what happened if the system couldn't properly detect a threat? A sniper on a distant rooftop, for example, or a long-range nuclear missile?

Keep focused, I told myself, running after Akasha. This wasn't the time for theoretical musings, which had defined my entire career. It was the time for action.

Atop the landing pad was the broad, imposing shape of the gunship, barely visible through the haze. It wasn't a model I'd ever seen before—Hegemony-made, most likely. It rocked slightly in the wind, but never quite "shifted." Then I saw why.

A series of long, thick cables had been stretched over the gunship, anchoring it firmly to the landing pad's base. *Shit.* Just as I turned to Akasha to point this out, however, I found her handling the problem of her own volition.

She knelt down beside the first cable, pressed the carbine's barrel to it, and fired. There was a loud, vicious *snap*—not from the weapon, but from the cable itself. The coiled material split apart and flailed in the wind like a whip.

"Not bad," I shouted over the screeching storm. "Now do that again!"

Akasha sprang into action, hurrying to the next cable while I assessed our problem on the ground.

And it *was* a problem. An ever-growing problem, in fact. There were already four soldiers making their way toward us, and the carrier wasn't far behind. It was only a matter of time until the alarms brought out the rest of the garrison and overwhelmed us.

Still, my damn HUD refused to project an encounter message.

So I decided to take things into my own hands.

Raising both pistols, I aimed at the nearest soldier. They were about fifty meters away and closing fast.

Just as my sights landed on them, the HUD lit up with its standard blue boxes. In short order, it also framed the soldiers running behind them—and the carrier.

Chanzig's Soldier (HUMANOID) (4)
Armored Carrier (VEHICLE) (CREW QUANTITY UNKNOWN)
CALCULATING . . .
Combined Estimated Kill Points: 96,000

While holding the pistols steady, though, I noted that the blue boxes were inconsistent. They fizzled and jumped around as though trying to compensate for the veil of sand. That was the least of my worries, though. What mattered more was holding off these bastards until Akasha had done her work.

I let off four rounds at the soldier in front, two from each pistol. Not a single one landed. So much for my tough-guy dual-wielding act. Slipping the left-hand gun back under my poncho, I stabilized my weapon and took aim at the same soldier's neck area. Then I squeezed the trigger twice.

One round kicked up the dirt just behind my target, but the second slammed into his upper chest. He staggered, likely caught off guard by my mere presence. But he wasn't done—far from it. The body armor had absorbed my bullet like a champ, and it didn't take more than a second before he dropped to a knee and brought his rifle to bear.

In that second, though, I pulled in a breath and fired again. The round pinged off his rifle in a spray of sparks.

I tried to readjust, to aim at the tiny pink blob between his vest and helmet, but there was no time. His rifle opened up on me with a chattering three-round burst. I hit the landing pad and rolled, wincing as a shower of shrapnel pelted my hand. Modri hadn't been lying—these sons of bitches lived to fight. They wouldn't go down quietly.

"Akasha!" I screamed, but there was no hope of her hearing me over the storm and the gunfire.

I wormed to the side, crawling desperately toward a row of pipes that rose off the landing pad's edge. My only cover. But even as I squirmed forward, bullets zinged and ricocheted off the pipes. A few even thumped into the spongy material around me.

Clutching the pistol to my chest, I rolled onto my back and began scooching away from the pad's edge, hoping it might further shield me. Akasha was on the other side of the pad, angling the carbine to shoot through another anchoring cable. While squinting at her work, though, I spotted a blue-framed silhouette in the corner of my vision.

The first of the soldiers—the one I'd managed to hit—was scaling the pad's ramp, sweeping the area with his rifle. His aim moved toward Akasha.

On pure instinct, I extended the pistol and fired four rounds. The first popped against his helmet and knocked the man to the side, but the others drilled right through his jaw and cheeks. He dropped to his knees, thrashing, then collapsed.

That bought me a moment to catch my breath—well, *a* breath. There were still three others and a carrier en route, and I didn't think the others were stupid enough to follow after seeing what I'd just done.

Suddenly, Akasha came bolting around the back side of the gunship. She waved at me.

I got to one knee, keeping the pistol cradled, then began creeping back toward her while remaining vigilant of what was in front. A good thing, too, because a helmet with blue lines around it appeared a second later. They were easing their way up the ramp, using the landing pad's edge as cover.

When I spotted the tip of a rifle barrel, I loosed a volley of shots at the soldier in front. The rounds slammed into the landing pad or whistled past their head, but it did the trick. The helmets shrank back down.

Still, suppression could only keep elite fighters out of action for so long. When they realized they were up against an archaeologist and a semi-blind captive, things would get hairy. I had to move. Seizing the opportunity, I whirled around and dashed toward Akasha's position.

Bullets soared past my head, carrying supersonic whooshes as they went. I hunched lower and kept moving. Akasha was close now—ten, fifteen meters. Then something slammed into my back. I went down hard, the wind knocked out of me and searing pain moving through my chest. Popped lung, probably. My pistol clattered away, lost to the storm.

But even as I lay there, squirming to get up, I felt strong hands grip my shoulders and start dragging me back over the landing pad.

"How many remain?" Akasha asked as she pulled.

"Three," I said, fighting for every half-breath. "And . . . a . . . vehicle."

She yanked me against one of the gunship's panels and set me upright, turning my mask side to side to ensure I was alright. Apparently satisfied, she stood and tugged on a few hydraulic releases connected to the rear-entry systems.

"We're almost in," she said with unnerving calmness. "Please hold them off with your weapon."

Talk about zero empathy. But with bullets slamming into the gunship's other sides and twanging off the pad around us, there was no room for discussion. I lifted my poncho, cursing and aching, and retrieved the spare pistol. Then, with what little mobility I had, I lay on my side and twisted to peer under the gunship's landing struts.

Two soldiers were advancing, while the third remained back at the ramp with his rifle at the ready.

I didn't dare fire, though. They needed to get closer. If I shot too soon, the one at the ramp would spot me and give me a full-metal overdose.

"Akasha . . ." I growled when the onrushing soldiers came within fifteen meters.

Right on cue, I heard the pop-hiss of the gunship's entryway unsealing. The rear ramp clanked down onto the landing pad, narrowly missing my foot.

The noise seemed to light a fire under the two soldiers' asses, because they broke into a run straight toward us. Time to shine. When the first man came around the corner of the main engine, I dumped five shots into his center mass.

He cried out, but released a reflexive burst of return fire as he back-pedaled. The bullets thudded into the landing pad just beside my thighs.

I gritted my teeth. "Akasha!"

"You are too impatient," she whispered as she leaned overhead, hooking me under the arms and easily pulling me up the ramp. "Prepare to fly."

All I could do was grunt, keeping the pistol outstretched as she dragged me down the gunship's central aisle. The flurry of the ion storm turned to the dark, sterile interior of the *definitely* stolen Hegemony vehicle. Auxiliary lights fluttered to life at my sides, and the rush of wind was overtaken by the hum of the onboard filtration systems.

It was a pleasant shift, but only temporarily. Because before I'd even made it halfway down the aisle, a soldier leaned out of cover at the doorway. I fired three times, managing to clip his shoulder twice—but it wasn't enough.

He sprayed wildly into the vehicle. His shots tore up the padded seats all around me and burst against reinforced bulkheads.

"Cease fire!" another soldier howled. "Akasha's onboard! You'll clip her!"

"She's escaping!" the other called back.

"Doesn't matter! Chanzig'll skin us if you draw her blood!"

Without warning, Akasha released me and hopped over my prone body. She turned back briefly, giving me a confident nod. "Get the ship started. Ramp open. I'll take care of them."

I lowered the pistol. "Are you nuts? Get out of the way!"

She didn't respond. Instead, she took a few casual steps back toward the enemy. Just before she reached the pressurization vestibule and ramp, she rested the carbine on a nearby seat and raised both hands in surrender.

"We've got her!" one of the soldiers yelled.

I just sat there for a moment, stunned at her lunacy. Then I got it. She was a distraction. A valuable target they wouldn't dare risk firing through.

Sucking in a breath that bubbled with blood, I crawled toward the cockpit and pulled myself up using a raised console. Behind me, the soldiers shouted orders at a silent Akasha. *How the hell is this going to work?*

By some miracle, I managed to slump into the main pilot's seat and begin flicking on what seemed to be the most vital instruments. After a few failed tries, I managed to boot up the engines and get the display online.

Just outside the viewpane, I saw what awaited us if we didn't make it out. The carrier was parked at the bottom of the ramp, unloading troops in twos and threes. More squads of soldiers were jogging across the courtyard. To my astonishment, the newcomers became framed in red rectangles, accompanied by a never-before-seen message.

[NEW COMBATANTS DETECTED]
[ENCOUNTER DESIGNATION CHANGED: SLAUGHTER EVENT]
Chanzig's Soldier (HUMANOID) (9)
UPDATING . . .
Combined Estimated Kill Points: 162,500

Well, that answered the question of how the system accounted for reinforcements joining the fray. Not that I'd ever had it.

"Power down the gunship immediately," a voice commanded over the compound's loudspeakers. "You will be spared if you comply."

"Alright, Modri," I said, still fiddling with the controls in a blur of fear. "Now's your time to shine."

Nothing.

I scowled. "Listen, I'm sorry I shushed you, and sorry I talked trash about your flying . . . but I really need you right now. So, come on out and do your tendril-thing."

Again, he was silent.

Then it hit me: I was out of luck. With an encounter active, the chok'tal—including Guide and Modri—was unable to do anything beyond projecting the relevant combat data.

I'd have to fly.

Bear in mind that I couldn't even locate the acceleration levers, nor the altitude joystick. It was a good thing Akasha had told me to keep the ramp down—I didn't have the first clue about how to raise it. But I was too deep to try anything else now. With confidence that I had no right to possess, I began wildly turning dials, toggling switches, and palming entire grids of sensitive-looking buttons.

Nothing happened—until something did.

The gunship's VTOL engines swiveled and ignited with reckless gusto, slingshotting the vehicle directly to the right. We skidded off the platform and began spinning wildly over the courtyard, our velocity picking up by the second.

"Shit, shit, shit," I hissed, my hands hovering uselessly over the controls.

If I touched anything, I risked crashing the gunship. But *not* touching anything would have the same result. With every erratic, nauseating spin, our trajectory swung closer and closer to the minarets lining the compound. One clip of a turbine, and we'd be plummeting back to the sand in a fiery wreck.

Things weren't any calmer in the back of the vehicle. I heard the scrapes and thumps of conflict, followed by a soldier howling in agony.

Akasha couldn't help me, even if she had some rudimentary knowledge of flying. She was far too busy saving us from our unwelcome boarding party.

"Think, Dak, think," I whispered, eyes glazing over the controls.

They all seemed to bleed together. So many lights, knobs, dimmers, charts. I'd given my brother plenty of flak for spending six years of his life in the Hegemony piloting academies, but now I understood where all that time had gone. This thing was a mechanical nightmare.

While probing the console with my hands, however, I flicked back some sort of rubber hood. A joystick elevated out of the panel.

"Here goes nothing."

Gripping the joystick, I attempted a gentle flick to the left to counteract our spin. The gunship responded by tipping, not turning, pitching us down toward the carrier. With a squeal, I gave it another flick to the right. It evened us out, but just barely. The gunship's nose scraped past a minaret, and then we were flailing through the haze again.

Curses ran through my head like a mantra. Was this *really* how I died? How I'd be remembered? Still in a panic, I searched the console for some sign of the VTOL instruments.

Just as we swung around for another minaret pass, I spied an embedded tablet that showed a top-down diagram of the gunship. The engine turbines were indeed tilted, painted with a bright red glow. Beneath the diagram were directional arrows that resembled a mosaic. But I had no time for guesswork.

Even now, the gunship was hurtling toward a minaret it wouldn't be able to avoid. Collision course guaranteed.

I took a deep breath, located the arrows I thought might save our skins, and pressed.

The gunship evened out, but we were still sailing forward. Still aiming right for the center of the minaret. How the hell were we supposed to pull up? My mind went blank. Joystick, arrow? Joystick, arrow?

The panel lit up with warnings as the minaret approached. Red lights flared. Collision alerts bleeped.

"Oh, screw it."

Out of options, I jerked back on the joystick and thumbed a random arrow. The gunship lurched skyward, rattling with fresh power as the engines went into overdrive. The tip of the minaret passed beneath the nose like a waiting butcher's knife. Then we were soaring, twisting wildly in the grips of the storm's high-pressure currents.

Lightning snaked outside the viewpane. Thunder jostled the cockpit. Before I knew it, the gunship was out of my hands, riding on a flow of temperamental winds. But at least the compound was gone. Ahead, there was no ground, no sky. Just a churning mass of sand, flashes, and darkness.

ENCOUNTER INCOMPLETE
Kills: 1
Kill Points Awarded: 21,000

"How's it going?"

Akasha's voice made me jump in my seat.

"God," I said sharply, "can't you walk a little louder?"

She sat down beside me, her back straight and shoulders squared. She looked like she'd gone for a leisurely walk instead of thrown down with Chanzig's soldiers. "May I ask where you learned to fly?"

I glanced at her sidelong, a weary smile on my lips. "Little place called the Amber House."

She either didn't get the joke or didn't care for it. "Do you know where you are heading?"

"Not at all, but I have a plan for that." Probing my mind, I called out to Modri in a state of humility. *Okay, I admit it . . . you're a good pilot. Now will you get out here and help me?*

"*I'll consider it,*" Modri said. "*Hegemony gunships are my bread and butter, after all. But I think we need to have a good, long chat about this Akasha broad. She's got a real chip on her shoulder about me. Well, the whole chok'tal thing in general. Did you hear her? Seems like she can kill us. I mean* us. *Not just you.*"

That can come later, I thought back. *Just . . . pitch in for now.*

"Fine. Gimme the command."

As before, I surrendered control of flying to Modri and held my hands out above the console. The tendrils' emergence hurt a tad less this time, probably because I was already swimming in adrenaline due to my punctured lung. In a matter of seconds, they slithered into the data ports and began their work of stabilizing the gunship.

Akasha tensed in her seat. The space between her brows began to glow through the blindfold once again. "You are entrusting the chok'tal with our lives."

"Relax," I told her. "It's a Polyp . . . and it's on our side."

Suddenly, the cockpit's loudspeaker system crackled to life. And what came out of it was none other than Modri's voice. "I have a name, you ingrate. Real pleasure to meet you, Akasha. I'd give you a peck on the cheek, y'know, if I had a body . . ."

20

In a profoundly ballsy and dangerous move, I decided to mute Modri—again. Why was it ballsy and dangerous, you ask? Because he was still flying the gunship. At any moment, theoretically, he could decide to say "screw it" and send us nosediving into the red canyons below.

I didn't believe he would take such drastic measures now, though. Especially since it had been ten minutes since I shushed him. We were out of the storm, flying in a random direction that took us over dry riverbeds and craggy, cave-filled basins.

Besides, how could he blame me? He'd spent far, far too long trying to hit on Akasha, a woman who was already two steps away from obliterating him and every other consciousness contained in the chok'tal. With or without a body, the man was clearly a horny devil. I could only imagine what sort of soldier he'd been in his actual life.

Thankfully, Akasha hadn't risen to his challenges. She'd just sat there in her meditative equipoise, occasionally looking in my direction as though begging me to shut him up.

And now, as we flew on, we both sat in that contemplative silence. The puncture in my lung seemed more or less healed, seeing as there was no longer a wheezing sound every time I inhaled. Even so, I was concerned about the bullet that was probably still lurking somewhere in my guts. Oh, well. Modri could fill me in on that sort of danger later.

"My name is Dak, by the way," I said, unprompted. "I . . . just thought you should know that. In case you didn't see it in my mind."

Akasha glanced over. "It is an unusual name."

"My parents wanted to be creative, I guess."

Again, there was that awkward silence. There was so much I needed to ask her about, so much to process and consider, but I just couldn't bring any of it up. There was an imposing quality to the woman. An unapproachable, intimidating aura that kept my lips glued shut. She'd helped me escape alive, sure, but I knew she could end me just as easily.

"You are the first Purifier who has wished to remove the chok'tal," Akasha said, making me perk up. "This is most unusual."

"How many have you known?"

"Many." She looked down at her lap, where she'd gathered her hands in the same meshed configuration. "All that I found, I killed."

"Just like that? Not even letting them explain?"

"I do not need explanations from Purifiers. They are hosts to the chok'tal. They are driven by power and bloodlust."

I leaned back in the seat, twiddling my thumbs. "Yeah, that doesn't exactly describe me."

She nodded. "That is why I find you . . . strange. Some beings, such as Chanzig, have crossed entire galaxies to find this boon of eternal life."

"It doesn't seem eternal to me," I said darkly. "Maybe I just play things long-term, but . . . I know it's not sustainable. You only stay alive as long as you keep upping the body count."

"There is wisdom in your words. But desperate creatures do not care for such logic."

"I guess not." I sighed. "What happened to those 'many' chok'tal? You know, after you killed their hosts?"

"The question is not applicable. I killed both host and chok'tal in one strike."

"But I was told—"

She shook her head. "I am the only one of my kind. I would not expect you to have heard of my capabilities. Nor do I expect the chok'tal to be aware of them."

"What do you mean, only one? As in, a chok'tal hunter?"

"The last of my species."

"Oh," I said quietly. "But that means your species . . . evolved to find and kill these things?"

"No. Not exactly."

"Well, don't leave me hanging."

She settled back in the chair. "If you wish to understand what I am saying, you must know the entire history of my people. I do not know if your mind can comprehend such things."

"Harsh. I'm an academic, you know. I think I can handle it."

"Is it really so necessary for you to acquire this information?"

"If we're going to get this thing out of me and shut down the whole 'game,' then yes," I said, scooting closer to her. "We're allies now, Akasha. In my mind, anyway. I came to get you because you're the *only* person who seems to have a bond to the chok'tal. The only one who seems capable of doing something to stop this insanity. I don't mean to be rude, but you said it yourself: You're the last one. You're a dying breed. If it's up to me, I won't let you go extinct. I'll do what I can to take your knowledge and help you put it into action. So, whatever you can tell me . . . I'll gladly receive."

She studied me for a long while, her fingers working in those cryptic patterns. Then, when I thought she'd decided to shut up for good, she angled toward me and opened her mouth hesitantly.

"Most of what I know about my people is not my experience," she said softly. "I was born long after they fled the homeworld. Long after they had been hunted and butchered." She bowed her head. "I was chosen to be the bearer of the lifesong . . . a living keeper of their history, their guidance, their quest to rid this universe of the chok'tal. Thus, I shall speak of them to you. But before I begin, know that I do not remember them as they truly were. I cannot even recall the faces of my parents. I am merely the one who remembers what was passed down."

I nodded solemnly. "Alright."

"My people were honest and slow to anger," she said with an unusual, mechanical cadence, almost as though reciting some religious litany. "They did not shed blood out of cruelty. They prized wisdom and learning above all else. They cared for their world and all worlds around them, seeking nothing but the wellbeing of living creatures."

She paused for a moment, making some sort of prayer gesture with her hands. "My people desired to understand the cosmos and the forces behind it. Thus, they worked with the sacred arts. They performed ceremonies . . . mastered the energy of the body . . . created elaborate mandalas, all in an effort to make contact with beings beyond our reality.

"One day, their prayers seemed to be answered. Creatures made of the most beautiful liquid metal fell from the heavens."

I stiffened. "The chok'tal."

"Yes," she said, her voice guarded. "Several of our elders, shamans with keen minds, accepted the chok'tal into their bodies as a blessing. At first, my people were overjoyed. Their power and energy were limitless, and they quickly vanquished the beasts that had preyed upon our cities for a thousand years. But such glory did not last. Soon, these shamans declared authority over our people. They slaughtered those who resisted. At the apex of their power, the strongest among them opened a gateway between this world . . . and the world of something unspeakable. The world of the Unmade."

"The *what?*"

"We had no name for the being beyond the gateway," Akasha said. "It had no body, no qualities that could be described, so we termed them the Unmade."

"And you think *that's* what made the chok'tal."

Akasha nodded.

"But . . ." I started, thinking. "But that means any Purifier could technically open a gateway to its dimension, right?"

She seemed to ignore the question. "My people did not survive the opening of this gateway. As soon as this shaman activated the link between worlds, horrible beasts began pouring across our lands and seas. The shamans slaughtered what they could, but there was simply too much. Within days, our planet collapsed. Cities burned and weapons were drawn. There was no time to seal the gateway. The chok'tal brought out a savagery that had lain dormant in the hearts of my kin.

"When my people understood the terror they had encountered, they abandoned the homeworld. They bombed their own planet to ash and scattered in the nine directions, struggling to escape the tide of slaughter. Most did not get far. Those that survived formed a community in the distant stars, dedicating themselves to halting the curse of the Unmade.

"Over hundreds of years, they cultivated perfection in both mind and body to become warriors. They studied the chok'tal and learned of their nature, their composition. Then, with the help of great machines, they altered their own forms until they had achieved a kind of symbiosis with the chok'tal. Through this process, they gained powers to aid in their holy quest."

"Like the ability to kill a chok'tal," I guessed.

Akasha nodded. "Not only this, Dak. They became capable of seeking out the chok'tal using their mind. They could feel its presence . . . even if it hid inside a cunning host. With the help of these gifts, they proceeded to hunt down and destroy every abomination."

"But . . . I don't get it. You're here . . . so what happened to the rest of them?"

She bowed her head. "In time, the chok'tal learned what our people were doing. Their hosts, the Purifiers, feared that we might eventually come for them. As such, the Purifiers joined forces and searched for our world. I was only a child when the elders came to my family, warning that the chok'tal would soon arrive. On that day, my world changed.

"We could not risk the Purifiers seizing our memories and using them for evil. We knew too much about the chok'tal, about the Unmade. So the decision was made . . . my people would abandon their physical bodies. They would upload their minds into a cube, a device capable of preserving them and all the wisdom of their ancestors. But not only this. With this cube, and all the powerful minds it contained, a capable warrior could locate the energy of a chok'tal from across the galaxy."

"You mean . . . you," I said quietly. "You were the one they chose to use the cube."

"Yes," Akasha said, her lip quivering. "I was the strongest of my kind. My parents, my teachers, my elders . . . their minds exist only in the cube. For many years I carried them with me, locating and dispatching chok'tal one by one." She looked up. "Until Chanzig found me."

I squinted. "How?"

"I do not know. I can only form theories," Akasha said. "I believe that he touched the world of the Unmade. He was not of their world, however, so they would not accept him. His body was mangled by the attempt, but his mind . . . his mind learned secrets that no man should know."

"You mean, he got the same kind of 'gifts' that your people did?"

"Perhaps. I believe he is like me, able to sense the presence of the chok'tal . . . and those who hunt them. I cannot say. All I know is that he managed to find me and imprison me, hoping I might aid him in locating what he seeks."

"That's it!" I said, almost jumping out of my seat at the revelation. "He wants a chok'tal so he can enter this, uh, world of the Unmade or whatever it is. He needs it to pass through the gateway."

"That is also what I have come to believe."

Another question popped into my head. "But . . . how did he make a gateway without a chok'tal?"

"Knowledge cannot be destroyed, only suppressed," she said darkly. "I believe Chanzig found a gateway created by another advanced Purifier. His only obstacle is that he cannot cross its boundary without the chok'tal."

"You think he still has it?"

"I am unsure." Akasha let out a long breath. "Yet I know that he *cannot* obtain a chok'tal. My people never learned what the Unmade desired from us, but it is clear that they reward cruelty. A man such as Chanzig becoming their champion would be . . . unthinkable."

"Agreed on that." I rubbed my chin. "Back at the nomad camp, the leader said Chanzig was trying to become a 'judge' or something. Any idea what that means?"

"It's possible the Unmade promised him something for entering the gateway."

"So . . . he's a puppet?"

"I cannot say," Akasha whispered. "None of our people ever crossed the gateway. We did not even dare to try entering it. The world of the Unmade is indescribable to beings such as you and I. It is another dimension, and yet . . . the space *between* dimensions."

"Right. So, the Unmade might be run by a bunch of power-hungry gods, and Chanzig is their prophet here in the flesh . . . trying to win their favor."

She nodded. "He will do anything to find a chok'tal and achieve that goal. But what I truly fear is what he would do after returning from the Unmade."

"Do you think any other Purifiers know about all this? You know, the Unmade and the creatures inside of it?"

"Perhaps. Why?"

Wheels began turning in my head. "Go back to the cube that contains your species. What happened to it?"

"Chanzig took it."

"What, to find chok'tal specimens?"

She shook her head. "Chanzig doesn't even realize the cube is capable of locating chok'tal. Only I am capable of communing with it, and I ensured that ability was well hidden."

"So . . . why bother keeping you captive? If you didn't use the cube for him, and your whole mission was to *not* let him find a chok'tal . . ."

"It was not a question of whether I wished to help or not; my body reacts involuntarily when the chok'tal is detected." By way of illustration, she pointed to the area that had glowed when I first met her. "Chanzig does not know the true function of the cube, but he *does* know that it holds value to me."

"It's collateral to him, then. A way to keep you in line."

Akasha looked up and out the viewpane. "Yes. If I refused to board the scavenging ships, he'd threaten to destroy the cube . . . and thus, the minds of those who exist within."

"So, you went on the same jobs I did. How did you get out of working?"

"It was a miracle of sorts," she explained. "I was injured while exploring a volcanic world. Chanzig decided I was too valuable to leave the Amber

House. As such, he did not allow me to leave the planet or even step outside of my chamber. Instead, possible chok'tal specimens were brought to the Amber House for examination."

I nodded, beginning to grasp the true extent of her torment. "So, when I came to meet you . . . you thought I was just another scavenger trying to sell Chanzig a chok'tal."

"Correct. I believed that Chanzig would have his prize . . . and with no further need of my people, he would wipe them from existence."

By this point, I was almost quaking with anger. It was bad enough to torture people, and even to hold Balnos' family hostage . . . but to consider destroying an entire species out of spite? It was unimaginable in scope. At the same time, though, it explained why Akasha hadn't just killed herself or refused to help Chanzig. It wasn't just about her life—it was about the lives of her entire people.

"But this means he still has the cube," I said, reining my emotions back in. "If we get our hands on it, we can find other chok'tal."

"To destroy them?"

"Ah, sure. But I was more thinking about chatting with other Purifiers. They might know all of this, if not more. You know, like how to safely remove the chok'tal."

"Such things are important to you, I am sure, but they are beyond my realm of concerns," Akasha said. "I agreed to come with you for my own aims, Dak. I wish to fulfill the quest of my ancestors . . . and to preserve their minds."

"If he still has it, we'll get it back. I promise you."

"You presume, as I do, that it truly exists."

I gazed at her for a long, perplexed moment. "What are you talking about?"

"As I said, Chanzig has the ability to toy with the minds of others. It is possible that he's corrupted my memory . . . made me believe that he still owns it."

"We can't afford to think that way. This is a lead, Akasha. A real, solid lead."

She shrugged. "It is all I have left."

"Then we'll use it. We have to go to his fortress, kill him, and find your cube. I mean, your people's cube. You get what I mean."

"You speak as though such things are simple."

"Not simple, but necessary." I sat back in the chair, pondering the insanity of what I was proposing. "We're the only ones who can do this, Akasha. Nobody else will go against him."

"You must realize what you are asking of me."

"What, a war?"

"No. You are willingly bringing a chok'tal to his territory. If you fall—"

"I won't," I interrupted, only half-believing the words myself.

"But if you do . . . I will make good on my promise. I will kill you and the chok'tal. You must understand this."

I gazed into her blindfold, quite certain there was no exaggeration in what she said. She had trained her entire life for this mission. For killing people like me. Going against Chanzig was, in some way, like signing a contract that allowed her to murder me at any time.

But what else did I have?

"Okay," I said finally. "Together, we'll bring the fight to Chanzig. And we *will* end him."

"The gateway, too."

"Huh?"

"It is not enough to kill him. We must also destroy the gateway. So long as it exists, it is a threat. If even one Purifier manages to find it or recreate it . . ."

Seeing her point, I nodded. "Alright, the gateway, too."

"This is a promise?"

"It's a promise, Akasha. I won't fail you."

I didn't realize the magnitude of this promise until an hour later, as we flew over the lonesome, fire-dotted flats toward Chanzig's megacity. The radiation threw off the navigation instruments, but Modri was doing an admirable job of keeping us on the right track. Or so I hoped.

Akasha had gone to meditate in the back part of the gunship, leaving me all alone with my constant companion. Well, *companions*, if you counted Guide and all the other personalities crammed in there too.

I figured it was a good time to get Modri's take on the whole thing. Mentally, not through the loudspeakers, of course.

"If it were up to me, we'd have left her back at the Amber House," Modri said, grunting. *"She's a looker—for an alien, anyway—but she's bad news."*

You heard her, Modri. She's our one shot at actually finding other Purifiers.

"For what? So they can kill you and soak up the points from it?"

No, so we can figure out how to remove you without killing either of us. That sounds like a win-win to me.

Modri made a dismissive *tsk* noise. *"All I'm sayin' is that her and all her people spent hundreds of years learnin' to hunt down and kill things like me. You really think she's gonna work to save your ass if things go bad? She's got her own agenda. And Guide and I aren't on it."*

Slow your roll, okay? Now, you might not remember this, but your little tablet was all about trying to find a good use for the chok'tal. Akasha might be our ticket there. If I can somehow get in contact with this "Unmade," I can get to the bottom of what this is all about.

"So, what is it, then? You wanna get the chok'tal out of you, or you wanna chat with the chok'tal's creator and become a hero?"

I don't know yet, Modri. I'm just trying to fix this for everybody.

"And you think killing Chanzig is your best shot? You heard it yourself: He's got one of them gateways in the fortress."

So what?

"So . . . why help her get that damn cube when you can skip the middle-man and enter the gateway? You've already got a chok'tal in you. Maybe that's the path to victory. Y'know, the way you win the glorious game."

Do you know anything you're not telling me?

"Nope. Truth be told, I never even knew there was such thing as a gate-way. Either Guide's forgotten how to form one, or I didn't get to a high enough rank."

I squirmed a little in my seat, praying Akasha couldn't hear this discussion through scanning my brain waves or something—especially because I saw the value of Modri's logic. He was right; Chanzig *did* have a gateway that could theoretically be accessed by a Purifier. And that, in turn, was theoretically a path to winning this "game."

Adding to that, the fact that Modri didn't know anything about a gateway was a sign that this opportunity was . . . rare. He'd pointed out two possibilities—Guide being unable to make another gateway, or the gateway being an uber-special ability—and neither were very good. If it was the first issue, and Guide simply couldn't instruct me on how to form one, I *needed* this gateway, because it was a piece of endangered knowledge. And if it was the second option, well, I was even worse off. Modri had reached an incredibly high rank, and he still hadn't accessed that power. What chance did *I* have to exceed him and find out for myself?

Akasha wanted to destroy Chanzig's gateway, but did *I*? Hard to say. What if Modri was on to something, and the answer to my predicament was waiting inside there? What if destroying it was also destroying my one route to a solution?

I didn't know what that answer was, but Akasha herself had alluded to Chanzig becoming a "champion" if he somehow entered the world of the

Unmade. Was it possible that the Unmade had created the chok'tal to find such a person? To choose a "winner" amid the bloodshed? Of course, I had no interest in being praised by an extradimensional being, but I *did* have an interest in the possibility of them rewarding me by safely removing the chok'tal. A very vested interest.

"*You're thinkin' about it, aren't you?*" Modri pressed.

Let's put it on the back burner, okay? I replied. *We have plenty of time before we cross that bridge.*

"*It always feels that way,*" he said, laughing. "*Always . . .*"

21

We flew for the majority of the day, touching down in gullies and former blasting pits whenever Modri detected another ship's presence on the radar. It was an effective strategy, if one that left me a tad confused. We were flying in a high-end, stolen vehicle that rolled out of the factory with a host of tracking chips, and not a single enemy ship seemed capable of detecting our presence. Why would Chanzig, a former Hegemony intelligence operative himself, be so careless as to disable these features within his fleet?

Modri had assured me that there was no such mechanism in our gunship—none that he could detect, anyhow—but I still didn't quite trust it. Chanzig had total authority over his world: surveillance grids, gene-sniffing checkpoints, surface-to-air missile grids . . . if someone coughed halfway around the planet, he'd know about it within an hour. It shouldn't have been so easy to make our getaway and continue roaming the surface. Especially not in such a pricy ride.

As it turned out, there was a reason for this. A reason I would soon discover.

In the meantime, we had a plan that seemed feasible, at least at first glance. We would fly to the outskirts of Chanzig's megacity, ditch the gunship, and hitch a ride on one of the many trams that shuttled laborers to and from the field refineries. I wasn't too informed in this area, but Akasha spoke with confidence about the operation. Seeing as she had far more experience with Chanzig that I did, I was inclined to trust her.

The plan reassured me somewhat as we drew closer to the megacity. It loomed on the horizon like a mirage, all skyscrapers and swarms of aerial traffic. True to Akasha's description, hundreds of tram lines snaked out of the urban center in every direction. From this distance, the whole affair reminded me of a gangrenous tumor surrounded by infected veins.

Modri flew low and fast over the gamma-irradiated flats, reasonably sure that this would cloak us from Chanzig's scans. For all his failings as an interstellar pilot, he was an impressive gunship operator. I was tempted to ask how he'd acquired such experience, but I resisted—the last thing I needed (or wanted) was another tale about the "good old days" of exterminating local populations.

"So, what about disguises?" I asked Akasha, who sat in the copilot's chair and studied the megacity with her eyeless vision. "I'm not judging, but you're wearing a pretty recognizable outfit."

She looked over. "I could say the same to you."

"Hey, at least I'm impersonating someone on Chanzig's side. You're an escaped fugitive."

"We can procure disguises easily in the outer districts," Akasha said. "The laborers all wear simple, baggy garb. If you trade them one of your weapons, they will be more than satisfied with the exchange."

"That, or they'll turn us over to the local enforcers for an extra ration ticket."

Akasha gave a thin smile. "We are not the only miscreants on this world, Dak. The city's underbelly is a dark, devouring place, filled to the brim with those who have been cast out of Chanzig's higher society. A pair of strangers seeking refuge will not draw any particular attention."

"It will if Chanzig has put out an alert for us."

She slowly turned to face me. "Does he believe you still live? The other scavengers are dead. Why would you be an exception?"

This was the awkward part. Over our last few hours of flying, I'd given Akasha the low-down on who I was and why I found myself in this piss-poor situation. I'd told her about the jobs, the jungle, the cavern, the ruins, the betrayals, the crash, the nomads . . . everything and anything I'd gone through, right up to the very moment of me heading to the Amber House. But there was one tiny, crucial detail I'd left out—not intentionally, mind you, but because it had been in a moment of such emotional overdrive. And that detail, of course, was me leaving Chanzig an "I'm coming for you" message inside Liura's prism.

When I explained this, Akasha's body tensed up.

"You did *what*?"

I shrugged sheepishly. "I was feeling manic, okay? I just wanted to say something that would scare him."

"Did you disclose that you had the chok'tal?"

"Why are you grilling me? Can't you read my memories?"

"Not all memories are available, even to one who can probe the mind," she said. "I see patterns . . . significant flashes . . . threads of a life. But I cannot view the entire tapestry at will. So I will ask you again, Dak: Did you disclose that you had the chok'tal?"

"That's . . . a yes."

"You bumbling fool!" Akasha said, rising from her chair so swiftly I was sure she'd evaporate me. "Do you have any idea what you've done?"

"It was a mistake."

She bent down and stared at the gunship's main display. The vehicle was running solely on semi-automation at this point, since Modri had engaged a set-it-and-forget-it system. "Tell the chok'tal to redirect its course. We cannot go to the city."

"Akasha, relax. We're not going right to its doorstep."

In an effort to prove my point, I gestured out through the cockpit's viewpane. The city was still many, many kilometers in the distance, and—

A sparkling red light was speeding toward us.

"Shit," I whispered. "What is that?"

Realizing Akasha wouldn't know any better than me, I reactivated Modri and thought, *You see that?*

"*Get me back in the pilot's seat,*" Modri growled. "*No time to explain.*"

I didn't ask him to. Instead, I dutifully thrust my hands out over the console and gave mental permission to take over flying. He didn't waste any time, instantly slithering out of my hands and into the electronics via his tendrils.

"Turn us around," Akasha said, more to the console than to me.

"No can do, missy," Modri replied through the loudspeakers as he— against all common sense—accelerated toward the red streak. "That's an A7-G. We nicknamed it a twinkler."

"Intimidating name," I said, though my heart's hammering stripped the words of any humor.

Modri dipped lower, bringing us perilously close to the wave-like rock ridges on the terrain below. "If that thing clips the gunship, we're all goin' down. Insurgents used to use 'em to crash our ships for capture missions."

"How do you crash a ship, then capture it?" I asked.

"That's what a twinkler's for, Purifier. Knocks out the main engines like an EMP, but it *also* deploys all the gadgets for softenin' a crash and forces the auto-land mode. Puts a sleep to ship real nice and steady."

Akasha's brows tensed. "I have never seen Chanzig use such a weapon."

"Never?" I said.

"You know his nature," she said bleakly. "He does not care for preserving things. He revels in their destruction."

After a few seconds, I caught on to Akasha's hidden meaning. But Modri beat me to the punch.

"He knows you're in this thing," he said. "He's tryin' to take you in alive."

My lips curdled with grim understanding. "So . . . why the hell are you flying *toward* it?"

Modri laughed. "Well, this one time on a little colony called—"

"Skip the story."

"Fine, joy-killer. We figured out that you can't outrun the bastards. You might get far, but they'll still tag your exhaust trail. Gotta just put your head down, pray, and speed right past 'em if you wanna get out alive. They usually hit something."

"That makes no sense!"

"Hey. Were *you* an elite reformer? No? Then shut up and let me do my thing."

"There's . . . there's got to be weapons on this thing. It's a gunship, for crying out loud!"

Modri scoffed. "The rotary cannons are all unloaded. You two managed to jack the only gunship in that compound that wasn't cleared for duty. Now, there's two missiles in the tubes, but those bad boys aren't gonna do a thing when it comes to interceptin' the twinkler. They're not seekers . . . just the point-and-fire type."

"So, we have to fly right at it?"

"Uh, yeah? You deaf?"

Akasha just eased back in her seat, clearly not comfortable but also in no position to alter the chok'tal's plans. She then casually fastened the emergency buckles.

Not sure what else to do, I followed suit. The red projectile—the "twinkler"—was screaming toward us at unimaginable speed. At a distance, it hadn't seemed too fast, but as we drew nearer its true velocity became apparent. The same went for its destructive potential. As the meters separating us dissolved, the twinkler looked more and more like the condensed heart of a neutron star. It was blindingly bright, even in the midday sun.

"You two ready?" Modri asked, as though we had a choice.

Akasha tossed an expressionless look my way.

"We're ready," I said, inhaling deep. "Please don't mess this—"

At that instant, Modri swung the gunship hard to the left. The twinkler sizzled closer, curving to match our trajectory. It was almost on us. Huge, crimson, radiating heat so intense that it seemed to melt the air. The gun-ship's projectile-collision systems blared in alarm.

The twinkler did a final spin, preparing to smash head-on into our—

"Now!" Modri yelled.

Every engine light across the display flashed from amber to red. Zany streaks flew across the charts and gauges, indicating dangerous levels of power. The ground was so close that our lateral thrusters tossed up sand and mica. But even as we thundered forward, the twinkler kept coming, kept curving, eager to swallow us whole . . .

Until Modri rolled up in a stomach-evacuating maneuver. For one hor-rifying, wordless moment, the gunship craned skyward and gazed up at a cloudless expanse. Then we swung back down, leveling out as an impres-sive shockwave rattled the rear turbines.

"Hell yeah, baby," Modri said, entirely too pleased with himself. "You hear that twinkler go *boom*? Damn, it takes me back to the good times."

It took me a few moments to realize we hadn't died. Unclenching the armrests, I looked over at Akasha, whose meditative prowess apparently wasn't strong enough to take away the same fear I felt. She, too, was rigid in her seat, pulling in long and generous breaths.

"Well, uh . . ." I said, probing for something to say in the aftermath, "that wasn't great."

"You kiddin'?" Modri countered. "I ain't no pro behind a gunship con-sole, Purifier. From where I'm sittin', that was fan-friggin'-tastic."

"It didn't solve the problem of Chanzig gunning for us."

"You're too high-strung. Both of you. Chanzig's probably just pumping twinklers out at anything that's flyin' near the city. Throw enough darts, and you'll hit the target."

Just after Modri spoke, however, a foreign voice came through the gunship's speakers. "Throttle down and land the gunship *immediately*. By order of the Supreme Chairman Chanzig of the Kagu System, you have been marked for arrest. Failure to comply will be met with extreme force."

I blinked at the console. "Modri . . . how did they get this frequency?"

"Okay, so maybe his ships are a little more connected than I thought," Modri said. "It doesn't mean there's any bark to their bite. Probably just an automated message being pumped out of the city transmitters."

As if in response, the dashboard lit up with unintelligible warnings.

"Modri?" I said warily.

"Uh, well, it ain't the greatest news," he said. "Better if you look yourself."

The rear-camera display blinked on, courtesy of Modri's control. I leaned closer to the screen to take a look. Akasha, in her typical stoic fashion, just sat there.

The image on the screen was grainy, probably as a result of the twinkler's crash and subsequent explosion. But I didn't need crystal-clear pixels to understand what had caused the console's warnings. Whistling through the air, hot on our trail, were *dozens* of twinklers. Their burning trails led back to a series of tubes half-buried in the sand—some kind of city-defense system, it seemed. And even as I stared at the image, jaw dropped in disbelief, yet another row of mortar-like tubes sprouted up from the sand below us and unleashed their payload.

"Looks like we're goin' on a city tour," Modri said, once more revving the engines to red levels. "Akasha, I've got a job for you."

"I don't like the sound of that," I said, glowering.

"What is it?" Akasha asked.

Modri hummed in approval. "Get your ass up, take the carbine, and head to the rear ramp. You're gonna do a little shooting practice."

"No, no, no." I shook my head with vigor. "That's a me job, Modri. Let her stay here."

"Oh, yeah?" Modri said. "And who's gonna fly the ship?"

"There's got to be another—" I stopped, suddenly realizing Akasha was no longer in the seat beside me. When I turned back around in the chair, I found her halfway down the aisle, the carbine locked and loaded in her hands.

"Y'know," Modri said, "I'm startin' to change my mind about that girl. Maybe she's a keeper after all."

All I could do was bite my tongue and grimace, keeping my hands steady for Modri's benefit. My gaze strayed back to the rear-cam screen. In it, things weren't much better. The twinklers were closing in with absurd ease, and the quantity of them had doubled since last I looked. Our best shot at stopping them was an alien meditation junkie with almost no firearms experience and a blindfold over her eyes.

This sort of nonsense had somehow become my new normal.

But the twinklers, and Akasha's quest to deal with them, weren't the largest issue. No, that lay directly ahead. If you'll recall, our plan had been to land at a safe distance from the megacity, find disguises, and quietly infiltrate the streets without anybody knowing. That had all gone out the window with Chanzig's countermeasures.

Now we were hurtling toward one of the city's main roads—a ten-lane, smog-wreathed stretch of cement jam-packed with ground vehicles and foot traffic. Even this massive street was dwarfed, however, by the scale of what surrounded it. Within minutes, we'd be trapped in a forest of ridiculously tall skyscrapers. Lost in a maze that consisted of flashing lights, cracked silicate windows, and flaking metal.

There was no hope of simply "blending in," either. All the air traffic had vacated the area, presumably following the orders of the same people who had told us to land. We were the only ship for kilometers on end.

And then I saw it. Far in the distance, rising against the heavens, was a steep onyx ziggurat that had been burned into my memory. Chanzig's fortress. It dominated the world beneath it. In that moment, it stole everything: my thoughts, my breath, my hopes. Even from so far away, it carried an omen of death. It was more than a structure; it was a titan, a physical embodiment of Chanzig and his monstrous power. How could we ever hope to assault such a monolith?

My musings were interrupted, though, by the sound of the rear ramp unsealing. Noises from the urban hell below streamed in, only to be covered by the pops of Akasha's carbine fire. The orchestra of chaos worsened as we plunged straight through the first of the skyscrapers. We were in the belly of the beast. The concrete wilds.

"Uh, Modri, I don't think this is so bright," I said.

"Take it easy . . . as long as nothin' worse shows up, we're fine." After a brief pause, he sucked in a breath. "Okay, it might be time to worry."

It didn't take long to notice what concerned him. Nestled among the rooftop terraces, plazas, and towers below were comically large miniguns mounted on rotating bases. These guns spooled up and tracked us as we raced overhead. But we were moving too fast to do anything about it. Too fast, in fact, to even consider cutting down the infinite branching streets around us. With each passing second, Modri covered hundreds of meters. City blocks and buildings and domes whipped by, all condensed into nauseating blurs that were gone before you could look at them.

It felt like a suicide run, but then again, what could we do? The twinklers, despite Modri's best efforts, were still creeping up on us. And Akasha's fire, on the rare occasions it managed to land, did little more than shave glowing red flecks off the missiles.

"What's the plan?" I shouted at Modri.

"Plan?" he said back, snorting. "Not dyin' is a good start."

Right as he spoke, a new alarm rang through the cockpit. This one was accompanied by the top-down diagram of the gunship . . . and it wasn't pretty. Red slashes were carved through the diagram, and the cutesy-looking avatar representing our fuel levels was wagging a finger at us in disapproval. Great. Running on fumes with overheated turbines.

"So, uh, new plan," Modri said. "How do you feel about a controlled crash?"

The blood drained from my face. "In a *city*? Absolutely not!"

"Well, it's either a crash or twinklers. Take your pick, Purifier."

They were both trash choices, but the crash *was* less trash than being captured. If we were going to do it, we had to find the right place. A place where we had a chance of surviving. A place where—

My focus snapped to the dark, fog-shrouded void that opened up to one side below the gunship. It was a sharp drop-off from the ten-lane main street, and within its depths, I saw blobs of neon and chrome. That had to be the city's underbelly, the one Akasha had mentioned while we were flying here. She hadn't said much about it, only that it was overflowing with refugees and scoundrels and all sorts of people who had good reason to fear Chanzig.

And that was good enough for us. At the very least, we'd have some like-minded company while we figured out a better plan.

"Take us down there, Modri."

"No can do. We're cruisin' too fast."

"So slow down!"

"If I do that, the twinklers are gonna tag us."

"At least we'll crash down there, not up here."

Modri hesitated. "Like I said, Purifier, those twinklers will force an auto-landing. It'll probably try to fly you back up to street level. Then you'll get taken."

"And there's no way to disable the auto-landing?"

"Not without blowin' up the *entire* guidance system." As soon as he'd said it, he seemed to know what I had in mind. "Don't even think about it. If you gut the hardware, I won't be able to control this thing at all. It'll smash into whatever's in front of it."

"I'll handle it. Just drop the speed, turn down there, and keep the ramp open."

"This is a bad, bad idea, Purifier."

It was, but I didn't have the luxury of thinking over the extent of that badness. Even as we bantered, the apparent end of the underbelly came within sight. After a few kilometers—which seemed like plenty, but wasn't much in light of our speed—we'd lose our opportunity to steer down into the city's depths.

"Just do it," I said sharply, "or I'll retract your control privileges and do it myself."

"Bullshit. You don't know how to."

"I can crash just as well as you."

Modri sighed in exasperation. "Fine. Tell your little lady to prep for hard impact. We're takin' a dive."

Modri's past antics had already taught that me when he said to prepare, it was already too late. This proved true when I spun around in the chair and called out Akasha's name. Before she'd even looked back toward me, the gunship whined and lurched down at a sickening angle. The grav panels kept Akasha fixed in place—barely.

When I swung my head back toward the viewpane, I wished I hadn't. We were plunging down into a hellscape of searing lights, chemical fog, and burnt-out buildings. Modri threaded the gunship through webs of interlocking catwalks, all of them thick with hooded civilians. With each jarring turn, we sped over pools of caustic sludges and sprawling bazaars. Haggard, soot-stained faces stared up in terror as we swooped past.

"Here it comes," Modri said. "Impact in five . . . four . . . three . . ."

He didn't manage to reach two or one. The first twinklers slammed into our rear turbines with a strangely gentle *thunk* and a pulse of electricity, tickling the hairs all over my body. Almost immediately, the console's lights flashed gray. The gunship's speed slowed, reduced to a spirited crawl as we glided over yet another bottomless pit. A deeper underbelly, perhaps? Where did it end?

Akasha came dashing into the cockpit just as the remainder of the twinklers struck our hull and clamped on like buzzing thorns. "What's going on?"

"New plan," I told her, standing and retracting Modri's tendrils at once. "We're going to crash."

She tilted her head to the side. "That's not a plan."

"As a wise disembodied consciousness once said: *Trust me.*" I drew my pistol and formed a mental link with Modri, then asked, *What do I destroy?*

"That panel right above your head. Just, uh, stand back. It might spark a little."

I wasted no time in stepping away and aiming. The twinklers were already manipulating the engines, dragging us back up to street level for Chanzig's waiting forces. In under a minute, they'd have us back in custody.

"Cover your ears," I said to Akasha.

The moment she complied, I fired three rounds into the center of the yellow panel. Just like Modri had warned, sparks came leaping out of the holes. Followed by a gush of black, viscous fluid.

Akasha blinked at me. "Now what?"

"Um ..."

Thankfully, I was saved by a fresh wave of alerts and warnings cropping up all along the main display. The top-down diagram showed a total loss of control to the engines, and the gyro-stabilization modules—or whatever the hell they were—had totally disappeared.

In the same instant, the gunship's engines throttled down. We stopped ascending.

Then we started falling.

"The chok'tal," Akasha said slowly, "is not controlling the vehicle."

"Correct." I grabbed her hand and started tugging her toward the open ramp at the back. "We're going to have to jump."

"*Use her as a cushion,*" Modri suggested. "*Maybe if you—*"

That was all it took to earn him another shush.

The grav-panels, helpful though they were, gave the whole situation a weird air of normalcy. Because if you ignored the rushing wind and the sights beyond the open doorway, things seemed just dandy. You could almost imagine you were just hovering there.

But we weren't. Staring out the gunship's back, I watched the world zip past us, whirling and blurring. We were in full-on tumble mode. Tumbling where? I had no clue. But sooner or later, we were going to find out the hard way.

"We will not survive impact," Akasha said bluntly.

I gave her an equally blunt look. "You think?"

"It is my best guess."

Shaking my head, I held the edges of the doorway and leaned forward. The sheer force of our descent nearly ripped me out. Between the gunship's constant twirling and the acidic haze of the air, I couldn't see much. The only thing in sight that didn't promise immediate death was coming up fast—a network of tarps, canvas, and metal sheets.

"Grab on to me," I told Akasha.

"Pardon me?"

"Grab. Don't ask questions. No time."

Despite her clear reluctance, she did so. Her body was warm against mine, her heart beating with a steady and gentle cadence. Mine wasn't.

It was jackhammering so bad I thought it would pop right then and there.

I stole one last look over the edge, trying desperately to focus on the tarp-and-canvas blob below, then jumped out with Akasha in my arms.

21

Wind howled in my ears. The folds of my poncho and Akasha's robes snapped about, coiling us in fabric that would do nothing to shield our bodies. We were in free fall. Mad, reckless free fall. But even as we plummeted, barreling toward whatever fate lay below, I held Akasha close to me and encircled her with my legs and arms.

At the last moment, I had the forethought to activate Indomitable. That's what I later discovered, anyhow. I can't say precisely when I triggered it, seeing as I have no memory of actually landing. All I can recall is the play of hot air and fumes, the sensation of her hair against my cheek, the lights streaking by.

Then I was lying on concrete, pain pulsing through every part of my body. It took a monumental effort to even pry my eyelids open. Scattered around me were bunches of canvas and metal poles that had been snapped in half. Ripped sacks of flour and busted fuel jugs poked out beneath the mess. The Deathless Tsar's golden mask lay cracked in half near my hands.

My mind felt scattered, as though it had shattered on impact like so many of my bones. Each thought was a wispy, fading thing, running away the moment I tried to seize it. Gradually, memories rolled back in. I was on Kagu-9. In the underbelly. Some desolate rooftop market.

Fueled by whatever adrenaline had survived the landing, I sat up and brushed off my poncho. The flour and dust came away, but the blood didn't. And there was a lot of it. Half my torso was stained red, and my limbs were covered in massive splotches that would soon turn to hematomas. My legs were shot—the left one, at least. While trying to stand, I heard . . . and *felt* . . . the bone fragments scraping inside my skin.

But the agony was like a caffeine injection. It woke me up, reminded me that I was far from being out of harm's way. And with that reminder came a thought. A name.

Akasha.

I spun around, hastily swiping the last of the grit and blood out of my eyes. Where was she? All I saw were heaps of fabric and plastic. Had she made it? Had she let go and fallen? My stomach dropped.

Then I heard murmuring. Whispering. Glancing up, I found a crowd of shaggy-looking strangers gathered in a semicircle. They wore all manners of clothing unfit for the world above: hoods, helmets, cloaks, respirators. And sprawled out below them was Akasha.

"Get back," I growled, fighting against the pain to draw my pistol. When my hand came out from under the poncho, it was soaked in blood. So was the gun.

Most of the crowd shrank back, but a few remained squatted over Akasha, patting down the folds of her robe and gibbering with delight. God-damn looters.

One of the men had a blade in his hands, and was lowering it toward the woman's white but bloodstained fabric.

I fired.

The bullet punched through his hand and into his hip. He fell back, howling and cursing, his knife flailing wildly at the air.

"I said, get back." I let out a bloody cough as I rose, using the nearby canvas as my support. "She's not yours."

The gunshot—or the man's screams—forced a mass retreat from the looters who hadn't obeyed my first command. They melded back into the larger crowd, which I now saw numbered in the hundreds. It was a mass of hoods and aftermarket body implants, all gathered under the light of misfiring neon signs.

Limping like never before, I moved to Akasha's body with my pistol still outstretched. I did a quick three-sixty to ensure the crowd had pulled back in all directions, then knelt down and felt for a pulse. It was there, but weak. Then there was the matter of the steel fragment sticking out of her stomach. Looking closer, I saw that it had punched all the way through. A pool of bright blood was expanding under her.

"We're eatin' good tonight," one of the helmeted looters said, rubbing his hands greedily. "Both of 'em in one spot!"

Another, marked by a backpack with ten mechanical arms and goggles, slapped the first man on the shoulder. "Shouldn't touch them. That reward ain't real."

"The hell it isn't."

"Jandrin's right," a woman said, flicking through a tablet that was connected to her temples via wires. "We don't want Chanzig coming down here. Not again."

The helmeted man squatted and scratched at his scab-covered arms. "You do what you like. I think they'll fetch a good sum. And I ain't splittin' the bounty."

I just watched them, one hand on Akasha's throat and the other aiming the pistol. So it was true, then. Chanzig had already spread word of his two runaways. He'd enlisted the help of his entire world to find his prizes.

But I couldn't worry about that. Right now, my bigger concern was the madness of the crowd. Their movements were slight at first, probably out of fear from my first shot, but they soon grew bolder. People began stealing steps here and there, trying to test how close they could get before I aimed in their direction and forced them back. My intimidation wasn't enough, of course. There were too many of them. They encroached everywhere, creeping up like a pack of dogs trying to take down a larger predator.

Even if every shot was flawless, I didn't have enough bullets. Akasha's borrowed carbine was nowhere to be found, and I couldn't risk performing a reload with so many eyes on me. This was going to turn real ugly, real fast.

"Hold up," a man shouted, his voice deep and authoritative enough to ripple through the crowd.

Bodies began parting, and soon the speaker emerged, flanked by a pair of "soldiers" with ragtag gear and tape-covered shotguns. Definitely not Chanzig's forces. The man himself wore a sleek jumpsuit, a flat-brimmed leisure hat, and boots that looked far too expensive for this part of the city.

"Who the hell are you?" I wheezed.

He put his hands on his hips. "I'm Atrellu. Local peacekeeper for this tier. And I'll wager that you're the one on all the bulletins."

I let my pistol lower an inch or so. "Could be. What do you want?"

Atrellu grinned. "You fell into *our* turf, my friend. And you're about to bring the damn rain down on us. So, the question is . . . what do *you* want?"

The crowd kept their distance, but their stares only intensified. Clearly this guy held some powerful weight around these parts. If I pissed him off, he'd set the dogs loose.

"I need to get her treatment," I said, motioning to Akasha.

"Reasonable enough," Atrellu said. "You got the bux to pay for it?"

"I've got a gun. It's yours if you help her out."

"We could just take it from you right now."

I raised the pistol again, causing Atrellu's guards to aim at me. "Not without taking a few holes to the face."

"Easy, chief," Atrellu said, laughing. He gestured for his guards to relax, which they did—though not without a few nasty looks in my direction. "Here's the golden question, stranger . . . are you with Chanzig?"

"Not a chance," I spat.

"What's he want you for? Kidnapping the Cobalt Seer?"

Cobalt Seer? Noticing where Atrellu's gaze had landed, I glanced down at Akasha. Oh. I guess her skin was, from some angles, a shade of cobalt.

"You know her?" I asked.

The crowd broke into laughter, but Atrellu calmed them. "Damn, you really aren't from here, are you?"

"Obviously."

"So, what it's about, then? You kidnap her or what?"

I shook my head. "She wanted out. She wants to take down Chanzig. And I'm helping her."

Truth be told, I'd expected laughter at that one, too. But nobody laughed. Instead, the crowd shuffled about nervously, looking up and around as though in fear of a stray bullet.

Atrellu studied me with severe eyes. "Chanzig's own holy woman wants to off him?"

I nodded.

"Well, I sure didn't see my day going like this," Atrellu said. "There's a clinic not far from here. We'll take you. But I'm gonna need to hang on to that pistol. Collateral and all that."

I just kept staring at the man, trying to find any sign of deceit or malice. He was hard to read. But at the same time, I didn't have much room for negotiations. If I started blasting or turned him down, I'd surely die—and so would Akasha. Too much to chance.

"Deal," I said.

Grinning, Atrellu whistled and brought out more "peacekeepers" to clear the rooftop of the masses. They departed easily enough once the guns started waving. Then Atrellu strode over and extended his hand.

"If you betray me, I'll make you suffer," I said quietly, extending the pistol in a show of surrender.

Atrellu gingerly took the weapon from my grip. "Don't worry about that, stranger. We aren't like Chanzig down here. And we certainly aren't no friends of his."

Despite my cynical expectations, Atrellu's words proved genuine as they guided us through a string of tunnels, blocked-off streets, and checkpoints. Well, guided *me*, more accurately. Akasha was carried on a stretcher by a few civilians that Atrellu deemed medically proficient. Every so often, her stretcher bearers would apply a salve or inject her with something to keep her heart rate in check. It was more than I could've done. For my own trouble, they gave me a pair of crutches and a shot of synthetic adrenaline. No qualms about those.

But while limping onwards and observing my new "allies," thoughts started to bubble up. What were these people really after? Why were they helping me, a wanted fugitive, to hide a member of Chanzig's royal circle? Sure, they'd *said* they weren't on Chanzig's side, but it was hard to believe they could ignore the same impulses as the looters in that crowd. There was surely a substantial reward for turning us in. And even if there wasn't, it was effectively suicide to move against Chanzig's wishes in his own megacity.

These thoughts fell by the wayside when I began noting the efficiency of the operation. Atrellu had clearly messaged ahead to ensure we weren't obstructed along the way. Everywhere we went, there was already a team of Atrellu's forces on standby, their transmitters chattering away and signal jammers humming. At first, I'd taken this faction to be some sort of vigilante-justice mob, but my opinions were changing rapidly.

The farther we headed into peacekeeper territory, the more I understood their true role. They were insurgents. Not against the Hegemony, perhaps, but against their own breed of "master." Unlike the Hegemony's foes, however, these insurgents moved with subtlety. They kept their weapons stockpiled in abandoned apartment lobbies and under thermal-cloaking tarps. To Chanzig, they probably presented themselves as loyal militias keeping order in the underbelly. But down here, in their native territory . . . they were biding their time.

Atrellu must've noticed my wandering gaze as we walked, because he nudged me in the shoulder and smiled. "So, just between us . . . why'd you nab Chanzig's seer?"

"It's a long story," I said. "To make it short, Chanzig's got something of mine."

"Down in these parts, it's not uncommon to hear that."

I just nodded, keeping my attention on Akasha and her slow, shallow breaths.

"She'll be alright," Atrellu said. "We've got good doctors down here. A lot of them used to be triage forces in the Hegemony."

"Doesn't surprise me. Chanzig's got a thing for poaching their *talents*."

He chuckled. "Yeah, well, he takes the best and discards the rest."

"Discards?"

"Look around you. Everything below ground level is just his waste dump. A lot of folks came here looking for a better life, a decent wage . . . and now they're sucking fumes all day."

I nodded in understanding. "And you?"

"Me? Born down here. Out of the womb and into the mud, we say."

"Ever seen starlight?"

"Not a damn drop." He grinned. "We make our way, I suppose. Never bothered me too much."

We passed yet another cache of weapons, this one cleverly hidden in a drainage pipe.

"You've got to be bothered about something to pack that much fire-power," I said, jerking my chin in that direction.

Atrellu shrugged. "It's gotten a lot hotter in the last few months. More skirmishes, more unrest. Chanzig's hold down here is getting weaker . . . or stronger. Depends how you see it. One of these days, he'll either abandon us or wipe us all out. Looks like that decision's drawing near."

"And you're preparing to hit back."

"Preparing for whatever comes," Atrellu said, a note of warning in his voice. "Chanzig's a real bastard, but there's more than enough problems down here in the Dungeon without worrying about what goes on up there."

"The Dungeon?"

"That's the name of our tier. See, down here, it's a game of pushing down anyone that tries to crawl up. Full-time job. We call the surface Nirvana. The first tier belowground is Limbo. Next one down is Purgatory. After that comes our tier, the Dungeon. And then we've got the very bottom . . . the Abyss."

"What's down there?"

"Nothing good. The farther down you go, the worse it gets. The Abyss is the garbage pit of this whole place . . . literally. The assholes above us throw their shit down here, and we keep throwing it down to the darkness."

"So . . . it's just trash?"

"Yep, trash of all sorts," Atrellu said wearily. "And radiation. The Abyss is right on bedrock . . . which means they've got gamma leaks every few days. We soak up some of the rays, but not nearly as much as them."

"Remind me not to visit."

"Oh, nobody *visits* that place. Not by choice, anyway. We've had to sentence a few of our own folks to the Abyss . . . murderers, rapists, that sort of thing."

I blanched at the concept. There was an entire civilization down here. A society with its own strata, its own customs, its own ideas of law and order. It was hard to believe there was something even worse than this tier, but I had no reason to doubt Atrellu's testimony.

"Do the tiers cooperate on anything?" I asked.

He looked at me as though I were insane. "Like what? Turf wars?"

"No, as in . . . resistance. Chanzig did this to all of you. Doesn't anybody want to stop it?"

"Like I said, we're all in our own slices of hell. Too worried about feeding families to raise a ruckus. And the number one ruckus is pissing off Chanzig, because that'll lead to extermination squads ripping this whole place apart . . . again. Besides, we live on the scraps from up there. No production, no scraps."

"How long can that go on?" I pressed. "How much can people really take?"

He laughed. "Oh, people are mad, but they ain't mad at the same things. Mostly just each other . . . especially the lucky bastards living on the upper tiers."

As he spoke, the seed of an idea took shape in my mind. I was no tactician, especially not in matters of war, but I knew history. I knew what caused powerful men to topple. What brought empires of all varieties to their knees. And that magic ingredient was here, festering in the neglect and disease of the underbelly.

"If it came to war," I said cautiously, "what would you do?"

"War with who? Chanzig?"

"That's right."

Atrellu pondered it for a time. "Doesn't much matter what I'd do. There's a whole lot of folks in this tier alone that would gladly put a bullet through his skull. We do what we can to hold them back from all-out fighting . . . but that dam's fixing to break."

"Do you have a plan?"

"For what? War?"

"Yeah."

He just snickered. "Plans don't work against someone like Chanzig. See, as you head up the tiers, his forces have more and more control. You hear that weird signal in the air?"

As a matter of fact, I did. It was fainter down here, but it was the same hum I'd sensed after first landing on the planet. "Is it really neural suppression?"

"Who knows?" Atrellu said. "The deeper down you go, the less you hear it. Makes you wonder how much the folks on the surface really love Chanzig . . . and how many are under his spell. But it doesn't matter either way. Even if you wanted to take him out and somehow reached the surface, he's got a grid of turrets, missile batteries, auto-lasers. It'd be a damn slaughter."

"There's got to be a way to shut down those defenses."

"Yeah, it's real easy. You just have to flip the right switch in the fortress's security module. But that's the kicker . . . it's *in* the fortress."

"There must be a weak link somewhere. A glitch in the system. There always is."

"Not for a man like Chanzig."

"You're telling me that there isn't a *single* person down in these tiers who knows about his security?"

"Well, if you go by the rumors, they've got a guy in the Abyss who claim they spliced into Chanzig's systems and stole all his data. Passcodes, overrides, files, that sort of thing. But it's the Abyss we're talking about here. Nobody's gonna do business with that crowd."

"Not even for a shot at revolution?"

He looked at me with intense scrutiny, parsing my unspoken meaning. "Listen, no offense, but I'm not saying nothing right now. There's been plenty of failed rebellions. Nothing came out of them but blood and orphans."

"Maybe the people just need a leader."

"Me? Hah. I'm just another crab in the bucket."

I looked at him earnestly. "Everyone starts somewhere."

"We've all got our own struggles, stranger. Yours is with Chanzig . . . I get it. But we're already doing you a real solid by sheltering you. Especially sheltering her." Atrellu gestured to Akasha. "To these people, she's a hero. A martyr."

"What do you mean?"

"That poor sucker that caught your bullet? He just wanted a scrap of her robes. Proof that she's real."

"I don't get—"

"When there's no hope, all it takes is a glimmer," Atrellu said. "For plenty of these folks, the Cobalt Seer is their glimmer. There's . . . stories about her. Rumors that she went against Chanzig, got herself locked up in the wastes. They see her as a symbol of resistance."

"Is that why you're helping us? Getting her fixed up?"

Atrellu smiled again. "Before you start thinking I'm your best pal, let me put it in practical terms. It doesn't look good to have Chanzig find you two down here. And it *really* doesn't look good if she dies in our territory."

"You think anybody's gonna spill the news? Get a transmission to Chanzig?"

"Not a chance. They know what my forces will do to them if they go behind my back."

I gave a dark laugh. "Sounds like you've got your own iron fist."

"Brutality is the language these people speak. They never learned anything else."

I could only nod at the grim wisdom in that. Perhaps Atrellu and his forces really were the lesser evil, stomping down outliers so they didn't draw attention from the surface. How could I pass judgment on people who'd been raised in this hellhole?

"So, what'll you do with us after she's stable?" I asked.

Atrellu chewed the question over, scuffing his boots a bit as he walked. "My old man taught me to keep my mouth shut until I've got the facts. So, we're gonna wait until the Cobalt Seer wakes up and tells us her side of the story."

"What, you still think I kidnapped her?"

"I think you're a crazy son of a bitch for coming here in the first place," he said, giving me a cheeky sidelong look. "Us dangerous men always need to be vetted."

"I'm an archaeologist."

"Sure you are. I heard what you did at that compound. Word travels fast down here."

"Like I said, it's a long story." I sighed. "I'm Dak, by the way."

"Weird name."

"I get that a lot."

After another few minutes, we arrived at a dimly lit building with metal bars on the windows. The surrounding street was clearly popular, as evidenced by the mounds of empty bottles, bullet casings, crushed gadgets, and syringes scattered about. And judging by the raucous crowd that had been shepherded behind a concrete barrier in the distance, it was a popular spot. A team of Atrellu's peacekeepers had to hold back the tide with riot shields and stasis-field generators.

"Fans," Atrellu said as he looked that way. "They've all come to see their martyr."

I whistled through my teeth. "I guess word really *does* travel fast."

"Damn straight. Now come on."

He stepped up to the building's front doorway, where the peacekeepers were busy fitting Akasha's stretcher inside. The door swinging on its hinges was a battered, ultra-reinforced slab of metal that had clearly survived a few shootouts.

"*This* is the best hospital you've got?" I asked, incredulous.

Atrellu didn't answer straight away. Instead, he pointed up to the foggy, endless darkness that was the sky, where flying shapes hovered like phantoms. It didn't take long for me to catch his meaning: Chanzig's gunships were already prowling for us.

"It's either this hospital," he said pointedly, "or *their* hospital."

22

The inside of the peacekeepers' "hospital" perfectly matched what I would expect from a former Hegemony doctor. A combat doctor, to be precise. Stacked upon the wall shelves, framed in grubby lighting, were glass jars full of unlabeled chemicals. Smears of sort-of-but-not-really-mopped-up blood coated the tile floor. And sitting on a tray near the "operating table"—a repurposed pleasure-sim chair—were the doctor's cutting tools, all of them mismatched and chipped.

"Oh, there we go," the doctor cooed as he worked on Akasha, staring at her injury through a trinocular set he had strapped to his face. "She'll make it. Barely."

Atrellu elbowed me as though to say, *I told you so.*

The rest of the peacekeepers stood around the doctor with bated breath, leaning this way and that to get a better look at his work. To his credit, it was decent work—so far. He had already managed to remove the largest hunk of steel and staple her back together, and he was now analyzing the smaller cuts and fractures she'd received during the fall.

I wasn't exactly sold on the doctor's hygiene practices, but looking around the room, it was clear he knew his stuff. The peacekeepers had supplied him with a full assortment of high-end triage modules and alien machinery, most of which I couldn't even identify. All of them were powered by a grid of humming, unsafe-looking generators that had been stitched together with naked wiring. Chanzig certainly would've raided this place if he'd known what sort of treasures were stashed within.

While I was doing my inspection, the doctor pushed back on his hover-stool and peeled off his gloves. "Show's over. Patient needs to rest."

Atrellu clapped his hands, signaling for his forces to make an orderly exit. They filed out, though most cast a parting glance at Akasha.

"When will she wake up?" I asked.

The doctor flipped up his trinocular set. "Alien physiology and sedatives are hard to match up. Could be five minutes, could be five days."

"Just keep an eye on her," Atrellu said as he followed his forces to the door. He looked in my direction. "We'll set up checkpoints in the area, make sure she's allowed to heal in peace. For everyone's safety, don't leave this place unless we give you the all-clear."

I nodded.

With that, Atrellu stepped out the door and walked off with his peacekeepers. Then it was just me and the doctor.

"You are Hegemony," the man said, unprompted.

I frowned. "Highborn, but not Hegemony. I didn't serve."

"A shame. You would have made a fine soldier."

"Doubtful."

He just shrugged and rinsed his hands in a dirty basin. "So . . . shall we take a look at you?"

My immediate response was to agree, if not outright beg him for a cocktail of pain meds, but my better judgment held me back. Nobody down here, not even Atrellu, knew I had the chok'tal inside of me. It was *possible* that Chanzig sympathizers would rat us out because we were wanted, but frighteningly *likely* that anybody—even Chanzig's critics—would rat me out if they knew what my body contained. Even this doctor.

"I'm alright," I said, suppressing a grunt of pain as my leg shifted. "In case you're wondering what happened to—"

He clicked through his teeth. "I'm not. It's not my job to ask questions."

"That works for me." I sat there for a moment, thinking. "While I'm here . . . I did have a request."

"Hmm?"

"Do you have something that could analyze radiation damage? Maybe treat it?"

It was a long shot, but it would've been stupid not to at least ask. After all, I'd gotten into this whole mess because I needed treatment. As it stood, I was hypothetically still dying—meaning even if I got the chok'tal out and lived, I might still be taken out by the long-term radiation. At the very least, I wanted to know how bad it was. Chanzig had said he was the only cure for my problem, but was that really true?

The doctor headed back to his hover-stool, studying me with violet eyes—the ultimate hallmark of a Hegemony pureblood. "In regard to treatment . . . absolutely not. I am no miracle worker. But on the topic of your former question . . . I do have something that could map damage. I presume it's for you."

"Correct."

"Very well, then." He scooted over to a pod-like machine with some kind of metal-coil grid on the front. "How did you receive this radiation?"

"It was a dig site. I, uh . . ."

My mind stopped. Went blank. For the first time, or so it seemed, I couldn't recall a single detail of the incident. All these years, I had walked around with the confidence that I remembered that day with ease. I had never actually bothered to probe it, to actively dredge it up and dissect what had gone wrong.

"Never mind," the doctor said. He beckoned me to come over. "This module will pass a stream of ionized— Bah, you're no medical expert. Forget the explanation. Just stand in front of it, lift your arms, and let me check the results. I'll be able to tell you how severe the damage is."

I did as he asked, hobbling over and standing in the correct position. It was a task and a half to simply elevate my arms, but if that was the price of certainty . . . I would accept it.

"Good," the doctor said. "Now close your eyes and exhale."

"Shouldn't I be wearing some sort of . . . radiation shield for this?"

He sneered. "If you're asking for this procedure, I think a bit more radiation is hardly an issue."

"Point taken."

Right after I closed my eyes, I felt a mild heat wash over my face and hands. Then there was a strange tickling deep in my bones, my innards.

"Done," the doctor said.

All at once, the heat and tickling vanished. It had barely been five seconds.

"That's it?" I said.

"Efficiency over duration. Sit down and try to stay conscious. I'll check the results."

At first, I wasn't sure why the doctor mentioned the bit about staying conscious. But within a few seconds, I got it. A splitting headache appeared, followed by jittery pangs deep in my marrow. I didn't even want to think about how much radiation had just been added to my tally.

"Huh," the doctor said, flicking through a few slides on his terminal. "Must be some mistake . . ."

I pulled my chair up beside his. "What's up?"

"Nothing."

"You can tell me the truth."

"No, that's just it. There's *nothing*. No sign of radiation." He studied me from head to toe. "Are you a hypochondriac?"

Part of me wanted to jump for joy—the chok'tal and its Anima had cured me. It had straightened me out on a deep, chemical level, ironing out all the kinks the radiation had done. Once I got the chok'tal out of me, I'd be home free. No radiation, no early death. But another part knew I had to stay quiet, reserved. I had to invent a plausible reason for the clean results.

"Well, I did have this experimental treatment done a few months ago," I lied, rubbing my chin in thought. "Maybe that—"

The doctor cackled. "Whoever sold you that treatment was a quack."

"What?"

"When I say there's nothing, I mean *nothing*. This module is calibrated for maximum sensitivity. It's able to detect the precursors and lingering— Again, why do I even bother? What I'm trying to say is, if there had *ever* been radiation damage to your body, it would have shown up here. But there's none. The only rays you've absorbed are due to walking outside on a bright day."

My breath slowed. "It's a false negative, right?"

"I thought so . . . until I checked the full-spectrum readings. There's your good news, sir. You're radiation-free and always have been."

It made no sense. Even if my internal Anima had been responsible for healing the damage, there should've been some sign of it. Some remnant or aftereffect. After all, Guide had said it would take several days to heal every wound on my body—and I had a strong hunch that didn't include long-term radiation. Even now, there were still those puckered patches on my back from where Liura had shot me in the jungle. If those relatively minor injuries hadn't been fully handled, how could I pass this test with flying colors?

There was only one option, and it chilled me to the core: Chanzig had lied to me. He'd promised me treatment for an imaginary condition. But that wasn't the worst of it. My mind worked faster, slicing through memories with determination, trying to reach the root of the radiation incident . . .

Only to find that there was nothing. In fact, it occurred to me that I hadn't even thought of my "injury" until after I'd met Chanzig for the first time. Had those memories been dissolved, just like Guide and Modri's, or had they been *implanted*?

Suddenly, there was another haunting epiphany. Akasha's words on the gunship came rushing back to me, this time with renewed importance: *Chanzig has the ability to toy with the minds of others. It is possible that he's corrupted my memory.*

How hadn't I seen it before? How hadn't I noticed such an obvious blind spot in my own mind? If this was true—if Chanzig really had warped my own memories to suit his goals—what else was an illusion? Was there any region of my history that I could trust?

"You ought to lay down," the doctor said, evidently having watched me this whole time. "You look a tad pale. I have some medication for that . . ."

"No," I said. "I need a clear head right now."

"Suit yourself. Just don't pass out and crack your skull open on my floor. I've no patience for cleaning up today."

In a vague trance, I wandered over to one of the cleaner-looking cots and flopped over. Nothing about the room seemed very real. The only things I could trust were the pain, my own breathing, and Akasha. Especially Akasha. She was in the same predicament as me, and perhaps my only way of figuring out what the hell was going on here. Delirious and mind-fried, I closed my eyes for just a moment, hoping to nap before she woke up. We had a lot to discuss.

"Wake up. Too much sleep is poison for the mind."

Akasha's voice hit me like a sledgehammer, wrenching my eyes open and forcing me bolt upright on the cot. I whirled around in a panic, but she was quick to lay a hand on my shoulder and ease me back down.

"There's no fighting," she said quietly, "but you should move and allow the blood to cycle. You've had ten hours of rest."

"*Ten?*"

She nodded. "The doctor is rather impressed with the rate of your recovery. He suspects you have tissue-regeneration implants."

I sat up, rubbing at my eyes and trying to figure out how I'd slept for so long. Worried I was dipping into my Storehouse Hours, I checked my rank timer. *Phew.* Still another three hours left on my standard timer. While shifting about, I sensed that most of the pain was gone. The blood flow had ceased all over. I'd need to ask Guide or Modri, but it was fairly clear that sleep *did* have an effect on Anima.

Thinking of my own injuries, though, reminded me of Akasha. She was awake, sitting here, very lucid. Her midsection was wrapped tautly with gauze.

"You're—okay," I said, still too groggy to speak like a normal person. "How do you feel?"

"The body is pained, but I am in acceptable condition."

"That's, uh . . . good. I think."

She looked me over. "How is your mind? The doctor said your composure was weak."

"I'm fine. Just got some . . . interesting news."

"Regarding?"

I leaned past Akasha, searching the adjoining rooms for the doctor. He was nowhere in sight, but I heard running water somewhere at the back of the building. Washing up, maybe.

"You mentioned that Chanzig can 'toy with minds,'" I whispered. "How do you know that?"

Akasha pursed her lips, then said, "Because I have seen it happen to others."

"Like who?"

"Servants of the Halcius Hegemony, mainly."

"You mean soldiers?"

She nodded. "They came to this world seeking various things: wealth, power, recognition, sex, narcotics, legacies. Each of them had their desire amplified by Chanzig's power. He reached into their minds and warped them, filling them with grand visions of what they would receive for service."

"So, he was lying to them. Offering them dreams."

"Yes." She furrowed her brows. "You suspect something similar happened to you."

"Maybe . . . I have no idea how to explain it. I thought I remembered something real, but when I tried to recall it, it wasn't there. Can you . . . take a look?"

"I shouldn't, Dak."

"Why not? You already did it when we first met."

"That was different," she said coldly. "What I saw was merely what lurked on the surface of your mind. What you allowed me to see, even if you didn't know I was accessing the memories. To access a specific moment is . . . perilous."

"I'm ready for it."

"No, you misunderstand. It's perilous for *me*. Every time one enters the mind of another by force, there are risks involved. One can never know what defenses guard the inner world."

"You don't have to force anything," I said. "I'm letting you in."

"You have neither the training nor the mental control to do that. Your mind is a wild beast, and you are asking me to step inside its cage."

"Please, Akasha. I need to know what happened to me. What Chanzig did."

She seemed to consider it for a long while, her head lowered and fingers working in cryptic circles. Finally, she lifted her hands to my temples. Her palms were hot against my skin.

"Close your eyes and relax," she instructed. "Don't focus on anything. Stay in the center. If your attention wanders, come back to the feeling of my touch. Do you understand?"

I closed my eyes and nodded.

For the first few seconds, I sensed nothing beyond her palms and the room's humid air. Then I felt an eerie presence, a thread of energy working in the space between my ears. It was as though an invisible finger had found its way to my brain and begun probing at my gray matter.

Then Akasha's touch turned cooler. Firmer. Her skin vibrated at a frequency I couldn't quite grasp. Little by little, those vibrations worked through my head. They seemed to agitate the pockets of fat and water I called my brain. As the sensation continued, I stopped feeling motion of any kind. Hearing, seeing, thinking . . . all of these dissolved into a formless, boundaryless expanse that was neither black nor white, nor any color in between. It reminded me of dying . . . of when the chok'tal had first seized my body.

Akasha screamed, and I was thrust back into reality.

When I opened my eyes, I found her several feet away, trembling and raising her hands to me like I'd attacked her.

"What?" I said, confused and more than a little alarmed. "What did you see?"

"There are no words to explain," Akasha said as she struggled to catch her breath. "It was just a void, Dak. An endless void. And within that void were . . . nightmares."

"What does that mean?"

"I don't know."

"Was it the chok'tal, maybe?"

She shook her head. "I've glimpsed many Purifiers' minds. This was unnatural. The work of Chanzig."

I scooted over, motioning for her to join me on the cot and settle down. But she didn't move. She just stood there, shaking and panting.

"There had to be something you could use," I whispered. "Anything."

"All I know is that you are not who you believe you are. There were fragments of something horrible . . . something unspeakable."

"I don't understand."

She stumbled her way into a chair and sat down, hugging herself tightly. "Death. Torment. Annihilation."

"You . . . you mean you saw that? In me?"

"It felt like a thousand years," she said softly, "and yet my mind could not contain the experience. It came in flashes. In droplets."

I just stared at her, completely lost for words. I was an archaeologist. A good, decent man. Sure, I'd killed a few people in the last day or two, but I hadn't done it out of cruelty. I'd taken their lives because I had to. Akasha surely knew that. Whatever she'd just seen had nothing to do with my activities since acquiring the chok'tal—it was something buried deep, unable to surface in my own mind.

"I need to know more," I said, moving closer to Akasha. She shied away from me. "Where does Chanzig keep his data? His records on the chok'tal search?"

"I don't know."

"You have to! You worked with him. You—"

"I was *taken* by him," she snapped. "You forget your place, Dak. I am not your servant . . . I am nobody's servant."

My mouth fell open, a half-cocked reply on my lips, but I never got time to answer. There was a colossal *bang* in the streets outside—two, maybe three blocks away—followed by the cries of automated alarms.

Akasha jumped up from her chair and rushed to the window. I followed.

Outside, Atrellu's peacekeepers jogged down the street with rifles in hand. Smoke from the nearby explosion wafted out into the road. Within seconds, the sounds of a dozen weapons exchanging fire rang out.

"I have a feeling who that is," I told Akasha.

She nodded, but her attention was quickly pulled to something at the other end of the street.

Atrellu. He was running up to our building's entrance, still flanked by his usual detachment of peacekeepers.

"Time to move!" he shouted as he banged on the door. "Company's arrived."

23

As we hunkered down in Atrellu's safehouse, which was less than five blocks from the "hospital," I grew more and more restless. Peacekeepers and random volunteers hurried into the building, lining up to receive a gun from the community's impressive stockpile. There had to be hundreds of weapons there, all stacked next to a towering mound of rifle magazines and other ammunition.

"Just give me one," I told Atrellu yet again, only for him to ignore him and keep handing out firearms. "Trust me . . . I can help."

"We're not firing back yet," he said. "These are just insurance."

"For what?"

"In case things go from bad to worse."

It was hard to see how things could possibly get worse for the people outside. Beyond the safehouse's reinforced, soundproofed walls, Chanzig's forces were rampaging through the streets and putting bullets in anybody who crossed their path. There were no windows, so I couldn't directly observe, but all signs suggested this was a massacre. Guns chattered away incessantly, blasts shook dust from the ceiling, and civilians came limping inside with blood all over their clothing.

"Atrellu, please," I said, only staying in my seat because peacekeepers with guns stood around me. "If we don't do anything, they're going to wipe you all out."

He stopped midway through handing out another rifle, turning on me with anger blazing in his eyes. "You brought this on us. We're gonna do what we've always done best . . . which is looking out for our own. Don't get in the middle of it."

Seeing my frustration, Akasha put a warning hand on my thigh. "This is not our fight," she whispered.

I glared at her. "You're right . . . it's everybody's. Chanzig is running roughshod through this city."

"We are outsiders," she said sternly. "This man may seem cruel, but he knows the hearts of his people. Not all problems may be solved with death."

"All? No. But some, like this? Absolutely."

Unable to help myself, I stood and walked up to Atrellu. The peace-keepers aimed their weapons, temporarily triggering my HUD's threat-detection system, but Atrellu waved them down in short order.

He looked at me with plain exhaustion. "What now?"

"You and I both know this is going to get worse," I said flatly. "Much, much worse. If Chanzig doesn't get what he wants, it'll be war."

"I already told you I'm not picking sides. Not yet. And definitely not until I talk to the Cobalt Seer."

"We need to at least have a plan."

"What *we*? There's you, and there's us. Got it?"

He went back to handing out guns, but I stopped him by pushing down the barrel of the next rifle he handled. "I want you to listen to me," I growled. "This might all be my fault, but there's someone even worse than me who caused *my* problem. That's Chanzig. All of you down here"—I paused to turn and indicate everyone in sight—"have suffered long enough because of him. Tell me that you at least have a strategy. If you won't carry it out, I will. And Chanzig can come for me."

Atrellu set the rifle down and sized me up. "Alright, you want to talk like a big man? Here's a starter for you. Chanzig isn't the only problem. You'd be hard-pressed to even reach Purgatory."

"What if I did?"

"Then you'd have to reach Limbo."

"And?"

"Then you hit Nirvana, the surface. Get chewed up by the gunfire and missiles. So, how's that sound, tough guy?"

My hands turned to fists. "It sounds like it's doable."

"Spoken like a true outsider."

"You said there was someone in the Abyss who could crack the security."

Atrellu gave a bitter laugh. "I said there were *rumors*. Even if they exist, once you go down there, you ain't coming back up."

"Give me a name."

"You're out of your mind."

"Maybe," I said, stepping closer, "but as you said, it's *my* fight. My struggle. And if there's a solution down there—something that can help you push upwards—I'll get it."

"What, and risk drawing Chanzig's whole army down there?"

"That's right."

Atrellu and his peacekeepers chuckled.

"Sit down, boy," he said sharply. "You're living in your imagination. This isn't some action sim-vid . . . it's reality. If you don't back up and let me do my job, I'll show you just how real things can get."

We stared at each other for a moment, all sound drained out of the safehouse. I could feel the weight of countless eyes upon me. This was the time to make a move, to show Chanzig what I could really do. But given the broken state of my body, not to mention Atrellu's disdain, I couldn't risk anything too rash. The peacekeeper did have a point: This wasn't my fight. If I went in with guns blazing, I'd be risking the life of every civilian on this tier.

With fire in my chest, I turned and started heading back to my chair.

Before I'd made it, however, a fresh wave of explosions rattled the floor. The civilians inside the safehouse shrieked and held their children close. Even before the debris had stopped raining down along the streets, an amplified voice rose outside. Only it wasn't just one voice; the words came from a multitude of sources, probably the loudspeakers hooked up to walls everywhere.

"Dak Korasa, you have been summoned by Supreme Chairman Chanzig of the Kagu System. Step out immediately, unarmed, and turn yourself in to the nearest enforcer. You will not be harmed if you comply. If you resist or continue sheltering, we *will* escalate."

Again, the eyes in the safehouse fell upon me. My breath caught in my throat.

"Stay where you are," Atrellu said quietly. "They don't know you're here. They're just testing the waters."

But Akasha's face told a different story. Despite her covered eyes, I could sense the same fears that lurked inside me. She knew it would be a bloodbath, if not outright extinction, for these people. Even if the peacekeepers were willing to discount the deaths as acceptable casualties, I wasn't—and neither was she.

I turned back to Atrellu. "I'm going outside. You can shoot me if you want, but I'm going."

"They're going to torture you," he hissed.

"I know. But at least I might finally get my meeting with Chanzig."

"You can't go," Akasha said. "If you—"

"You're staying," I said, already sensing her unspoken intent. "I'll tell them you died on impact."

She stood and seized my shoulder. "That's not what I am saying. You *cannot* go, Dak. Chanzig will have access to what lurks inside of you. I will not allow that."

Atrellu raised a brow, but didn't inquire further.

"I'll take that place," she said quietly. "Chanzig will peel open any mind in his custody. I'm able to withstand it. You are not."

I shook my head fiercely. "There's no way I'll allow that."

"You don't have to." With a sad, strange smile, she lifted her hands to the side of my head. Horrific understanding washed through me, and I found myself paralyzed, not quite sure what to do as searing energy built up in her palms. "I am sorry I must do this, but I made you a promise." My entire body went slack. Pain sizzled up and down my spine. I could feel the chok'tal squirming, fighting for life, as my consciousness began to fade. She was really doing it. She was killing me. "I do not believe you are a bad man, Dak, but—"

A shockwave ripped through my body.

Suddenly, the pain of Akasha's hands ceased. The energy was so intense that it took me a moment to realize what was happening. Smoke and sparks swirled in the air, and I was lying on my side, half-buried in a pile of broken wood and cement dust. The ringing in my ears filled in the gaps: I'd just survived an explosive charge.

Dimly, I saw silhouettes moving through the haze. Their flashlights cut bright beams over the rubble, exposing dismembered bodies and the smoldering remains of the safehouse's door. It was an entry team. Chanzig's team.

Chanzig's Soldiers (HUMANOID) (3)
CALCULATING . . .
Estimated Kill Points: 52,000

"Any visuals on him?" asked one of the soldiers.

"Negative," another said, putting two bullets into the body of a man that dared to raise his arm for help. "All peacekeepers."

"Got something!" a third soldier shouted. "Looks like the Cobalt Seer. She's unconscious, but breathing."

The first soldier said something into his transmitter, then moved to help his comrades lift Akasha's body.

All I could do was watch. My body felt like molasses, throbbing like never before. Even breathing was a struggle in the smog. Much as it pained me, I had to let the soldiers do their work. If I tried to attack now, armed with nothing but my mangled hands, I'd only succeed in eating the bullets from three rifles.

As the soldiers headed outside, Akasha carried between them, I felt a hand on my leg.

"Stay . . . down," Atrellu managed in a hoarse whisper. "They'll move on."

The soldiers' footsteps faded, and I found myself quaking with rage.

"I can't let them take her," I said, barely hearing my own voice.

Atrellu tightened his grip on my calf. "Be smart about this, Dak. Both of you are dead if you go out there."

I spat out a mouthful of blood. "I'm already a dead man walking. After the hell I went through to find her, I'm not letting her go that easily."

"You don't know what you're getting into."

"I do. Chanzig."

"That's just a name to you. You haven't been inside his torture cells."

Risking more broken ribs, I struggled up to my knees, then my feet. Blood carved red trails through the dust on my poncho. But I wasn't concerned about that. There were bigger things to worry about, such as the continuing gunfire in the streets. The message demanding my presence looped again, suggesting Chanzig's men wouldn't stop until they'd either ripped this place apart or found me.

"If I take them out, I'll lure the rest to the Abyss," I said as I clutched my torn-open side. "And if I don't . . . at least they'll have their corpse."

Covering his own grievous belly wound, Atrellu groaned and reached over to the weapons pile. He fished out what appeared to be a bulbous pistol with two barrels.

"Take it," he said, offering it with a trembling hand. "We call it a One-Two. Tuck it away until you need it. Shoots two shells, one per trigger squeeze. Very short range. Don't waste your fire . . . they won't give you time to reload."

Nodding with appreciation, I took the shotgun-pistol and slid it under my shredded poncho. It fit neatly in the sling meant for standard handguns.

Then I moved across the destroyed room, stepping delicately over corpses and people that would soon become corpses. Both knees screamed with pain, and I could tell the blast hadn't done any favors to the still-healing break in my leg.

"Dak," Atrellu said, stopping me as I entered the doorway, "give 'em hell for us."

"Oh, I will."

Outside was a scene of utter carnage. Bomb craters and piles of collapsed structures littered the street. Peeking out beneath the rubble were bodies of all shapes and sizes. Here and there, teams of Chanzig's soldiers deployed batons on some and wrangled others into manacles. Roaming packs of gunmen aimed at anything moving.

Maybe it was the wrong time, but I figured I had to perform a rank-up before I dove into my next suicide mission. The three hours remaining didn't worry me—no, I was more interested in gaining another power to tear Chanzig a new orifice. Leaning on the blackened doorway, I shut my eyes and pulled up the Status Display.

STATUS DISPLAY
PURIFIER RANK: 4
RANK-UP AVAILABLE: Rank 5 (3200 KP required)

Kill Points: 30,000
Genofacturing Points: 127,000

Rank Points: 0

Rank Time: 3 Hours, 28 Minutes, 14 Seconds
Storehouse Time: 3 Hours, 0 Minutes, 0 Seconds

Anima: 180%
Dominion: 0/2

Knowing my time was short, I triggered the rank-up to 5. This left me with a fresh batch of twenty-two standard hours, 153,800 Genofacturing Points, 200% Anima, and the crown jewel . . . another Rank Point.

I hastily tabbed over to the upgrade trees and browsed my options. Seeing as the jig was up and combat had turned to all-out slugfests, I skipped right over the Assassination tree. Modri would have some strong words for me—if I survived. But right now, I didn't need his guidance. I needed strength. Power. With my body as beaten up as it was, the Annihilation tree was my choice.

ANNIHILATION [Tier II] (*3 Rank Points required for Tier III access*)
Indomitable (REQ Rank 1): Further increases skin toughness, bone density, and muscle mass. (1/3)

Overclock (REQ Rank 5): Boosts the response time of fast-muscle fibers, temporarily heightening speed and strength in the desired area. (0/3)

Bloodlust (REQ Rank 3): Accelerates healing through the consumption of humanoid blood plasma. (0/3)

Tooth and Claw (REQ Rank 1): Strengthens nail and teeth density to optimize melee combat. (0/3)

Whether due to my delirious state or some new level of sadism, I considered Bloodlust with *extreme* interest. Nothing would've pleased me more than sucking the red stuff out of Chanzig's troops and using it to fix my body. But I wouldn't get a chance to do that, even if I managed to catch one of his soldiers without their armor on. There were too many of them, and they carried too many guns. Drinking blood wasn't an easy thing to hide.

Tooth and Claw was much the same. Too visible, too ineffective. My injuries had sapped whatever fight I had left in my hands. And Indomitable . . . well, I already had some of that. Beefing myself up wouldn't stop all their bullets.

That left Overclock, an option I hadn't been able to pick due to its prior level requirements. It promised me exactly what I craved: speed and strength. No matter how banged-up I was, I needed that sort of push. I took it with barely a second's hesitation.

With that out of the way, I closed my Status Display.

It was time for blood.

Before I'd even taken five steps outside, a gunship came swooping overhead. It hovered directly above, fixing me in the beam of a high-powered floodlight. Like any good surrendering combatant, I raised my hands and lifted my face toward the light.

It didn't take long for three squads of soldiers to come racing up and begin shouting commands. As I got down on my knees, fingers laced behind my head, a second gunship landed some distance away. Unlike the other gunships, this one was marked with a crimson slash over the cockpit. Some type of commander's ride. It was further distinguished by the fact that it was made for on-world transport use, not space combat, as evidenced by the side panels that slid back to reveal the crew area.

Once that gunship had powered down, an armored man with a velvet beret stepped out and stood at attention. He just waited there as the soldiers that held me at gunpoint shouted more commands: *stand up, walk here, keep your hands up.*

I did as instructed, silently obeying as they led me to the commander's gunship. It took all of my willpower to keep the hatred off my face, but I managed—that is, until I saw Akasha lying inside the gunship's crew area.

She was facedown, her legs bolted to an anchor on the floor and hands bound behind her back with magnetic clamps. Standing around her were even more soldiers, all training their rifles on her head.

"You must be Dak Korasa," the commander said as I approached. He had a clean-shaven, very punchable face that spoke of prep schools and cosmetic surgery. The highborn lilt to his voice was the cherry on top of his dickwad sundae. "My name is Lieutenant Thirmen. I must commend you both on surviving this long. Supreme Chairman Chanzig will be pleased that you kept his seer alive."

"Pull your men out of this place," I said bitterly.

Thirmen smirked. "You will have the opportunity to ask that of the Supreme Chairman soon enough. I simply obey his orders."

"Tell them to pack up . . . now. If you don't, I'll start swinging. Then you'll have to kill me . . . and Chanzig won't be happy about that."

The smirk dropped. "Why do you believe you have such robust bargaining power?"

"Because I know what I'm worth. Especially to him."

Thirmen studied me, seemingly to find out if I was serious. He must've decided I was, because he snapped a gloved hand. The surrounding soldiers retreated from their myriad engagements and made their way to the gunships that sat farther down the street.

"Satisfied?" he said.

"How do you live with yourself?" I replied. "Killing these people. Abusing them. They've done nothing to you."

"I could say the same of my comrades, many of whom you've already slaughtered like hogs."

I tipped my head in acknowledgment. "Withdraw from this tier, and I'll go peacefully."

"Oh, I'm certain you will." Thirmen lifted his wrist-mounted transmitter and gave a few hushed commands. Moments later, the gunships in the distance spooled up and ascended into the dark skies. "Come along, little dog. You have an appointment with the Supreme Chairman."

Much as I wanted to, I didn't resist as the soldiers nudged me onwards with their rifle barrels. They pushed me up and into the troop bay of the gunship, ordering me to sit a few seats away from Akasha. Three of the soldiers worked in tandem to secure my wrists with the same magnetic clamps and buckle my seat strap.

One of the three then started patting me down, beginning with my shoulder. My heart froze in my chest.

"Stop," Thirmen told the soldier with disinterest, boarding along with the remainder of his troops. He sat directly across from me and crossed one leg over the other. "The Supreme Chairman's orders were clear. The fugitive is *not* to be touched without cause until he's been delivered."

The soldier withdrew his hand, plainly confused, but not as confused as I was. What kind of genius prevents their forces from patting down a dangerous, chok'tal-wielding man who's known to be armed? Then it occurred to me: a man worried that his precious alien parasite would find a way to slither out and change hosts. Chanzig had likely never encountered a *real* chok'tal, so he wasn't sure about its properties. For all he knew, it could leave my body and hide in someone else's at will.

Thirmen meshed his hands on his lap as the gunship began to lift off. "Such a clever trick, wearing the face of a dead man. We had to torture four nomads before they told us the truth of what had happened."

I stared at Akasha, trying to keep my face neutral. "Do you realize that you're serving a tyrant?"

"We are serving the *only* source of order on this entire world. The flock should be grateful for the shepherd's stick . . . it keeps them out of wicked pastures."

"You know how many times I've heard that quote from Hegemony bootlickers?"

Thirmen smiled, all but confirming that he, too, had once been a soldier in the Hegemony's ranks. I was beginning to grasp why Chanzig had poached so many of their military members—they were zealous, official, not overly prone to questioning authority. The perfect cogs in his corruption machine.

Sulfuric fumes washed through the gunship's open side panels as we rose higher. Soon the lights of the Dungeon were gone, and we moved through a black, formless ocean.

"You mustn't be too coarse," Thirmen said. "If you keep up this behavior, I doubt Supreme Chairman Chanzig will allow you to view the main event."

I scrunched my brows. "Main event?"

"Oh, yes. Haven't you heard? The Cobalt Seer will have the secrets ripped out of her for all to see. She'll scream until her last breath."

"You're lying," I seethed. "He needs her."

"*Needed* her. The Supreme Chairman has informed me that you've brought him the marvelous treasure he's sought for so long. The same treasure the Cobalt Seer was hired to locate. And having found you, what need does he have for this unruly whore?"

I tried to surge forward, but the soldiers at my sides pinned my shoulders to the seat. As they held me back, I spotted something peculiar . . . something I had only seen on a few of my assigned jobs from Chanzig. Stashed beneath the seats were glossy, rectangular pads with red triangles on them.

Parachutes. Or something like it. The prerecorded safety videos aboard Chanzig's skiffs hadn't been very clear about that part.

"Ah, ah, ah," Thirmen said, wagging a long finger. "Control your urges, little dog. I would simply *hate* having to tell the Supreme Chairman that you care for the seer. He would make her death infinitely more painful."

"Just wait for what I'll do to you."

Thirmen's confident mask slipped—just for a moment, but it was enough. Beneath his bravado and control, he was *scared*. Scared of the bloodstained, valuable prisoner sitting less than a foot away from him.

When his soldiers noticed the crack in his demeanor, he put on a sickening grin.

"You still believe you're in charge," he said. "But you can't do a thing, can you?" Leaning over, he began stroking Akasha's hair. "She's quite a beauty . . . for an alien. How fortunate that the Supreme Chairman only ordered that we keep our hands off of you, and not her."

That was the last straw.

Mentally, I triggered Indomitable. Blood thumped through my skull. My skin bulged beneath the poncho. Bones creaked and ached as they hardened despite numerous fractures. Then I flipped on my new ability, Overclock.

The effects were immediate. Even while shifting my hands to my waist, making the subtlest of movements to avoid suspicion, I felt the explosive force deep within my muscles. The fibers in my flesh contracted with superhuman speed, turning me into something closer to a rabbit than a man. I'd only have one chance at this—it *had* to work.

Using my left foot, I nudged the rifle of the soldier sitting beside me. The stock slid outwards, causing the barrel to topple over and strike Thirmen's knee. He instinctively pulled back from Akasha, looking down at the barrel, then at me, then—

I brought my right foot up to my chest, only to kick across the aisle with vicious force. My heel crunched into Thirmen's nose. The back of his head struck the bulkhead with a terrible *splik* noise.

Before I'd even pulled my foot back, my peripheral vision filled with the details from my HUD. The gunship interior lit up with red frames.

[SLAUGHTER EVENT]
Chanzig's Soldiers (HUMANOID) (3)
Chanzig's Commander (HUMANOID)
Chanzig's Pilots (HUMANOID) (2)
CALCULATING . . .
Combined Estimated Kill Points: 93,500

Thirmen screamed, clutching at his nose and its fountain of blood, but I was already on to my next maneuver. I fished under my poncho and fought to draw the One-Two gun as the soldiers all around me leapt into action. A few managed to seize my upper arms, but I didn't need them—just my wrists.

With speed that boggled even me, I flicked the One-Two to my left and fired under my arm. The blast was concussive, taking out my hearing and nearly breaking my wrist in the same moment. The Overclock was probably the only thing that saved my tendons.

Sizzling armor fragments and blood burst all over the gunship's interior. Still buckled in, the wounded soldier pitched forward and cried out. It wasn't a fatal hit, but close enough.

Suddenly, the gunship swiveled hard. There were no grav-panels in this thing, so *everybody* was flung against their straps—even Akasha, whose body pivoted around the floor's anchor point.

The pilots were on to the brawl.

As I wrestled against the soldier to my right, Thirmen furiously swiped away his own blood and lunged forward. But thanks to Overclock, I was faster. I blocked his hands with my shin, then twisted in my seat, delivering a straight and absurdly powerful sidekick to the man's throat.

He slammed back, choking and gasping.

Just as I turned to the two uninjured foes, however, a rifle butt crashed into my temple. Bone shattered, and within half a second blood began coloring my right eye's vision. But I was too high on the pain to give a damn. Too overloaded with rage for Chanzig and his legions of barbarians.

Letting out a primal scream, I threw myself back toward the soldier who'd gotten me. He tried to rifle-butt me again, but I turned my shoulder in at the last moment, catching his blow and earning nothing but a popped-out joint. He reared back for yet another strike. In that moment of inaction, however, I managed to angle the One-Two up on my lap and fire diagonally up at the soldier's helmet.

The entire top half of his head was obliterated. The corpse slumped over, leaking cerebral fluid all over my lap as I undid my seat buckles.

There was no time to gag, though. The last soldier in Thirmen's squad, seated across from me and to the right, had managed to raise his rifle and aim at my face. He barked an order I didn't quite hear. His finger was on the trigger.

Out of the corner of my eye, I also glimpsed the copilot drawing his sidearm.

This was a fight I couldn't win. Not here, not now. Even if *everything* went to plan, there was no way I could seize this gunship without crashing it. These men were diehard soldiers for Chanzig. They would send us into a nosedive before letting me jack yet another vehicle.

Thirmen, struggling for breath and covered in blood, stared at me with eyes of wrath. "An impressive display, Mr. Korasa . . . but all for naught."

I dropped the empty One-Two on the seat beside me. "Thanks. But I'd like you to tell Chanzig something."

"Pardon me?"

"If he kills Akasha . . . his 'Cobalt Seer' . . . he'll never find what he's looking for. And don't get any ideas about the people down here, either. If you want me, you'll have to come all the way down."

"What in the burning hells are you—"

I never gave Thirmen the chance to finish his thoughts. Ducking my head, I sprang out of my seat and barreled right into the soldier with the rifle. Their gun went off the moment we collided, deafening me once again and ripping holes in the ceiling. The soldier managed to buck me off, sending me sprawling to the floor beside Akasha, but I didn't mind—it gave me the perfect opportunity to snag the one thing I desired: the glossy parachute pack.

Once I had my hands on it, I rolled onto my back and began delivering kick after kick to the two men above me. Thirmen caught a hard one to the jaw, and the soldier had his rifle bashed against his chest repeatedly.

Growling through the helmet, the soldier undid his own buckles and scrambled down after me. He threw a round of punches that thudded against my skull and snapped my collarbone. I swallowed the pain as I swung back, catching his helmet visor with an Overclock-amplified elbow. The silicate visor cracked, but he just kept coming.

Within seconds, he'd managed to pull a knife out of his thigh sheath. He lifted the blade and angled it over my face. I tried to raise my cuffed hand, but he pinned them with his knee. My usable leg was jammed up against the seat. The metal glinted in the light, and—

Gravity flipped as the gunship took yet another dizzying turn. The pilots were trying to shake me up, but it didn't quite work that way— everyone who wasn't buckled in took the brunt. Including the soldier on top of me.

We both slammed up and against the cockpit bulkhead, our tangle of thrashing arms and legs battering the helpless commander beneath us. Then we rolled off, still breathless, slashing and snarling and straining. The soldier's knife flashed again. But before it could land, there was yet another abrupt course correction from the pilots. Only it wasn't a hard turn to the side or a sudden dive.

The crazy bastards *rolled* the gunship.

We slid along the floor, picking up speed as the roll turned to a full-scale loop. But by the time I realized what was happening, it was too late. The soldier screamed, flipping over me and toppling out through the open side door. I grasped at the chairs, the harness loops, even Akasha's anchor—anything to keep me in place—but it was fruitless. My bloodied, bound hands scraped over the polished metal as though it were slicked with oil.

At the last moment, I spied the parachute pack I'd torn out from under the seat. It was teetering on the side door's edge, just about to tumble into the void. With a silent prayer and far too much adrenaline, I snatched it ...

And plummeted down into the howling darkness.

24

T*his* is the fall that I remember the most. Coincidentally, it's also the one I wish I could forget. I plunged through the layers of steam and smog, my body twirling like a leisure-ship gymnast, doing everything in my power to hold fast to the parachute pack. But it was enough of a challenge just to figure out which way was up. The air snapped at me, intermittently freezing and boiling, sometimes clearing enough to reveal flashes of life in the passing tiers.

My only solace was the belated system update, which probably came as a result of the falling soldier hitting something.

ENCOUNTER INCOMPLETE
Kills: 2
Kill Points Awarded: 18,250

RANK-UP AVAILABLE: RANK 6

The seconds went by . . . and by . . . and by, and still my broken hands struggled to open the damn parachute. It would've been easier if my hands hadn't been cuffed, I'm sure. My panic swelled when I detected a change in the *sound* of my fall. A quieting of the wind that buffeted my poncho. In a matter of seconds, I'd hit . . . something.

At last, I dug a nail into the pack's plastic coating. In a state of pure frenzy, I tore at the wrapping, peeling it away in bits and pieces. My hands moved on autopilot, and my mind was far away, already imagining the splat I'd make.

Frantically feeling around the parachute's compressed bundle, I found a latch. A tab. Whatever it was. It was right on the bottom of the bundle, stiffly glued in place. No matter how I explain it here, you'll never understand how much sweat went into pulling that damn thing. Between my wounds, the fear, and the violent force of the fall, it took every last drop of focus. I was screaming with exertion when it finally came undone.

In a flash, fabric inflated and burst out like a white mushroom above me. It kept unfurling, expanding, until—

Oh, shit.

Until that moment, I hadn't remembered the most vital part of any parachute system: one had to be wearing it.

The parachute puffed up and caught the wind, jerking my shoulders even farther out of their sockets as I held on for dear life. My fingers went numb, but I could feel the tiny bones within shrieking for relief. Blood streamed down my quaking arms.

But by Halcius, it had worked. I was slowing. Dropping gracefully into the void. Until I wasn't. Out of nowhere, one side of the parachute crumpled and twisted the wrong way. I lurched to the side, swinging like a fleshy pendulum beneath it. Then the entire thing coiled up on itself, collapsing and sending me back into freefall.

All I could do was scream. It was an unconscious, animal reflex as I headed into death.

Splash.

At first, I had no idea what I'd struck. All I knew was the pain that rocketed up through my feet and into my hips. Disoriented, I assumed I'd turned to jelly from the impact. But after a few seconds of muted sound, sensing the hot and stinging fluid all around me, I realized I was sinking. Drowning, more accurately.

The sudden urge to *breathe* exploded in my mind. Pressure built up in my face and chest, and I began flailing wildly, blindly. Which way was up? Which way was down? Snippets of random memories came back to me, including the words of a swimming tutor on my homeworld: *Note the direction of rising bubbles.* But that advice was useless. There were no bubbles. I looked about, but there was only blackness. A searing, boiling blackness that felt like salt being rubbed into my eyes.

All I knew was that this wasn't water. It was too thick, too abrasive. Already, my lips and nose felt as though they'd caught fire.

With no option and my lungs gradually compressing, I did the only thing I could and began swimming upward with sloppy kicks. What I took to be up, anyway. But within seconds, a thin, billowing force pressed down on me. *The goddamn parachute!* Running on mindless terror, I waved my shackled arms to clear away the obstruction.

My heartbeat was like a steel drum in my ears. Every pore of my flesh felt ready to burst from the pressure. My throat convulsed in greedy spasms, torn between the urge to breathe and the need to block out the sludge that had seeped into my mouth.

A deeper blackness began to overtake me—not in the fluid, but in my own mind. I was fading. Dying. All I could do was kick . . . and kick . . . and kick. Every other body part seemed to throttle down, sending its energy to my legs. Then that eerie peacefulness came over me, almost as though inviting me to end the struggle and take a deep breath. To sink into the universe of nothing.

Just when I was about to open my mouth and drink up my fate, however, I felt the distant thump of my heart. I felt the fear nestled within it. Modri's voice came back to me, reminding me to listen to it with great reverence.

The fear is what keeps us alive.

Clinging to that faint heartbeat, I gave every ounce of effort I had left in me. In fact, I went beyond it. I reached into the dark expanse of the mind, dragging out the same power that had sustained life since the birth of the stars. The bestial urge to live.

Suddenly, the liquid washed over my hair. Something cool tickled at my forehead. *Air.*

I lifted my head back and forced my lips up to the surface. The first sound I made was that of a newborn animal, shrieking out into the unknown above me. My breaths came in long, wailing gulps. Tingling flooded my entire body as the oxygen returned, taking me back from the brink of unconsciousness. Soon enough, other sensations returned—not all of them welcome, such as the chemical burning all over my skin.

But I remained there, treading water and breathing, grateful for the pain. Like my galloping heartbeat, it reminded me that I was still alive. Still kicking. Literally.

After a few seconds of drinking up as much air as possible, I kicked a bit harder and opened my eyes. Well, I tried to. Whatever hellish fluid surrounded me clawed at my eyes, and my cuffed hands were little help in clearing away the burns. Eventually, though, I was able to look around in spite of the pain.

There wasn't much to see. I was floating in some sort of black lake, the surface of which was only visible due to glowing green crystals that poked up through the fluid. These crystals also lent enough light to confirm that I was, indeed, stranded at the very bottom of the Abyss. Above me was the expected curtain of darkness, and although there were several walls far in the distance, all of them were corroded, eaten away by the same caustic sludge that held me prisoner. Floating among the crystals were mounds of discarded metal and rubber.

Things looked bad, but I had to keep myself focused. I ran through a quick analysis of what I knew about this place's shape. Unless the Abyss was shaped like a dome, with a single hole at the top and a wide, wide base, there had to be solid land somewhere near me. Ignorant though I was, I imagined the underground tiers of Chanzig's city to be closer to a cylinder. No matter how large this "lake" was, there had to be a livable area somewhere nearby.

Of course, it was also possible that I'd had the rotten luck to fall even *deeper* than any residential tier, landing in some sort of toxic pit where the Abyss's residents threw their garbage. For all I knew, I could've been at the bottom of a hundred-meter shaft from which nobody returned.

This was my prevailing theory, in fact—until I heard something softly splashing near me.

I turned in the fluid, straining to see between the shadows and my stinging eyes. A large, dark shape was moving closer. A boat, I realized. It was a junky, patched-together collection of metal sheets and rivets, guided by a pair of makeshift oars.

Sitting inside the boat, faintly illuminated by a lighting coil, were two children. A boy and a girl. Both wore baggy plastic suits and had respirators strapped over their mouths. As they came up beside me and leaned over, I noted that their eyes were covered by thick goggles.

"H-Hey," I said, trying to speak without drinking down the sludge. "Can you . . . get me out?"

The boy and girl exchanged a look. Then the boy squatted down near me, waving the lighting coil around to perform a cursory examination.

"Fortress?" he asked.

I tried to lift my hands onto the edge of the boat, but the boy raised his oar to put the kibosh on that plan. "What?"

"Did you work in the fortress?"

"No?"

The boy looked at the girl again, then back to me. "Why are you down here?"

"I'll explain. Just . . . please get me out."

The girl tapped the boy on the shoulder. "Maybe he's been exiled."

"I think so," the boy said. "Should probably just leave him. He'll dissolve in a few hours anyway. Or get eaten by the sludge-squids."

"Wait!" I said as they began to turn away. "I'm not a bad guy. I swear."

The boy giggled. "So what? We're out here to make some coin."

"Doing what?"

"Collecting stuff to sell. Duh." To prove this point, he reached into the boat's junk pile and held up a half-melted circuit board. "This baby's gonna make us some good, good coin."

"We're already gonna be late," the girl said, sighing.

"If you get me out," I said, struggling not to slip back under the surface, "I can get you coin. I promise."

This seemed to pique the boy's interest. "How?"

"Whatever you want," I said.

"Got something to barter?"

"No, but—"

The boy just made a *hmph* sound and turned to the girl. "Let's get back to the hub. Told you nothing good ever lands in here."

They both shuffled around in the boat, returning to their original rowing positions.

Despite my manners, I let out a growl and hooked my hands over the side of the boat. The vessel tilted slightly, provoking an immediate shout from the boy.

"You want me to beat you with the oar?" he called.

"Just take me," I pleaded. "I can—"

I was halted when the girl climbed over to me and began prodding at my magnetic wrist-clamps with a stick.

"Look at this," she said with mild curiosity. "Guess he really is an exile."

The boy brought the lighting coil back up and took a closer look at my restraints. "*Ooooh*, well, aren't these nice? 'Member when papa found cuffs like these?"

"Yep, yep," the girl said. "We ate *good*."

Sensing their strange yet very convenient interest in the cuffs, I decided to play my hand.

"If you get me out of here, I'll let you keep them."

"I dunno," the boy said. "You seem a little dangerous. We shouldn't be taking random exiles in our boat."

I sighed. "I'm not an exile. Just someone that ran into Chanzig."

The girl let out a gasp. "You *know* the Chairman?"

"Uh . . . sort of?"

"Wow. What's his face look like?"

Luckily, before I got drawn into the girl's infinite-question game, the boy waved his hand to cut her off. He looked at me with discernment. "You promise you aren't gonna try to kill us? And we get to keep the cuffs?"

I nodded enthusiastically. "Anything I've got is yours."

The boy glanced at the girl sidelong. "What do you think?"

She hummed. "He's got the cuffs on. We can still slit his throat if he starts getting mean."

It hadn't occurred to me until that moment, but there was a very real chance that these kids were *dangerous*. After all, they were residents of the Abyss—the worst of the worst people, as Atrellu had said. What was stopping them from just killing me and cutting the cuffs off with a rusty blade? Nothing, really.

But all of these concerns went out the window when the boy offered me his hand. "Welcome aboard, weirdo. Don't touch none of our stuff."

As it turns out, it's easy to avoid touching stuff when your fingers look like partially skinned vegetables. The "lake's" battery acid–like fluids had left every patch of my skin red and peeling. Even as I sat in the back of the kids' dinky boat, hissing with every dab of the towel they'd given me, I could feel the caustic brew chewing away at my soft tissues. If not for the 200% Anima, I can guarantee my eyes and tongue would've been meaty slush.

The only thing that kept my mind off the agony was Akasha. I couldn't stop thinking of her. After the little stunt I'd pulled on the gunship, who knew what they would do to her in custody? Even if Chanzig presumed I was dead—fat chance, since he knew what the chok'tal could do—he would make her pay for her role in all of this. And if he presumed I was still alive, he would torture her to extract every last drop of information she'd gained in my presence.

Looking back, I wasn't even sure why I'd been so stupid aboard the gunship. My original plan had been to get to the fortress and take out Chanzig in the flesh. But seeing Thirmen touch her like that had set off a hidden trigger deep inside of me. There was a certain kinship between her and I . . . an undeniable link that had been forged by our shared connection to the chok'tal. More than that, I had drawn her into this mess. I'd gone out of my way to make her a fugitive. I had to make it right.

But for the moment, I had to keep my head low and focus on what I *could* do, not what I *wanted* to do. Trying to climb my way up to the surface and assault Chanzig's fortress alone was, as Atrellu had said, an impossible scenario.

That being said, it was only impossible because of the current circumstances. The security network that governed Chanzig's automated defenses was my number-one hurdle. The number-two hurdle, of course, was a lack of manpower. In order to take the fortress, I'd need the help of everybody down here. The ones willing to pick up a gun and spill blood, anyway. But what would make them risk everything to fight?

As I mulled it over, I kept coming back to the same pipe dream I'd had in the Dungeon: I needed to shut down the security network. If I could somehow knock out the turrets and missiles and everything else that guarded the surface, I stood a fighting chance at marshaling the underground population and creating a certified rebellion.

After all, Chanzig *definitely* didn't have enough boots on the ground to stop a full-scale uprising. Atrellu had mentioned that the largest barrier to an uprising was the greed and resentment baked into this place. Each tier hated the ones below it, and the people had been conditioned—probably over hundreds of years—to accept their place or take the punishment. What they needed was spirit. A sense of passion that assured them they *could* take back their lives from Chanzig.

And maybe, just maybe, I could be that spirit.

It was a lofty ambition, especially given my present issues, but it seemed right to me. It was the only thing that could cure my guilt from what I'd done. Intentionally or not, *I* had brought Chanzig's forces to these tiers, the same way I had gotten Akasha trapped in my schemes. The least I could do to heal this broken society was give it the kind of hope it had never known. I could use the chok'tal for good, feeding it with the blood of the wicked.

This line of logic did startle me a bit—it sounded eerily similar to the rationale used by dictators all across the 'verse—but I trusted I had the heart to carry out my mission without slipping into madness. Perhaps there *was* a reason the chok'tal had found me.

That reason was justice.

While pondering all this chok'tal business, I suddenly remembered that I'd kept Modri shushed for far, far too long. I cringed a bit as I mentally woke him up.

"Look what you've done now," he said, not missing a beat. *"Covered in cancer gunk, saved by a pair of kids who probably still piss in their beds."*

Oh, you would've done better? I thought in reply.

"Purifier, I wouldn't even have been within ten systems of this shit. You know how maddening it is, just watchin' your stupid ass make mistake after mistake?"

What do you want me to do? Apologize for shushing you . . . again?

"I'm over that. Y'know, I'm still thinkin' over the news you got from the doctor."

It took me a moment to remember that, even while shushed, Modri and all the other minds inside of the chok'tal still had the ability to view my consciousness. It was voyeuristic, to say the least.

So, what's your take? I thought.

"My take? Probably the same as yours. You got screwed by Chanzig."

That's it?

"What the hell's it matter? You're stranded at the bottom of a living toilet. We've gotta figure out how to get you alive and off this world . . . fast."

Off the world? We're not done here yet.

"Listen, Purifier . . . it's well and good that you wanna kick Chanzig's teeth in, and maybe even help some of these poor lil' peasants . . . but you've gotta wake up. This is the real world, and the chok'tal don't give a damn about you being a good person. You just need Kill Points."

I gritted my teeth, almost taken aback by what I was hearing. *You were the one who said I should figure out what the chok'tal's true purpose is. Where am I going to get answers if it's not on this planet?*

"Just do what I did for a little bit. Head off-world, start a war with some tribes, turn the survivors into your mercenaries. Then you can come back and take names."

I'm not going to murder people just to make an army.

"Suit yourself. Guess my advice don't matter much . . . seeing as I've gotta put up with your incompetence whether I like it or not."

That's the spirit, I thought, smirking.

"So, what's your big plan?"

First, I get these cuffs off. Then shower. Then I find whoever's got the security network access down here.

"That peacekeeper prick said it was a rumor."

Better than nothing. Besides, I'm already down here.

Modri sighed. *"Alright, we'll do it your way. At least you were smart enough to take Overclock. But we've gotta discuss your next rank-up . . . because you ain't gettin' far without genofacturing."*

Honestly, it hadn't even occurred to me during my last rank-up that access to genofacturing products was even an option. But Modri was right: It had become unlocked the moment I hit Rank 5. And as much as I resented his brusque nature, he had been an efficient and successful Purifier. His advice on upgrades was worth taking.

"Home, sweet home," the boy said suddenly, plucking me out of my thoughts.

I looked over to see that a "shoreline" of some kind was now within viewing range. It was more like a seawall, lined with drainage ports that presumably kept the sludge-lake from filling up too high. All along the shore were lanterns that glowed a sickly yellow and illuminated clouds of tumbling fumes. There were also dozens of other scavenging boats, most powered by steam or unstable, irradiated cores that dangled off their backs.

Deeper inland, there were signs of life: thumping music, moving bodies, blots of neon and open flame.

I looked at the children. "This a city or something?"

"Not *a* city," the girl said, laughing. "*The* city."

The boy nodded. "Papa used to say that if you aren't in the city, you're in *Naraka*."

"It's some old alien word for hell," the girl added.

"Naraka, huh?" I said.

Again, the boy gave a nod. "You know, the zone that's outside the city. We call it Naraka. The *real* bad stuff happens there."

"What happened to your father?" I asked.

"Dead," the girl said flatly. "He went into Naraka."

The boy chuckled. "That idiot."

I had no way to know, of course, but I had a sneaking suspicion that the man I sought—the one who had access to Chanzig's security network—would be found in Naraka. And if I was going to go in there, I had to be ready . . . or I'd just be another dead idiot.

25

After the children had guided their boat into its assigned berth, a few scraggly-looking people with rags for clothing came running up. As it turned out, these people were the children's *hired hands*—yes, hired by the children. They bowed to their young masters and immediately set about offloading the junk the kids had collected, making sure to offer a few forced smiles here and there. Once they'd managed to pile all the scrap onto a squeaking cart, they proceeded to rinse the whole load down with buckets of water and then take off running to who-knows-where.

"Hard to find good help these days," the girl said, practically snorting with disgust as their "employees" faded into the crowd. "Bunch of freeloaders."

"Gotta respect a kid with ambition," Modri put in.

These two seem like little psychopaths, I mentally replied.

"I'd call 'em entrepreneurs."

Semantics.

"Hey . . . it doesn't look like an easy life down here. They're doing what they have to."

Yeah, I said, wishing I didn't agree. *But that's what Chanzig's done to these people. You can't see this and think I should still flee the planet without doing something.*

"Meh. I've seen worse."

I just rolled my eyes.

Sad as it was to see, the children weren't alone in their little business. Similar scenes took place all along the dockside. Crews pulled up with their loads of junk, and skeletal laborers who looked a few pounds away from death helped to secure the cargo and send it off into the city. It seemed that their entire economy was indeed run on the scraps from the tiers above.

Then again, what else could they extract or find of any value? There wasn't even any soil for growing crops. The "ground," if you can call it that, was some mysterious mixture of rusted metal and mineral crusts. Maybe this place had once been Chanzig's family mine. Maybe it had been a massive torture pit. The end results were the same.

After berating one of the slow-moving workers responsible for hauling the boat out of the sludge, the children whistled at me like I was a dog. They then led me into the hustle and bustle of the downtown district, each holding one of my arms as though I were their prisoner. They seemed almost glad to be doing it, as though a captive was a symbol of status. And down here, maybe it was.

It's hard to the describe the Abyss. Every face was different, individualized through the processes of mutilation and mutation. Some passersby had metal rings grafted into their foreheads and chins, while others had an extra hand, scales, or one of infinite other genetic oddities. The radiation that seeped up from below had created something approximating a new species.

But the people themselves weren't what made the Abyss so bizarre. It was the culture they had built. To a surface-dweller like me, it seemed clear that they had *some* type of organization and moral compass—but I can't say a word about what it was. Everywhere I looked, there was some fresh and incomprehensible sight: people hollering about knockoff body implants, columns of cult members marching past one another, illegal animal hybrids pacing around in levitating cages. At one point, I even spied a disembodied brain mounted on mechanical spider legs trying to locate a strip joint. The entire downtown area was like a surreal, never-ending circus put on for the amusement of absolutely nobody. And amid all that insanity, no one paid much attention to my chewed-up skin or the fact that I was being led about by a pair of kids. I was small potatoes.

After several minutes of navigating this carnival of debauchery, my "saviors" led me into a two-story club near the main square. Hanging above its door, spelled out in letters made from scavenged junk, was the name SIN4LIFE. Classy, no? A flickering screen claimed that it offered "Girls Guns Gore Guys Grub Goodstuffz."

This eclectic range of services drew an eclectic range of customers. Just outside its door were groups of all sorts: drunkards, half-machine merchants, dancers, fiends, and . . . a man feeding batteries to the mouth-shaped tumor on his neck.

But the children just barged right through the gathering. To my surprise, most of the club's patrons even made way for them out of deference—or was it fear?

Inside, it was more smoke than air. Not just one sort of smoke, either. The faded lights revealed a multicolored haze, its hues and density warping by the second as people puffed their drugs of choice. Bone-rattling, otherworldly tunes thumped out of speakers installed directly below my feet. While shouldering my way through the crowd, I felt nothing but sweat, gun barrels, and leather. No wonder Modri began asking me to hang out here and let him experience some "good times" through my body. Another temporary shush for him.

Fortunately, this madness didn't last long. After crossing the main floor and taking a few turns down a side passage, the three of us arrived at a bulky-looking door set into the concrete like a bunker entrance. Judging by the welding marks, it had been opened without permission several times . . . probably with explosives.

The girl reached up and banged the flat of her fist on the door.

Seconds later, the peephole in the door slid open. A pair of wide, bloodshot eyes with yellow pupils appeared there. "Yes, youths?"

"Need your lock-popper, Kumil," the boy said before lifting my arm. "We found *this* out there today."

Kumil's yellow eyes flicked over me. "I see . . . and what are you gonna do with it?"

"The popper?" the boy said.

"No . . . *it*. This body."

"Him," I corrected. "I'm a human, not a couch."

"Down here," Kumil said, laughing, "you're whatever a seller says you are."

I glared at the children. "I'm *not* for sale. You'd better honor our deal."

The boy seemed oddly disappointed by my words, but eventually sighed and nodded in Kumil's direction. "He's right . . . had a deal. We're just selling the clamps, not the body."

Kumil narrowed his eyes, appearing even more serpentine. "You're certain? I know a chap down in Naraka . . . always looking for some fresh bones to chop." He studied me further. "Or maybe you could lease him out for bloody-knuckle work. He looks like a bruiser."

"Just the clamps," the boy said, plainly wishing it were otherwise.

"Suit yourselves. Your wasted profits."

"Don't remind us," the girl groaned.

"If I pop those clamps off," Kumil said, "I expect thirty percent from the sale."

The boy folded his arms. "Twenty."

"Twenty-five," Kumil countered.

"Twenty-two."

"My lucky number. You have a deal."

Before I could even assess what had just happened, the peephole slammed shut, a few chains clinked, a series of bolts came undone, and the door squealed open.

Kumil stood before us in all his . . . glory. That's the only word that comes to mind, because I'm certain that in Kumil's world, he was indeed glorious. It's just a shame that most sane individuals wouldn't agree with his sense of taste.

You see, Kumil had taken genetic modification to such an extreme that I couldn't discern his birth species. Those piercing yellow eyes were only an appetizer. His head was covered not with hair, but rows of small, gasping "gills" that each seemed to possess their own mind. Rather than ears, he had bundles of cartilage and wire—some sort of hearing amplifier, I guess. Grafted skin of various origins and textures covered his neck, hands, and face. All of this was bundled up in a luxurious, blue satin bathrobe . . . and nothing else. I can only assume his lack of footwear was an attempt to show off his webbed feet.

"Please, do come in," Kumil said, offering a quarter-bow and stepping aside to usher us in with pizzazz. He smiled wide to reveal a mouth full of wriggling teeth that were closer to a whale's than a human's. "I hope you don't mind the, ah, mess . . ."

It didn't take long to spot the mess in question. Kumil's cramped little workshop was packed with barrels of ice and nitrogen bricks, all of them providing refrigeration for severed limbs. Streams of curdled blood ran along the tiles and into drainage grates. Outside this charming storage situation, he also had a variety of blades, laser-scalpels, and other "fun" tools hanging on the walls. I didn't even want to know what the human-sized, liquid-filled chambers were for.

"*So*," Kumil continued, scooping up a half-empty martini glass as he headed back toward his instruments, "you believe the popper will work?"

The boy nodded as he manhandled me toward a dented metal table. "It looks like the same kinda clamps as last time, so yeah."

"How often do you two do this?" I asked in annoyance, unable to help myself.

"What? Rescue dum-dums?" the girl asked.

The boy giggled.

"Alright, I believe my latest acquisition shall suffice!" Kumil said, returning with a small, pistol-like device that had a suspiciously long needle at the muzzle. Its fuel cell vibrated incessantly as he toyed with the trigger. "My first attempt with it, no less. How nice to finally have a test subject."

Each child held a different wrist, apparently believing they could actually subdue me if I decided not to play along. I decided to let them roll with it.

"Easy with that thing," I growled at Kumil. "It'll just get them off, right?"

"Naturally," Kumil said as he knelt down and searched for something on the cuffs.

"Yeah, don't go exploding them or whatever," the boy said. "And don't mess up his hands, neither. Because I don't want no blood getting in the lock. Not like that other time."

I just sighed and bit my tongue, knowing that my only two options were to play along and risk a hand injury . . . or go into combat mode, where I'd probably wind up forced to maim or even kill two children. Option two was probably easier, but I wasn't enough of a monster to justify it.

Having apparently found the magical spot he was looking for on the manacles, Kumil inserted the "popper's" needle. Then, with devilish glee, he activated the tool.

The needle began vibrating so fiercely I could feel it in my wrists, even through the cuffs' thick alloy. I did my best not to move, mostly out of fear that one wrong twitch would cause the supersonic needle to slice my hand off. And let me just note, it was *not* easy to sit still. The needle sounded like a kettle about to explode from pressure. It whined louder, louder, and louder . . .

And then stopped. Giggling, Kumil shut off the popper and retracted its needle. A thin wisp of smoke curled up from the locking hole.

"So . . . it's done?" I asked.

By way of response, Kumil tapped on the joint at the center of the cuffs. Both locking rings popped open, and I wasted no time in plucking my hands free.

"That's gonna fetch a *nice* price," the girl said, marveling at the cuffs.

Kumil set them down on the table. "Little bit of acid damage, but nothing we can't buff out."

I glanced awkwardly at the three strangers. "Am I free to go now?"

"Sheesh, I already forgot you were here," the boy said, curling his lip. "What are you waiting for? Applause?"

Rubbing my tender wrists, I stood and stared at the children. "I'm waiting for some information."

"That wasn't part of the deal," the girl said.

"I'm looking for someone," I said, ignoring her. "Rumor is that they have access to Chanzig's security network."

All three of the Abyss dwellers burst out laughing.

"What?" I said. "I'm serious."

Kumil placed a semi-clawed hand on my shoulder. "Friend, here's what you need to know . . . There are no such things as 'rumors' in the Abyss. If you hear it, it's true. But trying to find the source of that rumor . . . well, it's like looking for the end of a rainbow."

I stared at Kumil's hand until he pulled it away. "What about you, then? You heard of a guy like the one I mentioned?"

"Possibly. But you wouldn't want to go looking for them."

"Why not?"

"No offense, but I don't believe you're the type to succeed." He studied me from head to toe, all but scoffing. "Even if you didn't currently look like a bag of half-chewed meat . . ."

I frowned. "Let me guess. This guy's somewhere in Naraka."

"Where did this one come from?" Kumil asked, looking to the children with delight. "He's so confident for an outsider. I like that pizzazz."

The boy hardened his eyes. "Kumil's too nice to say it, so I will. You wouldn't make it in Naraka."

"I just need a place to start my search," I said.

"We don't like to toss around names down here," Kumil explained. "It's just bad for business."

It took all my restraint to avoid choking a name out of the gene-twisting weirdo. "Listen, if you give me something I can use, I'll pay you for it."

"Pay? Hmm? What can you offer?"

"Naraka's a dangerous spot, right?"

Kumil nodded, humming with anticipation.

"Well, I'll probably get my hands dirty. So, if I find something shiny, it's yours."

The girl leaned against a nearby vat of chemicals. "They'll eat you alive. Naraka ain't nice and courteous. Y'know, like *this* city."

It was mind-boggling that they considered this place *better* than somewhere else. Maybe I really was being overconfident about my ability to navigate the underworld . . . of the underworld. But I wouldn't back down now. After all the blood, bullets, and burns I'd endured since getting the chok'tal, I felt ready for just about anything.

"Let us break this down a tad . . . slower for you," Kumil said, smiling so warmly it *almost* seemed like he wasn't calling me stupid. "The Abyss used to be a massive, thriving area. Sort of. Well, thriving may be too strong a—"

"Get to it," I growled.

Kumil raised his hands in supplication. "Things in the Abyss weren't perfect, but they also weren't hellish. When times became truly desperate and the rations stopped arriving, however, certain . . . bad forces began claiming territory. The peacekeepers from the upper tiers came down to keep things under control, but by that point, it was too late. All they could do was establish a safe zone with the rule of law."

"This city, you mean."

"Yes, very good." Kumil did a mocking little clap that I'm sure he thought was genuine. "And everything outside that zone of control, the area the peacekeepers *couldn't* save, became—"

"Naraka," the boy said bitterly.

"Alright, fine," I said. "So, Naraka is run by cartels and freaks. Got it."

Kumil clicked his tongue. "Actually, the freaks are here in the city—and quite a pleasant group, if you ever get to know them."

I sighed. "The point is, Naraka is dangerous. Violent. I already got all that from these two *swindlers*." The children were taken aback by my choice of phrase. "I'm offering you a deal. You give me a spot to check out, and I'll come back with stuff."

"Whose stuff?" Kumil said, wary.

"Does it matter? If I see something shiny, I'll nab it for you."

"Ah, I see. You wish to give me stolen goods from psychopathic butchers."

"Basically."

Kumil grinned so wide I could see all three of his tongues. "As I said previously, I don't know *precisely* where to find the man you're seeking. But I know some . . . who know others . . . who used to know others . . . that had heard of this character."

"Do we have a deal, then?"

"Of course. But what if you don't come back?"

"Oh, I will." I moved closer to Kumil and stared into his yellow eyes. "But if you try to set me up, and I survive it, you'll wish I didn't return."

The children just chuckled.

"Hey," the boy said, "if they drop his corpse around here, save us the teeth. I'm making necklaces as a side hustle."

Oh, kids.

Half an hour later, I found myself standing outside SIN4LIFE, staring up into the smog that blotted out any hope of sunlight. The only things in my possession were my (destroyed) clothes, the chok'tal, and the name of a place in Naraka. The last was the most important. Kumil wasn't what I'd term a "trustworthy" fellow, but he did seem to know his way around the Abyss. He'd even drawn me a map on some coffee-stained paper. According to its directions, the gate out of the city and into Naraka was just a short walk away. From there, I needed to find my first target: a guy he'd called "Sudamo."

But before I headed out, there was some housekeeping work to do. And by housekeeping, I mean upgrades for the chok'tal, of course. Time to call out the housekeeper.

Hey, Modri, I thought, *you there?*

"*Always here. There's nowhere else to go.*"

Comforting.

"*So, you really gonna head into that Naraka place? You haven't even got a gun.*"

Yeah, about that. I've been doing some thinking about rank-ups . . .

"*Really? Why start now? You seem to love wingin' it and disregardin' my good advice.*"

I groaned. *I was chewing over what we talked about on that ship. You know, about saving up Genofacturing Points. What do you think about power-leveling?*

"*Power-what?*"

It's a term from simverse games, okay? Again, purely academic knowledge on my end. The point is, it's a method where you disregard everything except levels. Or, in our case, rank-ups. Just try to get as many as possible.

Modri considered it for a time. "*What about it?*"

Well, so far, I've been gaining a ton of Kill Points and delaying rank-ups as long as possible. It's given me a lot of points, but I've got a feeling I'll need to be a lot stronger to take on Chanzig directly. Might not have time to keep putting off the upgrades.

"*Duh,*" Modri said. "*The system's designed for you to scale up as you move along. Take out one or two idiots, do a rank-up, rinse and repeat. You jumped into this shit headfirst. No wonder you've got a stash of Genofacturing Points.*"

I've got a plan for that. Gonna make myself some gear.

"Finally . . . but why are you askin' about power-levels or whatever?"

I want your input, I explained. *Seems to me that I have enough Geno-facturing Points for the time being. And when I go up against Chanzig, I'll probably earn a few hundred thousand, depending on how long the battle goes, so I'll stockpile plenty there . . . But what I really* need *is the power to fight them in the first place. You know, good upgrades and all that. It seems like Naraka is the perfect power-leveling zone to get those.*

"Huh? How do you figure that?"

Well, it sounds like everybody there is a piece of trash. Murderers, thieves, monsters.

"Y'mean everybody's a target."

I half-nodded as I walked through the crowd, still uncomfortable with using such overt language. *The point is, there should be lots of individual groups that want to kill me. And I was thinking, after I take down one group, I could pause, do my rank-up, and move on to the next one. That way I could snag a bunch of new upgrades and be ready for Chanzig.*

"Well, ain't that weird . . ."

What?

"You're finally thinkin' like a Purifier," Modri said, almost cackling. "It's all about the points, chief. Forget honor, forget mercy . . . Points."

The reasoning struck me as cold, sterile, and yet . . . accurate.

How do I know when to stop, though? I asked.

"You never stop. That's what it means to have the chok'tal in you."

No, I mean . . . the power-leveling thing. What's too high a rank before I fight Chanzig?

"Just get those kills and keep me online so I can coach you," Modri said. "No need to worry till you're hitting a hundred thousand and up for KP requirements. But by that point, you'll be a walkin' death machine."

And that's a good thing?

"You bet. Just get your next rank-up in, buy Genofacturing, and get started on makin' your gear. Then we'll head to Naraka and wake those pricks up."

26

Although I'd gotten fairly comfortable performing rank-ups while out in public, the vibe of the Abyss made me doubt that I could get away with it unscathed here—especially when I planned to spend a decent amount of time working on genofacturing, which was sure to be attention-drawing. This being the case, I opted to buy a room at a hotel that seemed closer to a morgue.

The humanoid fabrique serving as a receptionist didn't bat an eye at my burnt skin or numerous bloodstains. The only thing they cared about was payment. And seeing as I didn't have any hard currency on me, my payment came in the form of bartering. The receptionist took my beaten-to-hell poncho *and* my boots. These items, they claimed, were worth a total of two hours in the hotel's worst room.

Well, good enough, I supposed. All I really needed was a locking door, four walls, a shower, and enough space to engage in genofacturing.

That was exactly what I got. Unless, of course, you count the mold growing on the floors or the weird stains on the mattress. Oh, or the tar-like shampoo in the shower. But enough about that. It was time to get down to business.

First up, I dropped into my Status Display menu and activated Rank 6.

STATUS DISPLAY
PURIFIER RANK: 6
RANK-UP NOT AVAILABLE (12,800 KP required)

Kill Points: 0
Genofacturing Points: 165,560

Rank Points: 1

Rank Time: 21 Hours, 59 Minutes, 59 Seconds
Storehouse Time: 3 Hours, 0 Minutes, 0 Seconds

Anima: 220%
Dominion: 0/3

Finally, I had three whole Dominion slots. I couldn't envision a scene where I had to use all three of my current abilities, but sooner or later, I'd be glad for the extra help. Who knew what power I might gain through upgrades farther down the line?

Alas, there wasn't much use in contemplating that right now. I already had my heart set on Modri's pick, Genofacturing, which sat near the top of the Mutation upgrade tree.

Genofacturing I (REQ Rank 5): Enables creation of a Genofacturing Spore and all Stage-I products. *Does not require a Dominion slot.*

With zero hesitation, I dropped my Rank Point into the upgrade. Easy. It was a bit frustrating to see that I still required two more Rank Points in Mutation to access the next set of upgrade choices—mainly because I also needed two in every other upgrade tree. In short, I was digging a lot of holes, none of them very deep.

Sooner or later, I'd need to carefully plan out my upgrade investment plan. A bad or careless choice could come to haunt me when ranks and points became scarcer. Even now, I sensed that every upgrade would eventually play a vital role in my success or failure—even if its only role was to serve as a foundation for better abilities. After all, if the chok'tal worked like most other recreational games, there would be some over-the-top, spectacular upgrades that required a high rank and specialized path to reach. Waffling around with random picks to suit my current encounters was probably fine for the being time, but I needed to start thinking about long-term optimization. How did I want to "play" this brutal game? What would I excel at?

The questions swirled as I dropped my Status Display and sat on the bed.

"So, Modri," I said, feeling secluded enough to speak out loud, "what do I do?"

"You should know the drill by now," he replied. *"Just focus hard on the idea of a Genofacturing Spore. Try to visualize a little cube on the floor in front of you."*

"You're joking, right?"

"Why would I be jokin' about this?"

"Well, for starters, where's it coming from? Am I gonna give birth to it through my—"

"Don't be stupid. You vomit it out."

I just stood there for a moment, unsure if I'd misread his sense of humor.

"I'm not kiddin' with you," Modri added. *"It sucks to choke it up, but once you've made that damn cube, you just gotta take it everywhere you go. I mean, you can make another, but I doubt you'll wanna ..."*

Just based on his description, I was already nauseous. But more than that, I was confused.

"You left me your Genofacturing Spore back in the jungle," I said. "But wasn't it, you know, bound to you? Locked with your genes? You said that nobody could use another Purifier's genofacturing stuff."

Modri made a *tsk-tsk* noise. *"I said nobody could use the genofactured* products. *The spore don't belong to nobody. You could've used mine, I could've used another guy's. But, uh, normies—the non-Purifiers—can't use 'em for much of anything. They just look like blobs."*

"So, in other words, if I'd been able to get that spore back from Liura ... I wouldn't have to vomit one up right now."

"Basically."

"Fantastic." Yet another reason to detest Chanzig and his legions. "Is it gonna fit out of my mouth? I mean, I saw the other one, and it was—"

"It'll grow once you spit it out," Modri interrupted. *"Just stop talkin' and get to hurlin'. You're wastin' too much time."*

Every single word Modri uttered made me question my decision to actually take part in genofacturing. I mean, did I need it? Probably. But did I need it *now*, and need it bad enough to eject a large spore from my own body? That was harder to decide. After all, if I royally nailed this whole "shut down the security network" thing, there was a good chance I could just loot Chanzig's vault and get my own hand-me-down spore for free ...

Oh, screw it, I thought. It was time to stop procrastinating and avoiding discomfort. After all, I was a Purifier now. I'd spent the better part of my life avoiding any unnecessary pain, even to the point of requesting anesthetics for having my blood drawn. If I wanted to survive, I needed to shed those old habits. I needed to embrace the suck.

Full of machismo but not sure why, I mentally engaged the intention to create a Genofacturing Spore.

The results were immediate. Deep in my stomach, I felt a cold, aching pit, almost as though I'd drunk too much water. Then the pit moved. It wriggled up through my guts, growing in size and tickling my intestinal walls along the way. I started to cough involuntarily. But that created a problem. You see, coughing evolved as a way to remove objects from the throat. And when a human throat senses that an obstacle is getting harder to remove, the natural response is to cough even harder—and then start panicking.

In a matter of seconds, I was a red-faced, choking mess, rolling around on my bed and punching my own stomach to get the damn spore free. Each time I tried to inhale, I sensed the hard, ever-expanding blockage. All I could do was pray as I flopped about like a fish, my air winding down and torso throbbing.

Then, just as the tunnel vision set in, the spore surged up into my mouth. I could feel it squirming, probing around my tongue and teeth. One of its delicate little tendrils swept over my uvula. And *that* was the exit ticket.

I'll spare you the details of what happened and skip right to the end result.

The Genofacturing Spore sat on the floor below me, covered in slime I won't even attempt to describe. While staring at it, wet-eyed and traumatized, I found myself rocked by a wave of dizziness. I sank down onto the bed and flopped back.

"Ah, good old post-spore syndrome," Modri said.

"Huh?"

"Yeah, it's like givin' birth. You just spat out around six thousand calories."

"I *what?*"

"What'd you think? You just made it out of fairy dust and magic? C'mon, Purifier, this is science. Calories out needs calories back in."

"You couldn't have told me this . . . before I did it? I feel like I'm dying."

"You are. Well, starvin' is more accurate."

"What the hell am I going to eat? I already sold my poncho and boots to get this room. And I'm *not* working my body on the corner."

While on the topic of my body, I decided to lift up my shirt and see if there was any visible consequence to the caloric drain. Indeed, there was. Before the chok'tal, I'd been on the skinny side, though with a few pounds hanging on my hips. Now, I was practically a twig. I could see the curvature of my hipbones and all my abdominal muscles. No wonder my healing probably hadn't been as proficient lately. There were no excess calories in my system, so the chok'tal had been giving me just enough resources to stay alive.

This Genofacturing Spore had been the last push. A significant one, at that. Given all the running, jumping, shooting, and general worrying I'd done over the past few days, I was probably deep in caloric debt. If I wanted to do anything other than enter hibernation mode, I'd need to eat—and fast.

"I sure hope the guys in Naraka have some fried stuff," I said as a migraine kicked in. "Maybe shawarma . . . or chocolate . . ."

"*Stay focused,*" Modri said. "*This is what genofacturing is for.*"

"What do you mean?"

"*Just trust me and get started, would you?*"

"Oh, fine." Although it was the last thing I wanted to do, I sat up and moved the plushy spore onto the bed. Various fluids came gushing out of it. "Gross."

"*It'll keep expanding for an hour or so. Ignore it. It'll work normally, even if it takes a while to heat up.*"

"So . . . all these 'products' will come out of this little spore?"

"*Yep.*"

I stared at it, skeptical. "But it doesn't make sense. You said Guide and the chok'tal don't like to waste energy . . . but this thing has enough internal energy to run for millions of years. And if I just keep making spores, that means the chok'tal has to waste energy. And that means—"

"*You heard your girlfriend,*" Modri cut in. "*All of this was made by beings from another dimension.*"

"So?"

"*So, you need to stop usin' your science brain . . . and start usin' your badass brain. No think, just make.*"

"Whatever you say . . ."

"*You know what you're doin' here?*"

"I think so. I got the prompt to use yours back in the jungle."

"*Show me what you've got, then.*"

Remembering what I'd done last time, I studied the spore until a green box labeled it GENOFACTURING SPORE. Only now, there was an additional option listed next to it:

ACTIVATE?

Naturally, I did.

A screen similar to the Status Display appeared, only this one didn't consume my entire consciousness. Instead, it floated in place above the spore, much like a holopane for anybody with the proper implant. Fittingly, the top of the screen read GENOFACTURING SPORE. Below it was a message and a list of menus.

[*Stage-I Products Available for Genofacturing*]
Genofacturing Points: 165,560

Product Categories:
Armor
Blades
Pistols
Shotguns
Rifles
Light Machine Guns
Shields
Utility Tools
Rations
Ammunition
Explosives
Tonics
View All Stage-I Products

Hot damn. Despite my fatigued state, a rush ran through me. For the first time, I'd be able to put my formerly useless Genofacturing Points to good use. Judging by the list of categories, I wouldn't be starving (or shoeless) much longer. In fact, all of my material concerns faded. It was like I had an infinite resource machine—provided I had the points, of course. It suddenly made sense why Modri had pushed so hard to acquire this upgrade and start crafting.

Although I was tempted to scroll through each category, marveling at all my options, I knew it would be a naïve and disappointing decision. Every game, no matter how robust, always started players off with the most basic, borderline primitive selections for crafting. It was best to just rip off the bandage by doing "view all."

So that's what I did. But to my (pleasant) surprise, my options went far beyond making a sharp stick or an intestine-based sock.

Genofacturing Points: 165,560

[All Stage-I Products]
Select individual products for further details.

Armor:
Keratin Arm Covering Pair (6500 GP)
Keratin Boots (8000 GP)
Keratin Chestplate (10,000 GP)
Keratin Glove Pair (4000 GP)
Keratin Helmet (12,000 GP)
Keratin Leg Covering Pair (8000 GP)

Blades:
Spinal Knife (10,000 GP)

Pistols:
Lucky Squeeze (40,000 GP)
Plopper (25,000 GP)

Shotguns:
Plaque Spitter (60,000 GP)

Rifles:
Clean Exit (50,000 GP)

Shields:
Bone Buckler (35,000 GP)

Utility Tools:
Bile Salve (5000 GP)
Cartilage Carabiner (4000 GP)
Flesh Patch (6500 GP)
Glowpod (3500 GP)
Membrane Gauze (4500 GP)
Sinew Rope (6000 GP)

Rations:
Balanced Glob (7000 GP)
Carbohydrate Glob (5000 GP)
Fat Glob (10,000 GP)

Protein Glob (5000 GP)

Ammunition:
Clean Exit Round (20 GP)
Lucky Squeeze Round (25 GP)
Plopper Round (20 GP)
Plaque Spitter Shell (40 GP)

Explosives:
Dazzler (4500 GP)
Stinger (4500 GP)
Scorcher (8000 GP)
Eraser (12,000 GP)

Tonics:
Anima Boost I (10,000 GP)
Dominion Boost I (8,000 GP)
Kill Point Boost I (20,000 GP)
Rank Timer Delay I (40,000 GP)

It was a decent amount to choose from. More than decent. But as I skimmed up and down the list, trying to mentally prioritize what I needed most, I found myself at a loss. How was I supposed to budget my Genofacturing Points with so many seemingly vital options?

Armor was, of course, a key focus. Anything that could stem my blood loss and keep me intact would be invaluable in Naraka. But wasn't the best defense a good offense? Many of my prior injuries had been sustained in fights where I'd had to rely on my hands or otherwise "borrow" a weapon. If I had a proper gun, maybe I wouldn't run into as many life-threatening situations. A pistol was closest to my price range, but I'd need to inspect them individually to decide on one.

But on the other end of things, I *needed* food, and plenty of it. Sure, food identified only by its macronutrient wasn't exactly appealing, but a "fat glob" was sure as hell better than hearing my stomach whine all day.

Clearly, my priorities needed to be in this order: food, weapon, armor . . . and then whatever else. And the top of that "whatever else" list was Tonics.

Modri's words about saving up Genofacturing Points were still fresh in my mind, so I didn't want to go buck-wild producing every single thing from that section. In fact, it was probably best to just ignore them entirely for now, unless Modri commanded me to make some. The names suggested they enhanced the focus of each tonic—in other words, Kill Point Boost probably made it easier to gain more points, Rank Timer Delay offered more time . . .

This was all well and good, but seeing as Tonics were relatively cheap and not Polyps, I figured their effects were temporary. Translation? They would be a waste in situations where I didn't need them. It was best to focus on the essentials now and pick up temporary buffs when I found myself in sticky situations.

The next "whatever else" category was Utility Tools, seeing as I didn't care much about a stupid shield or a knife. Once again, the names were anything but tempting, but I could see the value hidden behind their grossness. A rope and carabiner could've gotten me out of several tight jams, and the medically oriented products would be a godsend between fights. I mentally noted this before moving on to my last "whatever else" zone: Explosives.

The names were of absolutely no use, seeing as they all revolved around blowing stuff up. But that was fine; I would just waste my precious time reading descriptions of items that the system should've included at first glance. Explosives were a wild card for me, and not only because of my clumsiness. Thus far, all of my kills had been more or less intentional and done in openly hostile areas. It was a big step up to start carrying grenades and remote-detonation devices, especially in a residential area. Blood on my hands was okay . . . but not civilian blood.

And with that, I resolved to come back to explosives at a later time. My final priority list seemed just peachy: food, weapon, armor, utility tools.

I told my plan to Modri, and amazingly, he approved of it. Apparently, he'd ranked the importance of each category with a similar thought process to mine. It felt damn good to finally be on the same page as the crusty old killer.

After fetching a pencil and some crumpled paper from the room's trash bin, I sat down to do some quick calculations. I was hell-bent on getting a complete set of armor, so that was an expense of 48,500 GP right off the bat. Not too bad.

After confirming that fat globs restored eight thousand calories—though at the cost of causing indigestion and intestinal distress—I marked myself down to buy one of those, three of the five-thousand-calorie balanced globs, and another pair of the four-thousand-calorie protein globs. In total, the "meal" came to 41,000 GP. Again, not terrible.

Then I got down to the real brass tacks: a weapon and ammunition. Modri's suggestion was the Plaque Spitter shotgun, but at 60,000 GP, it was a bit outside my current price range. His back-up pick, the Plopper pistol, seemed more agreeable. After all, it was less than half the price and could easily be concealed.

Curious, I checked the Plopper's description in the spore menu.

Plopper (25,000 GP): An organic handgun that fires phagedaenic rounds. Rounds require direct contact with biological material to inflict damage. Eight-round magazine.

Well, that didn't help much. What the hell did *phagedaenic* even mean? I turned to Modri for clarification.

"*Oh, just buy it,*" he said, sighing. "*It's a killer gun. Probably the weapon I used most in the early ranks.*"

Frowning, I jotted down a note to buy it. If it was good enough for Modri, it was surely good enough for yours truly. Besides, 25,000 GP wasn't too much of a hit to my wallet. Maybe it really was just a budget gem.

Last up on my tally were the utility tools. I selected these conservatively, opting for one bile salve, one flesh patch, two membrane gauzes, and a glowpod. Another 24,000 GP accounted for.

All in all, my shopping total was 138,500 GP.

"So, uh, what now?" I asked Modri.

"*Now you print 'em out,*" he said. "*Just select each option, stand by, and let it squeeze out. Each product takes about five minutes—less if they're small—and pops out of the orifices.*"

"Orifices?" I said, gagging.

"*Oh, grow up. You see a lot of body parts as a Purifier.*"

"I wish you weren't right."

Feeling more grossed out yet hungry than ever, I placed my first enter into the spore: one balanced glob, served medium-rare. My remaining GP shrank down to pay, and the reddish glow in the middle of the spore increased to a steady burn. Various juices and tissues squirmed within as it worked to form the glob.

"*Hey,*" Modri said, "*old Purifier trick . . . Enter all your products now. They'll form a queue. That way you can catch a nap while it prints everything.*"

Not a bad idea for once. After entering all my orders and losing most of my GP, I settled down in the vinegar-smelling bed and shut my eyes.

It was time to enjoy what felt like my last decent sleep. Because once I woke up and resumed my crusade to take down Chanzig, there would be no rest. Only blood.

27

When my allotted two hours of hotel time was up, I marched to the front desk and returned my key. The mechanical receptionist didn't bat an eye as they finished up the paperwork and told me to have a pleasant day.

"Seriously?" I said, planting both keratin-plated hands on the desk. "Not even *one* comment about my new outfit?"

The fabrique's black optical sensors examined me for a while longer, then throttled down.

"My programming dictates that I cannot insult a guest's attire. Therefore, I have no comment to make."

"You're a real piece of work," I growled. "You're lucky I don't file a complaint with your manager."

"I am the manager."

"Well, who manages you?"

The fabrique turned to me and stared for a good five seconds, then swiveled to the other customers in the check-in line. "Next guest, please approach. We apologize for any stupidity on display."

None of the waiting customers dared say a word about me, though. Few even looked up from their tablets or implant feeds. They all had the good sense to respect a man who looked like an armored tooth.

Satisfied that I looked at least somewhat intimidating, I kept my helmeted head high and marched out of the hotel with my shower curtains slung over one shoulder. Right about now, you might be wondering why I had shower curtains. The answer was simple: the stupid Genofacturing Spore lacked any option to create a rucksack, which Modri assured was available with stage-II product access. This being the case, I'd taken the only waterproof thing in the entire room and turned it into my own bag. Bundled inside were my medical gadgets, the globs of food, the

Genofacturing Spore, the Plopper, and about a hundred rounds of ammunition. Yes, a hundred rounds of raw ammo. Much like rucksacks, additional gun magazines or bandoleers couldn't be made at stage I.

"*Y'know, I almost always covered that keratin armor with somethin' like a cloak,*" Modri said as I headed through the downtown area. "*It's not exactly . . . pretty.*"

"But it's functional," I said.

"*It can stop a few bullets, but it ain't gonna stop a railgun from skewering you.*"

"Can you just let me have this moment of triumph?"

Modri didn't seem to get it, but this was a huge milestone for me. My first set of armor had been stripped off of me less than twelve hours after getting it—and it hadn't even been mine. It had been Modri's old set, or so I gathered. He wasn't able to give me his *real* armor due to the genofacturing's "you make it, you wear it" rule.

But *this* armor—this glorious set of keratin armor, which perfectly fit my body—was all mine. Was it beautiful? Objectively, no, maybe not. My initial description wasn't far off. All the plates were rigid, cold, with the exact texture and appearance of an off-white tooth. The helmet was nothing more than an overgrown extension of my skull, lacking a visor of any type, while the boots felt like a frozen prison for toes. And yet . . . subjectively, it was stunning. Perhaps this is because I almost felt like I'd given birth to the armor. In some sense, I suppose I had. Through my mouth, anyway.

The point is, by the time I made it to the gates separating the city from Naraka, I felt like a certified badass.

"You're a certified dumbass," the guard said, cackling with his buddy as they looked me up and down.

I folded my keratin-plated arms. "You don't know the first thing about me."

The other guard snorted. "We get one like you all the time. New in town, wanting to make a name . . . so they decide to 'clean up' Naraka with bombs and bullets. I swear, not one of you makes it a day."

"How would you know if I'm ready?" I said.

In unison, the two guards stepped back at their sandbag checkpoint and pointed to the collection of signs hanging over the gate. I read them with some chagrin.

NO, YOU'RE NOT TOUGH ENOUGH FOR NARAKA
TURN BACK NOW OR DIE

NARAKA DEATH TOLL SINCE LAST MONTH: 506
NARAKA EATS BABIES

Okay, so maybe I wasn't treating Naraka with the proper respect. But this wasn't a lark for me, nor some crazy scheme to prove my manhood. It *was* a crazy scheme, yes, but not *that* kind of crazy scheme. No, I was doing this for the sake of Akasha and everybody else on Chanzig's world—as well as myself. So, no matter what these guards thought of me, I was going in.

Besides, maybe it was all hyperbole. Maybe the sandbags, floodlights, barbed-wire walls, four layers of doors, rows of buried landmines, mutant sniffing hounds, and rocket turrets were just for show, a way to scare people out of emigrating to Naraka. Maybe.

"Open it up," I told the guards. "If I make it back, I'll buy you both a beer."

The two men looked at each other, perplexed.

Then the first sighed and headed for the gate's release levers. "Suit yourself, pal. I either get a beer or a dead idiot out of this. Win-win situation."

Once on the other side of the gate and across the minefield, I got my first taste of Naraka. And for the record, I'd like to state that it was dreadful. But maybe we have different interpretations of the word "dreadful." For you, a pastry that's too dry might be "dreadful." I am not referring to that kind of dreadful. Here, the term dreadful represents the feeling you get when you find a pair of decomposing corpses impaled together on an iron stake.

And indeed, that was what I found. Hence, dreadful.

The bodies had been left in a sort of cleaning, almost as though welcoming visitors to Naraka. They were surrounded by mounds of bullet casings, bones, and shredded clothing, which I soon realized had been constructed to serve as fortifications.

"Seems a little unnecessary," I whispered to Modri. "Who'd want to come here, much less conquer it for its land?"

"*Same people that are livin' here, I guess,*" he replied.

Everything about Naraka was just *wrong*. And that included the landscape overall. I'd expected it to be a "bad part" of the city, but still connected in some shared urban sense, but it wasn't. Instead, it was a vast, barren stretch of rubble, its horizon illuminated by flames. There were a few buildings amid the destruction, but most seemed to have been "occupied" by warbands of one kind or another. The strangest feature in sight were massive iron pillars that stretched from the ground into the darkness overhead. After several kilometers of walking, I realized what they were: supports meant to keep the tiers above from collapsing. It was a tad chilling, knowing that the inhabitants of Naraka essentially controlled the trigger to an uncontrolled demolition.

Anyway, I steered clear of all this, creeping through the junkyards and ruins to find the location Kumil had given me. According to him, it was a small compound about ten kilometers to the southwest. It would be hard to miss, on account of its raging party and blue strobe lights.

This turned out to be accurate. In a land of screaming and distant explosions, it was a fairly peculiar sight. The compound itself occupied a "valley," which I strongly suspected was the aftermath of some ancient blast. Dozens of blue lights shone up into the smog, and even from a range of a kilometer away, I could hear the stomping feet and out-of-sync chanting. Something about their jubilant attitude unnerved me. After all, how crazy did one have to be when deciding to attend a party in Naraka?

"Stay quiet for this one," I said to Modri. "No offense, but I need total calm on this job."

Crouching low, I descended the valley's junk-crusted slopes by weaving between wreckage and towering debris. The idea was to get a general feel for the place. After all, this would be my first meeting with anybody in Naraka, and Kumil hadn't seemed sure whether this source was a friend or a foe. That meant I had to plan. To know whether I was gearing up for a cocktail chat or an hour-long firefight.

Eventually, I found a spot about a hundred meters away from the compound. From that range, I could easily see the foot traffic leading in and out of the main doors. Most of the visitors were what I expected: big, covered in experimental body mods, a few spliced with alien DNA. Admission was handled by a team of three guys with rifles. That didn't seem like much, until I realized that the arriving patrons more than happily stashed their guns in a trough nearby.

What the hell was this place? A nightclub, a bar, an underground fighting ring?

Whatever the case, I wasn't going in there without a gun on my hip. The only problem was how to smuggle it inside. At least, it *was* a problem, until I heard a few passersby coming down the switchback trail to my left. Their voices faded in as I hunkered down and listened.

" . . . in any event," a man said. "Zadano's got another shipment coming in next week."

Another guy huffed. "Yeah, well, Zadano's run this place into the ground. I oughta put a few bullets in him."

"Not while we're enjoying a good time here, please."

"Oh, killin' him *would* be a good time . . ."

The two broke into laughter as they marched past. I stayed down until their footsteps faded into the music, thinking. *Zadano . . . Zadano . . . Zadano.* Where had I heard that name? Then it hit me: I hadn't. Well, not that variety of it. But Kumil had told me to come here and see a guy named "Sudamo," so it was close enough. It sounded like he was the head honcho.

With that, a plan formed in my mind.

I marched down to the compound's entrance, shower bag bunched up and held plainly in my hand. The three guys in charge of things turned toward me, but none of them aimed.

"I'm here to see Zadano," I said with a husky, biting voice. "Got that, uh, *thing* he wanted."

The largest of the three, who also happened to have ram's horns growing out of his cheeks, turned to the others. "You hear anything about this?"

The guard with no skin over his teeth shook his head. "Nah, but Z's always got stuff comin' in and out."

"Maybe we oughta call it in," said the ram-faced man. "You know, protocol."

The third guard—who was actually quite normal-looking—let out a groan. "Forget that shit. Too much paperwork."

No-skin-teeth man chuckled. "Never seen armor like that."

"It's custom," I grunted out. "Very exclusive. You wouldn't know about it."

All three of the guards just blinked at me. I was saved by the normal-looking guy, who just peeled the gate back and waved me inside.

Once I was through and my tough-guy routine was over, I let out the biggest exhale of my life. Damn, I hated having to be "intimidating" on command. It was exhausting. So exhausting, in fact, that I was tempted to just go balls-out with the Purifier schtick and show off my skills. But that would be best saved for *after* I had upgrades cooler than getting puffed up and growing a pus-bubble.

As I entered the main building's courtyard, I became even more confused. It *was* a party, yes, but not a normal party. It was a luxurious event—the kind of thing rarely seen even on Hegemony citizen worlds.

Everywhere I looked, scoundrels, murderers, and thieves walked about with beautiful aliens as arm candy. The aliens were more or less all humanoid, with the occasional tentacle variety mixed in for fun. What truly united all the aliens was their elegant apparel. They wore glittering dresses, velvety shirts, shoes that probably cost more than my lifetime salary. This, of course, was contrasted by the mud-and-blood aesthetic of their partners.

The odd couples lounged about on furniture and chatted away under the crisscrossing streams of fountains, all enjoying a romantic and absurdly beautiful evening here under the gloom of Naraka. A few of the rough-and-tumble attendees even seemed to have seduced their alien partners, leading them upstairs for . . . whatever was going on.

I was just stumbling about, confused and amazed by all of this, when a gold-plated fabrique wearing a tuxedo tapped me on the shoulder.

"Hello, sir," the fabrique said. "I've been informed you are here to see Mr. Zadano."

I nodded sheepishly. "Yep. That's . . . me."

"Very well, sir. Please follow me."

This was a twist, but I wasn't unhappy about it. All in all, this was a pretty classy joint. Drinks flowing, music blasting, laughter abounding . . . I sure was glad I didn't have to go "Purifier mode" on the fine folks in here. Moral concerns aside, it was best to keep my profile as low as possible. Not the easiest in a keratin suit of armor, but I'd make do.

The fabrique led me up a flight of stairs, then escorted me to a set of oak double-doors attended by two clones with white gloves. Once again, I was impressed. Who knew culture could survive so far underground?

While knee-deep in appreciation, though, the cloned door guards stepped up to me and activated humming sticks. Metal scanners, I wagered. All I could do was pucker up, breath held and mouth dry, as they waved the sticks all over—including my shower-bag.

"Clear," the guards said as one.

After a gentle knock, the fabrique opened the doors and stepped aside to allow me entrance.

I did so, though not without a dose of confusion. Had the Genofacturing Spore *really* made my Plopper pistol with zero metal? If so, it was incredible—and terrifying. Granted, the biological weapon already looked like an overgrown, floppy organ that was entirely too phallic. So maybe it didn't need metal to be terrifying.

But I set those thoughts aside upon seeing the man on the other side of a rosewood desk. He was a rather large man—one who had decided to stuff himself into a blue satin suit about three sizes too small. His nose, ears, eyes, and chin all appeared to be solid chrome, lending him the appearance of a very confused fabrique who'd decided to try on a fleshy mask.

"Mr. . . . Zadano," I said, crossing his luxurious office in a few excited strides. "It's been too long."

He awkwardly stood, extending a hand as I made my way closer.

The moment the double doors closed behind me, however, I stopped in front of his desk and put my hands on my hips.

"Mr. Zadano, I was sent here by Kumil," I explained. "I'm looking for a special someone here in Naraka."

Zadano looked momentarily perplexed, then sat down in his chair and leaned back with a peeved expression. "I thought you were here with my delivery."

"Oh." I hefted my shower-curtain bag. "This?"

His chrome eyes widened. "Is that it?"

"I don't know. Is it?"

"Oh, stop playing games and show me my powder."

Well, this was a problem. I don't know exactly what I was planning, strolling into a random compound leader's office with a bag, but I decided to roll with it. He seemed like he *really* wanted the imaginary powder in the shower curtain.

"I'll turn it over," I said, "*if* you help me out with the guy I'm seeking."

"Guy? Bah, why didn't you just say so?"

I squinted at him. "Come again?"

"Guys, girls . . . it's not a problem either way. Since you came all this way to drop off my dust, I'll even let you get a free hour."

"What are you talking about? Is this some kind of speed-dating thing?"

Zadano's wicked smile thinned. "Is this your first time as a courier? New route or something?"

"Uh . . . yeah. That's the problem. I'm . . . new to Naraka."

"Ah, sonny, you should've explained. I apologize for giving you a hard time. My name's Jin Zadano, and I run Zadano's Oasis. That's . . . well, this place. Which I'm sure you probably know, since it was your job to come here." He stood again and went to his drinks table, where he began mixing top-shelf liquor with medicines of all sorts. "Now, you wouldn't know this, but the Oasis is the hottest joint in the whole zone. We have a zero-murder policy here . . . and everyone loves it! One of the only places in Naraka where you get all the lust, none of the wrath."

I nodded along, more confused than ever. "That's great and all, but I'd still like to ask about my next, uh . . . delivery. I don't know them very well."

Zadano tested out his nasty cocktail and gave it an approving moan. "What's the name?"

"I don't have one. Just his . . . description."

"Well, go on, then."

"He's a splicer sort of fellow, I guess," I said, already sweating. "You know, breaks into classified systems. He got his hands on Chanzig's security network somehow. Copied all the access and whatnot."

Zadano took the glass away from his mouth. "You shouldn't go talking about that sort of thing down here, sonny."

"You know him, then?"

"Nope, and nobody should. So, that's enough of those questions." He pulled back on his metallic grin. "Now, about the guys and girls . . . which one do you want?"

"Neither. I'm just—"

"Oh, come on. It's your first run here. I like to treat the couriers well. So, what'll it be? I can get you one of each. Two girls, two guys. Whatever you want!"

"Listen, I just want to know about my next client. Please."

"And *I* just want to pretend you never asked. Okay? Is that okay?"

Zadano was panicked, but by what? I hadn't threatened him. Armor or no, I was just a seemingly unarmed courier in his office. There was something deeper at play. Something I could exploit.

"What do you think I came here for?" I asked quietly.

Zadano started breathing faster, and sweat the color of burnt oil dripped down his cheeks. "You're . . . one of Chanzig's men, aren't you? One of the guys from the clean-up crews?"

"You tell me."

"I— I swear . . . I didn't even know he was in this zone. If I'd known Chanzig was after him, I wouldn't have—"

Scowling, I stepped closer to Zadano and smacked the drink out of his hands. It was time to play hardball. "What do you know about him?"

"N-Nothing! I just . . . I know he was trying to help Chanzig find something."

"Go on."

"They were looking for some sort of . . . parasite, I guess."

"I need more."

Zadano sniffled. "I know he was Hegemony . . . Aquatic Research or something."

"Exotic Research?"

"Yeah, that one!"

I breathed in deep as the pieces of the puzzle came together. This guy wasn't just some splicer who'd managed to breach Chanzig's database—he was Chanzig's old informant. The one who'd experimented on Modri. The one who'd tracked Modri. The one who'd led Chanzig right to the planet where I found the chok'tal. He was *here*, camped out in Naraka. The only question now was . . . what went down between him and Chanzig? Why had he fled to the lowest part of the planet with Chanzig's sensitive data? Was it collateral for his own life, or something else?

"So," I said, reining Zadano back in, "where can we find him?"

"Uh . . . um . . . the last I heard, he was about six kilometers east of here. He was hiding out in that gambling den. Argennia—that's the name! He was at Argennia."

Firmly holding Zadano's gaze, I gave a nod and let the bag drop back down to my side. That was easier than I'd thought. No bloodshed, only answers. If only everything could've gone that way.

"So . . . that's it?" Zadano said, trembling so hard his entire chair shook. "Am I free to go?"

I shrugged. "Sure, why not?" Just as I turned to leave, though, another thought came to me. I faced Zadano and scrunched my brows. "Just out of curiosity . . . go back to those guys and girls you mentioned."

He gripped his armrests. "What about them? Still want one? Or two? Five?"

"I think I'm fine. I just wanted to know how you managed to convince so many fine young aliens to work for you."

"Uh . . . that would be our benefit program."

I sighed and reached into the bag, rummaging around. "Okay, let's try the truth. There is no benefit program, is there?"

Zadano looked to be on the verge of robotic tears. "No."

"You're not paying them, are you?"

"No."

"And they're slaves."

"Indentured workers."

"Slaves," I repeated as I pulled out the Plopper and aimed at him. "That makes *you* a slave master. What do you think should happen to you?"

"Uh . . . I should . . . retire?"

I groaned. "This is just so upsetting. Here I was, thinking I'd be able to go on my way and finish this mission. But you just *had* to offer me a slave, and now I know all your dirty secrets. And, honestly, morally speaking, I think I need to kill you now."

He began blubbering in his chair, clasping both hands in what I assumed to be prayer. It looked more like a mutated seal asking for treats.

"And the worst part is," I said, thoroughly annoyed, "that I won't even get any points for killing you. You're not armed, so you're counted as an innocent. Which is both ironic and completely wrong."

Just as I started squeezing the trigger, however, the doors burst open behind me. In that same instant, I spotted Zadano's sausage finger—right on top of the panic button. The half-machine slave master was already bringing his own firearm up from under the desk.

Jackpot. More Kill Points for me.

As I spun around and dove to the side, the HUD lit up my targets with blue frames.

Jin Zadano's Guards (HUMANOID) (2)
Jin Zadano
CALCULATING . . .
Combined Estimated Kill Points: 42,500

I'd had better, and I'd had worse. The guards opened fire just as I slid down behind one of Zadano's ugly avant-garde couches, tucking my knees to my chest. Bullets ripped through the hardwood floor around me.

"Hah!" Zadano shouted. "You stupid, stupid dog of Chanzig! He doesn't rule things down here! We do!"

Unwilling to engage with the prick any longer, I leaned out of cover and fired at the door guards. The Plopper bucked in my hands, each round screeching out and leaving a blood-like mist in the air. Three of the six shots managed to hit home.

I swung back behind the couch, ready to pause and reassess, only to hear the worst screams I've ever experienced. Had I popped a liver or something? Half-curious, half-determined to kill them, I leaned back out and took aim.

Only to find that my work was done.

Both guards had collapsed—one in the doorway, one on the hardwood just inside Zadano's office. They thrashed and howled, their blood smearing all over the floor as they cried for help. It didn't take long to realize why. Each of my Plopper rounds had left a head-sized hole in their bodies

. . . and not *just* a hole. They were gaping, gushing wounds, with the surrounding flesh sizzling and melting away by the second.

I stared down at the Plopper in horror. It was "breathing," which Modri said was its way of venting excess heat between shots. What sort of acid was this thing spitting?

Within seconds, though, the two guards fell silent.

"So, that just happened," I called to Zadano. "Maybe you'd like to just drop your weapon and surrender now?"

Zadano scrabbled about behind his desk, presumably to get a look. Then he wailed.

"Yeah, it's pretty bad," I said. "You finished?"

"Fuck . . . you!" he screamed, letting off a few random shots that pinged into the couch.

Not long after, I heard the hollow *clink* of a gun that was dry on bullets. Raising the Plopper, I stood and circled over to Zadano's desk. The worm of a man was curled up in the fetal position, one hand blindly groping at his drawers for more ammo.

"I'm assuming I'll still get points for this," I said, aiming at his legs, "but I'm good either way."

Zadano screeched as the first two rounds ate away his calves.

I shifted my aim to his knees. "You're a businessman. You know how much pain is involved in 'working your way up.'"

Two hours later, I walked out of Zadano's Oasis with a proper backpack, wads of currency, six guns in decent condition, and far, far too much blood all over. I could lie to you and say I spared a few of Naraka's finest slave patrons, but I didn't. The majority of the bastards were so high off their own powder that they didn't even see it coming—meaning no Kill Points. The few who fetched their guns to fight back came to regret it.

And as for the rescued slaves . . . well . . .

"Just take this," I said, passing their de facto leader all the currency I'd kept in my bag. "Split it up among yourselves, use it to rent somewhere safe in the city. Tell them that if anyone gives you a problem, one of Chanzig's men will come for them. In a few days, things will change."

The alien girl looked at me, all six eyes misty with confusion.

"Not all humans are like them," I said quietly, "or like me. There are good ones."

She didn't say anything back, but I swore that her eyes spoke a language of their own. That, or I was somewhat high on all the vapors that had been floating through the Oasis. After some time, the column of former slaves marched out of the valley and back toward the city's gates.

I turned back to Zadano's Oasis, which was still burning bright with chemical flames. Half of me was disappointed I hadn't been able to pull off one good stealth job . . . but the other half was elated to have seen justice delivered. I mean, these assholes had maintained a two-level basement full of cages and mind-wiping terminals. They'd taken the last shreds of respect from people who didn't have much to begin with. They'd turned suffering into their pleasure.

They were just the scum on the top of the pond.

Satisfied with my first house call in Naraka, I set course for the joint known as Argennia.

28

It was strange, traveling through a land with neither night nor day. The only time-keeping instrument I had was the chok'tal, and seeing as checking the time there meant I also had to face my own mortality, I wasn't a fan of the method.

Instead, I tried to keep pace by talking with Modri.

"The guy seemed legit to me, Purifier. It sounds like my old nemesis is hiding out here."

"But why? I mean, they must've had a falling out, right?"

"Probably?"

I sighed. "Just makes me wonder what that guy is hiding. What he knows about the chok'tal."

"Oh, you're gonna teach him real good about the chok'tal. I'm gonna love watchin' you go to town on him."

"Easy. I'm not trying to become a torturer."

"Okay, sure, but when you flipped that guy and shot through his jaw in the black room . . . hot damn!"

"Hey, listen . . . I know you like recounting stories of all the gory stuff I did in there, but let's try to keep it light between encounters. Okay?"

"You're just too squeamish. Never knew you were such a force of death."

"I'm not. I was just helping those slaves."

"Maybe you were . . . but you enjoyed it. I could feel it. All that righteous anger . . . that bloodshed in the name of justice . . ."

I stopped and leaned against a pile of crushed ships. "I don't *enjoy* any part of this. I'm not like you, Modri."

"Keep sayin' it. I don't believe it one bit."

"The only thing that's cool here is this holster," I said, pausing to examine the truly *awesome* leather holster I'd looted from a kill in the Oasis. It made the Plopper feel right on my hip. And speaking of which . . . "Modri, what the hell did you make me buy the Plopper for?"

"*Huh?*"

"That thing *eats* people's flesh!"

"*Uh . . . yeah. Pretty neat, right? Just need one hit, and that thing chews 'em right up!*"

I gagged. "Why didn't you tell me I'd be committing war crimes?"

"*Thought you'd have gathered that from the 'phagedaenic rounds' part of the weapon description. It refers to a flesh-eatin' ulcer.*"

"How am I supposed to know that!?"

"*Oh, pardon me. I thought you were one of them book-smart fellows. Guess not.*"

Equally disgusted and impressed by my new weapon, I dropped the topic and kept moving along. "So, I'm thinking it's time to rank up."

"*Already?*"

"Yeah, like we discussed. Try to buy one of the *good* upgrades before I get to Chanzig."

Modri laughed. "*I like this approach. Upgrade, wipe out a rat's nest, upgrade again . . .*"

After briefly looking around, I spied a cave-like hollow inside one of the nearby junk mounds. I crawled inside and pulled a few pieces of rubber near the entrance, creating some seclusion for my rank-up session. The last thing I wanted was to wake up while being served at a cannibal buffet.

With my newfound privacy, I sat down and pulled up the Status Display for a rank-up to 7. All the kills in Zadano's Oasis had fattened me up good with points.

STATUS DISPLAY
PURIFIER RANK: 6
RANK-UP AVAILABLE: Rank 7 (12,800 KP required)

Kill Points: 83,500
Genofacturing Points: 27,060

Rank Points: 0

Rank Time: 14 Hours, 38 Minutes, 4 Seconds
Storehouse Time: 3 Hours, 0 Minutes, 0 Seconds

Anima: 220%
Dominion: 0/3

As expected, my Genofacturing Points were a bit on the slim side, but at least I had all the gear I'd need for the foreseeable future. Satisfied with the overall state of things, I triggered the rank-up.

STATUS DISPLAY
PURIFIER RANK: 7
RANK-UP NOT AVAILABLE (25,600 KP required)

Kill Points: 0
Genofacturing Points: 97,760

Rank Points: 1

Rank Time: 21 Hours, 59 Minutes, 58 Seconds
Storehouse Time: 3 Hours, 0 Minutes, 0 Seconds

Anima: 240%
Dominion: 0/3

That was the easy part. The hard part, by contrast, was deciding which upgrade path to focus on. Modri had extolled the benefits of the Assassination path over and over, but where did that leave genofacturing? I'd seen the upgrade selection enough to know that access to stage-II products—what I *really* needed to keep cranking out better gear—was probably locked behind the next tier of Mutation. This was a tricky point, because while I could technically pull off my strategy of power-leveling and unlock Genofacturing II in the near future, I wouldn't have many Genofacturing Points to use for crafting in the end.

Further complicating things, I was beginning to see great value in the Annihilation tree. Modri wasn't a huge fan of it, but then again, he'd been a murder machine *before* the chok'tal latched on to him. Perhaps he'd been powerful enough to survive without relying on those upgrades, and therefore saw them as worthless. Besides, how far had he even gone with that path? If he'd spent all his points in Mutation and Assassination, he'd probably missed some really, *really* overpowered upgrade in Annihilation.

Then again, that was the great risk of the whole thing. The chok'tal played it coy, keeping the next tier of upgrades locked and unviewable until you'd gotten enough of the current tier's choices. This made it extremely hard to put all your eggs in one basket . . . and also made it hard to justify putting your eggs anywhere.

Modri wasn't much use here, seeing as he couldn't remember all the upgrades he'd chosen as a Purifier. And believe me, I asked him about those. Many times.

All I knew for certain was that I needed to focus and pump the next few Rank Points into *one* upgrade path, thus unlocking a new tier. If my theory held true, that tier increase would open a new set of options. A quick re-check confirmed that I needed two more Rank Points in any given path to reach my goal.

Deep down, I knew I wanted Mutation. Not exactly because of the genofacturing, but because it was the most outlandish, the most mysterious. Assassination and Annihilation were both upfront about their goals of killing people, and while that made sense, given the "kill or be killed" mandate, it also meant I'd have to play the game just like every other Purifier. All of Guide's former hosts had probably been soldiers of one kind or another, and as such, I'm sure the more violent upgrade paths had suited them just fine by accentuating their existing "talents."

As for me, though . . . I was just a normal guy. I'd always relied on my brain instead of my fists to sort out problems. Assassination had initially seemed like a good pick because it allowed me to fight from the shadows, but maybe I'd gone about my thinking process all wrong. What if my soft, intellectual nature wasn't a hindrance, but a different sort of strength?

Mutation seemed to emphasize a Purifier's range of options. Between the night vision, the thermal cloaking, and the environmental mastery, it allowed a Purifier to step outside the box and devise their own solutions. Who knew what was possible farther down the path? Hell, maybe I'd be able to grow wings and fly.

Anyway, the point is, Mutation somehow became my top pick for upgrades. I pulled up the path description, weighing my options.

MUTATION [Tier II] (*2 Rank Points required for Tier III access*)
Polyps II (REQ Rank 3): Enables bonding with a second Polyp. *Does not require a Dominion slot.*

Omniphile (REQ Rank 3): Increases homeostatic efficiency in harsh environments. (0/3)

Nocturnal (REQ Rank 1): Enhances night vision when active. (0/5)

Well, it sure did look a lot more barren without the Genofacturing upgrade. Even so, I had to pick one. I knew right off the bat that I wasn't taking Polyps II, mainly because all of my Polyps were currently locked away in Chanzig's vault. And as for Omniphile . . . who cared? I wasn't duking it out on an arctic world or in some volcanic wilderness.

No, I was in a land of darkness. And that naturally lent itself to Nocturnal.

Not entirely happy with the choice but also resigned to its inevitability, I bought the upgrade and closed the menu. Ready or not, it was hunting time.

I made my way to Argennia, trying out Nocturnal a few times here and there. Admittedly, it was a lot better than I'd imagined. In my head, I'd envisioned it as similar to most night-vision gear, which simply cranked up ambient light. The problem with this approach is that it blinds you when you look at an area that's bright—such as a flashlight beam. Nocturnal, in contrast, kept most light levels the same, but cranked up the brightness of dark areas.

This meant that as I traveled through the shadowy expanse, I spotted about twice as much as before—including packs of ambushers and predators hiding among the rubble. By the time I came within sight of Argennia and its surrounding cityscape, I'd already taken out four bastards and stacked up enough Kill Points for my next rank-up. Who knew this whole "kill or be killed" thing was so easy?

Wanting to capitalize on any kills at Argennia, I found another hideaway, pulled up the display, and performed a rank-up to 8. Then I invested another point into Nocturnal, unlocking the next Mutation tier. This left my Status Display as follows:

STATUS DISPLAY
PURIFIER RANK: 8
RANK-UP NOT AVAILABLE (51,200 KP required)

Kill Points: 0
Genofacturing Points: 104,790

Rank Points: 0

Rank Time: 21 Hours, 59 Minutes, 59 Seconds
Storehouse Time: 3 Hours, 0 Minutes, 0 Seconds

Anima: 260%
Dominion: 0/3

Wanting to check out my new upgrade options (even if I couldn't buy them yet), I tabbed over to Mutation and checked the details.

MUTATION [Tier III] (*3 Rank Points required for Tier IV access*)

Genofacturing II (REQ Rank 10): Enables creation of all Stage-II products. *Does not require a Dominion slot.*

Telekinesis (REQ Rank 8): Forms a weak quantum link between your mind and any inanimate object within 10 meters. (0/3)

Blindsight (REQ Rank 6): Projects a sonar signal up to 20 meters from your nervous system, rendering a three-dimensional readout of any environment. (0/5)

Polyps II (REQ Rank 3): Enables bonding with a second Polyp. *Does not require a Dominion slot.*

Omniphile (REQ Rank 3): Increases homeostatic efficiency in harsh environments. (0/3)

Nocturnal (REQ Rank 1): Further enhances night vision when active. (2/5)

Well, well, well . . . now we were cooking. I set aside my first new pick, Genofacturing II, seeing as I had neither enough points nor the rank to acquire it right now. That left two intriguing additions: Telekinesis and Blindsight. Just as I'd hoped, the chok'tal was finally offering me the "exotic" sort of powers that were advertised as part of the Mutation path.

Blindsight seemed to have the most obvious use, especially in confined environments. If the ability was anything like a ship's sonar waves, I'd be able to spot enemies through walls, floors, or ceilings, then change my tactics accordingly. It was a neat upgrade, and definitely an asset worth considering.

But on the *other* hand . . . Telekinesis. The chok'tal was offering me a power that human mystics had spent hundreds, if not thousands of years trying to acquire. Even the most advanced techno-charlatans—the ones who'd installed MindForge implants in their brains—could barely move a fork across a table. There was a risk that the chok'tal's version of Telekinesis was similar, but I didn't worry much about that. After all, it had overdelivered on every upgrade so far.

Even as I closed the display and got up, preparing to crush some skulls at Argennia, I was filled with fantasies of flying rifles and self-powered carpet levitation.

"Come on, baby," I said as I headed toward my target. "Daddy needs a new pair of Telekinesis shoes."

Argennia wasn't nearly as classy as Zadano's Oasis—not outwardly, anyway. It was part of a larger settlement that seemed to revel in chaos. Even as I approached its walls, I saw a number of atrocities: people being led about in chains, animals dueling to the death in spiked pits, organs being harvested from still-living victims under bridges. *This* was the true face of Naraka.

The one upside of this madness was that it stripped away whatever vestiges of hesitation I still had. This was a fallen place. A world of brutality and sadism. Whoever was down here, engaging in this sort of cruelty, was not in the wrong place at the wrong time. They'd willfully come here to take part in the festival of pain. And that meant there was no shame in putting them out of their misery. In fact, erasing them from existence was probably a net positive in the cosmic scheme of things.

This being the case, I didn't bother doing the whole "I'm looking for this guy" act I'd done back at the Oasis. Instead, I walked up to the front door and started blasting. Four guards went down in a flash, but the music inside was so loud that nobody heard the kills. With their bodies still sizzling, I stepped over the blood and proceeded.

To this day, I have no idea what Argennia was. Zadano had called it a "gambling den," but that was like calling a house an "eating area." Gambling was just one of many, *many* rackets taking place within its depths. They had cage fights, opiate lounges, murder rooms—don't even ask—and a dozen other lawless pastimes, most of them profiting from abject misery.

Within ten minutes, it was just a building full of bodies and blood. My work was made even easier by the fact that Argennia loved their combo of soundproofed rooms and deafening tunes. Even if I went to town on one room of lowlifes, the lowlifes in the next room over had no idea until I kicked their door down.

While reloading my Plopper, I discovered I'd accrued about 60,000 Kill Points. A comically low number, considering all the violence, but I supposed it made sense. Half of my victims had tried to fight back with fists or broken bottles, and the other half hadn't been able to penetrate my keratin armor with their pistols. Sure, I had a few cracks here and there, but nothing permanent.

I felt unstoppable as I jogged up to the head honcho's office.

To my surprise, the worm hadn't even locked the door. He was cowering in the corner, shielded by about twelve "dancers" and other semi-clothed women.

"Step out," I growled, "so we can have a chat."

One of his bloodshot eyes poked through the crowd. "Are you the guy who took down the Oasis? I'll pay whatever I've got, alright?"

"I don't want your money. Just information."

"Uh . . . okay?"

"Where's the Exotic Research Division traitor who has access to Chanzig's security network? And don't play dumb. You know who I'm talking about."

The boss whimpered. "We, uh . . . yeah, we don't talk about him."

"So, you do know."

"Even if I did, I'd die before I said shit to you."

I waved my Plopper pistols at the malnourished, trembling group around him. "Ladies, please move out of the way. Your employer and I have a few topics to discuss . . . in private."

Despite my best efforts, I didn't get much out of the Argennia boss aside from a lot of screaming and yet another name. Another den of sin that was rumored to have once . . . maybe . . . possibly . . . had contact with the man I sought.

Right about now, you're probably thinking, "We get it . . . you ripped your way through a bunch of shady spots in Naraka to find Chanzig's informant."

You're absolutely correct.

Over the next day and a half, I went on an unhinged murder spree. Torture clubs . . . pleasure-pod arcades . . . You name it, I dismantled it.

After the third or fourth spot I hit, things paradoxically got easier. There were less patrons mulling about, and the bosses seemed almost eager to tell me what they knew. Now, I never got a clear answer as to why that happened, but I have a theory that word got around in Naraka. And what was the word? *Tell the armored tooth what he wants to know, or you're gonna die.*

Naturally, I won't bore you with all the details of how this process went down. Instead, I'll skip to the good part. The part where I finally learned the name and definitive location of Chanzig's informant.

I was in some no-name warehouse deep, deep in Naraka, my Plopper pistol overheated from firing so many rounds into goons.

Clutched between my fists was the neck of Rimdul Swator, an alien man with an obsessive desire to buy and consume the flesh of children.

"I swear, it's legit!" Swator screamed as I held him back over the catwalk's edge. "He's *there*! I'm telling you the truth!"

I let him dangle above the bloody grinder below. "How can you prove that?"

"I— I've got a transmission dated from yesterday, with the location data and everything! He sent it from his personal terminal . . ."

"And how do you know him?"

Swator gulped through my grip. His lone, cyclopean eye widened with fear. "He, uh, pays me . . . to keep him sheltered."

"How does he pay you?"

" . . . Food."

"As in, children?"

Swator gave a nervous giggle. "I'm really more of an omnivore . . ."

"Pull up that record and get me his location," I said, pulling him back onto the catwalk. "If you have it done in five minutes, I might consider letting you live."

Swator wasted a few seconds just staring at me, occasionally checking out the Plopper, then took off running toward his archive room. I, on the other hand, just sat down in the nearest metal chair and wiped the sweat off my brow. Killing sure was hard work.

A short while later, Swator raced up to me with a flickering gadget of some kind. "Here! Here! It's a . . . tracker, of sorts. It'll take you right to him!"

I yawned and looked him over. "Didn't we agree on five minutes?"

"I . . . well, I wanted to add it to this device. You know . . . to make it . . . easier for you."

With one brow raised, I took the device from his hands and checked out the data. Sure enough, its target location was only a few kilometers away.

"Thanks for going the extra mile," I told him. He grinned. "But unfortunately, Swator, a deal is a deal. It's very important to be punctual."

Before he even understood what was happening, much less had time to scream, I put a Plopper round straight into his face.

On the way out of the warehouse-slash-cannibalism farm, I dragged Swator's body to a pen full of mutated boars and tossed it in. It just seemed right. Poetic, in some way I can't quite put into words. The boars seemed to appreciate their snack.

"*Damn,*" Modri remarked as I departed. "*That was ice cold, man.*"

I shrugged. "He deserved it."

"*No, I mean the last few encounters in general. Not a single drop of mercy. You've even made* me *cringe a few times.*"

"It's for a good cause."

"*What, becomin' Naraka's next premier business owner?*"

"Try again."

"*Givin' me the sweet, sweet pleasure of seeing you find that informant and gut him?*"

"Ha, ha, ha. You're a funny guy. Just keep a lid on it while I pick my next upgrade."

"*Ugh, don't tell me you're still hung up on Telekinesis.*"

"What? It's remarkable."

"*It's useless,*" Modri said, annoyed. "*Oh, wow, you can move a cup . . . or throw a piece of fruit! Watch out, bad guys!*"

"Did you even take it while you were a Purifier?"

"*How am I supposed to remember?*"

I ignored him and headed to a small ridge overlooking the warehouse, seeking out a spot for a final rank-up before my encounter with the informant. A *lot* had changed about my Status Display in the last day or so, and I wanted a full look before I went any further with my insane quest. The earliest Naraka spots I'd taken down had given me a full rank-up each, but the last few ranks—due to the system's ever-doubling requirements—were proving to be a pain in the ass.

STATUS DISPLAY
PURIFIER RANK: 9
RANK-UP NOT AVAILABLE (102,400 KP required)

Kill Points: 96,400
Genofacturing Points: 116,790

Rank Points: 1

Rank Time: 12 Hours, 18 Minutes, 46 Seconds
Storehouse Time: 3 Hours, 0 Minutes, 0 Seconds

Anima: 280%
Dominion: 0/4

Ugh. Just a few thousand points away from a rank-up—a real bummer when you're about to throw down with a foe that might actually award a decent amount of KP. But whatever. At least I now had my fourth Dominion slot, close to 300 percent in Anima, and an additional Rank Point to spend.

You're probably wondering why I opted to hang on to the Rank Point instead of just instantly buying Telekinesis. The answer is simple: I knew Telekinesis was awesome. Too awesome, in fact. If I'd purchased it any sooner, I would have been more focused on trying to throw small objects than doing my job—also known as killing.

Thus, I'd held off on buying it. I wanted to wait until I had a nice, quiet moment—like this one—to assess my options on a more practical level.

Very soon, I'd have to take on Chanzig and his entire army. And as much as I loved Mutation, I wasn't certain it had the "oomph" in the head-to-head gunfights I knew were coming. The only upgrade in Mutation that seemed directly suited to combat was Genofacturing II, which would allow me to theoretically produce better armor and guns. The only question was . . . would I have enough points to make what I wanted?

As I sat there, contemplating this, a strategy began to emerge. Thinking fast, I took the Genofacturing Spore out of my rucksack and set it down in front of me. Then I activated it, pulled up the menu, and tabbed to the Tonics section. A quick look at the Kill Point Boost concoction confirmed most of what I'd expected.

Kill Point Boost I (20,000): Doubles the amount of all Kill Points gained for six hours. All encounters affected by this boost must end within the six-hour window to gain increased points.

Six hours wasn't too bad—I'd been expecting closer to two—and neither was the whole double-KP thing. What *did* sting a bit was the price tag. 20,000 GP was nothing to scoff at, considering the Plopper had only cost 5000 more. In essence, I was buying a six-hour ticket to even more Genofacturing Points. If I somehow failed to find a good encounter or couldn't finish it in that time, the investment would be worthless. But if this informant guy was worth as much KP as his other former Hegemony comrades . . . *cha-ching*.

Of course, there was one other colossal problem. Several of the bosses I'd killed here in Naraka hadn't fought back. A few had grabbed a shovel or something equally dumb, netting me a few thousand KP, but the majority had gone without a squabble. If the informant just let me kill him, or somehow took his own life, I'd be shit out of luck.

But this "game" was all about chances. Risks. Having gained some confidence in my plan, I purchased the Kill Point Boost and let it form. Then I closed the spore's menu, went back to my Status Display, and unlocked Telekinesis.

I'd get to it later.

If all worked out as intended, I'd chug my boost tonic, kill the informant, and get my hands on *something* to take out Chanzig's security grid. That way, I'd be ready for a balls-to-the-wall confrontation when I finally climbed back out of his hellhole. Preferably with Telekinesis.

"Hang tight, Akasha," I whispered. "I'm coming back for you."

29

Back in childhood, I'd fallen victim to a fairly serious viral infection. My cure had come in the form of a medicine that was so vile its smell could wake up unconscious patients. You can probably imagine the taste. That medicine was, by far, the most disgusting and undrinkable liquid ever created by mankind.

But this Kill Point Boost tonic gave the medicine a run for its money.

It ran down my throat like one long, unbroken chain of phlegm, its flavor somewhere between rotting apples and stomach acid. The texture was better suited to industrial lubricant than a beverage. Somehow, some way, I gathered the strength to swallow it. My intestines immediately went into revolt, but I pushed through it.

A message appeared on my HUD.

Tonic Active: **Kill Point Boost I** (5 Hours, 59 Minutes, 58 Seconds)

For better or worse, I was now committed.

I stood in the center of a junk canyon, the walls around me made of crushed iron and half-melted plastics. According to the tracker I'd received, the informant in question was less than half a kilometer away. He was *here*, hiding among the wreckage with his treasures.

"I can't believe you drank that without pluggin' your nose," Modri said. *"You really are a sociopath."*

"I was hoping the flavor wouldn't be so bad."

"Aw, shucks. I guessed you just missed the cherry variety."

I sighed and kept following the tracker's guidance, my Plopper held close at my side. I'd been traversing these canyons and rubble cities for the better part of an hour, feeling much like a rodent trapped in a scientist's maze. The paths seemed to loop back in on themselves and steer you away from critical junctures. Only now, I felt I had some grasp of the principles. I'd made enough mistakes to know which routes were dead ends and which were viable.

Arriving at yet another crossing, I opted for the left-hand path. But before I'd taken three steps, Modri called out in my mind and brought me to a stop.

"What now?"

"*Look down,*" Modri said gruffly.

I did. At first, there was nothing in sight. But Modri wasn't known for pestering me without good cause—most of the time. After a few more seconds of searching, aided by my trusty Nocturnal vision, I spotted what had triggered Modri:

A tripwire.

It was hardly perceptible, given that it was as thin as a hair, but it existed. It had been strung across the path at ankle-height, similar to the tactic I'd used against Balnos and Kardinal. Upon squatting down and squinting, I found that the wire was connected to a bundle of black plastic-wrapped explosives behind some cardboard.

"Well, look at that," I said to Modri, whistling. "Looks like we're going in the right direction."

"*Just watch with me,*" he replied. "*I know these types of soldiers. If there's one wire, there's probably fifteen more. They're thorough.*"

I nodded. "Makes sense that you'd know how this guy thinks, I guess."

"*Yeah, he's a real sick son of a bitch. Had a thing for needles and scalpels. Come to think of it, I guess Naraka's his perfect playground.*"

Grunting in assent, I stood and continued creeping along the path. I stepped over another tripwire within twenty seconds. "Say, Modri . . . what exactly *is* the Exotic Research Division? Did he work with rare animals or something?"

"*Not exactly. Exotic, in Hegemony lingo, means 'unknown potential.' His crowd was always workin' on some new invention, some genetic mod designed to create the next variety of human.*"

"Doesn't seem to gel with the Hegemony's 'humans are supreme' stance, does it?"

"*Funny thing is, from this guy's point of view, it probably lines up. The boys in Exotic Research thought us normal humans weren't livin' up to Halcius' divine vision. In their eyes, humans were meant to be more. Y'know, super-people.*"

"Ah, sweet hypocrisy," I muttered, stepping over yet another tripwire. "I can't believe they thought the chok'tal was their path to a better human."

"That's what they told us in the official reports. But you know how bureaucracy is with tellin' the truth."

"What, you think there's something else?"

"I don't think any government tryin' to find a warmongering alien parasite has the best of intentions. And definitely not the pricks who carry out that search."

"A point we can firmly agree on."

Another few tripwires later, I heard a jumble of noise. The tracker device confirmed that I was now a tenth of a kilometer away from the informant. Shushing Modri for absolute focus, I crouched down and made my way to the next turn.

Once in position, I heard a variety of industrial sounds: saws whirring, electricity crackling, hydraulic presses rising and lowering. But between these sounds was a voice. A low, paranoid voice—one that seemed to belong to a man conversing with himself.

" . . . didn't believe," he muttered with an insane cackle. "None of them believed you. But your day is coming, God of Flesh. It is *coming*. In fact, it's already here. Or was it yesterday? No, no, it's here today. Always today!"

The name "God of Flesh" gave me temporary pause, but in all honesty, it wasn't much more bizarre than the other things I'd been exposed to on Chanzig's world. Weird or not, this seemed to be *my* guy. The tracker even confirmed it, filling the screen with a repeating dot that roughly corresponded to the voice's origin point.

Morbidly curious, I leaned farther around the corner.

The junkyard clearing had the appearance of an arena, complete with "stands" made out of stacked wrecks and chunks of intact buildings. The "seats" were illuminated by haphazard floodlights hanging from electrical cords. I would say the seats were empty, but that's not strictly true. See, each seat was occupied by . . . stuff. Some contained whole corpses, while others were merely piles of steaming gore. Others still had been claimed by the bodies of deactivated fabriques. It was a theater for ghouls.

Their "show," if you'd like to call it that, took place in the bloodstained central pit of the arena. This area, too, was framed by repurposed lights of varying brightnesses and colors. But as you might expect after hearing about the audience, the main event wasn't much to see.

Scattered across the pit were operating tables, empty fluid-drip bags, body parts, and frothy nitrogen tubs. And at the very center of it all, a hunchbacked man in a surgeon's bodysuit worked on his latest patient. His procedure was being filmed by a dozen cameras, which then projected the up-close, low-resolution image to a collection of vidscreens all around the arena.

From the looks of it, our fine doctor was busy transplanting a kidney into a corpse's throat.

When I found myself ready to vomit and unable to take his humming any longer, I stepped out into the arena. A motion-sensing light trailed my approach, but the doctor seemed too absorbed in his work to notice.

"Excuse me," I called out. Nothing. "Excuse me!"

With a startled yelp, the doctor dropped the kidney onto the sand. He then whirled around on me, wiping the blood off his visor with an equally bloody glove.

"You," he growled, "you have interrupted a *very* important operation!"

"Yep, it sure did look that way." I walked a bit closer. "I've heard you have something that could help take Chanzig down."

"Oh, look at this, dear friends . . . A dog of Chanzig has come to pester the God of Flesh!" he roared to his dead audience. He mimicked the sound of booing. "You serve a false master! How do you answer for your crimes?"

"I just want to talk."

"They always do. Talk, talk, talk . . . and not one action of virtue is accomplished! You run your mouth like a festering roast!"

"Alright, I have no idea what that means," I said, shaking my head. "Let's get right down to it. Did you gain access to Chanzig's systems? Download the data somehow?"

"Oh, I bet your *master* would love for me to tell you that!"

"I don't work for Chanzig. I want to take him out."

The God of Flesh squealed with glee. "You've come to volunteer your flesh, then, haven't you?"

"No? I—"

"This . . . is my army!" he bellowed, again gesturing to the crowd. "I have built them to overthrow the false god . . . the idol they call the Undying One! That traitorous, filthy rat will have to answer to the people now . . ."

"Wait . . . you're trying to take Chanzig down, too?"

"But of course! I am the one true god . . . the sculptor of skin! And I have waited so, so long for my day of reckoning. We will rise up like vermin to tear down his monuments!"

"Okay, I like the energy," I said, trying to rein the madman in a bit, "but maybe we can start with the basics. Do you really have something to take down his security?"

"Even better. I have something to *fry* his security!"

"Oh. That actually is better."

"Bombs, dear child. Electromagnetic pulses perfectly synchronized to the frequency of his networks." He began pacing in a circle, snickering to himself here and there. "One blast . . . at the right range . . . and it all goes *poof*!"

For the first time since seeing this guy, I started to believe he was a verified genius. I mean, sure, he'd definitely lost his marbles between Chanzig and living down here, but if he'd really made an EMP that could target Chanzig's security network . . . how could I complain?

"Where are the bombs?" I asked. "I can help you with that."

The God of Flesh tore off his surgical hood, revealing a face ruined by skin grafts, burns, and acid splashes. "Observe my miracles, child! Look at this pure, unadulterated beauty. And you believe I need your *help* to accomplish my aims!?"

Okay, I'd have to take this delicately.

"No, not at all," I said. "I just . . . admire your work so much. I wanted to assist you. Please."

He studied me for a moment, nodding and making small comments under his breath. Then he exhaled. "Very well. But before you become my apprentice, you must know of my strife. You must suffer the devilry Chanzig has brought upon this world!"

"Can't we talk about that while heading out of Naraka?"

"Silence!" he screamed. After a few coughs, he reestablished his (sort of) calmness. "All who have joined my army have listened to my story and agreed with me. You, too, must hear the tale! This is your initiation."

"Alright. Get it over with."

The God of Flesh made a self-satisfied little *hrm* noise, then proceeded. "The great devil, the one known as Chanzig, came to me as I toiled away in the Halcius Hegemony. Well . . . wait. Actually, he was in a cell. And I visited him . . . I digress! He filled my head with beautiful visions of a world that had gone beyond the flesh. A world with gorgeous people everywhere . . . *everywhere*! And I was so sick of the decay . . . sick of the ugliness and flaws . . . that I agreed to help him."

As the God of Flesh spoke, I mentally compared his ramblings to what I already knew of him. So far, so good.

"In order to cleanse this world and remake it with beauty, he required an artifact," the man continued, back to his pacing. "I searched high and low for him. I combed the stars. And at last, I found it! I did . . . until I didn't. That bastard of blood . . . Jekra Modri! I curse your name, Jekra Modri!" He took a few seconds to just howl incoherently at the smog above. "Ahem. Where was I? Yes, the bastard Jekra Modri! He fled, but I could not find him."

Once again, everything added up. Now it was time to fill in the wild blanks from *that* to . . . well, all *this*. Corpses included.

"The God of Flesh was eventually discovered in his attempts to find the bastard Jekra Modri," he whispered. "I was locked away with no light and no sound and no meat, labeled a traitor and a spy. The devil Chanzig rescued him and brought him to the land of his brothers. This land! But it was not a land of milk and honey. It was all a lie!

"Even after I slaved away, working and cutting to help the devil Chanzig . . . he decided to betray me. He took away my beautiful creations. He chewed the tender flesh of my mind. He sought to kill me and hang my body from his fortress! But I did *not* die! I stole his secrets, and I fled!" He suddenly crouched and smeared a handful of bloody sand into his face. "Through the soil of Naraka, I was reborn. Down here, I prepare my legions for war. I shall reclaim my seat as the God of Flesh . . . and with the artifact he desired, I will be free to shape all bodies exactly as I please!"

"Oh," I said, not quite sure what to say to the panting, sweaty madman. "So . . . Chanzig betrayed you because you couldn't find that alien artifact, and now you want it for yourself?"

"Yes! You understand! Unlike the others, *you* understand!"

"But if neither of you found it, how will you get it?"

The God of Flesh's face soured in an instant. "Curses! I must have overlooked this stage of my plan . . ."

"Ah, well. It's all good. Happens to the best of us. So, can I take those EMP bombs and get started for you?"

"Absolutely *not*! You cannot handle those until you are a member of my army."

I blinked at him. "And how do I do that?"

"Sit on my table," he ordered, shoving the previous "patient" off into the sand. "I shall make you beautiful, like all the others!"

A quick glance at the hundreds of bodies in the audience told me that was *not* a good idea. But it also didn't seem like a good idea to kill the guy with no warning. He was crazy, without a doubt, but it was clear it wasn't all his fault. His mind had been broken by Chanzig. Filled with delusions of a world that perfectly matched his ambitions.

Wait . . . that was it. Modri *had* been right. Chanzig's whole mode of operation was tempting people with the exact things they desired, even if that thing was impossible. Eternal life, a world of infinite beauty, an impossible radiation therapy. All of them were unreal, hallucinatory things, yet strong enough to overpower the rational mind.

In that sense, all of Chanzig's leaders were victims themselves. They had all been sold a bill of goods by their supposed "master."

"Say, maybe you can just show me the bombs first," I suggested. "Then we can decide what to do together."

The God of Flesh stared at me for a long, long while, occasionally glancing at the audience. He even leaned over at one point as though listening to their whispers. Then he clapped his hands and pointed to me.

"You, good sir, are a liar and an agent of devilry," he snapped. "My army has just told me of your true intentions. You are here to kill me and allow Chanzig to corrupt my beautiful body. And that shall *not* happen!"

"Excuse me?"

Suddenly, the God of Flesh bent down and retrieved something from under the operating table. Well, actually, two things. Both of them were semitranslucent nano-carbon swords. Yes, *swords*.

I sighed. "You've got to be shitting me. Just when I'd *like* to let someone live for a change . . ."

[NEMESIS EVENT]
God of Flesh (HUMANOID)
CALCULATING . . .
Estimated Kill Points: 17,500 (TONIC BONUS: 17,500)

I lazily lifted the Plopper, ready to deliver one good round to the doctor's face and end his suffering. But before I could even aim, the madman pulled his surgical hood back on and charged at me, screaming and swinging.

When he came within ten meters, I opened fire.

The Plopper rounds smashed into his hood's visor and . . . did nothing. Aside from a few spurts of dark, ink-like fluid, there was no sign I'd even hit him.

The gun's description bounced back into my head:
Rounds require direct contact with biological material to inflict damage.

Oh, great. I was about to be killed by a sword-wielding maniac who'd named himself the God of Flesh, all because I'd failed to read the damn manual for my own weapon. Not the best way to celebrate my career as a Purifier.

There was no time for a pity-party, though, because one of the nano-carbon swords was already slicing toward my face. I rolled backward and to the side, coming up on one knee just as the blade swiped past my nose. It didn't stop there, though. The blade's continuing momentum took it cleanly through the operating table I'd just stood at, cutting it in half.

"Come and die, vermin!" the man screamed.

Frantically holstering the Plopper, I fought to get my rucksack off and pull out one of the many *normal* guns I'd scavenged. But the God of Flesh didn't allow that. He came flying toward me, howling and gibbering, whirling the swords so they raked the sand between us.

All I could do was drop the rucksack and dodge. This time, one of the blades bit through the keratin on my shoulder, cleaving off a solid chunk. Another inch closer, and he'd have sliced through an artery.

As I backpedaled, ducking some swings and outrunning others, I activated Overclock and Indomitable. The expected rush of power and bulkiness hit me at once, but it was far less useful than I'd anticipated. All the skill and grace in the world wasn't enough to counteract a madman's out-of-control swinging.

With a screech, the God of Flesh thrust both blades at me. I hopped back in the nick of time, then surged forward, hoping to grab one of the weapons before he reeled them back in. I almost got the left one, but he was faster with the right. He pulled back for an overhand strike. Now or never.

Seizing the opportunity, I rammed into him and wrenched back the hand gripping the raised blade. A tendon popped. The man shrieked and let go of that sword, but not before spinning around with a reckless slash from the other.

The blade carved right through my side, easily butchering the obliques. Pain flared through my torso, but I couldn't give in now. I had to press the attack.

When the God of Flesh tried to bring the sword around for a follow-up blow, I stepped in close and delivered a superpowered punch straight to his face. The visor cracked, and he crumpled under the force of the strike. The second sword fell from his grip.

Before the man could recover, I snatched up both swords and held them at his throat.

"This is over," I whispered. "I'm sorry for what happened to you, but it's done."

He lifted his throat. "Go on, then. Kill me, vermin!"

Not knowing what I could possibly say to ease his suffering, much less to make him stop fighting, I took his advice. Both blades sliced through his fabric and flesh with barely any resistance, and soon blood was spurting all down the front of his bodysuit.

The God of Flesh fell back, spasming on the sand. He rasped out something through the blood.

"What?" I said, kneeling down to try to hear him.

"Face," he gurgled through the shattered visor. "Show me . . . your face."

It was a strange request, seeing as my helmet already exposed about half of my features, but I decided to honor it. He was dying, after all. He deserved a last bit of respect.

Once I'd pulled the helmet off, I held it under my arm and stared down at him. "There you go."

A wide, bloody smile appeared on his face. "It's . . . *you*. So . . . beautiful."

"Me? Huh?"

"Just . . . as I remembered. So very beautiful. A creation . . . all my own."

And with that, the light faded in his eyes.

NEMESIS ENCOUNTER SUCCESSFUL
Kills: 1
Kill Points Awarded: 35,000
Storehouse Time Awarded: 1 Hour, 30 Minutes

RANK-UP AVAILABLE: RANK 10

As I stood up, trembling, the first thing I did was reactivate Modri's speaking privileges.

"Did you . . . hear him?" I said, still transfixed by the body. "He recognized me."

Modri just sighed. "*Crazy son of a bitch. He was even more gone than when I saw him.*"

"But he knew me, Modri. He knew my face."

"*He was just ramblin' on, Purifier. People say a lot of batshit stuff when the oxygen's leavin' their brain. I've had people call me their mother.*"

"Seriously? He called me his creation."

"Look around this damn arena. He probably sees everything as his creation."

I nodded, trying to shake off this weirdness. "Maybe you're right. This place gives me the creeps."

"Me, too. Only good part of comin' here is that I got to see my tormenter get a taste of his own medicine. Well, his own swords, actually. Even better."

"Yeah, I'm sure that's fantastic . . . to you."

I shook my head, but started to get another idea from Modri's mention of the swords. Sure enough, there were two sheaths under the table where the God of Flesh had drawn his weapons. Feeling a bit like a graverobber but certain I'd use it for better purposes, I looted one of the swords, sheathed it, and forced it into the rucksack. The handle portion poked out through the top flap, but that was fine.

Then I headed toward the arena's back door, which seemed to lead to the interior of a large trash dome.

"Where you headed?" Modri asked.

"The *real* reason we're here is for those EMP bombs. Seems our psycho friend was doing a little bit more than just saving dirt on Chanzig."

"No kiddin'! It sounds like he was plannin' a full-on rebellion."

"Good idea, poor implementation."

The doorway leading into the dome, as it turned out, was more like a tunnel. It extended several meters through a layer of highly compacted junk, its sides overflowing with busted pipes and frayed wires. When the tunnel finally opened up, I found myself in a room that must've served as the God of Flesh's workshop . . . and home.

It had a packed-dirt floor, a soiled mattress, and a heap of spare parts. Lying next to the parts were bundles of wires and circuitry that I assumed to be the EMP bombs. But these objects were really just accessories to the room's main feature: a row of blinking terminals, all of which were connected to a collection of vidscreens hanging from the walls and ceiling.

"And they say madness doesn't have taste," Modri commented.

"I'd stand by that statement." After gingerly packing the EMP bombs in my rucksack, I headed over to the terminals and assessed them. "Ever worked a system like this?"

"Few times. You?"

"Never. They look like Hegemony tech."

"That's 'cause they are. Just do what you did with the ship. Stick out your hand, give me access privileges. I'm not a splicer, so don't go expectin' any miracles, but I can play whatever's in here."

That was good enough for me. I was grateful to have the EMP bombs, but more than anything else, I wanted to know what Chanzig's informant had preserved on here—especially if it involved me. The way he'd looked at me and recognized me still had me shook. It was the same way Liura had looked at me back in the interrogation room. People were keeping secrets, and I wasn't stupid enough to believe it was only Chanzig.

Modri's tendrils snaked out of my wrist and into the terminal's open ports. A few vidscreens flickered or displayed static as he probed around.

"Anything specific you're after?" Modri asked.

"Yeah, but I'm not sure what I'd even call it," I said. "Read me a summary of whatever you find. If something seems promising, pull it up for me."

"Will do."

A few seconds later, Modri began recounting the terminals' contents. *"Alright, looks like this Flesh God guy was pretty, uh, prolific. Is that the word? There's a lot of shit here."* He mumbled a bit to himself, then started in earnest. *"I'm seein' pretty much everything Chanzig could've ever wanted to store. He's got all of the informant's research data on the chok'tal—and me—plus charts, statistical models, flight plans . . ."*

I scratched my chin, thinking. "That's probably all his own stuff. I'm more interested in the private files Chanzig had in the fortress."

"Ah, yeah, there's some of that, too. He's got a list of all the people who traveled here for scavenging work, the crew rosters, plus all the missions he assigned."

"Maybe it's some kind of directory. Start with whatever this guy had on Chanzig."

"Already did . . . and hot damn, is it a jackpot. Looks like the God of Flesh kept some of the files he created while still in the Hegemony's Exotic Research Division."

"Like what?"

"Well, he's got a vid from six or seven years back. It's labeled 'Chanzig After-Action Report.'"

I nodded stiffly. "Play it."

"You got it."

With bated breath, I turned my attention to the vidscreen right above me. There was a wash of static, then a grainy video feed showing the interior of a Hegemony confinement cell. A bald man sat inside the cell, separated from the camera by a stasis field. He was shackled to the walls, and his skin appeared to be flaking off in large patches. His eyes and ears were ringed with dried blood.

"*Is that Chanzig?*" Modri asked.

"I'm not sure," I said absently, transfixed by the man's face. I'd never seen Chanzig as a human being before, but this had to be him. Before his "condition" got much worse, that is.

Back on the vid, a hand moved into frame on the left-hand side of the screen. Then the owner of the hand began speaking. "Tell us what happened when you encountered the gateway. Every detail."

I recognized the voice as belonging to the God of Flesh. This had to have been recorded while the surgeon was still employed by the Hegemony. Back before he'd been hunting Modri.

"It . . . it was glorious," Chanzig whimpered, his lips cracked and burned. "I led the team to its entrance . . . but the others were too scared to enter. Too timid. Too mortal. I was the only one with the spirit to step inside and receive its grace."

The interviewer—AKA the God of Flesh—cleared his throat. "What happened to the rest of the team?"

"The gateway told me what I had to do," Chanzig said, staring directly into the camera's eye. "It spoke to me in whispers from another world. It said there could only be one. The rest were too weak to see its beauty."

"Are you saying you killed your own team?"

"I put an end to their weakness. But don't weep for them, Doctor. They will be reborn in the next world. The better world."

When the interviewer spoke again, his voice was strained. "What did you see when you entered it?"

"More than words can express," Chanzig whispered. "It was a realm of infinite beauty, infinite light, infinite power . . . I was overcome. My mind was flooded by its brilliance. Blinded by it. And then I heard the voice of the realm's creator. They told me that I was not ready, and that I had tried to walk where no mortal is allowed. I had tried to claim victory without the Sacred Guide to prepare my mind. *This* is my punishment for pride." He nodded toward his mangled arms and legs. "But I will return to it. I will remake this world."

"Thank you," the interviewer said with a strange note of . . . awe? "Interview is concluded at zero-nine-twenty standard hours."

I folded my arms, not quite sure what to make of this first entry.

"*That gateway really scrambled his marbles,*" Modri said.

"You're not wrong," I said, humming to myself. "Did you see what I did?"

"*Which is?*"

"Chanzig was using his mental manipulation here. He was implanting desires in the interviewer."

"How do you figure that?"

"It's obvious. Listen to the interviewer's voice. I think this is the moment Chanzig converted him."

Modri grunted. *"So, this is when the God of Flesh started lookin' for me."*

"That, or pretty damn close. Chanzig must've asked him to help fulfill the prophecy with a chok'tal. And *that* launched a new project in the Exotic Research Division. On paper, it was probably to create super-soldiers for the Hegemony. But in reality . . . it was just a ploy for Chanzig's gain."

"You really missed out on a career as a detective," Modri said, laughing—until he stopped abruptly. *"I found something on me."*

"Really? What is it?"

"I dunno. Seems to be some kind of file about my physical performance. Ah . . . uh-huh . . . I see. This is one of the files those assholes made while testin' me in the facility."

"But what exactly is it?"

"Not much, really. They've got a few notes about my obstacle course runs, reflex measurements, eye movements . . . Oh, hold on. What the hell . . . ?"

"Speak up."

"They've got a full scan of my nervous system. Twenty-four hours of twitches, scratches . . . any movement from my muscles."

"Why would they need that?"

"No idea."

"Alright, try something new," I said. "I want to know what he has on me. Can you run my name in the directory?"

"I'll give it a whirl." A minute or so later, Modri let out a confused groan. *"Name's Dak Korasa, right?"*

"Yeah."

"Says here that you traveled to Kagu-9 about three years ago. No other comin' or goin' records."

"That doesn't make any sense," I said. "The first time I came to this world was a few months ago."

"Yeah, well, the only other thing I've got is some kind of file labeled 'Korasa Analysis.' It was made before your first visit . . . three and a half years ago."

Perplexed, I gestured for him to pull it up on the screen.

It wasn't a video, but rather a hard copy of some kind of psychological profile. Over three pages were devoted to descriptions of my childhood and education, most of which had apparently been recorded through my self-reported testimony. Only it wasn't *just* psychological. It included everything: my blood type, my genetic sequencing, my metabolic rate.

Most curious was the note at the bottom of the page, which read:

Research Summary: Dak Korasa is an optimal candidate for the program. With a 99.8 percent genetic match to Jekra Modri, as well as confirmed shared ancestors, he is almost guaranteed to provide a stable foundation for our research. Additionally, Mr. Korasa does not appear on any Hegemony genetic-flagging algorithms. This means he would be able to pass any future retinal checks or other testing methods without raising suspicion.

Further Considerations: We feel compelled to mention the fact that Mr. Korasa is suffering from severe radiation damage, and may die within the next year. Fortunately, Mr. Korasa is willing to provide past samples of his DNA as a secondary option, should our primary course of action fail. We do not believe there is any treatment capable of saving his life. As such, we should begin our program immediately.

"Holy shit," I said quietly, trying and failing to understand what I'd just read.

"*Holy . . . shit,*" Modri echoed.

"We're related."

"*Me . . . to you?*" He made a gagging noise. "*No offense.*"

"Is that really all you can think about?" I snapped. "I don't know what any of this is. We know I didn't have any radiation damage . . . but this is saying I did. And that I probably died from it."

"*Who cares about that? The real question is, why are they mentioning me? Why the hell is it important that we had a genetic match?*"

There was no answer to satisfy any of this. The more I read, the more confused I was. All I'd gathered so far was that Chanzig had found the gateway to the Unmade, converted the God of Flesh to his cause, and then . . . found me. But why? Even if I did have some genetic connection to Modri, what was my role in any of this?

"He *must* have more on me," I said. "Try checking out the crew rosters, especially the ones that have Balnos, Liura, and Kardinal listed."

"*Good news and bad news,*" Modri said. "*I found all the crew logs . . . but you're not listed on any of 'em.*"

"And the others are?"

"Yep."

I took a deep breath. "It doesn't add up. Why would he have a psych report on me, then list me as arriving here three years ago, but not include me in anything since then? Three years ago, I didn't even know Chanzig existed. There's no way I came here."

"Well, if it helps . . . this cache also has surveillance vids. Looks like Chanzig has a file attached to each note in the security logs."

"You mean . . . there's a vid of me meeting with him? Three years ago?"

"That's what it says."

"Pull it up, then."

This vid showed what appeared to be the interior of Chanzig's fortress. The camera had been pointed away from his nanite chamber, instead capturing the floor's elevator and lobby-like conference area.

The elevator doors opened, and two figures stepped out. One seemed to be an officer in Chanzig's employ, judging by the armor and rifle, while the other was . . .

Me.

"Is that who I think it is?" Modri asked.

"I don't know," I whispered. "I'm not sure who it is myself."

The man, who I'll refer to as Dak Two for simplicity, approached Chanzig's nanite chamber. His face—*my* face—and his expensive-looking suit became bathed in a mysterious glow from beyond the glass.

"This is Dak Korasa, sir," the officer said. "He's here to speak about his treatment plan."

An ethereal laugh came through the glass. "Good. Very good. Please allow Mr. Korasa and I to speak in peace."

The officer gave a half-bow and headed back to the elevator, while Dak Two just stood there, shifting his weight awkwardly.

"Mr. Korasa," Chanzig said once the elevator doors had shut, "it is so pleasant to finally meet you."

Dak Two cleared his throat. "L-Likewise, sir."

"Do you know why I've called for your expertise?"

"I've heard a bit, sir."

"How advanced is your condition?"

"I'm not sure," Dak Two said softly. "The doctors said it was the worst they'd ever seen. But I'm able to work. I'm a hard worker."

"I'm sure you are. But don't worry overmuch about stressing your body, Mr. Korasa. It's what's inside that matters."

Abruptly, the vid shut off.

"What the hell was that?" I managed.

"*Not a damn clue*," Modri replied. "*You sure that wasn't you? Seemed kinda similar. Y'know, what with the pencil-pusher look and whatnot.*"

"I know how I look, Modri. But I don't remember that. Is there anything else with me?"

"*Nope, but I think I found the name of the God of Flesh. Looks like he's listed in the archives as Dr. Gabran Markazian. And there's quite a few vids with him . . .*"

I nodded, trying desperately to forget what I'd seen and find something useful. "What kind of vids is he in?"

"*Let's see . . . There's a lot of 'project meeting' files here. Oh, and some things about 'experimental designs.' Wait. Hold up. There's something interesting here.*"

"Play it."

The vidscreen winked on again. The setting was the same, right down to the camera angle and level of lighting in the chamber room. Once again, it began with the elevator doors opening. The only difference was the man who stepped out: the God of Flesh, also known as Dr. Markazian. This was clearly an old video, as the doctor's face was relatively normal.

Markazian was covered in surgical scrubs, and his hands were pink from washed-off blood. He stalked up to Chanzig's glass chamber in a fit.

"What is it now?" Chanzig asked, mildly bored.

Dr. Markazian shook his head. "We lost Korasa."

"Come again?"

"He died on the table. It's like I told you. *Just* like I told you. The nervous systems aren't compatible due to his age. Not to mention the radiation . . ."

"Your job was to make them compatible."

"The statistics are only a prediction, not a reality. I warned you again . . . and again . . . and again. A forty-four-year-old man has far too many neural connections for what you requested."

The crackling lights behind the glass came nearer. "I suggest you mind the way you speak to me, Dr. Markazian."

The doctor visibly gulped. "We're still looking at alternatives."

"You said that you'd run all the tests, didn't you? Mr. Korasa was the closest match."

"Yes, he was, but you have to remember . . . you're trying to fuse two individuals. This isn't an easy process. And by now, there might be a better match on the market."

"Failure after failure," Chanzig said coldly. "First was your attempt at creating a virtual intelligence. Next was your foray into imprinting a clone with his nervous system. Then came your little adventures with neurons. How many years will you waste? How many donors?"

"Experimental research takes time."

"You are running out of it, Doctor. Your behavior makes me question how badly you wish to find the Sacred Guide and complete me."

"No . . . don't say that," Dr. Markazian said, half-pleading. "I got you the gateway, didn't I? I've delivered on every promise thus far. I just . . . need to make the creation stable."

"It only needs to last until the Sacred Guide is found."

"That could take months, sir. With all due respect, it's more prudent to spend the extra time creating a sustainable organism. We can't handle another creation with a mental breakdown or genetic flaws. They need to perform under pressure."

"Do you know what will happen to you if you keep disappointing me?"

Dr. Markazian peeled off his gloves, his jaw working in tight circles. "There's a final option we haven't tried yet."

"Elaborate."

"We could start from the foundation. We have all the raw materials we need, sir. It's just a matter of assembling them properly."

The vid cut off again.

Modri wasted no time in whistling. *"You died? That's hardcore."*

I tried to speak, but my mouth was bone-dry. "I . . . No, I never died. Not in Chanzig's fortress, anyway. I don't know what this is, but I don't like it."

"It sounds like they were doin' some kind of procedure on you. Tryin' to make you one of the good doctor's little creations."

Much as I wanted to reply, I just couldn't find the words. In some ways, I now had more questions than I'd come with. For instance, it made sense why the God of Flesh had recognized me . . . but not *how*. This vid seemed to indicate that I—or whoever the hell my clone was—had indeed died a long while ago. Why wouldn't the doctor have mentioned that? And furthermore, why had he called me his creation? It was clear he and Chanzig had made *something* . . . but what? And if they had, was *I* really their creation? It was all a jumble. As I stood in that plastic-smelling, cramped room, I found that I had no idea who I was or what I was doing there.

But I *would* find out.

30

By the time I reached the gates back into the city, I was pissed. Pissed at my own confusion, pissed at having been roped into this mess, pissed at everybody and everything that had come together to make this maelstrom of lunacy.

This might explain why I was so terse with the guards.

"Open the goddamn gates," I barked. "I'm on my way to kill Chanzig."

With little more than a nervous glance between them, the two men stepped aside and worked to open the mechanisms. On the other side, I found the pair of guards who'd first let me out into Naraka. They were midway through chuckling at some asinine joke, but their grins faded when they saw me, my bloodstained armor, and the overstuffed bag of guns on my shoulder.

"Rain check on those beers, assholes," I said, tossing them a particularly shiny pistol as recompense.

They didn't say a word; in seconds, they were both brawling on the dirt, punching and clawing at each other to secure the loot.

I headed back to Kumil's place at a brisk walk. Along the way, nobody dared to speak to me. Few even had the balls to look in my general direction. Those that did look, however, were quick to murmur and speak in hushed tones. It appeared my cleanup job in Naraka had made quite a ripple in this slice of hell, too.

Upon reaching SIN4LIFE, I shouldered right through the dazed crowd of fiends, went to the back passages, and banged on Kumil's door. I must've been knocking like a demon, because the slippery fence unbolted the peephole in three seconds flat.

"What do you—" Kumil froze upon recognizing me. "Uh, hold on. Let me just, ah, let you inside . . ."

As soon as he opened the door, I barged past him and dumped my entire rucksack on his metal table. I took a moment to gather up all of *my* stuff and place it back in the bag, of course. But Kumil didn't seem to mind. He stood at my side, slack-jawed and bug-eyed, his gaze roaming hungrily across the assortment of weapons and flasks and other trinkets I'd taken from my enemies.

"You . . . gathered all this? By yourself?"

I nodded. "I'm leaving these here with you as repayment. Give some profits to the kids."

"Wait— You *found* that splicer?"

"More of a slicer, but yeah, I did. He's dealt with."

Kumil swallowed hard and tried a gentle pat on my shoulder. "Nice . . . work. Just out of curiosity, how many people did you—"

"No details," I interrupted. "Listen, Kumil, I've got a job for you. I want you to take these guns and sell them at half price to anybody who's willing to fight. There's going to be a revolt in a few hours."

"Eh?" Kumil started smiling. "You're joking, right? Is that it?"

"Not at all. I'm taking down Chanzig, just like I said I'd take down the guy in Naraka. So, start selling these guns. And if I find out you fleeced anybody, I'll come back and have some words with you."

I turned away before Kumil could say or do anything, confident he wouldn't be brazen enough to defy my instructions. After all, he'd seemed to be on the verge of soiling himself the moment he opened the peephole. If he'd survived this long down in the Abyss, he knew how to stay out of trouble.

It took me almost a full hour to locate the spiral stairwell linking the Abyss to the Dungeon. The entire construction was a rickety, wavering column that creaked with every step. There were no guards at the Abyss entrance, but it didn't take long to discover the reason behind that. You see, about halfway up, the stairwell became littered with corpses. Some were fresh, others a few days or weeks old. Within ten minutes of tedious climbing, I was in total darkness on all sides. Below was a shifting smog, and above was a milky night. My only comforts were the bodies under my boots.

As I climbed, I had the opportunity to reflect on my plan. And by "plan," I mean my total lack of a plan. I'd spent the entire return journey from Naraka seething, imagining all the ways I'd skin Chanzig or burn him alive. But none of those ideas featured the in-between segments that took me from planning a rebellion to actually *winning* the rebellion. Anger alone was not enough to overcome a tyrant in his own dystopian city.

And for that matter, could I even be sure the EMP bombs would work? Their inventor had once been a powerhouse of intellect, sure, but in his last days, he'd been reduced to a slavering heap of a man. For all I knew, his brilliant EMP bombs could be nothing more than a bunch of tape and a radio antenna.

All in all, my ambition of toppling Chanzig felt about as solid as the terrible staircase I was climbing. Who was I to think I could stroll into a land of madness, kill a few goons, and bring about systemic changes? I wasn't a savior; I was an archaeologist. At least, I'd seen myself as an archaeologist. Now I wasn't so sure what I was. My name, my face, my history . . . all of it had been called into question by the files on the terminals. The only thing I *knew* was mine, through and through, was my intention to get justice.

"*Not even gonna do a rank-up?*" Modri asked, startling me.

I stopped and held fast to the rusty railing, which seemed about ready to snap. My thighs were on fire.

"Can you warn me before you talk?" I said.

"*You want me to talk . . . to warn you I'm gonna talk?*"

"Maybe dial up your volume slowly. Like a transition."

"*Okay, but then you'll just assume you're hearing voices.*"

I sighed. "I already am."

"*Fair enough. But hey, listen. I think you oughta hit Rank 10 before you head up there. Maybe some of Chanzig's forces are still lurkin' about, and you can soak up enough Kill Points to hit 11 before you actually start the fight.*"

"I was just thinking about that fight, actually. I'm . . . not feeling great about it."

"*Oh, come on. Not another 'cry me a river' festival.*"

"I'm just being realistic. Maybe we're rushing into this."

"*Purifier, if I'd called off every mission I felt I was rushin', I never would've done a damn thing. That's what being a hero is all about. You're never ready, but you act anyway.*"

I raised a brow as I continued climbing. "You're saying you were a hero for invading worlds full of innocent people?"

"*You're not much better, are you? How many people are gonna die in this rebellion?*"

"Alright, you're not getting high marks for pep talks."

"*You brought it up. I'm just bein' fair.*"

"Touché." Again, I stopped and leaned against the staircase's central column. "It's just . . . I always saw myself as doing something great. Being someone great. But when I saw what was on those vids, it just took the wind right out of me. What if I'm nobody? What if I'm just some creation of a mad doctor?"

"Oh, so now you want *my pep talk?"*

"I don't know what I want," I said quietly. "I just want to know who I am, and to know what I stand for."

"Lemme tell you a little story," Modri said after a considerate pause. *"Back in my old unit, we had this one guy named Butcher. Real nasty son of a bitch. He'd always pick fights with the other reformers, get disciplinary hearings, that sort of thing. You couldn't even give him a compliment without catchin' a fist to the face."*

"How does any of this relate?"

"Be patient. It'll get there." Modri cleared his nonexistent throat. *"So, one day, Butcher gets put in our squad for a mission. We're supposed to take out an insurgent cell at some pump station. Now, it's all goin' good and dandy . . . until we get ambushed. Butcher takes a shrapnel canister to the head. He's bleedin' all over, leakin' brain juice and all that. He lived, but c'mon, he was basically a vegetable."*

"Still not getting the link."

Modri made a shushing noise. *"A few months later, ol' Butcher rejoins the teams. He's happy as could be, smilin' and jokin' with everybody. Compared to the Butcher we used to know, he was a different man. We found out later that he'd undergone some neurological procedure. Surgeons patched up a few wires wrong, and that changed everything. His whole life, his personality, memories. . . . None of it was the same. He ended up retirin' and becomin' some sorta chef."*

"You think that happened to me?"

"No, you dolt. Pay attention. What I'm sayin' is, it doesn't matter who you've been. It doesn't matter if you've got villas here and a gold toilet there. Everything can get taken away, right down to your mind. So, in reality, you don't own shit. Not even your body. The only thing that's yours, the only thing they can't take away, is what you do in this exact moment." He was silent for a long moment. *"Anyway, how's that for your stupid pep talk?"*

"It was perfect," I said sincerely, a second wind softening the pain in my legs as I pushed onwards. "Just perfect."

Around two hours into my ascent, I heard the bustle of the Dungeon filtering down from above me. I'd never been so happy to hear the creak of aging trams or the chatter of intermittent gunfire.

Before going the rest of the way up and finding Atrellu, however, I decided to do my rank-up in accordance with Modri's advice. After all, there was a very real chance one of the Dungeon's peacekeepers would shoot me out of habit. Having another 20 percent in Anima would help make sure I didn't end up like the many corpses on the staircase.

Sitting down and slumping against the central support again, I called up my Status Display.

STATUS DISPLAY
PURIFIER RANK: 9
RANK-UP AVAILABLE: Rank 10 (102,400 KP required)

Kill Points: 131,400
Genofacturing Points: 116,790

Rank Points: 0

Rank Time: 2 Hours, 46 Minutes, 13 Seconds
Storehouse Time: 4 Hours, 30 Minutes, 0 Seconds

Anima: 280%
Dominion: 0/4

Cutting it a tad close for timing, but whatever. The more disappointing thing was that I hadn't been able to soak up more Kill Points since imbibing the tonic. Silly me had assumed that the God of Flesh would yield over fifty thousand, especially considering the fact that "God" was in his name. But alas, I had just enough to bump me over to Rank 10 and add a little extra onto the GP pile.

I activated the rank-up to 10, and the 300% Anima readout instantly lifted my spirits . . . almost as much as Rank 11's 204,800 Kill Point requirement depressed my spirits. It wasn't the worst situation, however. I was about to launch an apocalyptic war against Chanzig, and that was guaranteed to bring the points rolling in.

Right now, the only choice of any consequence was which upgrade to pick. And I already had a solid guess for which one I'd take.

Genofacturing had clearly made a difference in my efforts to cleanse Naraka—even if the Plopper had a bit of a fatal flaw against armored foes, the keratin armor I'd printed had saved me from countless pistol rounds, melee blows, and blasts. In fact, I was beginning to suspect the armor itself had some of the chok'tal's magical properties, as several of the scratches and dents seemed to be leveling out and repairing themselves.

To put it simply, even genofacturing at stage I had granted me access to the kinds of tools a Purifier *needed* in their journey, especially if they didn't have access to a high-end armory. I could only imagine what sort of wonders stage-II genofacturing would bring.

Not needing to debate any further, I spent my Rank Point on Geno-facturing II. The only outward change in the Mutation tree was at the top.

MUTATION [Tier III] (*1 Rank Point required for Tier IV access*)

This was an unexpected surprise, mainly because I hadn't paid any attention to Telekinesis and its contribution to unlocking Tier IV. The quality of upgrades for Mutation had undergone an astonishing leap from Tier II to Tier III, so I was practically salivating to see the next selection. Maybe I'd gain the ability to make someone's head explode by staring at them.

But anyway . . . that was all in the future. The post-Chanzig future. Returning my focus to the present, I closed out the Status Display and continued up the staircase.

After about a hundred feet of ascent, I heard boots stomping around on the steps overhead. Through the metal grating above, I barely discerned a group of soldiers. Not Chanzig's soldiers—they were too informal and prone to laughter—but Atrellu's peacekeepers.

"Hey," I called up, hoping they wouldn't fire through the floor, "I've got an important message for your boss. Mind if I visit?"

The guards' conversations dried up in an instant.

"What's your name?" one of them called down.

"Dak Korasa. Atrellu knows me."

"Doesn't ring a bell."

I rubbed my temples. "I'm, uh, that guy that fell out of the sky a few days ago with the Cobalt Seer. And then fell down to the Abyss. In general, I just fall a lot."

"Oh, yeah!" another guard said. "That *is* him! I recognize the voice!"

"He's *alive*?" a third guy put in.

"Well, dead man," the first guard said, leaning over the railing to peer down at me, "I think it's time you rejoin the land of the living. Come on up before one of the ankle-chewers gets you."

Frowning, I resumed my climb at a jog. "Ankle-chewers?"

"If you haven't seen any, you're probably safe. Probably. Just hurry."

Thankfully, I made it to the top without having my ankles chewed off—or being shot to hell. The latter was a very real concern, seeing as Atrellu's forces had surrounded the top of the stairs with a maze of sandbags, towers, turrets, and even artillery pieces. They assured me that the display was mostly a show of force, but there were enough bullet holes and scorch marks around the area to poke a hole in that statement.

A pair of peacekeepers led me through the shuttered streets and foggy alleys. Most of the Dungeon was in disarray—worse than it had been prior my arrival, that is. Roofs and doors were blown apart. Stacks of rubble filled former marketplaces. And although the peacekeepers didn't point them out, I spotted several warehouses and empty lobbies full of wrapped bodies. The marks of recent conflict were everywhere, including the blistered faces of children that walked past. Chanzig's troops were gone, but their impact certainly wasn't. They'd come down here to instill an air of fear and death, and they had succeeded.

Atrellu's new headquarters were surrounded by block after block of barricades and checkpoints. The peacekeepers manning these stations had haggard, weary stares, and most had amp-sticks hanging out of their lips. A few were even slumped over their heavy weapon tripods, slumbering away under the drone of a distant raid siren.

Atrellu, however, still had some fight left in him. Even as we approached the main building, I heard the man frantically shouting orders.

"Then move that unit to the next station!" A pause. "What do you mean we don't have enough troops? Call up the reserves. Okay, call up the reserves of the reserves."

My peacekeeper escorts led me up the building's steps and through the front door.

Inside, it was just as chaotic as I'd expected. Transmission operators were hunched over their terminals, sending or receiving encrypted packages. Officers with holo-maps argued over pixilated details. Quartermasters fumbled to load rusty shotguns.

Atrellu was at the center of the storm, pacing about and shouting into his relay headset.

"Sir?" one of my escorts said, causing Atrellu to absently lift a finger. "Sir?"

This time, Atrellu spun around with wrath on his face. "What is— Oh."

He stared at me as though I were the first human he'd ever encountered. "Is . . . that you?"

I shrugged. "I've been asking myself that question a lot lately."

He gave a little grin, walked over, and shook my hand. "Looks like Chanzig's little cult is wrong. The Undying One is standing right here."

"Sorry it took me a while to come back," I said, slipping my rucksack off. "I had to make a little detour."

"What, to get some tooth armor?"

"Close, but I've got something better."

I fished out one of the EMP bombs and handed it to Atrellu. He accepted it gently, turning it end over end in awe.

"You made a bomb?" he finally asked.

"Not just a bomb," I said. "It's an EMP that targets Chanzig's security grid."

Atrellu eyed me warily. "How did you get this?"

"Let's just say I took a quick trip to the Abyss. Naraka, to be precise."

"You're shitting me."

"I wish I was. Would've been a lot less blood." I walked over to his table and plopped down the other bombs. "You have anybody who can test these things out? I'd like to iron out a few details before we use them."

"Whoa, there," Atrellu said. "What do you mean by *use* them?"

"You know . . . to take down Chanzig's grid. Kick things off."

The chatter in the room around me stopped. All the peacekeepers looked over, their gazes dripping with discomfort.

"We're not in any position to do anything extreme," Atrellu said softly. "Matter of fact, we're still cleaning up from that last strike. It'll be weeks before we can even consider something like this."

"Weeks?"

"Yessir, and that's just to *consider* a plan. We need to do recon, get our operatives on the higher tiers, scope it all out . . ."

I folded my arms. "We don't have that sort of time."

"Down here, all we've got is time, okay? I get it: You want the Cobalt Seer back. But rushing up there with some slapdash bomb isn't gonna fix anything."

"I'm offering you a chance, Atrellu. This is the moment you've all been hoping for. You've got a real shot to knock out those defenses. A real way in."

He laughed. "You have no idea what a real rebellion is, do you? Even *if* we stormed up there, dragged Chanzig out, and seized this town for ourselves . . . it'd be anarchy. You wanna talk about fighting him? It'll take us at least a year, Dak. We'd need time to vote on things, get leadership organized, set up distribution chains, territory agreements . . ."

My hands turned to fists, but not out of anger at Atrellu. I understood his position. He was a man of the people, and no decent leader would feel comfortable throwing waves of bodies at an enemy like Chanzig. But for me, an outsider, there was rage at the whole situation. Chanzig had built a literal hell for these people, and he'd built it so effectively they couldn't organize enough to climb out.

"Let me be the test, then," I said quietly.

Again, the room fell silent.

Atrellu squinted at me, unsure. "What are you talking about?"

"We need to test these bombs. Let me take one and surrender myself to Chanzig. If it works . . . you'll know. And if it doesn't . . . well, you'll also know."

"That's suicide, Dak."

"Maybe. But living down here is a slow death for everyone. So let me do this for all of you. Let me take the fight to him and see how he bites back."

Atrellu shook his head, chuckling. "You really have a death wish, huh? How do you expect to get up there without getting blown into bits?" I started to reply, but he waved a hand to cut me off. "It ain't Chanzig I'm talking about. The troops on the upper tiers are nothing to play with. It's like I said, Dak . . . everyone's out for themselves."

The harsh reality of Atrellu's remarks pressed down on me. He had a point. How was I going to make it up to Chanzig's front door carrying an EMP bomb? Getting captured wasn't even a problem—it was finding a way to *reach* the people who would capture me. If I drew the attention of anybody on the tiers above this one, I'd blow my cover long before making it to the goal.

Then it hit me . . . Don't fix a strategy if it ain't broke.

"Are those gunships still coming down here?" I asked. "I fell into the Abyss, but they probably don't know where I landed, right?"

Atrellu nodded. "They've been combing all over the tiers. Putting up rewards for your body."

"So, if someone found my body, they'd come down to pick it up."

"Yeah." His eyes bloomed as he picked up on what I was thinking. "Hell, no. We are *not* doing another fake surrender."

"It's not a fake surrender," I said. "It's a hijacking."

"Even worse."

"Have some faith in me. I've done it before."

Atrellu let out a long breath, fidgeting with his hat. "You know what you're asking of me, right? You want us to spark another conflict. When they realize that gunship was taken *here*, in the Dungeon . . ."

"The other option is that I walk straight up there alone. And I'll do it, too. I'm short on time."

"What the hell is your rush?"

"Long story," I said, smirking. "So, what'll it be? Either way, I'm going to Chanzig. I'm going to make him pay—or try to."

"Goddamn, Dak. You're giving me a few hours' notice to decide if I want to overthrow the ruler of our planet."

I clapped a hand on his shoulder. "You'll make the right choice."

"Yeah, well, right choice probably would've been to shoot you dead when you crashed here."

"Too late for that," I said as I backed toward the door. "Check your charts, make your transmissions, get a feel for everything. Oh, and reach out to the Abyss. A guy named Kumil. Tell him you're with me and ask how many fighters they can send up. Then let me know when it's game time."

I strode out of the headquarters and toward the closest hotel feeling like pure gold. It was still a rough situation, all things considered, but man, I had *handled* that conversation. I'd let Atrellu and all the other peace-keepers know that I wasn't just talk; I meant business.

This sense of unshakable coolness lasted about three minutes. At the conclusion of those minutes, the thrum of countless engines appeared out of nowhere. In a flash of déjà vu, dozens upon dozens of gunships low-ered down and out of the smog, hovering in a circular pattern over the entire district. Floodlights framed me in the middle of the urban square. The nearest gunship, which had come down directly above me, dropped even lower to reveal a team of locked-and-loaded troops with Chanzig's uniforms.

"Well, shit," I muttered, raising my hands.

Even *I* wasn't dumb enough to risk a fight at the moment. All of my weapons were either holstered or crammed into the rucksack, and the gunship crews had clearly learned my tricks by now. They wouldn't hesi-tate to shoot the moment I reached for something.

Every peacekeeper in the area shrank back into the shadows, doing their best to minimize engagement with me. I couldn't blame them. To this place, I was an outsider—albeit a compelling one—that had thus far brought nothing except bloodshed. And even if they *did* think I could make a difference, there was no sense in dying on this hill. Better to retreat, regroup, and rethink.

Out of the corner of my eye, I spotted the surgeon who had treated Akasha and I upon our arrival. He stood in his little "hospital's" doorway, watching me with a muted yet content expression.

I knew that look all too well. It was the look of a man who'd just screwed you over and was taking pleasure in the act.

"Good, old-fashioned betrayal," I called to him over the gunships' whirring.

"Nothing personal, stranger," the surgeon yelled back. "It's not betrayal if you hardly know someone . . ."

"Is Chanzig paying you nicely for it?"

"No payment needed. You just bring too much noise to this tier. Once you're gone, things will be calm again. Sorry."

I met his eye as teams of soldiers rappelled or hover-booted down to ground level. "Don't sweat it, Doc. You're not the first man who's sent me to die."

A soldier appeared at my side, but before I could turn to them fully, their rifle butt came flying toward my face. Pain exploded through my nose. Wet blood sprayed out over my chin. Then another soldier clocked me in the back of the helmet, and it was lights out.

31

"Wake up, little dog. You've been a terribly disobedient visitor to this world, and you're in need of some correction."

As far as wake-up alarms go, the words of Chanzig's torturer were among the worst.

I opened my eyelids through a sticky film of gunk, only to immediately re-shut them against the room's harsh light. For some reason, my head couldn't move, nor could my hands, or ankles, or neck. Vaguely, I sensed that I was being held in a spread-eagle position. Everything was smooth and cold.

Oh, damn it, I thought with annoyance. *They stripped me and secured me to something metal again.*

Seriously, did Chanzig have a fetish for cold steel or something? I never did find out. But considering how bad the nudity-metal combination was, it might surprise you to learn that there was something even more atrocious about my situation. And that *something* was the voice of my torturer. It belonged to none other than the perverted bastard who'd captured Akasha using the gunship. The same one I'd gifted with a royal beatdown.

"Hello, Lieutenant Thirmen," I muttered through a coppery and aching mouth, my eyes still shut. "Hope you enjoyed the rest of your flight."

His footsteps thudded closer. "Look at me."

"Oh, I wish I could. I bet your face looks *terrible*, what with all those boot and fist marks. Turn down the brightness so I can take a peek."

Suddenly, his fingers clamped against my cheeks. He squeezed until my teeth ached. "You have so much wit in you. But I bet I can bleed that out."

Despite the grip on my face, I let out a laugh. "I don't think Chanzig would appreciate you harming his property."

"Oh, don't worry yourself with that. Supreme Chairman Chanzig doesn't even know you're here."

"Huh?"

He let go of me and began circling whatever contraption I was on. "I made a private deal with the surgeon who ran that clinic. He was more than happy to deliver you to me *personally*. I'm sure that when I eventually turn you over to my master, he'll be delighted that I softened you up."

"Or torture you to death, too. You don't know what you're messing with. He's *obsessed* with me. Platonically, I mean. Hopefully."

"Oh, yes, he is. He thinks you're something truly special. And yet . . . what makes you special is more than skin deep. In fact, all your specialness is deep, deep within. So no matter how cruelly I treat your skin, little dog, Supreme Chairman Chanzig will just be happy to see your insides. What's left of them, that is."

As bad as this was, I had only one thought about everything: *Why isn't my HUD going into combat mode?*

"Feeling a bit more playful than usual?" Thirmen said. "That would probably be the tranquilizers and adrenal inhibiters in your body. I took the liberty of helping you relax during your air travel . . . for the safety of yourself and all other passengers."

Damn. I was beginning to truly hate the biological consistency of the chok'tal. Apparently, it understood humanoid threat responses a little *too* well. No adrenaline, no sense of fight or flight. And thus no encounters. No Kill Points.

"Pacification," I said weakly, laughing in spurts. "Smart move. If I wasn't so doped up right now, I'd sure as hell be ripping your jaw off."

"That's why you'll never win, little dog. You're just an animal. A blind, hungry *thing* desperate to survive. You'll eat your own limbs to stay alive. But we . . . those who are faithful to the heart and mind of the Supreme Chairman . . . we will inherit this world and make it whole again. We will show who is eternal and who is *meat*."

I nodded for a time, trying to look deeply analytical. "That's some grade-A cult quoting."

"We'll see who's left standing when the Supreme Chairman remakes this fallen world." He returned to stand in front of me. "You know, most of my colleagues thought you were dead. They said that no mortal could survive such a drop."

"I'll wager Chanzig wasn't real happy about your performance."

"No," Thirmen said faintly. "He was not."

Again, I fought to open my eyes through the lethargy and stinging. The first thing that hit me was, unsurprisingly, the light. It had been pointed directly into my face. But once that initial shock wore off, I was able to get a good look at the man standing before me.

His nose had been flattened and split, its tip wrenched to one side. Dark, freckled bruising covered the entire center of his face, including the bags beneath both eyes, No more perfect features. That was all my work, and I was damn proud of it. But there were other marks, too, such as small burns and stripes where the skin had been ripped away.

"Yes, look upon me and weep," Thirmen said. "This is what Chanzig does to those who disappoint him. And you, little dog, are the ultimate disappointment."

"So, what's the plan? You want to torture me for embarrassing you in front of your boss?"

He smirked. "No, I want to torture you because of your conduct. You believed you could disrespect me without consequences."

"And *you* believed Akasha was the property of your master."

"Is she not?"

"No," I growled. "Chanzig doesn't own anybody, even if he thinks the world is his. So you, and him, and every other cultist are in for a rude awakening."

Thirmen stepped closer. "Akasha is his, as are you. Even now, she resides far, far above us, dwelling within his chamber. I'm sure he will enjoy breaking your mind even more than hers."

A seed of rage appeared in my chest, but even as it grew, it began to dissolve. This damn tranquilizer made it impossible to feel *angry*. To feel anything.

"Now, then, let's move on to more interesting topics." Thirmen moved away and went behind my contraption, allowing me a better look at the small room's white, circular walls. When he returned, he was holding the Geno-facturing Spore. "What can you tell me about this remarkable . . . item?"

"I *can* tell you plenty, but *will* I tell you? Not a chance."

"Oh, we'll see about that. You and I have all the time in the world."

"There's a time limit on everything," I said, winking. "Trust me on that."

Thirmen just hefted the Genofacturing Spore in his hands, examining its pores and ethereal red light. "Time doesn't seem to be a pressing issue for you. After all, you've managed to collect a great deal of trinkets during your travels."

"Why the interest? Hoping to impress Chanzig with them?"

"You speak in jest, but you're not far off the mark. You see, the Supreme Chairman's time of ascension is near. And when he claims his throne, he will need a second-in-command. A follower capable of carrying out his vision in this world."

"I guess you didn't hear what happened to the last guy who was Chanzig's assistant."

Thirmen stopped rotating the spore and stared at me. "You're referring to Dr. Markazian."

"Nowadays, he prefers 'God of Flesh.' Well, he did."

"You're implying you killed him, no?" Thirmen smiled. "No great loss. He was a madman, hanging on to my master's coattails for a chance at divinity."

"And you think you're different? I bet you're just like Markazian—a Hegemony puppet willing to betray your uniform for a better pension."

Thirmen's eyes hardened. "A pension? You believe I'm driven by wealth?"

"Most people are."

"For years, I served the Hegemony because of my devotion to Halcius," he snarled. "The one true creator, the source of all existence . . . a grand *lie*. You see, I was committed to Halcius through blind faith. I believed the words of my instructors and commanders." He glanced away. "But in the darkest hours, when my fellow soldiers were slaughtered by the thousands and abandoned by their leaders, where was Halcius? Where was his radiance, his purity? Nowhere."

I hadn't expected it, but the core of genuine anguish in the man's voice evoked curiosity in me. "What did Chanzig promise you, then?"

"To bring back my brothers in arms," he said earnestly. "Once the Supreme Chairman has completed his transformation, he will be capable of miracles. He'll resurrect them. All of them."

"Wait . . . you think Chanzig is going to raise people from the dead?"

"I don't think; I *know*. When I visited him in confinement, he filled me with visions beyond your imagination. He knew my deepest wishes, and he knew the way to fulfill them."

"What if you're wrong?" I asked with genuine concern. "What if he's been lying to you and all the others?"

"Spare me your doubts, little dog."

"I mean it. How do you know he can do anything he's promised you? For all you know, he could just be feeding everybody a diet of fantastical dreams."

"When he is made whole, there will be no barrier between dreams and reality."

I shrugged—tried to, anyway. "You're going to feel real stupid when I'm proven right."

"You won't be around to find out." He smiled and circled back around my contraption, fiddling with something metallic. "Now, I can tell you won't surrender any information willingly . . . which is fine by me. I was rather hoping you'd put up a fight." When he returned, he was carrying a pair of scalpels. "I've heard much of your miraculous healing abilities. My men say that you fight like a demon, and no matter how much you bleed, you don't perish. Let's put that to the test."

Without warning, he stabbed both scalpels up into my ribs. I let out a muffled cry, hoping I might deprive him of whatever sadistic joy came from skewering my organs. With every breath, the twin blades scraped against new flesh.

He reached down, wet one of his fingers with my blood, and licked it. "Tastes rather ordinary to me. But let's see if the flavor changes with pain."

I locked eyes with him, trying to keep my face neutral.

"Playing a tough soldier, are we?" Thirmen taunted. "I have just the thing for you, though I do believe it's in the other room. I'll go fetch it. Just make sure you don't wander too far."

He walked off, chuckling at his own terrible joke as he went.

When the door shut with a hiss, I went into action mode. There had to be something to get me out of here. Some upgrade I'd neglected, maybe, or a hidden chok'tal power I'd never drawn upon.

Speaking of chok'tal powers, I attempted something I should've tried earlier.

Modri? I thought, probing for his presence.

Nothing.

As the seconds ticked by, the dread set in. I was completely immobile, and all my thoughts came in slow, rambling waves. Maybe this really was the end. Despite all my cleverness, and my pain, and my sweat, I'd been outplayed.

All I could do was stare down at the scalpels, both of which jittered in rhythm with my heartbeats. It was maddening to think that my situation would be drastically changed if I could just grab one of them. At least then I'd have a weapon, or something to help break my cuffs. But seeing as my arms were firmly fixed above my—

Telekinesis.

The word broke through the fog of my mind in a flash. It was the one upgrade I hadn't played with, and now I deeply regretted that. Even if merely thinking "Telekinesis" was enough to activate the upgrade, what could I actually do with it in a matter of minutes? How would I learn to move things, or sense them, or whatever the hell was required? This time around, there was no Modri or Guide to lay such things out.

This would be a solo experiment.

Praying I could still trigger upgrades in spite of my weakened state, I shut my eyes, focused, and thought the magic word. At first, nothing happened—which was expected. Several upgrades needed a secondary component beyond merely thinking the name.

With that in mind, I stared intently at the right-hand scalpel. I thought Telekinesis again, straining my face in an attempt to move the blade. All I succeeded in doing was giving myself a semi-aneurysm. Obviously, there was something else here.

Think, Dak, think.

There was a mechanism to moving things. There had to be. Some system that translated thoughts into movements. Reflecting on it further, I contemplated how I moved my fingers, or my mouth, or anything else on my body. Before the movement itself, there was an intention to move. Tensing up didn't actually cause the body to act. It was the *intention* that mattered.

Although it was a long shot, I began testing my theory by staring at the scalpel and relaxing as much as I could. The sedatives helped with that. Next, I simply willed the scalpel to slide back. There's no other way to describe it, really—I treated the scalpel as though it were an extension of my body, a limb devoid of its own feeling.

Suddenly, the scalpel wobbled.

It hurt like hell, seeing as it scraped what I assumed was my spleen, but the pain was overpowered by the euphoria of success. I'd done it. I'd moved something . . . with my mind. If I hadn't been about to undergo torture, I would've thrown myself a party.

But alas, I *was* about to be tortured. With time ticking down, I kicked up my efforts to move the blade. With each push of willpower, the scalpel jittered a bit more. After about three tries, I saw blood along the metal. It was coming out.

Just then, however, I heard bleeping as someone worked to reopen the room's door. My concentration fumbled. Rather than smoothly withdrawing the scalpel, I yanked it clean out and lost control. The red-stained blade clattered to the floor just as the door opened.

"I hope I didn't keep you waiting too long," Thirmen said as he came around to me. "There was a bit of a delay with—" He halted, staring down at the scalpel and the surrounding flecks of blood. "How very curious."

"I guess you didn't stick me hard enough," I said.

"Perhaps."

Though it may have been my imagination, I swore there was a note of fear in him. A small, nearly invisible crack in his demeanor, expressed through twitches in his brows and lips.

"No matter," he continued, showing me a long, slender device with a needle tip. In many ways, it resembled Kumil's lock-popper. "Do you know what this is, little dog?"

"Not a clue."

"I suspected as much," he said, smiling at his new toy. "Long ago, when the Hegemony wasn't quite so soft, it had a special punishment reserved for traitors. Not just any traitors, of course, but the worst sort: the traitors who were citizens themselves. In the Hegemony's eyes, it was unthinkable that somebody could work to destroy the order of their own people, especially when everything they had—their wealth, their comfort, their security—had come from the Hegemony itself."

"Is this history lesson going anywhere?"

Thirmen's lips flattened out. "The Hegemony decided that if these traitors wanted to degrade their own culture, they were no longer part of it. And as such, they had no authority to represent themselves as citizens any longer. Aesthetic matters included."

I looked at Thirmen, then the needle-gun thing, beginning to understand what he was implying. "You want to stab my eyeballs?"

"I'll simply drain the irises' color and stain them with something new. Just as I did to myself. It's tremendously painful, little dog."

Studying his face closer, it became clear he wasn't lying. The pigmentation in his irises was bizarre to say the least.

"Did Chanzig make you do that?" I asked. "Just like he made you give up your life to come here and serve him?"

"I did it of my own volition. Once, I had eyes as purple as yours. But when I came here, I gave that up. I gave *everything* up." He lifted the needle closer to my face. "It's only right that you face my master as a proper servant. As of now, you are not a Hegemony citizen. You are nothing."

"Let's talk about this," I said, squirming as he brought the tip even closer to my right eye. "You don't need to—"

"You've spoken enough," he said, his voice distant and dead. "Forgive my shaky hands. I just get so excited ..."

As the needle came closer and closer, its point growing hazy, I focused intently on the metal. With every scrap of my mental power, I willed it *away*. Anywhere but inside my eyeball. Still, it continued to approach. Thirmen took hold of my eyelids and pried them apart, and soon my vision was muddy, clouded over by involuntary tears.

"Be grateful," he whispered as the needle loomed. "This is your rebirth in the face of death. A new face for the sacrificial lamb."

Move, I mentally screamed at the needle, desperate to summon the same force that had moved the scalpel. But there was nothing. Even as my mind coiled around the needle, I sensed Thirmen's force behind it. There was no contest between my newfound telekinetic power and a grown zealot's arm strength. No matter how much I pushed, he could resist me with the touch of a finger.

With no other options, my mind strayed to the last thing I'd focused on: the scalpel. I could still feel the faint bond with it. It seemed to absorb all my fear, my urgency. And as the needle's point came within a hair's width of my eyeball ...

Metal rattled against the floor.

Thirmen immediately froze up, retracted the needle, and looked down. His gaze lingered on the scalpel, which now appeared as ordinary as ever ... with one exception. Smears of my blood surrounded the blade. It *had* moved. *I'd* moved it.

"I should know better than to leave things where I might nudge them," Thirmen remarked, plainly alarmed but still trying to put up a façade of normalcy. "Allow me to handle this so we can continue uninterrupted."

As he bent down to pick the scalpel up, a vicious idea took hold of me. The odds of it working were slim, if not nonexistent, but it wasn't like I had millions of other options to try. This was my one shot to repay the bastard for all he'd done.

His hand came close to the blade, and I focused. I focused like never before. I felt every atom, every quark that comprised the metal. Ripples of latent power flowed out toward me, and I clutched at them, strengthening the bond between mind and matter.

At the last second, just as he went to grasp it, I flicked the scalpel upwards. It lifted in a violent streak, slicing clean through the skin between his thumb and forefinger. Then it twirled and flopped back to the tiles, bringing with it a thin spray of his blood.

Thirmen stumbled back, cursing and hissing, clutching at his injured hand. When his eyes finally met mine, I saw what I'd been waiting for: the terror. For perhaps the first time, he had a real taste of what I could do.

"Sorry about that," I said. "Clumsy hands."

With wide, vengeful eyes, the man stood and snatched up his fallen needle-gun thing. Then he came right up to me and flashed the grin of a maniac.

"You're free to display your parlor tricks," he whispered, kicking the scalpel far across the room. "It will just make *this* all the more satisfying."

Again, he lifted the needle in position and wrenched my eyelids open. This time, I knew it was over. No way out. No last-minute aces up my sleeve.

Just before the needle entered my eye, I resolved not to scream. He wouldn't get any satisfaction from his captive.

The point drew nearer . . . nearer . . . nearer . . . growing in size like a horrible moon.

"Let's drag this out," Thirmen said. "It's not the wounds that give delight, little dog . . . It's the fear."

Then everything went black.

My first thought was that he'd done it. He'd taken my vision with one bad jab from the needle. But that didn't make sense—he'd only been threatening one eye. Just as I was analyzing this, a low, wailing alarm filled the room. Soft auxiliary lights flicked on all around us, bathing the room in an otherworldly cherry glow.

And then, with the most beautiful mechanical sound I've ever heard, my restraints unlocked. My feet plopped down on the supports below me, and my arms flopped down to my sides.

Thirmen's eyes looked like marbles in the dim light: wide, dark, glossy with fear.

"Sir?" a voice crackled through the man's suit transmitter. "We've just suffered an attack on the grid. All systems are down. Looks like another uprising."

It was Atrellu—it had to be. Those damn EMP bombs had worked. If I hadn't been locked in this asshole's torture chamber, I would've howled out of sheer joy. But seeing as I *was* locked in the torture chamber, there was business to handle.

Thirmen didn't reply to his underling's message. In fact, all he managed to do was take a step back and begin panting as I stepped off the platform. The needle device shook in his hands.

"Now we can fight on fair ground, *little dog*," I said quietly. "I know you've left Halcius and the Hegemony behind, but you might want to say a few prayers now. Insurance for the afterlife."

In a show of surrender, Thirmen tossed the device aside and raised both hands. "You don't have to do this, you know."

"Oh, but I want to."

"I'm— I'm not a threat to you. I was just—"

"Following orders? Trying to scare me? I'd advise you to just save your breath. Whatever reason you give is just going to piss me off even worse."

"Are you . . . going to kill me?"

"Obviously." I cracked my neck and moved forward. "Thanks to your sedative, I won't even get Kill Points for this. But I think the reward is in the *doing*, don't you?"

He swallowed hard. "Can you . . . make it quick, then?"

"Let's just say I'll take a page from your book. 'You and I have all the time in the world.'"

32

Still bathed in Thirmen's blood, I lumbered over to the room's table and began reclaiming all my equipment. It was convenient that they'd left all my stuff here—armor, guns, and blades included—but it didn't make the process of suiting up any faster. The sedative was still slurping through my veins, and I'd used the last of my rage to rip my torturer apart.

As I pulled on the armored leg plates, however, a thought bubbled up through the chaos of the alarms and pounding feet in the hallway.

The neural suppression field was gone.

I'd first sensed it when the EMP bombs went off, but I hadn't put much attention it. Now, however, it seemed so obvious. The moment the field went down, Thirmen had lost his edge. It wasn't just my intimidation factor that had turned him into a coward—it was the loss of Chanzig's voice in his head. The loss of whatever brainwashing signal had turned his men into fearless zealots. In a flash, I understood how Chanzig maintained such strict order on the surface of his world. The Deathless Tsar, the torturer, Dr. Markazian . . . They had all been lured to this world by his powers, and upon arrival, they'd fallen under his spell of control.

It was time to end the source of that spell for good.

Once I was fully armed and armored, I sat the Genofacturing Spore on the table to make myself a shiny stage-II weapon. But when I tried to activate it, nothing happened. That damn sedative. It seemed that they'd dosed me up so strongly that almost *all* my chok'tal interfacing abilities were kaput. All I had were my upgrades—but how far would those go in a fortress full of cornered animals?

The thought chilled me . . . until I realized it wasn't true. I had something more valuable than any powers the chok'tal could grant: my survival instincts. The same instincts that had gotten me through the jungle, through the ship, through the wastes, through the Abyss . . . Here and now, they would carry me through Chanzig's death. My heartbeat was the only fuel I needed.

Wielding the Plopper in one hand and the nano-carbon sword in the other, I triggered the door's emergency release. The panel slid back in a spray of fog, revealing empty corridors lit by dull red bulbs.

"I don't know if you're there, Modri," I whispered as I stepped out, "but if you are, I hope you enjoy this. It's gonna get brutal."

I started by heading toward the sound of boots on tiles—maybe not the brightest move, given my tranquilized and solo status, but it would definitely lead to the heart of the action. And that meant a route to Chanzig. I moved down the corridor, swinging my Plopper from room to room to check for threats. Soon enough, I came to a junction point . . . and my first enemies.

The squad of four was jogging toward me, suited up and carrying rifles. It seemed that they didn't recognize me as a threat, however, because they hardly looked in my direction. Only when they turned the corner and one of them slowed did the trouble begin.

"Who's your commander?" the nosy soldier asked.

His comrades stopped and turned on a dime, staring at me expectantly.

"Uh . . . Commander . . ." I shook my head. "Oh, forget it. I'm too messed up to act right now."

Leaping forward, I slashed horizontally and severed the man's head just above his shoulders. This shocked even me, as I hadn't expected to hack through so easily. Nano-carbon was no joke.

Even as I stared in awe at the falling head, though, the other soldiers sprang into action. One opened up with gunfire, causing me to whirl around and take the brunt of the shots with my back panels. The rounds still punched into my back like a sledgehammer.

While turning, however, I rushed to the side and took cover behind the corner. One of Chanzig's men had run in the same direction as me, leaving us both in melee range. Before he could get a shot off, I plunged the blade through his chest and ripped upward, carving a straight line from his solar plexus to his collarbone. He dropped in place with a muffled scream.

The soldier who'd opened fire leaned around the corner and put two bullets into my chest plate. Whether due to our distance or the rifle's power, the plates shattered and sent me staggering back. Bits of powdered keratin misted in the air. Another bullet, and I'd be dead.

I simultaneously triggered Indomitable and charged forward, firing a quick pair of shots with the Plopper as I engaged. The biological rounds splattered on the man's helmet—no damage, but enough of a distraction to close the gap and ram the sword through his visor.

As I yanked out the blade, heaving from even this small exertion, I spied the last soldier out of the corner of my eye. He stood about ten meters away, kneeling with his rifle shouldered. No matter how fast I was, I couldn't win this bout. Just as he squeezed the trigger, I ducked back around the corner and hurried through the nearest doorway to take shelter.

I found myself in a triage room of some sort. Operating tables, medical cabinets, and multi-armed mechanical surgery rigs surrounded me. Wait . . . medical cabinets. This was probably where Lieutenant Sadist had found the tranquilizers. Which meant there had to be something to reverse it here.

Still watching the door with the Plopper, I moved low and fast through the rows of equipment, trying to find where they hid those sweet, sweet drugs. It wasn't too hard. They had entire bins full of narcotics: uppers, downers, overs, unders. And the thing I sought—synthetic adrenaline— was overflowing in one such bin.

At least, I assumed it was adrenaline. The labels were faded and described a long, intricate chemical compound. But they were also marked by all the same symbols I'd seen on Hegemony-issue adrenaline injectors. Good enough for me.

Grabbing one of the vials, I popped the protector cap off and immediately jabbed it into my neck. The rush was intense, immediate, and completely overwhelming. It felt like fresh life had been breathed into my corpse.

"Let's try it now . . . Can you hear me?" Modri asked.

I grinned. "Loud and clear, cous."

"I'm not your cousin."

"You might be, according to that genetic report."

"We'll talk about that later. Y'know, after you're not about to die. By the way, why'd you inject dextroamphetamine?"

My heartbeat galloped as I heard his words. Second by second, the world became more vivid, more lucid. "That wasn't adrenaline?"

"Nah, 'cous.' That was top-shelf amp-juice. You just took three times the dose for infantry."

"Oh, shit."

"Yeah, 'oh, shit' for the guys you're about to murder. Show 'em who's boss."

Deep down, I knew I wasn't some hardened killer, but the amphetamine made it extremely hard to remember that. With all the fury and energy of a starved tiger, I advanced toward the door.

The soldier popped out just before I reached it, only to be framed in a blue box.

Chanzig's Soldier (HUMANOID)
CALCULATING . . .
Estimated Kill Points: 11,000

With a growl so harsh it hurt even my ears, I rammed into him and drove him into the back wall. Then I slashed across his face with the blade—a shallow cut, just enough to shatter the silicate material. Before I knew it, I'd raised my Plopper and fired a round directly into the broken helmet. Steam and hideous odors vented through the visor as the man shrieked and collapsed.

ENCOUNTER SUCCESSFUL
Kills: 1
Kill Points Awarded: 11,000

"Damn," Modri said. *"That was . . . a bit excessive."*

"Yeah, no kidding," I replied, flicking the blood off my sword. "Now that we're done with all that, though . . . I think it's time for a little genofacturing."

"Shouldn't you be storming the tower while the fight's going on?"

"Everyone knows the hero has to have a badass weapon for the final fight. Even if you're someone like me."

Within three minutes, I'd hidden myself in a corner of the triage room and set the Genofacturing Spore on the tiles. After taking a deep breath and hoping I wouldn't be caught with my pants down, I activated the spore's menu.

[Stage-II Products Available for Genofacturing]
Genofacturing Points: 145,790

Product Categories:
Armor

Blades
Pistols
Shotguns
Rifles
Light Machine Guns
Shields
Utility Tools
Rations
Ammunition
Explosives
Tonics
View All Stage-II Products

There would be time to check out all my new goodies later—if I survived. For now, the most vital thing was a weapon. I couldn't risk taking my Plopper into combat here, mainly due to the soldiers' armor. If I encountered the next squad at a range too far for melee, I was screwed. What mattered now was firepower, and a lot of it. With that in mind, I checked just four categories: Explosives, Rifles, Light Machine Guns, and Shotguns.

Shotguns:
Plaque Spitter (60,000 GP)
Fungal Burst (90,000 GP)

Rifles:
Clean Exit (50,000 GP)
Prion Storm (85,000 GP)
Farstrike (120,000 GP)

Light Machine Guns:
Nail Chewer (150,000 GP)

Explosives:
Dazzler (4500 GP)
Stinger (4500 GP)
Scorcher (8000 GP)
Eraser (12,000 GP)

Once again, the lack of obvious names didn't help me in the slightest. But at least my selection pool was larger, and there seemed to be more versatility this time around—including the addition of my first light machine gun, or LMG.

I immediately struck the LMG off the list, though. I'd be mobile, and most LMGs tended to be large, bulky weapons that required a stationary position. That was what I'd heard from Liura, anyway. Besides, it was already 150,000 of my Genofacturing Points for the gun alone. The ammo would break the bank in no time, especially given how much of it an LMG ran through.

Tabbing through the rifle descriptions, I got a better idea of what both new choices were used for.

Prion Storm (85,000 GP): A compact, close-combat automatic rifle that deals damage over time on top of its normal kinetic effect. All rounds that strike biological material impart a fast-acting prion capable of killing the host in hours. Thirty-round magazine.

Farstrike (120,000 GP): A long-distance, bolt-action sniper rifle capable of punching through most targets. Fires a thick, highly volatile round that may be used for antipersonnel or antivehicle combat. Five-round magazine.

Both were intriguing in their own way, but also limited. Prion Storm seemed like an excellent weapon overall, though its emphasis on shooting prions that dealt damage over time rather than, say, piercing armor was concerning. I didn't need to kill Chanzig and his men a few hours from now—I needed them dead in short order. Conversely, Farstrike was an extremely appealing choice . . . but only for open environments. Here in Chanzig's corridors, a sniper rifle was a death sentence.

That left my final primary weapon category: Shotguns. I pulled up the description for Plague Burst, praying it wouldn't be a dud.

Plague Burst (90,000 GP): A semi-automatic shotgun that fires explosive, neurotoxic rounds. After initial detonation, a volatile gas cluster will blanket the impact area for a short duration. Purifiers are immune to this effect. Six-shell magazines.

It looked like we had our winner. The shotgun was perfect for close-quarters combat, and the added bonus of delivering a neurotoxic cloud—which I was immune to, of course—would help flush his troops out of any fortified positions.

Before I moved on to explosives, I queued up the Plague Burst and forty-eight shells. Which reminded me . . . *Magazines.* How else would I carry that many shells? Fortunately, Genofacturing II seemed to have opened up spare magazines. Only 500 GP apiece for the Plague Burst variety. Thinking logically, I got seven to hold the extra shells I'd purchased. With that finished, I resolved to get creative with it and pressed on with my original goal: getting stuff that went *bang*.

In short order, I checked each explosive's description.

Dazzler (4500 GP): A nonlethal grenade capable of blinding and deafening enemies. Five-second timer.

Stinger (4500 GP): A nonlethal grenade that releases thousands of paralytic thorns. Five-second timer.

Scorcher (8000 GP): A lethal grenade that generates flames and intense heat within a five-meter radius. Five-second timer.

Eraser (12,000 GP): A lethal fragmentation grenade. Five-second timer.

Well, Eraser was a bit underdeveloped, but it got the idea across. Not quite sure how to plan for grenade usage, I picked up two Scorchers and two Erasers.

The final cost for my last-minute shopping trip? 135,900 GP, leaving me with a paltry 9890. But if I didn't kick some serious ass in here, I wouldn't get the chance to buy anything again. This was an investment worth every digital penny.

"*So, you got a plan*?" Modri asked as I waited for the spore to finish up the products.

"Hardly." I leaned against the nearby wall, listening for any approaching footsteps. Distantly, I heard the thumps of constant explosions. The city was at war. "All I know is that I need to get up to Chanzig's office. He's at the top of this place."

"You'll figure out a way. I'm proud of you."

"You are?"

It was strange to see how my heart moved from his words. Maybe it was just the amphetamine injection, of course, but it warmed me in a way I hadn't expected. It really was like a father complimenting his child. Even weirder that we *were* probably related.

"Yeah, I mean, I'm still not jazzed about you taking Telekinesis, but ..."

"Hey, that was the only thing that saved my ass."

"I'm thinkin' the EMP bombs did that."

"Noted." I sighed. "I don't know what I'll find up there, Modri. I don't know what Chanzig's become since we saw him in that vid. He's certainly not a human anymore."

"You can take him."

"Maybe," I said quietly, "but I won't kill him right away. I need to know what this is all about."

"Bad idea, Purifier. Kill first, find out later."

"Seriously? You don't even want to know the answer to this thing?"

"What answers could possibly make you feel better?"

I paused at that. "What do you mean?"

"No offense, but your life is gone. You're a Purifier now. Does it really matter how you got here, who you are, what Chanzig did to you? It's like I told you back down there. You aren't your story."

I nodded at the wisdom in his words, but something in me just couldn't embrace them. "I need to know for my own sanity, Modri. If I'm going to die, I want to know what I am. I want to feel that this mattered."

"Do what you have to. Just remember to pull the trigger when you get the chance."

"You bet I will."

As the genofacturing products rolled out, I prepared. First up was the Plague Burst, which was smaller and sleeker than I'd expected. The entire weapon had the same organic design as the Plopper, with glistening, "breathing" components all over it. The heat-vent slides looked like gills surrounded by small bones, and the barrel resembled a span of dense muscle. Just holding it made me feel slimy.

Soon the ammo popped out, however, and I occupied my time by loading the many shells into spare magazines. Within minutes, I'd loaded the last magazine and stuffed it into my rucksack. I kept two other mags tucked in the shotgun itself, making use of the mouth-like holding slots near the stock of the weapon.

Things were looking good, but I had an important check to do before moving on. Crouching down again, I took a peek at my Status Display.

STATUS DISPLAY
PURIFIER RANK: 10
RANK-UP NOT AVAILABLE (204,800 KP required)

Kill Points: 11,000
Genofacturing Points: 9890

Rank Points: 0

Rank Time: 16 Hours, 5 Minutes, 21 Seconds
Storehouse Time: 4 Hours, 30 Minutes, 0 Seconds

Anima: 300%
Dominion: 0/4

Plenty of time to end the nightmare.

After a quick test of racking the Plague Burst, I felt ready. Again, probably the narcotics talking. But the source of my motivation didn't matter. I had a quest, a mission to fulfill before I left this world. I would make Chanzig explain *everything*, and then I would destroy him.

33

I had no idea where I was in the fortress, but I had a hunch Chanzig was still far, far above me. Because of that, my first aim was finding an elevator. There was a chance that EMP had knocked out even that basic function, of course, so stairs were the backup plan. A terrible backup plan, considering how many thousands of steps were probably in a place like this.

With the Plague Burst up against my shoulder, I moved down the corridors with enough flourish to make Modri jealous. He was shushed for the time being—easier to hear footsteps and voices—but I was sure he'd take delight in the spectating part of things.

Up ahead, there was noise. A lot of it. Gunshots, shouts, and echoing *booms* rolled out toward me, forecasting a battle around the next turn.

When I reached the corner and peered around, I wasn't disappointed. It seemed to be the fortress's grand lobby—a long, broad hall marked by ornate pillars and tapestries of Chanzig's face. There were dozens of soldiers stacked behind deployable stasis fields and cover, all aiming toward what I assumed were the front doors. Several casualties had already been pulled to the rear, but it seemed obvious that this defense unit wasn't budging anytime soon. Because of the lobby's gradual incline, the defenders had a natural high-ground advantage over the attackers.

Still, the fact that Atrellu and his forces had made it this far was encouraging. The EMP had clearly done its job in terms of disabling the turrets and other hard defenses. Now all that remained was taking the fortress and toppling Chanzig's statues. And I intended to play a starring role in that part of the planet's saga.

Sliding out a bit farther, I got a good look at the layout of Chanzig's forces. There were three or four heavy machine gun nests, a handful of grenadiers, sharpshooters in the upper levels, and even a virtual-reality operator controlling a flock of small, pistol-wielding drones.

My best bet was to wait for the rebels to make another push, then add to the chaos. I began mentally assembling an attack plan, marking targets and—

Gunfire broke out again, sapping any hope of thinking instead of blasting. When the noise reached overwhelming levels, I pulled off my rucksack, plucked out my four grenades, and put the plan into action. While staying behind cover, I leaned out and tossed each of the explosives in two-second intervals. The two Scorchers went down to the lower part near the front doors, since I wagered the attacking rebels could use the cover of fire to push up. The two Erasers, meanwhile, were chucked high up on the slope.

Using the grenades seem to trigger something in the chok'tal, because the entire lobby was lit up with neon red boxes.

[SLAUGHTER EVENT]
Chanzig's Soldiers (HUMANOID) (17)
Chanzig's Drone Pilot (HUMANOID)
CALCULATING . . .
Combined Estimated Kill Points: 225,500

The Scorchers went off just as I was preparing to throw the last Eraser. I'd expected it to burst in a spray of flame, but that was *not* what I got. Instead, the grenades began by pumping out a spray of thick, shimmering fog. For a moment, I worried that I'd gotten the nonlethal variants by accident. But then . . . the fog ignited.

The entire lower section of the lobby erupted in wild, blossoming white flames. The wave of heat blasted some twenty meters toward me, tickling my brows, and suddenly the entire area was a sea of screams and thrashing bodies.

I didn't have time to rubber-neck, however. The Erasers detonated at that very moment, thumping the ground and sending sprays of debris high into the air. Body parts and pulverized cement rained down in the confusion.

Before any of the soldiers could get their bearings, I rushed into the haze with my Plague Burst and began unloading on anything moving. The first victim went down with half a head, while the second and third caught the shotgun's payload right in their chests. I hurried on as soon as their red boxes disappeared, ducking behind cover as the enemies' return fire whistled overhead.

But the haze from the Erasers didn't disappear. Instead, it thickened with a creeping green smog. Glancing over, I noted that the Plague Burst's casualties were leaking those neurotoxic fumes. In a matter of seconds, I heard howls and wet coughing beneath the rifle chatter.

A good start, but I'd need more than a nasty cloud to take out this many troops. I ducked even low and ran behind the back of a fountain, hoping to cross the lobby and carry on by flanking the left-hand side.

Thankfully, the gas kept everyone at bay long enough to get in position. When the rebels started pushing again, I leaned out from behind cover and put a shell through a machine gunner's visor. The same neurotoxic fumes began spilling out of him, preventing his comrades from taking over the weapon's operation.

More bullets came in my direction, ripping into the nearby walls and chewing at the floor. One even zipped past my cheek.

Seizing the moment to reload, I plucked out the half-empty mag and popped in a fresh one. Then I leaned back out and took a shot at the drone operator near the back of the lobby. The shell pounded into the cement right near him, causing the man to instinctively drop behind cover.

Again, the bullets came. Only this time, they landed. One tore straight through the already-weakened keratin on my shoulder, burying deep in my flesh. I stuffed down the pain and tried to lean out again, but a second bullet cracked into my helmet. No penetration, but the bullet shattered and peppered my face.

I fell back into cover, hissing and prodding at my face. Judging by the ripped flesh and blood, the wound was superficial. I still had both eyes and both hands. That was enough to ruin these soldiers' days.

Drawing a deep breath to center myself, I triggered Indomitable again—along with Overclock. Then I sprang out of cover, running and gunning as the bullets whizzed past. After hurdling over a barricade, I found myself face to face with a soldier. One blast of the Plague Burst put him down for good. His partner, a man wielding a grenade launcher. He barely had time to swing his weapon before I put two shells into his chest and neck.

A volley ripped through the concrete near me, but I'd already dropped to the floor, crawling desperately for the next bit of cover farther up the slope. There was no way to go back now. I had to move forward or risk a sharpshooter drilling me in the back.

After reaching a bullet-riddled pillar, I stood up and took a quick peek. Sure enough, one of the marksmen on the upper level had noticed me and tagged my position. His shot ripped past my nose and left an inch-deep hole in the floor.

Instead of moving out, I waved the barrel of the Plague Burst in the shooter's field of view. The moment his bullet zipped past, I leaned around the pillar, shouldered the shotgun, and fired. It was a fair distance away, but the shell made contact. The marksman's body slumped forward over the railing and came crashing down.

As I took a moment to reassess, heart still pounding with adrenaline (and amphetamine), I looked down at the lower slope of the lobby. The rebel forces were beginning to pour in, firing haphazard bullets up at Chanzig's forces. It suddenly hit me that this wasn't a good thing. Even if those *were* Atrellu's peacekeepers, many of them probably thought I was dead, or in some labor camp halfway around the planet. If they weren't . . . how many would be able to distinguish Chanzig's troops from a random armored man? I had to haul ass if I wanted to avoid taking some unfriendly fire.

Rushing back out of cover, I went on another shooting run by rushing up the side aisle. As I passed each barricade, I let loose with the Plague Burst. Those who didn't die immediately would succumb to the neurotoxic gas.

I fired shell after shell, no longer feeling any pain through the smokescreen of the excitement. This was battle lust. Bloodlust. But I didn't mind it. I became a pure machine, seeking out and eliminating heads like it was my full-time job. Soon I was completely in the flow, dodging, firing, reloading, and flanking without a single drop of hesitation.

Within minutes, nothing remained except the final bit of resistance at the top of the lobby slope. The defenders had walled off the position with sandbags and stasis fields. It had to be a vital point.

As I crept closer, scanning the rubble for anything still breathing, I realized what they were guarding: the elevators.

After doing a final reload on the Plague Burst, I advanced on the fortified position. Bullets from both factions flew over my head as I moved in a crouch. When I reached the outer wall of the defensive ring, I brought the shotgun up and steadied my breathing.

Then, in one smooth and efficient movement, I stood and started unloading. The first round punched through a soldier right in front of me. I moved the barrel, shot, moved, shot. In seconds flat, the five occupants of the sandbag-and-stasis field position were nothing more than smoking meat.

Then there was silence—aside from the occasional shots from the rebels, of course.

SLAUGHTER ENCOUNTER SUCCESSFUL
Kills: 16
Kill Points Awarded: 202,250
Storehouse Time Awarded: 1 Hour, 30 Minutes

RANK-UP AVAILABLE: RANK 11

The thrill of reaching my next rank-up was powerful, but not as powerful as the post-battle crash. I wearily climbed up on the sandbag wall to scan for more enemies, but all I saw was the human wave pouring through the front doors. Just in time for some hard-won dictator-looting.

As I stood on the sandbags, however, voices rose from the mass below.

"It's him!"

"Look, it's the Tooth of Justice!"

"He's alive!"

All I could do was shake my head at the name "Tooth of Justice." God, was that an awful thing to be known as.

"This fight isn't over," I yelled, causing the crowd to freeze up and listen intently. "Your tormenters will fight to hold this fortress to their last breaths. Chanzig is still at the top. So, stay together, watch each other's backs, and remember to use discretion when shooting. After this is over, it'll be *your* city. Only destroy what needs to be destroyed."

The rebels muttered to each other for a few seconds. Then one of their members, a burly-looking fellow carrying a hammer, let out a maniacal cheer.

"Did you hear that, everyone!?" he hollered. "Burn this goddamn place to the ground!"

Now *that* got an enthusiastic reaction. Oh, well. These people had been cooped up in their own hells for generations—there was little hope of quelling them now. For better or worse, they would decide their own futures today. But only if I finished my own job.

I climbed down to the other side of the sandbags and rested there, gazing at the bloodstained elevator doors. The idea of stepping inside them filled me with dread. As a matter of fact, it unnerved me so much that I was debating doing my rank-up to 11 before I moved another foot.

But I couldn't. I shouldn't. If I survived this encounter and didn't earn enough KP to hit 12, I'd be stuck on Chanzig's planet without any ethical source of combat. I could fly to another world, sure, but who knew if I'd make it in time? No, it was best to save my rank-up for now—and use it *if* I beat Chanzig.

Dusting myself off, I stood and stepped in front of the doors. Nothing could stop me now.

Except Chanzig's voice, that is.

"Hello, Dak." The playful yet pitiless tone came through the elevator's speaker panel in a staticky blast. "It seems we've reached the end of this little charade."

Stupid as it was, I aimed at the speaker panel. "Are you going to surrender now?"

"Oh, what a grand idea. It looks like that would be most advisable in my predicament."

"Agreed."

It was absurd, hearing the voice of the man who'd ordered me dead and raised hell to find me—well, the chok'tal inside me, anyway. He spoke as though I was his child, his long-lost friend. What world was he living in?

"Let's make an arrangement," he said. "I'll open these doors, and you can come up and visit Akasha and I. We'll have ourselves a chat before you kill me."

"You sound pretty calm about all this."

Chanzig laughed. "What else can a man do when his world is crumbling? Come, step inside. You can even keep your weapons, if it'll make you feel any safer."

Before I'd even answered, the doors slid open to reveal a shiny chrome interior. I hesitated for a good while. This felt like a trap, and yet . . . what if it wasn't? What if Chanzig really was giving up the quest in this final hour? It was a naïve judgment, I'm aware, but there's no predicting the thoughts of a creature like Chanzig. Whatever humanity—and thus common sense—he'd once had was long gone.

"Alright," I said quietly, boarding the elevator with my rifle at the ready. "Any tricks, any games, and you'll never get the chok'tal. I'll make sure of it."

The doors slid shut.

"Don't worry, my dearest friend," Chanzig said. "I don't need any tricks to end this. The truth should be enough."

34

Despite spending the last few days fantasizing about, planning, and actively seeking this confrontation with Chanzig, I found that my resolve had crumbled about halfway through the elevator ride. It was hard to say if I really wanted this. Not the killing Chanzig part—I still longed for that—but the idea of finding out the whole truth.

I've found that for most people, truth is best kept in small doses. The moment you get too much of it, you want to put things back the way they were and return to the world of illusion. But you can't. The truth has a way of breaking things forever.

And for that very reason, I found myself in the paradoxical position of both wanting to know everything, yet also know nothing. What would happen, after all, if I found out I wasn't really Dak Korasa? Not the same Dak Korasa who'd willingly joined Chanzig three years ago, anyway. My entire life would be revealed as a fantasy. The friends, family, and accomplishments of my existence would be reduced to hallucinations. If everything came crashing down, what would be left in the rubble? What could I possibly cling to and call "mine"?

When the elevator dinged and opened its doors, however, all thoughts vanished.

I stepped out into a room that was simultaneously alien and very familiar. It was the same lounge-type environment I'd seen on Dr. Markazian's archived vids. A few chairs, a low table, beige floors and walls . . . and at the back of the room, spanning the entire wall like an enormous aquarium, was Chanzig's nanite chamber.

The man himself stood right behind the barrier, hands folded behind his back. Only it wasn't proper to call him a man any longer. He looked like a living glitch, a massive, humanoid-shaped bulk of dancing quarks and electricity. I had no idea how tall he'd been in his original form, but his current size was monstrous. He stood nearly three heads taller than me, with a barrel-chested frame that made me look like a strip of jerky.

His nanites swirled in the air around him like a cloud of sand, zipping in and out to mend a body on the verge of collapse. Several threads of the nanites were dense, trailing out of his back and along the floor like tentacles.

"At long, long last . . . we finally meet again," Chanzig said. "What a fine day for a reunion, Dak."

I aimed the shotgun, already knowing it wouldn't pierce whatever barrier he'd made. "Where's Akasha?"

"Easy now. Let's start with one thing at a time. How about a drink?"

"I'll pass."

"A man set on business," he mused, pacing along the barrier. "I can respect that."

"My only *business* is killing you."

Chanzig's glowing eyes seemed to sparkle with delight. "Before you proceed with that plan, please allow me to show you my vision. All your questions will be answered."

"How do you know I have questions?"

"Because your mind is like an open book to me. Your thoughts, your fears, your failures . . . I see all of them, Dak. And I can sense your curiosity about what you are."

I opened my mouth, only to find I couldn't speak. There was something *wrong* with his aura. Something that froze my mind up like cement.

"Come and speak with me," Chanzig said as he lifted his palm to the barrier. With a soft whine, the material turned to something resembling a liquid and parted to make a doorway. "It's cozy in here. I promise."

It seemed like a colossally terrible idea to follow his instructions, but something in me relented. To this day, the only explanation I have is his mental power. Nothing else explains it. I stepped on through the barrier, shotgun still up at my shoulder and ready.

Once I was through, every pore of my skin ached with a soft, never-ending burn. It was like the air itself wanted to devour me. Maybe the nanites were tasting me.

Chanzig resealed the barrier and stepped back, gesturing to the room around us. It was a relatively small space—or seemed to be, until I noticed the corridors that led deeper into branching rooms on either side of us.

While I stared at those corridors, wondering where Akasha might be, Chanzig moved to the floor-to-ceiling window at the back of this area. I followed him there and looked out.

Below, the city was in flames. Armored vehicles were overturned, crashed gunships smoldered in the streets, and mobs of rebels surrounded the fortress like vultures waiting to feed.

"I wanted to make an ideal society," Chanzig said, with a note of genuine disappointment. "A society in which, through loyalty and service, one could rise to the highest positions of power."

I glanced at him. "You made a world where these people had to eat each other to survive."

"Wisdom through suffering, Dak. That's what this life is."

"No, it's not. Not the way you did it." I faced him with gritted teeth. "You enslaved an entire planet for your own greed. You only cared if resources flowed up here . . . to you."

"What shall I say? The higher good is always what matters."

"And by higher good, you mean getting the chok'tal. Something to save you."

Chanzig laughed. "Save me? Oh, Dak, you myopic mortal. This body is nothing to me. What matters is the mind. The chok'tal within your body will bring about a new era for this world. All the ash and death below you . . . is just a dream. I will unmake it."

Much as I wanted to despise him, to turn my gun and shoot right now, I couldn't. There was something deeply sincere in his voice. He believed in his fantasies more than anybody else.

"Who am I?" I whispered. "And don't lie to me. I saw Markazian's vids."

Chanzig nodded calmly. "I'm aware you did. As I said, your mind is open and revealed to me. I'll illuminate whatever is dark for you." He turned and started heading down the right-hand corridor, and I followed. "I must say, Dak, that your little quest for answers has enthralled me."

"It would've ended sooner if your men weren't so incompetent."

He turned back to me. "You're referring to Lieutenant Thirmen, are you not?"

"That's right," I said. "They should've patted me down on that gunship."

"I instructed them not to," Chanzig explained. "You see, Dak, I don't want to kill you. I don't even wish to harm you. So, from that angle, I'm rather pleased you gave Thirmen a taste of his own medicine."

"You ordered my death."

"That was for something different," he said sharply. "But alas, I'll allow bygones to be bygones. You've exceeded my expectations."

"What 'expectations' are you talking about?"

"You'll understand soon enough. For now . . . let me say this. There is no greater joy in a father's life than seeing his offspring try to surpass him."

I stopped dead in my tracks. "*Father*?"

"Oh, relax. I'm speaking poetically." He let out a self-satisfied little laugh and continued on to the room at the end of the passage. "Hurry along, Dak. I have so very much to show you."

As I walked, I noted that trails of nanites followed him like slime. They slithered along the floor, merging with one another and branching off into fractal patterns that resembled long, thin threads of black. My attention followed one particularly long nanite trail as I stepped into the room, but that changed the moment I saw what filled the "gallery" around me.

Dozens upon dozens of large, liquid-filled tanks occupied the room, each of them containing a human being curled in the fetal position. Their bodies were various sizes, some misshapen and others conjoined. But my breath caught in my throat when I saw the face of a relatively normal-looking specimen in the front row.

It was *me*. All of them were.

"What do you think?" Chanzig asked, looking at me with a smile.

"What do I . . . think?" I said faintly. "What the hell are you doing here? What *is* this?"

"This, Dak, is your home."

"What?"

He patted one of the tanks affectionately. "All of these are my failed creations, but I just didn't have the heart to discard them. You were the only success."

"You're lying," I hissed. "I wasn't *made* here."

"No, you're quite right: You were made in the labs about six stories below here. But the fact remains, Dak—I gave you life. Just a short while ago, you were one of these floating marvels. Isn't it just remarkable?"

I heard the words he spoke, but it was as though they were another language. I just couldn't make heads or tails of any of it.

"I can feel your confusion," Chanzig said. "Allow me to assist."

He raised both hands and began emitting streams of nanites. These nanites coalesced as a solid cloud, then formed intricate shapes, then . . . people.

"What are you doing?" I asked.

"I've no need for digital archives," he explained as he refined the cloud between us. "My mind contains a living memory of every vid that's been recorded in this structure." He stared at me intently. "My former associate,

Dr. Markazian, didn't have *everything* on that little cache he stole from me. For the purpose of clarification, I thought I'd show you a few defining moments to fill in the gaps."

The nanite swarm soon crystallized into a clear rendering of this room. It was *like* a standard vid, but not quite—the angle suggested it hadn't been recorded by a vid at all. Instead, it had been saved directly into Chanzig's nanites like a cloud file. No pun intended.

In the vid, Chanzig and Markazian stood before one of the large tanks. Inside was me—or some version of me.

"When will you know if it's been successful?" Chanzig asked in the vid.

Markazian tapped on the glass. "A few days at most. Initial signs are good. The subject's brain activity suggests they've integrated Modri's nervous system without any complications."

"Are they ready for memory insertions?"

"Probably, although I'm a tad concerned about starting too early. The nervous system is still imprinting on their neurological structure. Tampering with memories now could cause . . . unwanted side effects."

"Such as?"

Markazian shifted uneasily. "There's a risk of Modri's nervous system going into overactivation."

"Speak simply, Doctor."

"Yes, of course. My apologies. You see, right now, in a psychological sense, this *is* Mr. Korasa—without any of his original memories, of course. A tabula rasa. But our uploads of Modri's nervous system will soon overwrite Mr. Korasa's. He'll walk, jump, and chew just like Jekra Modri. If we begin injecting memories too soon, it could cause the nervous system imprint to fight for dominance over Korasa's conditioning. In essence, it could bring out more of Modri than we've predicted."

"I see no problem with it," Chanzig said. "The more alike they are, the higher the likelihood of this subject doing *exactly* what Jekra Modri did on the planet. And by extension, the higher the likelihood that the subject follows the same trail and leads us to the Sacred Guide. Is that not our aim?"

"It is . . . but . . . I'm not referring to that, sir. I'm saying that the subject's entire behavioral pattern could be replaced by Modri's. They would do *everything* the same . . . including fighting."

"Ah, I see. Worried the subject will come to hunt you down?"

Markazian gulped. "It's a real possibility, sir. We should let the nervous system settle in, *then* begin granting them memories from Mr. Korasa's report."

"Unfortunately, Doctor, we don't have that kind of time. I'm beginning immediately."

"But . . . sir . . . we're already growing them at well beyond accelerated rates. We shouldn't tamper yet."

"Fortune favors the bold."

The nanite cloud shifted, but the room and angle was the same. Now there was only Chanzig, who stood in front of "my" tank with his hands lovingly caressing the glass.

"Your name is Dak Korasa," he whispered. "You are an archaeologist who graduated from the academy on Halcium Beta. You're a timid man. You enjoy coffee in the late afternoon . . ."

Without warning, the nanites dispersed, erasing the vid.

Chanzig smiled at me. "Do you see now, Dak? I *did* make you. Your name, your body, your skills in combat . . . all of them came from me."

I tried to parse what I'd just seen and heard, but I couldn't. It was as though I'd just woken up from a dream, or fallen into a lake of déjà vu. Everything felt simultaneously foreign and far too familiar.

"I . . . don't understand," I said quietly.

"I can't blame you. It's a rather convoluted tale, your birth." Chanzig sighed. "You see, Dak, when Jekra Modri fled from the Hegemony, I knew that time was of the essence. The Hegemony is too inefficient, too corrupt, to ever harness the power of the chok'tal. I needed to find Modri myself, and Dr. Markazian was all too eager to assist me."

"Because you hypnotized him."

"Hardly, but I'll explain that later." His smile widened. "Dr. Markazian brought much of his research to me. One of those pieces of research, as you've discovered, was a complete scan of Jekra Modri's nervous system and physical responses. You might call this the 'program' that runs an organism. How they react, how they move, how they think. If we could make such a program active, it would be able to mimic the chok'tal's host and trace their footsteps, thus leading us to our target. But of course, we couldn't simply clone Jekra Modri and insert this data. The entire Hegemony was looking for him. Even my own men, loyal though they are, would've run to the enemy and told them that Modri was in our custody. And if that happened, well, the Hegemony would've uncovered *everything* . . . Markazian's defection, my plans . . ."

"So, you found someone else."

Chanzig clapped. "Very good, Dak! But not just yet. We tried other routes . . . such as turning Modri's nervous system into a virtual intelligence, using a random DNA host, or inserting it into a pile of muscle tissue. No dice, however. We needed the right combination of biology and psychology to make the project work. The right 'hardware' for our 'program,' if you will. And after many, *many* failures, we located Jekra Modri's closest genetic match . . . which happened to be you. Well, your *original*, I should say. When I found Mr. Korasa, his radiation damage was extensive. Even so, he volunteered for this project."

"What? For a hope at treatment you couldn't provide?"

"It's not about the treatment, Dak. It's about the *joy*. Nobody cares about their actual life, nor how long they live. They care about the ending. They want to know that their life was perfect. And I was going to give that to Mr. Korasa."

"What are you saying?"

"Again, I *will* explain. But stay focused with me. We're coming to the key part." He meshed his hands and walked around me. "As you saw in the archive's vids, Mr. Korasa died while we were trying to integrate Modri's nervous system. A pity. Markazian then had the idea of using Mr. Korasa's DNA to create a template . . . a blank slate that could absorb Modri's data while in the growing process."

"You mean . . . I was just a clone to contain Modri's nervous system. A hunting dog to help you find the real Modri."

"Such an excellent summary, Dak. You may not be the real Mr. Korasa, but you absorbed his sharp intellect all the same."

"So, my memories . . . aren't mine."

"No. In fact, they're not even Mr. Korasa's. They're my version of his memories. You see, he died before we could properly extract that information, so I had to use his psychological report to gather the key details. Where you were born, how old you were, your parents' names . . ."

"But why would you give them to me?"

"Oh, come on, Dak. Don't ask what you already know. Markazian's vids explained it perfectly: a subject without any memories was prone to psychological breakdowns. We needed to have a healthy, functional subject who believed they were a real person. One who could function in a team without causing suspicion. Although I do believe Liura suspected your true nature . . ."

"Let me get this straight," I said, my deep, aching fear slowly turning to anger. "You sent me on scavenging missions knowing that I wasn't a real archaeologist. You just wanted me to subconsciously lead you to Modri."

"Yes, exactly. Now you're getting it."

"In exchange for my help, you wanted to kill me and trap my suffering in a recurrence prism."

"Ah, ah, ah," Chanzig said, wagging a finger. "Now you're getting confused. I didn't order your death because you were useless to me—I ordered it because you tried to betray me. You tried to escape from my empire."

"You were *never* going to treat me . . . because there was nothing to treat."

"Do you really think I'm so cruel? Do you think I've had men ripped apart and placed in recurrence prisms for no reason?"

"Yes."

He laughed. "No, Dak. As I said, I am fair. I reward loyalty and punish disobedience. Had you done the ten jobs I asked, I would've given you what Mr. Korasa always wanted: memories of a family, a quiet home, a life full of love and success. You would've spent eternity in a recurrence prism, yes, but it wouldn't have been marked by pain. You would've existed in bliss . . . forever. Safe with me."

"But it's not real," I snapped. "That's been your grand plan all along, hasn't it? To sell people dreams and kill them while they're blissed out in happy fantasies?"

"The fantasy *is* the reality," he said softly. "Don't you see it? At the end of your life, it doesn't matter what's a hallucination and what is true. All that matters is how it *feels*."

"No wonder you can't see that what you did to me is wrong. What you did to all these poor bastards in the tanks."

Chanzig shrugged. "I'm sorry to tell you the truth, Dak. You're just an instrument. A tool. A wind-up toy that lived beyond its purpose." His face brightened. "But you surprised me, friend. You truly did."

"By coming here and fucking up your plans?"

"You haven't 'fucked up' anything," he said. "You see, you awakened the magic ingredient that made you succeed where all other creations failed. Your *fear*. Your survival instincts. When the team left you for dead, Jekra Modri came alive within you. You turned into a warrior . . . and you found the chok'tal, just as I'd always hoped. You even brought it back to me. You're a *success*!"

I just stood there, not sure what to say or do. Which part of me was Dak Korasa? Which part was Jekra Modri? Who was *really* running the show of my consciousness? All I knew was that I didn't, and *couldn't*, know anything true. My entire existence was just a figment of Chanzig's imagination. A mind and a body merged for one man's vision . . . and yet, where was *I*? Korasa was the canvas, Modri was the paint. Both halves of the painting that was "me" had come from other people. There was no room to live as an individual.

But my pain was real. It was the one thing I could hold on to and call mine. The throbbing, empty hole in my chest reminded me that I was still alive. I existed.

"Oh, don't be so melancholic," Chanzig said. "I can feel the pit in your soul, Dak. But I can change all that. I can still reward you for your loyalty."

"There is *nothing* you can give me to end this."

"I wouldn't assume that. Come, I have more to show you."

Without waiting for me, Chanzig proceeded down the rows of tanks and into an adjoining room at the back of the gallery. I moved after him like a zombie, no longer controlling my own limbs. It was as though Chanzig's magnetic pull compelled me to follow.

There were no tanks in this new room. In fact, there was almost nothing. It was a large, vast space, almost completely black. But there was a strange pattern to the walls. They were . . . freckled, as though made of millions of tiny, tiny . . .

My heart seized up in my chest.

"Do you recognize them?" Chanzig asked, sweeping an arm around at the countless recurrence prisms that formed the walls and ceiling. "You're standing in a room full of half a million eternal souls, Dak. Some are suffering, and others are in bliss. Liura's somewhere here . . ."

"You're depraved," I whispered. "Is this what you did to all of your loyal followers? You shoved illusions into their heads and killed them while the prisms were recording?"

"I've shown them the world that exists only in their dreams. The most glorious, incredible experience they could ever imagine."

My throat seized up. "Did Balnos even have a family?"

"Of course not." He laughed. "Balnos' family died years ago. But that was his wish . . . to save his loved ones. Every being has such a vision, and I merely pulled it out of them. In my new world, all beings will be their own gods. All dreams will be made real." His eyes narrowed. "But those who oppose me, who attempt to keep this world stranded in ignorance, will forever exist in their own hell. This is simply justice. I take no pleasure in their punishment."

"But that means you . . ."

"Yes," he said, nodding slowly. "I *invented* the recurrence prism, Dak. The gateway showed me so much. Granted, these prisms are just a crude, mechanical thing . . . but once I am made whole with the chok'tal, I won't need them anymore. My mind will become the ultimate recurrence prism. I will be able to absorb all beings into myself, loving and punishing equally."

"You're not a god," I growled. "You don't have the right to play with peoples' minds!"

"It is not about rights. Rights are seized through power. For too long, this world has been a broken, corrupt place. It has rewarded devilry and lies. But I will make it fair. I will give each and every sentient being the eternity they deserve."

"You don't want to know what I think you deserve."

Chanzig grinned. "Just consider this, Dak. If you surrender to me now, and allow me to freely join with the chok'tal, I will give you *exactly* what you want. An endless dream better than reality. I can even make you believe that you've saved Akasha and killed me. Whatever you wish for in the bottom of your heart . . . I will make it real. You will live with me eternally in my empire . . . as an equal."

I wanted to vomit. To run. To shoot him through the head. But my body seemed frozen by his power. "Show me Akasha. Then I'll decide."

"Suit yourself," he said, leading me back out of the prism room and through the tanks.

I followed him in a trance, barely thinking as we moved down the corridor and back into the original space with the barrier. In fact, my mind was completely blank when he led me into the other corridor across the room. What other horrors did he have in this place?

At the end of the corridor, a sealed door slid open to reveal a sort of office. Just in front of me was Akasha, floating in a living cage made of nanites. A blade made of the same material was pressed against her throat, and some sort of golden cube floated above her. Most alarming, though, was the recurrence prism blinking on her neck.

And in the center of the room, producing wailing noises like nothing I'd ever seen before . . . was the dormant gateway to the world of the Unmade. The base resembled a mound of pulsating flesh and bone that gripped the floor using spider-like legs. Shimmering above it was the entrance itself, which had a watery, reflective sheen. Even at a distance, I could tell it was inactive, waiting for my touch. But not just waiting. Calling out.

The bulk of its energy poured out of the core, though I can't recall how it looked, for reasons that will soon be made clear. But what I will *never* forget was the light. The strange whispers coming through it.

"I now present the Cobalt Seer to you, Dak," Chanzig said. "If you grant me the chok'tal right now, I will let her go. She'll be free to wander the cosmos. But if you resist me . . . I will make her end painful beyond your wildest imagination."

35

In a split second, my mind absorbed all the details of the room. Akasha's cage was held together by a nanite rope that led into the walls. Chanzig was two meters away from me. The gateway was ten.

"Don't do it," Akasha whispered. "Don't give in to him."

"I have a counteroffer," I said to Chanzig. "Fight me to the death."

Chanzig folded his arms. "What a novel idea. But you realize, of course, what will happen to Akasha if I win."

"I know."

"I'm offering you bliss, Dak. Infinite bliss."

"But it's not real," I said bitterly. "This . . . all of this . . . is just your own madness projected onto the world. And I would rather die in reality than live forever in your imagination."

"Quite the risk you're taking."

I pressed the shotgun to my shoulder. "I've always been a gambling man."

Chanzig just studied me, smiling and giggling to himself. Then, without any warning, he teleported across the room toward me, a nanite-created whip cutting the air between us.

[NEMESIS EVENT]
Chanzig (UNKNOWN)
CALCULATING . . .
Estimated Kill Points: 304,500

I lunged to the side as his whip tore through the floor and walls, leaving a smoldering gash. In the same movement, I fired at Chanzig's center mass.

He teleported away from the shells, appearing at my side in less than a millisecond. All I could do was duck and roll as his nanite whip came around again, severing a chunk of my keratin armor at the shoulder. And as I backed up, trying to aim properly, he teleported in a zigzag fashion toward me.

Just before he reached me, I fired into the empty space where I knew he'd appear. The shell popped against his chest, spraying out a gush of black nanites that resembled blood. He staggered, allowing me to sidestep and deliver another shot to his neck.

Again, the nanite-blood sprayed. But he didn't stagger. He blinked into melee range, then slammed my chest with his open palm.

Before I knew it, I was sailing through the air and slamming into the back wall, all the air torn from my lungs. My ribs ached—surely broken—as I stumbled up and raised the shotgun.

I pulled the trigger just before he teleported, blasting the wall behind his former location. He appeared behind me and slashed across my back with his nanite-powered claws. Keratin shattered, the rucksack tore, and my flesh and muscle sprayed hot blood. The pain was excruciating. I cried out and collapsed to the floor, struggling to roll over before he could pounce on me. The Genofacturing Spore and nano-carbon sword spilled out of my bag, probably through the fresh rip.

But by the time I'd flipped toward him, Chanzig was gone. He materialized on the other side of the room, just beside Akasha.

"This is your last chance, Dak," he said as he swirled the nanites around the woman. "I've been having fun playing with you, but even I grow tired of games. Surrender now, and bliss is yours."

Gazing into his burning eyes, I triggered Overclock and Indomitable.

With that newfound vigor, I swung up to one knee and fired two shells. One hit the wall, but the other clipped Chanzig's leg, causing another black spray.

I went to fire again, but I was empty.

Shit.

Even as I fumbled to grab another magazine from the floor, Chanzig flashed to my side and slammed down on my helmet. My chin cracked against the floor, and I felt the crushed remains of several teeth rolling around on my tongue. Ringing filled my ears.

"You're nothing, Dak," he whispered in my mind. "You were just a means to an end. A project. And now it's time to retire you."

As my vision resolved, I saw the nano-carbon blade just below me. I feigned defeat for just a moment, swaying about on hands and knees. Then I grabbed the sword and flipped over, slashing in a wide arc as I came around.

The blade sliced through Chanzig's stomach, causing yet another gushing wound. He hopped back and began charging energy in his hands. I seized the opportunity to get up to my knees, roll, and move closer to Akasha.

But before I could reach her, the room dissolved into a dark forest. Mist blanketed the ground. All around me were skeletons and shriveled bodies.

Chanzig's silhouette appeared in the distance, just between a pair of gnarled trees.

"More mind games," I said, shaking my head. "You should know by now that those don't work on me."

"Perhaps," Chanzig said, his voice echoing all around me, "but you're now in *my* domain. The realm of the infinite mind."

Suddenly, the figure ahead of me swelled to monstrous proportions. It became a looming giant, a creature that towered into the clouds far above. A colossal hand made of darkness came swooping down from the heavens like a starship.

Only when its shadow came over me, blotting out all light, did I realize the danger. Even if it was all imaginary, death would be real. I had no doubt he could ensure that. I sprinted to the side, leaping over corpses and fallen branches. The pain in my ribs and head pushed me harder.

At the last second, I escaped its shadow. The hand smashed down into the woodlands behind me, flattening everything with a tremendous shockwave. The impact threw me onto my chest in cold mud.

But there was no time to recuperate. I scrambled back up, spun around, and leapt onto the gunship-sized finger behind me. Even as the hand lifted up, ascending with impossible speed, I began moving back toward Chanzig's wrist. The wind howled around me, and soon we were high in the clouds. The fleshy landscape before me became dark and foggy. Still, I ran through the biting cold. I ran through the pockets of lightning.

Soon I was on the forearm, then at the elbow, fighting for every inch of ground as I scaled the titan. When the air became thin and the arm lifted, I dug my blade into the flesh as a piton. Climbing like a mountaineer, I drew closer and closer to the shoulders.

Suddenly, the figure hunched over. Gravity inverted, and I thrust the nano-carbon sword as deep into the skin as it could go. I held on with all my strength as my legs swept out from under me, dangling over the raggedy clouds. Chanzig released a deafening roar and straightened, preparing for another tactic.

With that brief respite, I withdrew the blade and climbed higher . . . higher . . . higher. Soon enough, I reached the neck—a gargantuan pillar thrumming with glowing veins. Chanzig's face stood over me like a vengeful god, his eyes all fury and hatred.

"Fuck you, and fuck your dream world," I roared, sprinting along his collarbone with the blade extended.

The nano-carbon bit through his neck, severing veins that gushed like broken dams and ripping open his windpipe. A rush of dark, corrupted air came howling out of his throat.

Then, in a flash, we were back in the fortress. Back with Akasha and the gateway.

Chanzig stumbled back, his throat leaking torrents of the nanite-blood mix.

"You ingrateful, insidious waste of life," he said with a mangled voice. "I should have put you down when I had the chance."

"Too late for that," I said, grinning.

But before I could gloat, Chanzig zipped through the room toward me. He seized me by the neck, lifting me high into the air. Akasha squirmed in the cage beside me. A fire hotter than the sun chewed at my skin, seeping into my very bones.

"I'll now take what is mine," he hissed. "What I have worked so long to have."

The air bled out of my body. My legs kicked and thrashed, and the nano-carbon blade clattered to the floor below me. As the pressure and pain mounted, my vision grew hazy. All the feeling retreated from my fingers and toes.

Chanzig pressed his face to mine, searing my skin. "I'll make sure you suffer in eternity, Dak. Or should I call you Nobody? That's what you are. Nothing but empty space."

As my world vanished into tunnel vision and the familiar embrace of death closed around me, the only thing I sensed was my mind. My whirling thoughts, my fears, my survival instincts, all screaming at me to *live*. It was the same force I'd felt in the jungle. The same force that had pulled me through the Abyss and its caustic lake.

Distantly, I activated *Telekinesis*.

I probed downward, searching for the sword somewhere near my feet. It came to me as a light, airy presence. My willpower flooded the metal, and I could feel it vibrating at the smallest levels of energy. I sensed it rattling along the floor, struggling to lift . . .

It wasn't enough. I needed more power. More . . . fuel.

My mind circled to Chanzig. To the abuses he'd committed. The torment he'd put me through, and the corruption he'd fostered on his world, and the countless minds he'd imprisoned for his own sense of divinity.

Fuck you, Chanzig.

That wrath was the spark. It surged into the sword, driving it across the room with speed I'd never thought possible.

Chanzig's grip loosened. He stared into my eyes with a wide, devious smile.

"You poor fool," he said, giggling. "Your last attempt to slay me . . . and it does nothing."

He angled my head to the side, forcing me to look at the nano-carbon blade embedded in the wall.

I smiled back at him as my lips went numb. "Good thing . . . I wasn't aiming for you."

Chanzig's brows furrowed, but only for a moment. Grim understanding passed over him as he looked at the broken nanite rope leading to Akasha's cage. Her former cage, that is. Its binding thread had been severed by the sword, and as a result, it had collapsed into a thin cloud of nanites. Chanzig's eyes slowly tracked to the side, coming face to face with Akasha's outstretched hand.

"This is for my people," she said as she pulled off her blindfold.

All three eyes were blinding. Completely blinding. There was a flash of white light, and then Chanzig began screaming like a man being buried alive. His grip weakened. Every nanite comprising his body vibrated in midair, pulling apart and eroding into dust.

In one violent act of implosion, Chanzig completely evaporated.

ENCOUNTER FAILED

I fell to the floor, choking and sputtering. In my delirious state, I nearly missed the strange phenomenon that took place. A stream of glimmering, golden motes swirled in the air where Chanzig had once stood. And as I pulled in haggard breaths, the stream moved toward me. Into me. It sank down my throat and filled my lungs, infusing me with power that felt both raw and unstable.

A new message filled my HUD:

Morphic Imprint Gained: Mind Cascade

But there was no time to consider what it meant. By the time I'd come back to full consciousness, Akasha was standing over me and resettling her blindfold. She looked down at me and offered a hand.

Dazed, I accepted it.

"You took my kill," I said with a hoarse voice.

She just smiled faintly. Then, without explanation, she turned and retrieved the golden cube levitating on the floor. She held it in both hands, turning it end over end with clear reverence.

This was it: her people's cube. The thing she'd worked to find for so long.

Before I could ask any questions, though, an automated voice came over the speakers.

"*All personnel, please evacuate. Self-destruct sequence has been initiated by the Supreme Chairman.*"

Akasha and I shared a look.

"We need to leave," I said.

She nodded. "Not before I've destroyed it." Her focus strayed to the gateway.

"Akasha, wait," I said. "This could be our only chance."

"Don't even dare."

"Akasha—"

"We killed him to stop him from entering it," she hissed. "And I was prepared to kill you for the same reason. Do not make me."

"But if we leave it—"

"Turn away from it, Dak. Let me destroy it."

For a fraction of a second, we both just stood there, our eyes shifting from each other to the gateway. For her, it was a portal to hell. For me, it was my only possible shot at removing the curse of the chok'tal. Akasha's legs twitched, preparing to move, but I still had Overclock on. I sprinted directly for the gateway . . . and jumped into it.

The world froze just as my finger broke its mirror-like surface. A prompt appeared in my HUD.

[Gateway to the Endgame Realm] [UNCLAIMED]
Save Point Progress: 86%
Guardians Defeated: 18/25

Gateway requires claimant for activation.

No living claimant detected. Claim Gateway?
[YES / NO]

Panic overtook me, but there wasn't a good reason for it. Time was literally frozen. Akasha's glowing hand was still reaching toward me, fixed in space like a prop. I had all the time in the world to make a decision . . . and then live with it forever.

What did it even mean, claiming a gateway? Would I be able to take it around with me like the Genofacturing Spore, hopping in and out of the Unmade at will? I had no idea, but it seemed smart. I thought back to what Modri had said in the gunship: Gateways were a dying opportunity. Thus far, I'd seen no indication that I was any closer to making one of my own. The Purifier who'd made this gateway was surely dead by now, but in their prime, I was certain they'd been unstoppable. It was safer to claim it now and worry about Akasha's protests later.

With no shortage of hesitation, I selected yes.

[Gateway to the Endgame Realm] [Purifier Dak Korasa]
Save Point Progress: 86%
Guardians Defeated: 18/25

Activate Gateway?
[YES / NO]

If the last decision had been uncomfortable, this was downright torture. I was about to throw myself into a world of inhuman terrors and eldritch threats. There was no guarantee such a world would even have oxygen.

Still . . . this was what I'd come for. A chance to end this.

Yes.

A million hands began clawing at my skin. My vision went black, then red, then gray, then white . . . The colors circled around me as my body was broken down and remade. Time stretched. One second became a million years, then vice versa. In a matter of moments, I traveled through eons of spacetime. Screams and whispering voices pulled at my mind, trying to drag me into the formless chaos all around me.

But eventually . . . I landed. I staggered forward in several inches of red water. The sky above me was black, its horizons covered by alien structures that threatened to break my mind. A ceaseless, haunting chant swam through the silence.

Most distressing of all, however, was the looming tower far in the distance. It dominated the landscape much like Chanzig's, and yet . . .

No, I thought, suddenly realizing why the tower seemed so familiar. It was a more mind-twisting version of what Chanzig had built. Taller, darker, more ominous. It made Chanzig's building look like a cheap scale model.

What the hell was this place? Was *this* what Chanzig had found? No, I realized, he must've been sucked into the void that connected our world and this one. He hadn't had the chok'tal to pull him through.

But now I wasn't so sure anybody should be here. All around me, seemingly endless in all directions, was the blood-like water.

"You are not Chanzig," a voice boomed. It wasn't spoken in alltongue—not even language, really. It was as though the void had somehow found a way to interact with my mind directly.

I looked around, but there was nobody to speak. "Where are you?"

"I am everywhere and nowhere. Everything, nothing. I am the Unmade. And you should not be here yet."

A chill worked through my limbs. "I've come here to find you."

"Why?"

"To end this game. To remove the chok'tal."

The Unmade laughed—a horrid, hollow sound. "You have not yet *won* my game, mortal. I thought that Chanzig surely would've succeeded. He had the cruelty needed to triumph. He would've been a worthy victor, had he received my creation to enter the game . . ."

"He's dead now."

"So I've seen. How curious. It looks as though you'll need to take his place."

"Why don't you come out and tell me how to win, then?"

The Unmade's growl rattled my chest. "You're nothing but an insect."

"And what are you?"

"I am beyond whatever your feeble mind can imagine."

I shook my head. "I can imagine what you are. A sad, pathetic interdimensional being who torments mortals for fun."

"Is that what you think this is? Oh, you silly pest. The chok'tal is more than just a game for my amusement. Although it is also that . . ."

"What is it, then?"

"A meeting with my glory is earned, not given," the Unmade said casually. "Let us see if you can succeed where all the others have failed. Conquer this land and break down the gates of my tower. Then you may have your precious meeting."

"You mean . . . this *place* is the final challenge?"

"Is the name Endgame Realm not suggestive enough?"

"I don't give a damn what it is," I said. "I'm not playing this game any-more. I'm here, so show yourself."

"You heard me, whelp. Prove your worth through force. From what I have observed so far, you are not even a mote of dust compared to the Purifiers who have come before you. And yet . . . this situation is so . . . new. So unpredictable. It sounds very . . . entertaining for me."

"Well, it ends now."

"I think not," the Unmade said. "I've rather enjoyed the exploits of you and your blue witch. Your crusade to slaughter your maker, and her life-long journey to rid the world of my influence. You may not be the most powerful challenger, but you are surely the most unique . . . for the last million years of your universe, that is. Delight me with a grander show."

"No," I shouted, glancing about uselessly. "Come out and face me!"

The Unmade laughed. "You've wandered where you do not belong, Purifier. Eighty-six percent of the way to my abode . . . and at only Rank 10. At this stage of the Endgame Realm, even the smallest insect could rip you apart in its sleep. But as I've said, I've taken a liking to you . . . which is why I won't kill you just yet. There's no sense in destroying such a peculiar toy."

"Afraid of a little fight?"

"Hardly," it said. "I would rather save the stakes of life and death for a later time, when you are more capable of putting on a show. For now . . . I will just teach you a lesson about arrogance. Let your pain serve as a reminder of what you are meddling with."

Suddenly, the red waters around me erupted with movement. Bodies rose up, all of them maimed and bloated with unnatural shapes. Their eyes were completely dead. Pure white. Decaying flesh hung off their frames.

[SLAUGHTER EVENT]
Risen Abominations (ERROR) (ERROR)
CALCULATING . . .
Combined Estimated Kill Points: ERROR

Not sure what to do, I began slashing wildly at the oncoming horde. But I couldn't stop them. They occupied every free space, forming a living ocean that had no beginning or end. No matter how much I hacked and sliced, they continued to surround me. Soon they were piling atop me, scratching at my skin and tearing away plates of armor. Their teeth and nails raked over me. I cried out, but there was no sound . . . only the horrible chanting of this cursed dimension.

"Remember my words," the Unmade said, its voice chewing at the inside of my skull. "Go back to your measly three-dimensional world and remember this moment as you strive to pose a threat. I am eternal. You are meat."

Then there was blackness.

ENCOUNTER FAILED

When I opened my eyes, I was lying on the floor of Chanzig's office, my body wracked with incessant pain. Blood streamed from every slash on my body. My armor was gone, as was most of my clothing. Even my lungs crackled with trapped fluid.

Akasha loomed over me, her eyeless face utterly unreadable. She pressed a hand down on my forehead.

"Please . . ." I whispered. "Don't do this . . ."

Her lips softened, and her hand began to glow. The third eye beneath her blindfold lit up.

Just as death seemed certain, as her powers began burrowing into me . . . she stopped. She lifted her hand to the gateway and flooded it with energy. In a matter of seconds, the gateway was just a pile of ash. Any memory of it was gone.

She'd purged the image from my head. Purged it just as Chanzig had done to countless others.

"Come," she said quietly, kneeling down and working to pull me against her. "We must leave this place."

My head was too muddled to resist. I stood with her, leaning against her body as she led me toward the main hub and its barrier. When we arrived, I found that the transparent wall was completely gone. It had died with Chanzig's end.

"The . . . vault," I muttered, trying to speak around the wash of blood. "Polyps . . . I need . . . them."

Akasha shook her head. "There's no time. We have to reach the hangar and find a ship."

Much as I wanted to fight her, to be a headstrong idiot and recover all the treasures Chanzig had stolen from me, I knew I couldn't. I was on the verge of death myself. Blackness swam in my vision as Akasha tugged me into the elevators and shut the doors.

I slumped down to the floor, trying to process what Chanzig had shown me . . . and the Unmade . . . and Akasha's sparing of my life. But everything was so jumbled. It was as though the whole day had been a fever dream.

When I opened my eyes again, we were inside a vast hangar. Docked ahead of us was a massive starship—all chrome, except for a pair of black fins along the top. Beyond it, in the cityscape outside the hangar, the sky-line was on fire. Explosions rumbled and brought entire buildings toppling down.

"I . . . can't fly," I mumbled to Akasha.

"Chanzig has virtual-intelligence pilots in his personal ships," she explained. "We'll find a way. Just as we always have."

36

What happened between the hangar and entering orbit is lost from my mind. Not because it was erased by Akasha, but because of blood loss. When I finally came back to consciousness, I was lying in one of the ship's triage modules, my lacerated and bruised body hooked up to a dozen mechanical arms. Several tubes and wires ran out of a hole in my torso.

"You're awake," Akasha said. She was sitting in a chair beside me, half-hidden by shadows. The golden cube rested on her lap.

I swallowed through a dry mouth and nodded. "How long was I out?"

"Four hours."

Running some quick mental math, I comforted myself with the knowledge that I still had about eleven hours to do a rank-up.

"Where are we now?" I asked.

"In subspace," Akasha said. "I've charted a flight to a world I once knew."

"Dangerous place?"

"It's home to a monastic order that helped me train my abilities. They may do the same for you."

"You know I have a timer to beat, right?"

"It's a hostile world beyond their walls."

I nodded, satisfied. "That'll work." Lying back, I thought on recent events. My heart hammered at the mere recollection of what had happened. "Akasha, I have to ask you something."

"Why I spared you . . . even after you disregarded my instructions."

"Yeah . . ." I scrunched my brow. "How did you know?"

She looked away, seemingly avoiding my last question. "I have my reasons, Dak. You will learn them when we reach the monastic order."

"Am I a ritual sacrifice?"

"I cannot say what you truly are."

"That's not very comforting."

She took a long breath. "The brothers and sisters of the order granted me the knowledge to carry out my holy task. They have spent eons studying the Unmade and beings like it."

"You mean . . . there's more than one of them?"

She ignored my remark. "For over a million years, the order has sought something I considered impossible: a Purifier capable of using their techniques in the service of compassion. A Purifier who might save our world from unspeakable evil."

"And you think that's me."

"I cannot say. The order clings to secrecy. But before I left their walls, they told me the signs of such a Purifier. You possess them all."

"Well, what are they?"

"All will be revealed when we reach our destination."

I furrowed my brows. Her mention of "signs" had reignited my memories of Chanzig and the mysterious power I'd gained. "Does this have something to do with that Morphic Imprint?"

Akasha gave me a look of equal confusion.

"When Chanzig died, I absorbed something from him," I explained. "It's called a Morphic Imprint, I guess. I have no idea what it does."

"This surpasses my knowledge, Dak. It is a question better saved for the monastics."

I gave a stiff nod, simultaneously excited and terrified of what Akasha's hermit community might tell me. Or do to me.

"There's . . . one other thing," I said quietly.

"The gateway."

"Uh, yeah. Remarkable guesswork."

"I was not entirely forthright with you," she said softly. "I know far more about the chok'tal than I have explained."

"You mean, you knew Purifiers could claim gateways to the Unmade?"

"More than that, Dak. I knew that Purifiers could *create* gateways."

My jaw dropped. "How do I do it?"

"I cannot say. But the gateway that resided in Chanzig's fortress . . . was the same gateway opened by the shaman on my homeworld."

"You're sure?"

"I felt its energy," Akasha said. "It was the energy of my people. An echo in my mind."

I whistled. "Now it makes sense. Chanzig's 'helper'—Dr. Markazian—talked about how he'd secured a gateway for his boss." I thought on it, and my mind exploded with fresh concerns. "Wait . . . that means the Hegemony has been to your homeworld."

"I believe this is true."

"Do you think they're still there?"

She glanced away. "This is not known to me. But if they do continue to occupy its soil, nothing good will come of it. It is a dark place. A place that the Unmade may easily access."

"So . . . Chanzig somehow found your homeworld, entered the shaman's gateway, scrambled his own mind, and then directed the Exotic Research Division's search from behind the scenes. He used Markazian and all the other Hegemony officers as puppets to carry out his quest."

Akasha inclined her head. "I share this assessment."

"These, uh, monks you mentioned . . . how much do they know about opening gateways?"

"That is a question you must ask," she said. "Such answers were not given to me."

"But you're a certified chok'tal hunter. Why wouldn't they tell you?"

"They hold many, many secrets, and I was not privy to all of them. Much of their knowledge has been curated for one purpose, and one purpose alone."

I hummed, gaining a hint of understanding. "So, they're saving the best of their wisdom for this Purifier you mentioned. Their champion."

"That is what I have gleaned. But as I said, not all is known to me."

"How long ago did you leave?"

"A few thousand years ago."

All I could manage was to blink at her. "*Thousand*?"

"Rest, Dak," she said, rising. "Put your mind at ease. Heal. The monks will not go easy on you."

"Will do," I mumbled. My mind was still in overload from the revelation that Akasha had lived thousands of years longer than me. As she moved toward the door, I called out to her. She turned back. "Akasha, I just wanted to say—"

"Don't thank me," she cut in. "We are equal in the preservation of one another's life."

"So . . . friends?"

"Rest. I will check on your later."

Then she was gone, leaving me alone in the shadowy module.

I settled back and tried to relax, only to remember something I'd forgotten to do ever since waking up.

"Hey, Modri," I said. "Sorry about leaving you off for so long."

"Idiot."

"Excuse me? I just found out I'm half you. So you're really calling your-self an idiot."

"Nah, I'm callin' the Dak half of you an idiot. Besides, you didn't get me. You got my nervous system."

"Which makes me an expert killer."

"I saw your performance back there. Pretty sloppy, so let's not get carried away."

I smiled, somewhat grateful to have him with me again. I suppose our bond made sense, given what I'd learned.

"You wanna talk about everything?"

"Like what? The fact that I'm not really *real*, just some madman's creation?"

"Yeah. That."

"Surprisingly, not really. If I think about it too much, I'll go insane."

"Yep," Modri said, laughing. *"Welcome to the chok'tal life."*

"Speaking of which, what did you think of the Unmade's dimension?" I asked. "That was . . . your homeland."

"I think whoever runs it is a real prick."

"No kidding."

Modri grunted. *"I didn't even know that place existed. And maybe for the best."*

"Wait . . . what? You're telling me you didn't know there was an endgame?"

"Nope. Didn't even know about the gateway-making thing."

"Goddamn. How many ranks do I need to open another one?"

"Not a question for me, Purifier. Maybe Guide would know, but I doubt it. He's only equipped with information until Rank 15 or so."

I groaned. "Great. Adrift without a paddle."

"Hey, at least you found this endgame thing. From what you've said, it sounds like what I was after. Just thought it'd be more . . . pleasant."

"That place sure as hell wasn't the solution you sought," I whispered. "But you heard Akasha. There are people who think they've got it figured out."

"There always are."

"I'm guessing you also don't have a clue what that Morphic Imprint thing is."

"Bingo. You're in uncharted territory here, Purifier." Modri laughed. *"All I know is that you're gonna have to go back to the Unmade's den. You saw that progress percentage, right? That shit about save points?"*

"I hate to say it, but I think you're right," I said, sighing. "Something tells me what's waiting for us at one hundred percent: the big boss."

"So, what's your working theory? What's the Unmade up to?"

"You're supposed to be telling me those things."

"I'm just along for the ride."

"We'll find out soon enough," I said. "There's a time for everything."

"Fair enough. I guess now it's monk time."

"Sounds . . . relaxing, I suppose."

"More like boring. Did you know monks can't get laid? What are we gonna even do there?"

I rolled my eyes. "We're not going to—" I stopped, suddenly realizing all my memories of sex had been illusions planted by Chanzig. I was technically still a virgin. "Sex isn't everything, Modri."

"Maybe you should get Akasha's take on that. You'd make a nice pair. Two weird, obsessive loners, both bonding over their shared hatred of the chok'tal . . ."

"Oh, shut up."

He did.

"Sorry, I didn't mean it as a command," I said, scratching my head. "The point is, it's not time to think of a relationship. Like, at all. This is the time to hunt."

"Not much different from rollin' around in bed with a woman."

"How so?"

"Screwin' and killin' . . . they both get my engine runnin' hot."

I flopped back in the bed. "This is going to be a long flight."

Two hours later, I woke up rather surprised—I hadn't even known I was drifting off. Akasha's tender love and care—paired with Chanzig's top-shelf experimental drugs—had returned my body to some degree of normalcy. At the very least, I found myself able to sit up and stretch without ripping open any scabbed-over wounds.

Then the thirst hit me. When was the last time I'd had anything to drink? Still groggy, I limped out of bed and into the adjoining modules. There had to be a sink somewhere on this ultra-luxury yacht. Rather than a faucet, however, I stumbled across some sort of transmission room.

It was a cramped, dim space, its walls covered in layers of wires and transistor grids. I didn't know much about hardware, but I knew this was where faster-than-light messages arrived. Emergency warnings, course shifts, that sort of thing. But *this* transmission module drew my attention for another reason. It had belonged to Chanzig. Maybe he had something more in the ship's archives. Some clue that might help illuminate the madness I'd gone through.

After a furtive glance over my shoulder, I slumped down in the transmission operator's chair and booted up the console. The transmission inbox appeared instantly on the overhead screen.

Most of the inbox was barren, having been regularly scrubbed or otherwise kept clear. But there *was* a new transmission queued up. Judging by its six-hour-old timestamp, it had probably been sent and received just before we entered subspace.

The sender's information was blocked, but it was open for playback.

I activated it.

The face that appeared onscreen was that of a middle-aged man in a green uniform. A green *Hegemony* uniform. Both eyes were violet, and his scalp bore a large tattoo depicting an old sigil of Halcius. This was a true zealot. The sort of sociopath who ascended the Hegemony's ranks with ease.

"This is Anointed Reformer Laritas," he said in a deep, cold voice. "I'm sending this transmission in response to your request for immediate surface control on Kagu-9. As per your operator's instructions, I have sent this message to your personal terminal, as well as all modules connected to your fleet."

I felt the blood drain from my face. *Request for immediate surface control.* This must have been one of Chanzig's last ploys as his world collapsed: to call in the Hegemony's guns, even if he'd spent his entire life backstabbing them. If he couldn't own it, nobody could. The coward.

"We have mobilized our forces, and expect to be there within the hour," Laritas continued. "As for now, it is vital that *nobody* is permitted to enter or exit Kagu-9's orbit. Even your private vessels. Due to your . . . employment history . . . with the Halcius Hegemony, as well as various reports of strange occurrences related to classified information, we are treating this situation as an active containment breach. A full blockade must be established, followed by aggressive deployment. We cannot give any estimates as to projected casualties from our actions."

"*They're gonna get slaughtered,*" Modri whispered as Laritas began explaining troop numbers and maneuvers.

I jumped a little, having forgotten Modri was still here. But the surprise quickly returned to anger. "He sold them a lie."

"*Eh?*"

"He told them this was a rebellion. He covered his tracks with a fucking lie."

"Not unusual for Chanzig, is it?"

"There's got to be some way to reach Atrellu and his forces," I said, trying in vain to think of something. Even if I sent a transmission now, it would be lost in subspace, bouncing around relays for hours. By the time we arrived and the message sent, it would be too late.

"They're probably gone," Modri said quietly. *"Hate to break that news to you, but I know how the reformers work. That planet is gonna be ash."*

"But—"

"At least they died free."

A lump formed in my throat. There was some cold comfort in Modri's words, but I couldn't hold on to it. Directly or otherwise, I'd caused this. I'd sentenced those people to death for crimes they didn't commit.

But another part of me knew I hadn't done it. Not alone. Chanzig had forced my hand, and the Unmade had forced his. That was the root of it all. The Unmade. It had set this entire sick game in motion . . . and it would pay for that.

Back onscreen, Laritas finished describing the blockade setup. He lifted a hand to end the transmission, then stopped.

"By the way, Chanzig," he said, "I will make no exceptions to the containment order. If any of your personal vessels travel outside of the Kagu system, I will ensure they're hunted down and *processed* with haste. Do not test me."

Modri whistled as the transmission faded. *"Well, at least we're in an inconspicuous star yacht, right?"*

ABOUT THE AUTHOR

Curator Omega is an interdimensional traveler, archivist, and occasional author from the deep reaches of the void. He is best known for curating tales from the Cutthroat Cosmos, including the Purifier series. In his free time, he enjoys sailing in the hearts of dead stars and studying cookie recipes from extinct empires. He resides in the quantum flux right behind you.

9 781039 413146